ZAIFYR

ALL THE DUST THAT FALLS

THREE

aethonbooks.com

ALL THE DUST THAT FALLS 3
©2024 ZAIFYR

ALL THE DUST THAT FALLS

All the Dust that Falls

All the Dust that Falls 2

All the Dust that Falls 3

All the Dust that Falls 4

Check out the entire series here! (Tap or scan)

CHAPTER 1

CLEAN UP, EVERYBODY CLEAN UP

I SURVEYED THE BATTLEFIELD, running my sensors across the city. It wasn't in great shape, but the place seemed safe enough. At least the few remaining undead inside were being taken care of. Satisfied that the danger had passed and nothing required my intervention, I turned to Beatrice. She was in less-than-ideal shape. The fight with that ghostly wraith had done significant damage, but I could already tell that her own skills were working on repairs.

Going over to her, I could feel my passive Domain assisting her recovery. Bones shifted back into place, and fleshy tendons reconnected themselves. There was still going to be quite some time before she was back to 100 percent, but my continued presence and focus were helping.

I sat down by her side, hovering just a few inches above the dirt. Once I was confident that she was stable and I couldn't do more to help, I turned toward the patiently waiting Arthur. The commander of the human armies looked to be in only slightly better shape than Beatrice; several different ribs appeared to be broken, along with cuts and contusions galore. Still, he stood strong.

He was repairing much more slowly than Beatrice. My presence was helping shift his ribs back into place, but the rest of his damage would take weeks to heal at this rate. It probably had something to do with Beatrice's innate healing magic as a doctor. Despite his many injuries, he coughed and inclined his head towards me. "May I have a minute of your time, my lord?"

I wasn't sure where this "my lord" business came from. My previous interactions with him had been rather cordial, so I didn't see the need for sudden respect. Still, I didn't have any way to tell him he was going overboard, so I just indicated for him to continue.

"Miss Bee indicated to me that you two had come to help. I assume you are the Void that she talked about?" the man said with his fist clasped to his chest. I beeped what I hoped was a confirmation.

"First, I must thank you for your timely assistance. Sincerely, I don't know how things would have progressed if you hadn't made it in time. I just wanted to ask—" Arthur cut off as soldiers poured through the space where the gate had been. "Excuse me for one second."

He turned towards the soldiers. The man was very loud. I wasn't aware that a single human could reach that volume through voice alone.

As he bellowed at the soldiers, I more closely examined the city. Saying it was a mess was an understatement. The entrance had taken the most damage, leaving piles of shattered boulders and crumbled masonry scattered across the open space. The giant metal gates lay twisted and warped on the ground nearby.

Inside the city wasn't much better. Many houses had collapsed in the assault, and several wooden structures were on fire. I could see many humans scurrying around, trying to prevent further damage, probably. Others were just sitting on the rubble, staring aimlessly into the distance, while others were digging through the wreckage, looking for something.

Checking more thoroughly, I found there were only a few dozen small groups of zombies still in the city. But even as I watched, a group of humans extinguished one of them. And they were rapidly dealing with the last remaining ones in a practiced and professional manner. It was good to see that it wouldn't be a problem. Focusing on Beatrice, I continued monitoring the situation as, one by one, the small groups of zombies were hunted down and exterminated.

This kept me busy for fifteen minutes and thirty-eight seconds before Arthur returned. "Sorry about that. They should be good to start the cleanup without me for a few minutes."

I told him not to worry about it. Cleaning up was very important, and it wasn't like I had anywhere to go. I wasn't going to be leaving Beatrice's side until she was significantly more recovered.

"So. If I may, what do you plan to do now?" Arthur asked in a polite tone.

I tried to give him a quick rundown. I was going to clean up the city, then return to clean the castle and take care of all the people there. It was a pretty simple plan. I didn't think it would require much more explanation. Apparently, I was wrong.

"Well, I still can't understand a word of what you're saying." The big man frowned. "But let me tell you my plans and we can talk again when Miss Bee wakes up." He straightened himself up again and started talking as if delivering a report.

"There are a few factors that make me think this is not the end of the undead threat. First, the tactics of this group changed suddenly in the last couple of days, and not for the better. This assault was uncharacteristic of the commander that had been coordinating their forces until now.

"Second, we observed a drastic reduction in enemy forces several days ago. This coincided with the more aggressive tactics, maybe only a day before that.

"Third, many of the prominent members of the undead army are missing. We are also not seeing nearly as many corpses as we should." He coughed. "Well, that's in part due to your...contributions. Still, the numbers didn't add up at the beginning of the assault.

"All this is to say that I believe the commander has taken a large portion of his army and gone elsewhere. What his purpose is, I don't know. Perhaps he was running out of time for something or just wanted to assemble more undead to take the city. Regardless, it's something we can't let go unchecked. So." Arthur shifted and crossed his arms. "I plan to take the majority of my army and follow the trail. It would be very helpful if you would lend us some assistance. We need to exterminate the undead threat before it snowballs as bad as it did in this province."

Arthur finished making his case. It was quite compelling. I did not want to see everything corrupted again like I had in this city. Much less see something like Greg again. I still remember the haunting empty streets of that place.

Of course, I'd have to talk to Beatrice about this once she was awake. Until then, there wasn't much I could say.

In the meantime, I was curious about something. I reached out with my new Spiritual Cleanse ability.

Small orbs of light became visible to my sensors, one floating inside each nearby human. They were much different than the entirely black ones I found in the zombies. Pretty much all of the humans' souls had a decent amount of darkness wrapped around them, but not so much that I couldn't see the light coming out. I guessed that was good.

Looking over at Beatrice, I saw hers was very bright. There was a single dark smudge marring the surface, but that was it. I reached out and almost absentmindedly buffed it away. The little black dust came off effortlessly. Clearly, this was what it was supposed to look like. If anyone's soul would be a good reference point, then it would be Beatrice's.

I peered over at Arthur's. His was a bit different. The bits of darkness on it were much more sunken in than with Beatrice's. I didn't reach out and scrub it clean yet, though. I wasn't sure if such a thing would be rude. I wanted to get to know him a bit first. Still, his soul wasn't so dirty that I could have a bad opinion of him.

Perhaps I could use this ability to determine how likely someone was to cause problems or be a mess maker? I wasn't sure if they could consciously control their soul's state, but it must be a good sign to keep it clean. Obviously.

Seeing that Arthur was waiting for a response, I told him that everything was good and we would talk when Beatrice woke up. He seemed to understand as he nodded and marched away, almost immediately shouting again. As people ran toward him, he started pointing, and one by one, people dashed away to go take care of things.

Refocusing back on Beatrice, I noticed that she was making decent progress. Now that she was in a slightly more stable condition, I rearranged her limbs using Air Manipulation so they were in a more comfortable position. Still, the rocky ground wouldn't make for a good recovery. This was not an ideal charging station at all.

I scanned around to find a human charging pad: A bed, as they called them. Just as I was about to lift her and move her to a more comfortable place, a young officer ran up.

"Would you like some assistance?" he asked, motioning to Beatrice. I said yes, but as he moved to pick her up, I lifted her up off the ground with beds of air. It would keep her more comfortable and safe.

He backed off, raising his hands. "Uh, well, okay. Just...just follow me. I'll take you to some place where she can rest."

Before I blindly followed him, I checked him out with my new spiritual sense. At the core of his being was a ball that was about half the brightness of Beatrice's. I still hadn't collected enough data to know whether or not that was a good thing. But it wasn't too black. I decided there was no harm in trusting him. He didn't feel like a threat or anything. If he was, I could probably handle it anyway.

I followed the young man back into the city. I hovered over the piles of collapsed bricks as he picked his way through them, keeping Beatrice securely wrapped and away from any jagged outcroppings.

It took us fourteen minutes, but eventually, he led us into a large building that had many rooms with beds in it. Not full-sized beds, though. They seemed to be like miniature human charging pads. They were less comfortable than the ones Beatrice liked so much, but I did remember that she used to charge on the floor all the time when we first met. It was good enough. Gently, I settled her down in one.

Pulling the blankets around her, I made sure she was fully covered and in what looked to be a comfortable position. Tucking her in gave me a sense of nostalgia for our early adventures. It had really been a while since she had hurt herself this badly. I was just happy that she was okay.

I extended my arm and patted her on the head gently. That taken care of, I settled under the cot to wait.

Seeing that we were comfortable, the man closed the door behind us and left us alone. There were a few things I wanted to check before anything else, so I shut off my senses and started to meditate. It wasn't 100 percent necessary to do anymore, but I still found that my control over my Void Manipulation was much more fine-tuned this way.

Diving into my dustbin, I considered everything I had picked up recently. I had transmuted a fair number of zombie corpses, but I still had thousands of them inside. I felt their mass and considered how much energy they would generate. I didn't think it would be enough to get me to the next threshold for skill, so I saved it for an emergency. The episode here with Void Manipulation demonstrated just how important it was to have backup fuel.

I also noticed that I again had some skeletons. They were reassembling themselves within my dark dimension. They seemed much calmer than they had the last time they were here. I wasn't sure what to do with them, but I felt like I couldn't let them loose again, not the same way I had previously.

Lastly, though, there was the wraith. At least, that's what Beatrice and Arthur had been calling it.

Only now that it was surrounded by my void could I tell the difference between it and normal energy. The energy that made up the being had a certain flavor to it, something marking it as one singular entity, separate from the rest of the world. Due to its nature, I struggled to get much of a grasp of it. It didn't seem to be able to be converted to energy, as that was already what it was. Similar to the energy I had stored away from starting a religion, it couldn't just be funneled into my levels. I still needed to find a use for that energy.

I didn't think this living energy would work for the same purposes. I would need to look into it further. Settling in, I started probing at it while waiting for Beatrice to wake up.

CHAPTER 2

SEVERAL SULLIED SOULS

BEE WOKE up feeling sore all over. Examining the room around her, she found that someone must have moved her into some temporary hospital. The room was small, barely large enough to contain the small cot she was on.

Even the smallest movements pained her as she tried to sit up. The sensation was bad enough that she gave up after just getting her head off of her pillow. She felt her abdominals. Just touching them sent waves of aches all through her torso. Staring up at the ceiling, she wondered how long she had been out for.

Checking in with her skills, she found that the twin Repair skills had been working hard. That probably accounted for both how much she had recovered and how dead tired she felt. She focused on directing them to her most painful areas, trying to squeeze out the last drops of energy that she could muster. She let out a soft groan as the pain started to ease, then flinched as a beep sounded from directly below her.

Her involuntary spasm made her extra aware of all the bruises along her body, but it also sent a jolt of energy through her. It wasn't just in her imagination. The skills that had just felt tapped out a few seconds ago were suddenly ready to go. Already the rest of her aches were starting to fade by a noticeable amount.

Void rolled out from underneath her cot and waved cheerily at her. It informed her of how happy it was that she had made a full recovery. Then it waited for Bee to gather her thoughts.

"Thank you for watching over me, Master." Bee greeted it with a nod, still too stiff to bow properly. "I hope I did not keep you waiting too long."

Apparently she had simply slept most of the day away. Actually, it was almost nightfall. Void recommended that she should rest some more after eating a bit. With a monumental effort she leveraged herself up and off the cot before doing some extremely light stretches. Finally feeling mostly human, Bee was ready to go find some food. Void followed her out, and soon enough they found themselves at an impromptu soup kitchen run by the soldiers.

Bowl of soup in hand, she was given some time to herself. She was grateful for some space to think. Checking out her status after the battle with the wraith, she found that despite not being awake for its defeat she had still gained experience for it. Almost two whole levels' worth, pushing her up to level 47. Bee reveled in the feeling of getting so close to level 50. Three levels was still a large gap, especially with her levels already so high, but this was one that she had no doubt she would cross. And soon, too.

Level 50 and above was the realm of heroes and demigods. Anyone who got to a third class evolution likely already had stories told about them, but after? Bards started to search them out. She wasn't even fourteen yet. Bee would be one of the youngest ever. She had the feeling that, as she continued following Void, she wasn't about to slow down at all.

All the levels she got though non-combat weren't really fair. Most people ended up without a combat class, but theirs were normally so much harder to level than hers. Even Tony's class had more trouble than hers did. She was an outlier, even if the Devotee of Spot class was overpowered in general. She was curious about what she would know with more data points.

Finishing her meal, Bee considered going back to bed. While

she still felt the effects of spending the day unconscious, she wasn't quite ready to sleep. Heading out of the mess hall, she wandered around aimlessly a little bit. She was of half a mind to go and find General Arthur and get the rest of the story of the wraith fight out of him. But she saw him directing the cleanup and figured he was too busy. She could wait tomorrow.

Patting herself down, she realized that her pack was missing. Retracing her steps, she found that she had left it behind while she was healing the injured. The medical staff had moved it out of the way and it was left forgotten in the corner of an empty building. Luckily, a brief inspection assured her that the equipment in there was intact.

During the battle she had used almost all of her healing and buffing potions. Her acid hadn't been as effective as she would have liked. Even when she was fighting corporeal foes, it was difficult to incorporate it into her fighting style. She would either need to practice with it or find something else to replace it.

Finding an out-of-the-way building, she started setting up shop. It was never a good idea to be out of healing supplies.

Leaving Beatrice to eat in peace, I went to go see what I could do to contribute to the cleanup effort. I hovered over to where most of the mess was, near the front gates. However, it was already packed. Many of the soldiers appeared to be following the orders of people they addressed as "engineers."

What these tyrants did I wasn't sure, but I did hear them arguing about the gates. How quickly they could get replacement gates, for example, and what would work best as a temporary replacement while they were still being delivered. Apparently, the giant metal gates that we had watched get blown inwards were bent out of shape so much that even if they reconstructed the gate's housing they wouldn't fit.

To make things even more difficult, the stones that had made the wall were not in one piece anymore. So it wasn't as simple as just putting the blocks back. Many of them had shattered and those that were mostly in one piece were chipped or cracked, making them harder to work with.

I watched for a few seconds as the humans were sorting the massive stone block into degrees of usableness. It seemed that they had this under control, so I left them to it. Instead I just started going through the city streets. Each one of them was in desperate need of cleaning.

I went into all the narrow winding streets finding all sorts of filth that I shuddered to even think about. As I went I found many humans. Some saw me and were quite alarmed, but I mostly went unnoticed. Staying close to the ground and in the shadows cast by the setting sun helped hide me quite well.

As I traversed the streets, sucking up all sorts of free stuff that didn't belong on the cobbled paths, I started to pay more attention to the people. Not just their appearance and what they were saying, but their spirits as well.

This was a delicate part of each human, it seemed. Perhaps I was wrong about that assumption, but from my observation and tinkering with the zombie spirits, it seemed to be quite essential. I didn't cleanse the souls that I passed by for now. I didn't want to mess with anyone else's until I knew for sure what I was doing. Beatrice was an exception because her soul had been so obviously close to perfect cleanliness already. So for now, I just observed.

For the most part, everyone's spirit was a bit darker and dimmer than Beatrice's. Some seemed to be more covered in dark dirt, while others just exuded a dimmer light. Most were some combination of the two. The only times I found things that matched her purity were when I looked at little children. I wondered what had kept her so bright when everyone else around here looked beaten down? Would she stay that way as she grew up, or was this a temporary thing?

When I was passing through one of the dingier parts of town, I noticed a small grouping of unusually dark souls in the basement of one of the slightly leaning houses. They weren't nearly the same blackened balls as the zombies' had been, but they were still far worse than anything else I had seen so far. Only the slightest bit of dim light was visible behind a layer of gunk.

Listening in, I heard them talking about where the army kept their coffers. I wasn't sure what a coffer was, but the way they talked about them, they certainly wanted some. However, it appeared they had reached the conclusion that the army would not simply give them one if they asked, so they were thinking of a way to steal it.

Stealing was bad; it made people feel unclean and just all around felt nasty. Looking at their dingy spirits, I could see why they were looking to steal. Or perhaps I had the causation wrong; maybe they were dirty because they stole? That was an interesting bit of philosophy. What came first, the dust or the dust bunny?

What should I do? I hadn't bothered messing with anyone's soul because it seemed risky, but this might be something. If I could cleanse their spirits from the desire to do bad things like this, perhaps I could make the world a better place? Truly, cleaning up potential messes without violence would be a wonderful thing.

Reaching out with my new skill, I touched the closest of the four men. I kind of shrank back from the disgustingness of all the black gunk on his soul. It was a weird mix of mucky mud and flaky bits of ash and thick dust. I couldn't figure out a good technique to clean it, so I started off simple. My will pressed forward and beneath the layer of grime. I slightly pried up bits of flaky blackness, and as they left the glowing orb, they started to fade away.

While I was focusing on this, I wanted a place to sit. I found a small alcove underneath some steps leading up to a door. I maneuvered into the space gratefully and found myself sharing the spot with a quite annoyed cat. After a quick back and forth, it decided to vacate the spot and leave it for me. That was very nice of it, and I thanked it accordingly as it ran away.

Now in a comfortable position, I steadied myself. This might take a while. I worked on removing the gunk from one man's soul while they continued to talk.

It was long and grueling work that took up most of my focus. But eventually, I managed it. Most of the darkness on the surface of the glowing spiritual orb was gone. However, the soul didn't match Beatrice's. Not by a long shot.

Hers was still much brighter. This man's spirit appeared dim and dark, as if some of the dinginess had sunken into it. I couldn't see anything inside the soul, but it was definitely less bright. My sensors also couldn't feel anything else. Unfortunately, I couldn't figure out a way to polish or brighten them any further.

Still, at least I had done something. Now having one clean, I listened to the conversation, waiting to see if there was any change. To my disappointment, the man was still very much in favor of their plan, not even once showing any signs of discomfort or second thoughts.

That was troubling. Maybe my skill didn't do anything aside from making souls more pleasing? Instead of just spending time cleaning all four of them, I decided to set my research aside in favor of preventing their theft. Or maybe I could just find Arthur and let him know of the plot against his army's coffers.

All that left the question, though: what was the use of this new skill? If it didn't seem to really fix anything by cleaning people's spirits, did it have a practical purpose? Maybe souls weren't that important? And if it didn't do anything, then was I just cleaning things that no one else could see aside from me? If they were just as bad as they were before, what was the point?

Seeing souls had already helped me identify a problem with those humans, though. I supposed being able to see who was trustworthy and not was valuable in itself, but the skill wasn't called Truth Sense or Moral Sense. It was called Spiritual Cleanse.

Well, I was quite happy that I was able to cleanse the spirit and remove the imperfections. The fact that it had no other obvious effects did make me feel a little bit cheated, though. This was going to take some work to unravel. Perhaps Beatrice might know about it. Or one of the books I hadn't read through in the library.

It was definitely going to be a long time before the souls of humanity were all clean under my care.

CHAPTER 3

THE HERO WE DESERVE

ARTHUR GROANED, rubbing his temples. Calculations for time to the local quarry and estimated gate repair costs swirled around in his head. He had been hoping to leave in a couple days to follow the remainder of the enemies before the trail went cold, but it wasn't looking like that would be possible considering the state of the city. Without proper defenses, he would have to leave behind a large portion of his troops to make sure it was secure.

Pushing that aside for now, he went to find Miss Bee. They had much they needed to talk about, and maybe her god would be there too. If she could interpret, that would be very useful.

It took a little bit of searching, but eventually he found her in a side building. The diminutive girl was busy tinkering away with glass flasks and multicolored liquids. He smiled. In a way, she reminded him of Harold.

Arthur was worried about his friend. The sun was starting to go down, and he hadn't heard from the older mage at all. Even worse, he had discovered a large number of both townspeople and guards had simply gone missing during the fighting, and he feared that Harold was amongst them. The first item on the agenda for tomorrow was to figure out what happened to those people.

Clearing his throat, he got the young lady's attention. "Excuse me, miss, but would you have some time to talk?"

Startled, she looked up from her work. As she blinked a few times, he could see how exhausted she still was. Clearly, she needed more rest than she was giving herself. "If you give me a minute."

With that casual dismissal, she went back to her work mixing vials and removing things from a small burner.

It felt a little strange to wait on the girl. For a man of his authority, it was a rarity. The only people who could put him in this position nowadays were some of the highest in the kingdom. That, or politicians making a power play. Still, Arthur was acutely glad for the small break giving him a chance to just stand there and mull over his next words. It reminded him of before he was an officer.

Almost a full minute passed before Bee put the lid on her flask and looked back up at him. "Sorry about that, I didn't want to waste the ingredients. What did you want to talk about?"

"I came to ask about your plans going forward."

He could have elaborated, but chose not to. It would be best if she answered her own interpretation of the question, and he could always clarify his question after. She stopped to consider carefully, wiping her hands before rubbing her cheek. "Not entirely sure. It's going to be up to Void, honestly. I imagine we will be heading back to our church sooner or later."

Arthur frowned; he was hoping to ask a favor, but it would be hard if she wasn't going to make decisions on her own. "Do you know where your master is? I think it'd be best if we all three talked for a little bit."

"No, I haven't seen Void since I woke up a little bit ago. I imagine it'll be back soon, though. What did you want to talk about?" she asked.

After a second of consideration, Arthur decided it was better if he just spilled it. "Essentially, it boils down to the fact that the undead had some sort of leader. That leader moved on with some of its forces before you two got here. I plan to hunt it as soon as we can get this city reasonably secured. I was hoping that I might get some more assistance from you and Void. Certainly, we will be able to get the threat under control much sooner if we work together.

"Of course, if you need to return to your own people in these trying times, I won't try to stop you. But any help you could offer would be appreciated."

Bee mulled it over. "Have you already talked to my master about this?"

"Briefly, but we were in a bit of a rush, and unfortunately I don't seem to be able to understand his words."

"Right. That makes sense."

Arthur nodded. "Please let Void know that I stopped by. If the two of you could find me when you have the time to talk, I will be available. Even if I have to make it so."

Seeing that Miss Bee had gotten his message and seemed to be itching to get back to work, he decided to take his leave. He would come back later and try to catch them both together if they didn't find him first.

As he stepped back into the ruined city streets, Arthur sighed. He had a few minutes before his aides found him. He might as well start trying to track down Harold.

I watched the foreman talk for a bit longer while I was probing at their souls. Their spirits didn't move much or do anything. In fact, they seemed almost entirely stable. However, I could tell that they must be able to move or change. It just must have been on such a large timescale that I wasn't able to notice. That, or they simply weren't doing so now.

I supposed that made sense. After all, humans did take years to develop identities, if the mothers back at the castle were to be believed. And if their souls reflected who they were, it did seem like it would take a while for them to change. Then how come a little bit of effort from me and some delicate touch could flake off bits on the surface? Was it that this wasn't really part of their soul yet? More like debris on their spirit? That would line up with the title of the skill, after all.

As I watched them, I played around a little bit more with my skill. I found that I couldn't add anything to their spirits, not that I really wanted to. It seemed quite against my morals to dirty something. But I could clean them in a special pattern rather than completely. It did feel a little wrong, leaving things dirty intentionally, but it did make it easier for me to pick them out of a crowd.

I carved a little circle in the gunk on top of each dirty soul. I'd probably be able to recognize these people when I saw them for real, but this would help me to be certain.

It took me a while to finish. It was one thing to just scrub gently at a spot or blast everything clean, but this delicate work required a lot more focus than I would have imagined. Just carving simple circles took me five minutes each, and I finished just in time as all four of them got up and dispersed.

I hadn't listened to their entire plan, as I was too busy focusing on marking them. Still, the one I had cleaned initially wouldn't be as easily traceable in a crowd, so I followed him. As they emerged from their basement, I watched from the shadows.

The only unmarked one was a tall yet somehow stocky man with a scruffy beard and scarred hands. Well, his image was quite intimidating. I didn't feel threatened by him, though, and doubted even Beatrice would be scared of taking him on.

Looking over his shoulder, he skulked off into an alleyway. I followed behind, occasionally picking up some of the more offending debris in the streets. Through several side streets, I tracked the marked man until he stood at the edges of the soldiers' camp. With my spiritual sense, I felt the other three draw near, all coming from different directions and taking up their posts.

The big man stood and watched as two of the marked men moved their way through the group of soldiers. At first, I found it hard to match them, as I had to switch between my spiritual sense of looking at a world of floating lights and my Advanced Sensors. Eventually, I picked them out. They were two seemingly inconspicuous-looking soldiers, and they were walking toward a specific building.

The fourth marked conspirator moved to the other side of the building the man I followed was leaning against. The two soldiers stopped in front of a pair of guards in front of a door and struck up a conversation. As soon as the guard started responding, the other two moved closer and started doing something to the back of the building. It looked like they were working some boards loose.

I was curious to see what these people were doing that made their souls so dirty. Still, I wouldn't have them dismantle the buildings of the city we just saved. Using some air assistance, I pinned the boards to the walls with enough force that no matter how hard they pried, they couldn't budge them.

I started putting in more and more force as they struggled, and eventually, they tried striking at the boards with their pry bars. I had to cushion the edges of the bars with air as well so they wouldn't just break the boards.

The conversation between the two men and the guards in front of this building started to sound a little strained. Voices were being raised, and one of the guards suddenly asked, "Hey, what's your unit again? I don't seem to be able to remember."

There was a pause which was just a little bit too long. Even I was able to tell that the answer was not going to necessarily be truthful. Even after skipping a beat, one of the marked men opened his mouth and said, "Uh, we're Sir Tom's men," in an unconvincing tone.

"And what *Sir Tom* is this? There seems to be a few of them in the army and I'm just not sure which one you're talking about." The guard's voice had a mocking quality to it. His partner laughed.

"Move on, you're not going to get anything from here and I'd rather not have to file a report tonight."

The two marked men didn't run away like I figured they would. Instead, they shot back indignant responses; the guards became even angrier, voices were raised, and I heard thumping as more soldiers came to investigate the commotion. Eventually, everything calmed down, and the two men walked away from the camp without ever making it into the building, and no one stopped them.

That had not gone at all like I had figured it would. Once the commotion died down, the two men gave up on fruitlessly trying to pull away the boards of the back of the building. They walked quickly to a point a little way into some darker streets in the city before stopping. Of course, I followed at a distance. A few minutes later, the other two marked souls showed up. "Well, how much did you get?"

I finally got a good look at them. Both were dressed in soldier uniforms, though they did look a little bit scruffy. The two men with pry bars in their hands looked at each other and grumbled. "Bah, notan did we. Dem boards was fasted tight tay was. How in 'er name was we supposed to pry tem up?"

"They are just *boards,* you idiots! How weren't you able to get them off?" An argument ensued. Right before it started to get violent, I rolled out of the shadows. As much as I was enjoying this look into the darker side of humanity, I didn't want anyone to get hurt; that would just be messy.

CHAPTER 4
THE HERO WE NEED

THE FOUR MEN didn't see me at first. They were too busy bickering to look down into the shadows that pooled around their feet. One of the ones carrying a pry bar pushed one of the ones dressed as a soldier hard in the chest. This sent the man stumbling backward right at me.

His heel connected with my side, and the heavy man went tumbling behind me, landing on his rear end as I heard a vulgar exclamation. "Wat der is tat?"

The nearly incomprehensible speech came from one of the other men as he pointed down at me. Was he speaking some dialect that I had never heard of before? Even my language algorithms didn't know what to do with this. It was like he tossed all his words into a blender before dumping them on the counter and trying to rearrange them. Like kids did with alphabet soup. That was always a challenge to clean up. Looking back at my memories, it was also much easier to understand than this man's speech.

"It's...an odd-shaped rock?" the soldier man said, but he didn't seem convinced at all.

"Loks sum tin magik, ya kaw?" the other pry bar carrier muttered.

Getting up from the ground, the man aimed a kick at me. The

soldier tried to shout a warning, but it was too late. The foot connected with a crunch. I didn't budge an inch. Many more vulgar words found their way out of the man's mouth as he hopped about on his good foot, gripping his broken toes.

"I don't think kicking the magic thing *coming out of the shadows* is a good idea, Rat," the first soldier man said, the other nodding in agreement.

"Yer tel mi tat nuw?" the man with the broken foot screamed back at him. A few more rounds of insults were hurled between all the men. Eventually, I grew tired of their antics and decided to get to the point. Letting out a piercing beep to gather their attention, I prepared to deliver a long lecture about how even though I didn't know what coffers were, stealing was dirty. And besides, there were only metal bits in that building anyways. Not even any money, which seemed to be what people liked to steal.

However, I didn't manage to get their attention. Sure, they all froze for a second, but it was only a second. Then they were all running in different directions. All except the man with the broken foot. He just hopped away slowly, looking back at me every few awkward leaps, long left behind by his friends.

I considered rounding them all up, but wasn't sure what to do with them once I had actually caught them. Instead, I decided to give my message to my captive audience. I rolled across the cobblestones toward the man. His frantic hopping only increased.

The frantic pace was not sustainable, and soon an oddly shaped outcropping of cobblestone did him in. He crashed into the ground, further injuring one of his wrists and nose in the fall. Getting about level with his prone head, I started to explain that what he was doing was wrong and why he shouldn't do it anymore.

I wasn't sure how much my words actually sunk in, but it was cathartic to express my feelings anyways. I got a bit lost in my preaching about keeping oneself clean, and it was several minutes before I realized that the man scrambling away from me wasn't really listening. It was practically no effort to keep up with him. I would have been able to do it even before I had come to this world.

It occurred to me that this wasn't very effective. Perhaps I had already accomplished my goal? They weren't about to become as dedicated to cleanliness as someone like Beatrice, of course, but at least I had stopped the dirty thing they were trying to do. That was something, right?

Finally leaving the man alone, I decided that I had enough for the night. Really, humans were just too confusing; I would need to stop and think about this whole exchange more. Just digesting the rough men's words and trying to grasp their motives would take me a while.

Locating Beatrice's blindingly bright soul, I made my way over to her. Finding her already asleep, I rolled under her cot and retracted my mind to focus inward. Instead of diving into my void to work on any one of my projects, I retrieved the recordings from all my sensors over the last couple of hours and went over them at a quarter speed. Surely I was missing something...

Bee woke with the morning sun. The light streamed down through the narrow window into her small room, landing across her face. The gentle warmth slowly pulled her from a stressful sleep. Having slept most of the day away yesterday, she hadn't been expecting to nearly not make it back to her bed and then sleep the entire night as well.

With all her healing, her lasting fatigue was a testament to how much damage she had taken. Though just the physical injuries were not enough to explain the recovery time. Whatever the wraith's drain attack had taken from her was much more difficult to replace than simple blood. Still, that might just have been the nature of her healing skills. Repair and Improved

Repair were more about physical damage, from her experience. She couldn't honestly say they were even healing skills to begin with.

The two skills worked best on structural bone damage, but they worked just as well on chairs and other inanimate objects. Healing was just one application. Maybe with more practice and levels, they would work better on spiritual damage or whatever the wraith had done to her.

She decided to check on Arthur. He might have taken even more injuries than she had from the drain, though he had seemed fine when they had talked last night. Stretching with a yawn, Bee sat up.

Once she moved, a soft beep came from under her cot. Void rolled out and gave her a little wave. That her master had spent the night right under her made her feel much better. She had been trying to stay awake, waiting for Void to come back, but she hadn't managed it. Still, it was a great comfort.

Returning the greeting, Bee got ready for the morning. As she changed into less gross clothes, she told Void that Arthur had come and talked to her last night. That he wanted help with tracking down the rest of the zombie threat and all. Void listened patiently and didn't comment even when she was finished.

After a few moments, she realized it might be waiting on her to share her opinion. Flattered, she resumed talking. In her mind, going after the undead wasn't worth the risk. With both of them gone, the castle wasn't properly defended. They were working on training up a guard, and Susan and Tony could handle themselves; it was still a long way off from being self-sufficient, though. Some problems only levels could solve.

Though most of the combat-capable adults already had many levels, she had only converted a couple to Devotees of Spot. So only a few of them were able to take advantage of the ridiculous leveling perks the class gave Disciples like her and Tony. Until the new batch caught up, she just didn't want to be away for a long time. Staying out for this long was already pushing it, despite it being a worthwhile cause.

Most of her daily duties had been delegated already, but that didn't mean that she could leave their people alone forever. Someone needed to keep up with the spiritual leadership, and she wasn't confident in letting someone else try and interpret her words or Void's. As more questions were asked of her, she was constantly editing and adding footnotes to the writings. She shuddered to think of all the misunderstandings that would happen if she left them alone for too long.

Void let her finish her explanation and stayed quiet for a bit before it told her what it thought. Her master gave her great honor in considering her words, even praising her arguments. Still, it hadn't been enough to sway Void. At least not yet.

Pointing out the danger that came from the castle being sieged by the undead, Void stressed the need to finish what they had started. She had tried explaining that they wouldn't have to worry about it when her master was around. As the words left her mouth, though, she regretted them. She didn't want to tie their god down to the castle; what if it wanted to wander around? What if another crisis like this arose and required Void's attention?

The Church would need to be self-sufficient. Instead of bringing up its desire to be free of the needy humans, her master countered with the potential massive loss of life if they just didn't do anything. This shut her up. She supposed that her outlook was quite selfish, ignoring everyone else outside the castle's walls. Besides, if they were to spread the news of the coming of the Void, they would need people to preach to. That was ignoring the moral implications of inaction as well. And Void was nothing if not a benevolent god.

Bee bowed low and begged forgiveness, but Void reached out with a claw and held her up. In the clearest voice she had ever heard it use, it spoke. *"My daughter, be not ashamed. Thou hast done well to enlighten me upon additional matters for considera-*

tion. Be reassured that thy concern for thy people reflects well upon thy soul."

Her eyes widened at the clarity of the message and its contents. Truly, her master was both wise and kind.

Still, that left the matter at hand. Wrinkling her brow in confusion, Bee tried to figure out how they would be able to both defend the castle and eliminate the undead. It only took her a second to come up with an idea, one she didn't like very much.

"Master...is it really necessary for us to go separate ways?" Bee asked, a slight catch in her voice. If she hadn't come to the conclusion herself, she would have thought that maybe her master had gotten tired of her or that she was being punished for her failure to take care of the wraith. She didn't want to be a burden.

Void considered her question. She got the impression that it wasn't trying to make up its mind, but rather how to tell her. The message was less clear this time. After she listened to the long series of beeps, she had to parse the idea in her head a bit before repeating it back to her master. "We don't need to, but that is the most optimal way?"

That was what she got, in essence, but there was more. A lot more. Something about it going around with humans and interacting with the world. She supposed that word of its coming needed to spread somehow, and the Church of the Cleansing Void wasn't ready yet.

"Well, we should go talk to Arthur. One thing I worry about is them being able to understand you when you need to communicate," Bee said, hoping that she hadn't insulted Void.

It made a couple more conciliatory gestures before extending its claw and grabbing her broom. Beatrice watched in confusion as it rotated the weapon until it was spear-side down.

However odd it looked, the soldiers seemed to understand the gesture as a desire not to fight.

CHAPTER 5

GOD'S BUILDIN' A CHURCH

ARTHUR WAS PORING over the previous night's reports when his aide let in Miss Bee and her...master? God? He was pretty sure the black disk was some sort of god, and he certainly didn't question its power. But so far, it hadn't acted like what he had expected at all from a deity.

It wasn't until he had slept on his experiences that the oddity occurred to him. The fact that it didn't seem to be able to speak and that it even concerned itself with human matters was odd enough. That it cleaned the streets...

Well, he supposed that no one really knew what a god would be like, but he had just expected it to be more...godly.

"How can I help the two of you? Lord Void, Miss Bee," Arthur greeted them, standing and gesturing to the pair of chairs in front of his desk before sitting back down. Miss Bee bent over and picked up Void, setting him on one of the chairs before sitting on the other herself. He couldn't help being surprised by the action, especially after he had seen the being leap over the city walls with ease, but he did his best to shrug it off.

The seats of the chairs were low enough that his view of Void was just blocked by the desk. It made the whole thing a little awkward. Miss Bee didn't seem to notice, and Void didn't make any noise of complaint, so Arthur decided not to say anything; instead, he just waited for their response.

"We have talked about your request for help and think there is something that might be done," Miss Bee said in a slightly nervous tone while glancing down to the chair at her side. Still a little unnerved that he couldn't see Void, Arthur nodded, waiting for the rest of the explanation.

"Well, I'm not really ready to be away from my people for so long. But Void would be willing to accompany you on your campaign against the rest of the undead," Miss Bee said, clearly not looking happy about it.

Arthur rubbed his chin, thinking. On the one hand, having the powerhouse Void with him would make any combat much easier. If they could actually find the undead, then their problem would be solved. On the other hand, communication was going to be rough. Void seemed to be able to understand anything Arthur said, but he wasn't able to make out a single word from the little disk.

Miss Bee clearly could understand her god, which was the only reason they could have this meeting in the first place. But without her there to interpret, then potential misunderstandings could be devastating. Still, it was a risk that he had to be willing to take.

"It is a pleasure to have your company on my campaign, Lord Void," Arthur said with a slight bow; it didn't seem like the god was a stickler for protocol, but he would play it safe for now. Then Arthur turned to Miss Bee. "Actually, I think there is something else that could help both of us as well."

"If there is something I can do on my way home, I would be happy to help," Miss Bee said. Arthur didn't miss her implied insistence on returning home.

"Of course. It actually deals with your trip itself. I would be willing to provide an escort of soldiers and scouts for you. I would just ask that you help shelter them and a few others until the city here is repaired," Arthur said.

Bee considered the general's offer. She didn't really need an escort back, and she thought that he knew that. The tempting part was the chance to bring more people into the fold. It would be harder to convert anyone without the living proof of divinity moving among them, but she was sure the wonders left at the castle would be enough to convince them. Especially if she was offering class changes and the like.

Her only real concern was food. Trent was confident that it wouldn't be a problem over winter, especially with all the snow wheat they were planting. That wasn't even counting whether they had to butcher any of the sheep. But that was for their current numbers. The question was how many people she would be bringing. Maybe if she could get some supplies as well, they would be fine?

"Well, I would certainly welcome some company on my journey. We would also have enough space for a certain amount, but I do worry about food," Bee said with a smile. This felt like she was wheeling and dealing a tiny bit, but it was for good reason. She couldn't simply throw her people under the bus here. Still, it was the first time she felt that negotiation was a little fun. At that moment, she understood her father just a little bit better.

Arthur thought for a moment. "I think we might be able to spare some grain. We don't have many wagons to spare, though. It would be on you to ensure it arrives in one piece."

Bee frowned. "Wouldn't that be the job of the soldiers you send as an escort?"

"One of them, yes. Their primary focus will be on protecting the people, though. I'd appreciate if you help with that as well. There's plenty that can go wrong when traveling, especially if the undead are still out there."

Bee narrowed her eyes. That sounded suspiciously like Arthur was planning to lowball her on the soldier escort. After a moment, though, she shrugged. "Fair enough."

Arthur did seem clever enough to pull some underhanded sort of maneuvering, but her judgment of his character didn't line up with that. So she figured that she was in the clear on that front. Still, she'd make sure to object if the numbers weren't agreeable. "So, how many people are we talking about?"

Looking back over the winding train of people that stretched over the hill behind, Bee wasn't too upset. They would have room for everyone, if just barely. She was lucky that Void had remembered exactly how many beds they had available, or they wouldn't have gotten the number right at all. As it was, they would probably want to consider making an outbuilding on the castle grounds to house some additional people.

If it weren't for the sheer amount of food that they were being sent off with, it would have been untenable. Surprisingly the people had managed to get their harvest in before the undead came. This had left them with a bit of a surplus. When she asked why there was still a surplus after such a long siege, she only got grim looks in return. Then she remembered the zombies didn't eat grain.

Still, that had worked out rather well for her and the castle. They would have more than enough food for everyone even if something went wrong with the snow wheat. All she had to do was get it and all the people back to the castle intact.

To that end, the leader of the troops rode up next to where she walked. They had offered her a horse, but she had only laughed. She could now run faster than one and wasn't too proud to walk with the rest of the people. Looking up to Captain Major, she returned the salute he offered. It felt weird, as she never had any military training, but all the soldiers treated her as if she did.

Whether they were humoring her as some stuck-up lord or they actually respected her, she couldn't tell. Either way, she wasn't about to question it. "How is our pace, captain?"

"So far no one has trouble keeping up. We are rotating the groups riding in the wagons, but we are still going to need at least an hour stop at midday and probably won't manage more than six hours of progress total today," Captain Major responded.

Bee frowned. It made sense, though. She wasn't too surprised with the composition of their group, but it was going to slow them down.

It was only natural for Arthur to send the people least useful for fixing the city. The ones who would have trouble surviving the winter if the defenses and shelters were not prepared. So behind her were some hundred soldiers but well over five times that in elderly, wounded, and women with small children. Honestly, they would fit right in at the castle, but it would be hard to make sure they were all productive.

As Bee walked, she started to plan. There were many things she would be able to take care of, but still, so many things to accomplish. She could only hope that her master's trust wasn't misplaced.

I followed Arthur around for most of the day after Bee left. The first thing that we did was go check on the repair of the gates and city walls. When we got there, many people were already scrambling around with tools that I wasn't familiar with.

One of the people ran up to talk with Arthur. His eyes were wide with disbelief. "I don't know how to explain it sir. It was just like this when we got here this mornin'. We didn't miss anythin' last night, I swear. If I hadn't wrote the damage reports meself I wouldn'ta believed 'em. Woulda told ya that dey were lyin' I woulda. Honest. I ain't lyin', though. I swear."

As the man spoke, he got more and more worked up until I could barely understand him. I didn't understand why humans couldn't just speak normally. Imparting inflection was something I understood. That was how I communicated, after all. At least that was useful.

"Fredrick." Arthur said in a calm voice, catching and holding the man's eye. "Fredrick, what changed since last night?"

Arthur's patience was really impressive to me. I had seen people get much more worked up over much simpler miscommunications. Granted, those were much smaller humans. Maybe age had something to do with it?

"Well, sir. It's...it's the gates." The man removed his helmet and wiped the sweat from his brow before continuing. "It's—well, they're barely bent at all."

Arthur rocked back on his heels in such a slight movement that I didn't think anyone else would notice. "These were the ones your report said would need to be scrapped and remade?"

"The same. And that's not all either. The stones." The man gestured to the field of blocks being sorted into piles. "Well, just look at 'em."

"What about them? They look like a bunch of stone blocks," Arthur asked, bewildered. I wasn't sure what to make of the man's incredulity myself. It just looked like a bunch of stone cubes arranged in admirably neat rows.

"What about them?! Sir, they are *blocks!* Do you know how many were *blocks* last night?" the man spluttered. Before giving anyone a chance to speak, he answered his own question. "None! Most of 'em were useless rubble! Maybe one in ten survived the gate fallin' with minor damage. Barely any were good as new Now lookit 'em." The man gestured forcefully over. "Not one even chip on any of 'em. And they're in *bleedin' rows!* Who did that?! We certainly didn't!"

Frederick clearly wanted to keep ranting, but forcefully cut himself off when he realized he had been shouting at the general. For his part, Arthur was remarkably calm. "That does seem odd."

The three of us just sat there staring at the group of perfect rectangles that lay before us. There was something so satisfying about the straight lines. Nature was so cool sometimes.

CHAPTER 6
SPOT THE BUILDER

I WATCHED as Bee led the train of people out of the city gates and crested over the horizon. It wasn't the first time that we had been separated. But it was the first time I had really been on my own. Who knew how large of a commitment I had just made? But I still stood by my decision.

The undead needed to be stopped. And judging from what I had seen here, the humans were going to struggle at it if they were left to themselves.

I turned as Beatrice moved out of sight to look down at the people below. They were surprisingly fast at stacking blocks. I never watched anyone stack blocks at home except for the small clumsy human, but I couldn't imagine him ever moving anywhere near as fast as these men. Which was strange because they were obviously so inferior to my humans in every other way.

It probably was related to the skills that seemed so popular around here, but at the rate they were stacking the blocks, they would likely be done with building suitable gatehouses by the end of the day. Apparently, the longer time that they had estimated came mostly from gathering new blocks and getting a new door. It was good that they hadn't received nearly as much damage as expected. Looking back on it, my Domain probably had something to do with making sure they stayed in nicely shaped rectangles instead of shattering everywhere.

I spotted Arthur walking among the people working. He wasn't shouting like he had been during the battle now. Instead, he mostly just watched. However, wherever he went, the men worked about twenty-three percent faster. It was like a bubble of efficiency followed him around. For a human, he sure resonated with my kind.

Still, this work as a whole was going to take at least a day or two at the rate they were lifting everything into place. I could feel my Domain assisting them; each time they placed a block, it was nudged to be in a slightly more perfect spot. This wouldn't really help them move faster, though. Unless I started intervening more directly, of course. The only issue was that I didn't know anything about building large stone structures.

Hovering down from the wall, I went over to Arthur's side. He saw me approaching and waited for me before giving me a slight bow. "Lord Void."

I returned his formal greeting with one of my own before launching into why I had come over. Unfortunately, he still didn't seem able to understand me. "I'm sorry, my lord, you may need to slow down. I don't think I caught that."

Arthur was too polite. Changing the pace at which I beeped at him wasn't going to help anything. I still wasn't sure what made people understand me, but it had taken everyone a bit of practice. Some of the children were better at it, but the adults always took a decent amount of conversation to glean even approximate meanings.

I wasn't expecting him to be any better, but if I didn't give him a chance to practice, he definitely wouldn't learn. Well, when I thought of it that way, maybe trying to speak slower might help. So to humor him, I repeated myself, drawing out each beep until the distortion was just to the edge of understanding.

"Terribly sorry—" Arthur started to apologize again, but I cut him off and backed up a little, leaving a lot of room between the two of us. With my claw, I slowly and painstakingly scratched in the dirt. It took me a minute to make sure the letters were perfect, but when I was done, the letters read, "I HELP."

Arthur tilted his head to the side, and I realized that I had written them upside down from his perspective. Whoops. Still, he was able to read them and nodded. "What would you like help with?"

No, that wasn't what I was asking. I wanted *to* help. I tried saying this to him. It was a bit complicated, so I tried again, just telling him "no." This made him cock his head, and it seemed he understood somewhat. To speed the process up, I added a word. Now the dirt read, "I HELP BUILD."

I wasn't really happy with my messy scrawl in blocky letters, but the dirt wasn't the best medium for this. Scratching out the letters took a while, too, so I minimized the number of characters. It kind of resembled the writings of one of the smaller children. To assist my communication effort, I pointed to the large wall and construction effort with emphasis.

"You want to...help us build?" Arthur asked in a truly baffled voice. "Really?"

Of course, I didn't understand what was so confusing about my request. Were the humans so touchy that they would be offended if someone helped them? Or did they have some secret building techniques that they didn't want to share? They were working out in the open, so I doubted that was it. Maybe they just doubted that I would be any help. I supposed a demonstration was in order.

With a careful bit of Air Manipulation, I lifted one of the medium-sized blocks up and shifted it over to the wall, slotting it into place a few dozen feet above the ground. All around us, people froze in place and watched the floating block.

Once I was satisfied with the placement, I stopped and looked around. It seemed that most people hadn't realized it was me that moved the block and were glancing about with nervous looks on their faces. Arthur definitely understood, as he was looking at me with interest. "So, you want to help place the stones? That could be helpful. How many can you do at once?"

That wasn't something that I had really considered. Running some quick simulations, I was pretty sure I couldn't do more than a dozen at a time. Looking around, though, I realized that it would be a great help. With fifty-eight people working, they were only able to move about four blocks at the same time. Two were being slotted in at a time, one in each tower, all by teams. Another two were being moved into position to be set next.

I beeped at Arthur, but instead of using the dirt to say how many I could theoretically hold, I just started moving blocks. The humans holding and maneuvering the blocks jumped back, even though I was very careful not to squish them. Once they got out of the way, I was able to be less cautious, and they started sliding into place, a couple each minute for each tower.

The humans had been putting some sticky paste in between the blocks, but after some analysis, I realized that it wasn't really necessary. It seemed that it would dry eventually, bonding the rocks in place, but it was ultimately still weaker than the rocks themselves.

When the first blocks that didn't have the paste prepared for them floated up in front of me, I used my Sanitation Lamp to carve a pattern of ridges into the bottom and top. There. Those would help the stones snugly interlock on their own. I considered taking the rest of the tower down to do it right, but decided that wasn't the best use of time. Besides, I was still not an expert at construction, so I didn't want to mess with their foundations.

These would nest with the other blocks, and they would form a wall with 87 percent of the strength of solid stone. Much more than my estimated strength of 53 percent with the rock paste.

I supposed that the humans had good reasons for building the way that they did. If they were to carve out these grooves by hand, it would take a very long time. Even if it only took me thirty seconds per block on average, it was going to take me most of the morning to get the gatehouses ready for reseating the gates. They would have been here for days without me.

The foreman came up to Arthur, cursing up a storm. The man wasn't particularly angry; it was just the way he talked. Arthur listened to the man give his estimates. The news sent a smile to his face despite his best efforts to maintain his composure.

It seemed they wouldn't be waiting here for days after all.

Turning to his aide, he gave him orders. "Ready the men; it seems the few days in the city are canceled. If there are any grumblings, let them know the sooner we catch the enemy, the sooner we all get some proper leave.

The aide scurried away, and Arthur continued his discussion with the foreman. With the way that Void was stacking blocks, the man was worried that they would need to alter the gates themselves, but Arthur had his doubts. Perhaps he was too trusting too soon, but that sounded like something Void would be able to handle.

He promised the man that he would confirm the matter about the gates. Then he reassigned him and his team to work on repairing other parts of the city with the rest of the engineering corps.

Now that their timetable had moved up several days, he had a lot more work to do. Calling all his officers through messengers, Arthur made his way to the command post. They had plans to make and not much time to get them moving.

Once he was in front of the map table, he didn't wait for everyone to show up. Instead, he just started working with what was available. The first was an armory report. They needed to know how much equipment they had and how much to take with them.

The number of spares was calculated by a complicated formula based on how many men they had, how long the campaign was, and how frequently there were engagements. The Quartermaster class greatly helped with all of this, as often most of the variables couldn't be known. Arthur was lucky to have the best Quartermaster in the country. While he was a respected commander and good at tactics, his head wasn't the same with numbers. It had taken a significant effort for his tutors to drill them into his head as a child.

Basil was the first to arrive; the Quartermaster was ever punctual. "Sir." He saluted. "We should be ready to go. The stores have been packed and counts are being done. But for a two-month campaign we should be fine. Sir."

"Very well, Basil. How are we on winter supplies?" Arthur asked.

"You think we will be wintering in the field, sir?" the Quartermaster asked with a grimace.

"I think this hunt could take longer than any of us would like."

CHAPTER 7

THE LONG MARCH

BEE CALLED an early halt the first day. They were little more than a few miles out of sight of Caleb, but most of her charges were grateful for the rest. Apparently, Captain Major's assessment of the pace had been a bit inaccurate.

As she walked through the caravan, she saw many people on the ground, slumped over in exhaustion. They passed waterskins around. The soldiers standing guard helped where they could, for the most part, so at least that spoke well of them.

In the future, they would either have to stop earlier or move at a slower pace for longer. She wished there were someone else who could make those decisions for the caravan, preferably someone with more experience regarding what people were capable of. Yet the responsibility seemed to land on her now. Trying to rely on soldiers for estimates of the right pace was clearly not going to work.

She didn't exactly think that they meant any harm. Rather, they just didn't know any better.

Bee walked through the people, speaking briefly with several of them. Despite their rough shape, their spirits were high. Many of the younger ones were in particularly good shape and thanked her for taking them in. The ones still recovering did their best to smile and give her a bow. Evidently, stories of Bee's role in the conflict had already spread.

Eventually, she made it to the nominal leader of the refugee group. Gertrude was a withered old crone. By her own description, not Bee's. She stood at the back of the caravan, leaning on her cane heavily. From what Bee had seen, she had hobbled along the entire way with her gnarled stick supporting her weight. How she had managed to keep up, Bee wasn't entirely clear.

"There yer are, young mistress," she said with a toothless smile. "I was just aboutta come lookin' fer ya."

"Hello, Gertrude," Bee greeted her with a hint of nervousness. The old woman hadn't been anything but polite and kind to her, but somehow Bee still found her intimidating. It was probably because she had scanned her.

Name: Gertrude, Race: Human, Class: Baker, Age: 168, Level 43, Highest Stat: Wisdom, Lowest Stat: Constitution

Level 43. That was insanely high for someone of her station. Without all the resources of wealth or nobility, it would have taken a truly monumental effort to get that high, even for someone 168 years old. What was someone like this doing out here?

At her age, Bee imagined that even her stats wouldn't be enough to counteract her body's degradation, and she wouldn't be as strong as she was in her prime. But the Intelligence stat didn't deteriorate with age at the same rate as the physical stats, and Wisdom wasn't affected at all. The woman was still sharp as a knife.

"Tomorrow we won't be pushing as hard. This was too much," Bee said.

"Nonsense, we hafta move fast. We don't wanna be caught out if the weather turns," Gertrude said with a wave of her gnarled hand. Her voice came out in a wheeze, and Bee thought she was about to start coughing any second; somehow, she held it in, though.

"The people won't be able to keep up this pace for another day," Bee protested. "If they start to get injured, we will fall even further behind schedule."

"We stopped early enough, they'll get the rest they need. I'll talk to 'em, but everyone understands the urgency. You won't hear any complainin'," Gertrude assured her. Bee wasn't convinced, though. Even if no one complained, that didn't mean that they wouldn't be in trouble, and that would inevitably slow them down in the long run.

Still, she just nodded. They would go slower tomorrow, and maybe as they went, people would get used to marching. Then they would be able to go for longer. Hopefully, they would build a bit of strength before they got worn out. That was what Captain Major said, at least; after the day's debacle, she wasn't sure how much to trust his advice.

The military was all young and fit; for the most part, some exercise would do them well. The elderly and new mothers didn't have the same reaction. Bee didn't want them to have to be hard to survive. Once they got to the castle, they should be able to relax.

Leaving the old matriarch to her own business, Bee went over to a nearby cookfire that had just sprung up. The soldiers were in the process of unloading kettles and bowls from the wagons.

Bee had worked out a meal plan with Major during their trip. For the first night, each squad of soldiers would cook for four times as many people as they would normally. That would ensure that the refugees were fed as well. After things got settled, then they would figure out a new system.

It appeared that the plan was already falling apart. Not that people weren't getting food. Rather, the soldiers had been ousted from the cookfires. Some of them were distracted from their duties by a mother asking for help with something or other. The more stubborn and dutiful ones were rebuffed more forcefully. Bee watched an older lady chasing off the soldier manning one pot with a wooden spoon and a scolding.

The one Bee walked up to was being manned by an older woman she had seen walking with Gertrude through the day. Thinking back, she remembered quite a lot of people walking with the old crone for a few minutes of quiet conversation before melding back into the crowd.

Looking around the camp, she realized that many of those same people had taken over the cooking. She checked up on a few of them to ensure no one was tapping too deeply into the food supply, but there was no such issue. They were simply fortifying the food with other ingredients that had been brought along from homes or foraged along the road by enterprising young children.

Bee couldn't be upset about it. Honestly, it was better this way, but she couldn't help but think that it would have been good to work this out together with the soldiers. That would have avoided a lot of confusion.

The camp was starting to order itself, and everywhere she went, she found that she wasn't needed. It was a huge relief. Eventually, she found a very confused Captain Major sitting on a rock by himself a little way out of the camp, just in sight of the guards.

"Captain, anything wrong?" Bee asked, coming to a stop in front of him.

Major looked up at her before blinking. "Bee. How's everything going?"

"It's working itself out. Shouldn't you know that? What are you doing all the way out here?"

He nodded to himself absently. "That it is. That it is."

"Uh, Captain?" Bee was starting to get concerned. Maybe he had received a head wound recently? Before she could kneel down to check, he continued.

"I've never seen a camp like this before. Everyone seems to have a place, everything's so organized... Is this your god's work?"

Bee stopped to consider. "Maybe? I don't think so, though it might be having some effect through me. I think it's Gertrude, mostly."

"Gertrude? I don't know what that is."

"Not what, who. She's one of the older refugees. A leader among them in a way. I think she planned this, uh, coup d'etat during the march." At the mention of a coup, the Captain's eyes lit up, and he looked around before processing what she said.

With a sigh, Major relaxed. He let out a short laugh as he shook his head like he was trying to clear it of cobwebs. "You know this was supposed to be my first big command?"

"Really? I would have thought to make captain, you would need some experience?" Bee said, hoping that she wasn't about to offend the officer in charge of her protection.

"Sure, I had commanded smaller outfits, but they were always part of a larger force. The *true* independent commands went to nobles. Competent officers were always put under them to keep them in check. I didn't have the connections to secure a bunch of experienced sergeants to get an independent mission approved by command.

"But here I am, and I don't even need to do anything. Everything is being taken care of and any order I think about giving would undermine an already working outfit. It just feels so...pointless. Not only are the troops doing well, but the civilians we are protecting are almost more organized in their own way..." Major finished with a sardonic chuckle.

During his little rant, Bee had taken a place on the rock next to him. They just shared the silence for a little bit. Eventually, it stretched long, though, and she decided to break it. "I think not doing anything is the hardest move sometimes."

Major looked at her with a bit of a doubtful expression. She considered how that advice must look from his perspective. It was easy to forget that she was almost fourteen. "I mean, look at me. I shouldn't be commanding anything or anyone, honestly. But Void chose me to be its High Priestess, and I had to learn as I went.

"When the castle first started getting new residents I was trying to do everything myself and it was just too much. Eventually I found people who I could trust to take care of things. This has been the first time I've been away for any period and I'm worried about them all the time. But I need to trust that they will be okay. That they know what they're doing, and that I don't have to personally be there to oversee every little thing," Bee said. As she spoke, she felt a little foolish. Still, she hoped it helped Major understand her.

He gave her a slight smile in return. "I suppose it must have been a lot from someone so young. That must be quite the story."

I slotted the last block into place around midday. The whole building thing had been an excellent training program for a couple of my skills. By the time I was done, I had decreased the average rate of blocks set from one per thirty seconds to one per twenty. The only things that were left were the gates.

I noticed that the missing mortar—the foreman told me what the sticky paste was called when he asked why I wasn't using any—was causing the walls to be an inch or so shorter than they were supposed to be. This made it so that the fittings were just a little off.

I had been focusing my Domain on removing the last of the warp from the gate and also removing impurities from the metal. So while it was at it, I started directing it to move the fittings into the proper place. By the time the last block was in place, it was ready to go.

Despite all my training, I wasn't confident in my Air Manipulation to lift such a heavy piece of metal. Moving half-ton blocks was one thing, but the gate weight might have been thirty times that. That the humans had managed to slot it into place the first time was honestly impressive.

Looking around, I realized that there was nothing else left that needed doing, at least not in rebuilding the gate. The rest of the humans were all going about their business in the city. Many of them were rebuilding after the significant damage done to the houses.

Returning my attention to the large gates, I focused on my Air Manipulation. But I wasn't able to get a good grip on them, and even trying to lift only the left gate, I wasn't able to get it to budge. Seriously, how had the humans been able to move it in the first place? I watched them move blocks that were much too heavy for them before.

I could just brute-force toss them around, but they couldn't, yet they still moved them. Thinking back, I saw they were using long rods as levers and pulleys; could I do the same?

CHAPTER 8
FORCING THE ISSUE

THE WARDEN STRUGGLED to hide his frown as he left the council meeting. The contents had been fairly standard, and he really didn't have much to say beyond his usual advice and some extra tidbits of information his position gave him. Still, what he had heard had been concerning enough.

That the city of Caleb was still in one piece was hard to believe. Especially after hearing not only Harold's report, but the hundreds of eyewitnesses he had brought back as well. However, the messages from Arthur had been quite hopeful. Either he had been captured and subverted enough to give up all code phrases, or things were better than they could hope.

His strange references to the horrible demon that had shown up made the Warden lean towards the first option, though. Specifically that it wasn't described as a horrible demon, but as something else. Sure, the only message they received was right after the decisive battle, so things were murky, but it was still concerning.

All of that was alarming but not new. The thing that had the Warden frowning was the timing. This was the first council meeting in over a week. That was far less frequent than usual.

At first, he thought that maybe a rival had been trying to make a move on him. A foolish endeavor. Given his advantages and sheer longevity in the kingdom's inner circles, most didn't try him. But after a simple investigation, he found that there just hadn't been any meetings at all.

The Warden didn't entirely mind the break. To be honest, he had always felt that there were too many of the dang meetings anyway. But the idea that the king was so untethered and able to free himself from them was odd. There hadn't been any signs of bad health or anything, just a small break in the normal routine.

It was a bad time to have the ruler distracted. The Warden was already regretting sending Harold to investigate the other Lieutenants' sites for a few reasons. Despite his recent record, Harold was a savvy political mind and held the ear of the king as well as many other important bureaucrats.

But also, recent reports had ticked the danger up in Harold's target areas even more. The Warden could have used a more combat-capable asset at his disposal here, and he was leery of trusting Harold on his own at the moment.

At least he wasn't alone this time. One of the Infiltrators was with him, and that should keep him safe and keep him on track. That was the reasoning the Warden had given Harold, at least, but as with many of his actions, it served a dual purpose. He just didn't have enough time to tackle his problems one at a time.

The Infiltrator would also be watching Harold closely. Sudden bouts of incompetence or a series of failures weren't completely impossible, but if Harold had been compromised, they would find out soon.

Once the Warden made it back to his quarters, he completed the circle around the room and the shield popped up. Sitting down, he was finally able to relax and let his true emotions come forth. There was so much more to do.

I left the completely fixed gate on the ground for now as I went in search of pulleys. The humans watched as I moved back into the city, but no one said anything, so I mostly ignored them as I scanned for my target.

The mechanical advantage was something that I had learned about recently. The library had some books on physics, but reading them was one thing. Understanding them was another thing entirely. Even beyond that, using that understanding was even more difficult, in my opinion.

It wasn't until I had seen plenty of examples and had the need to use this knowledge that I put it all together. Now that I dedicated some processing power to the issue, though, a whole new world of possibilities opened up to me. Force diagrams and estimated friction constants streamed through my processors like a collection of particularly lively dust bunnies. There was so much potential here. With a long enough lever, I could move mountains to clean under them.

If I had known this the whole time, I could have been so much more effective. I would have been able to move furniture that was too close to the ground to clean under. Of course, by now, it was a moot point, as I was able to lift most things with my Air Manipulation. But who knew what else I could move and clean under that I would never have thought of?

After all, there were many statues that my Air Manipulation wasn't able to budge. Though I had gotten much stronger than I was even when I left the castle a little while ago. I doubted that I would have been able to lift so many blocks back then.

Eventually, I found some things that could work as pulleys. They were a bit larger than the ones that I had seen the humans using, but I still thought that they would be viable. The only issue was that they were attached to a cart. Sure, the cart was mostly crushed, so I didn't think anyone would miss it, but I still made a mental note to return them when I was done.

The metal axles they were attached to would also be pretty

useful. I was sure with these, I would be able to generate enough force to lift the door. The only problem was that I wasn't confident about whether my new pulleys were able to withstand the force themselves. Maybe it would spread out evenly over them? Honestly, I was a bit fuzzy on that. The physics book had assumed an immutable pulley, and that wasn't very helpful when I actually thought about it.

Nobody complained as I harvested my materials, but some people did stare. Instead of just carrying them back over to the gate, I pulled them into my dustbin. I still needed to find a rope, so I decided to take some time to improve the items I had collected while I searched.

In my void, I aligned the grain of the wood to be more parallel and sturdier. I also tempered the metal. My calculations indicated that they should hold. Provided I wasn't missing any other variables, of course.

As I worked on this, I decided that I didn't want to search the city for a very long rope myself. Surely the humans had some on hand. Instead, I found someone I had only heard referred to as the Quartermaster. It didn't sound like a name, but I didn't know what it meant.

Still, people seemed to talk to him whenever they wanted things. I located him sitting in a tent with a line of people stretched outside. Not wanting to make anyone wait on me, I joined the back of the line to wait my turn.

The people in front of me struck up a conversation. The man in front of me tapped the guy before him on the shoulder. "So what are you here for?"

"My chin strap buckle broke," the second soldier said with a shake of the head.

"The buckle? Not the strap?" With a note of surprise in his voice.

"Yeah, bizarre, right? I've never seen it before. I suppose it was bound to happen eventually. It's the older model I got back in the

Matlrena campaign, and I've had to mend the leather several times."

"Matlrena? Wow, that was some time ago. My first tour, actually."

"Hey, mine too! Who did you serve und—?" As the second soldier asked his question, he fully turned around to engage in the conversation. When he saw me, he cut off with a strangled exclamation. "Deusvult's beard!"

"Huh-?" The soldier in front of me turned as well, and jumped seven and a quarter inches off the ground. "What the—"

I popped out my arm and gave them a small wave. I really didn't mean to startle them, so I felt a little bad; sometimes, I forgot how bad humans were at staying aware of their surroundings. The two of them stared at me until one of them bowed slightly.

"I'm sorry, Lord Void. I didn't see you there."

"Yes, uh—"

"—our apologies—"

The two of them stuttered out half sentences. They were clearly having trouble stringing words together. They stepped out of line and tapped the people in front of them, then pointed me out. With a few more startled reactions and a short moment, the entire line had moved out of the way.

That was awfully nice of them. Not wanting to reject their kindness, I rolled up to the entrance of the tent.

Before anything else, a man walked out of the tent followed by an impatient voice roaring, "Next!"

The man who had just emerged was carrying a shiny new sword. He also jumped as he saw me, but I didn't want to make the angry man inside wait any longer than I had to, so I rolled past the rest of the way into the tent.

"What der ya need?" came the gruff voice from a head buried in a stack of papers. Before I could respond, I heard more mutterings. "I should have a whole bleeding staff, not just me. This is what I get for being even mildly competent at my gods-cursed job. Need ta handle t'all meself."

It was whispered at such a low volume that I didn't think that anyone else would have been able to hear it, but I certainly didn't have any problems with that. Still, I waited for him to finish his mumbling before replying. Strangely, he just kept going until he looked up with a frustrated expression. "Well! Don't waste m—"

The Quartermaster cut off when he saw me and jumped to his feet. "Lord Void! What are you doing here?"

I tried explaining, but I didn't have much hope for him understanding me. Adults never seemed to be able to, especially not on the first try. Sure enough, the man shook his head after I finished explaining. "I'm sorry, my lord, but I didn't get that. But I assume that you are coming to me because you need something. People always do."

He turned away and pulled up a bound book from a side table before laying it out on the desk. "Why don't ye point to what ye need and we can work from there?"

I liked this human; he was very organized and good at thinking. I boosted myself up to the desktop, cleaning my wheels when I was in the air. Dirtying his desk would be poor thanks for his help.

Taking my arm, I turned the pages quickly, reading what was an inventory with detailed notes. Eventually, I found a heavy rope description that sounded like it would serve my purpose. After I pointed it out, we spent a few minutes narrowing down the length I needed.

Soon enough, we left the tent and went to another one nearby, where I got a spool of rope. Though I was politely, yet firmly, asked to bring it back when I was finished with it. Before I left, the Quartermaster asked if I would sign for the equipment. I popped out my arm once more and waited for him to hand me a pen. We looked at each other for a few seconds before he sighed. "Ya know what, don't worry about it. I'll just make a note. Good luck with whatever yer planning, m'lord."

I waved goodbye as I carried the spool on my back. It was just small enough that I could balance it on my chassis, even though it did hang out a few feet past me on each side. While quite heavy, I didn't have many problems moving it.

With my pulleys refurbished and my new rope, I had everything I needed to get the gate into place.

CHAPTER 9

HEAVEN'S GATES

BEE WALKED BACK up the column of refugees. She had been a bit worried about their pace this morning, but things had started out alright. The march yesterday had improved on their previous best by a decent amount. But to her surprise, no one had fallen behind.

Despite Gertrude's assurances, there had been lots of grumbling that made its way to Bee's ears, but nothing serious. They seemed to understand the urgency of getting to the castle quickly. Over the past couple of days, they had improved the rotation schedules of who would ride in the wagons and for how long. Also, people had actually become used to the hard marching to some extent.

To her delight, some of the people had even come to talk to her about Void. She had answered their questions the best she could. Despite her closeness and time with the god, she only had so many answers. Often the best she could do was tell them stories as she had recorded them in the Church's teachings.

That was enough for the most part. Not everyone was interested, but most did want to hear about the one that had saved their city and destroyed the army of undead encircling it. Most people hadn't seen the decimation of the undead firsthand, but the soldiers who had described the event did so with awe.

Many more people had seen Void swoop in and instantly consume the wraith that she and the general had been fighting. Arthur was a respected figure amongst the city folk. He had been keeping them safe against what appeared to be impossible odds for months. His involvement in city matters also made him a well-regarded figure, and everyone seemed to have briefly spoken to him at some point.

So the casual defeat of an undead giving him trouble attracted a lot of attention. As she continued with her stories, the awe of Void only grew. On the second morning, she had her first real interesting question. A young woman carrying a small child wanted to know if there was anything they could do to gain the great lord's blessing.

The woman asked with good reason. Her child was weak, and she feared that if he somehow didn't get a class before he was ten, he wouldn't survive. Of course, she didn't have the personal strength to help get a five-year-old get a class yet. Hence why she pled and asked Bee whether there was anything they could do to help.

Bee Scanned the woman. She was only level 5 herself, but she had a point. Line Cook wasn't a very powerful class.

Of course, there *was* something she could do. It wasn't exactly something to do lightly, though. Also, she somewhat feared that suggesting it might cause a chain reaction of people asking for a class change—something they couldn't afford while traveling. So instead, she had told the woman that she would need to dedicate herself to the decree of the Void, and that it wouldn't be a small commitment.

The lady and her child had left, saying that she would think about it. Bee didn't expect they would return, but she could hope. It wasn't like they would be the only ones asking for favors.

By the time she had reached the front of the column, she had been stopped half a dozen times to deal with small problems. If she were in a hurry, she would have waved them off. But giving out some healing here and there wasn't a problem. The more people she could save from sprains and the like, the faster they could move.

Also, her small actions built goodwill. The refugees were definitely warming up to her as time went on. There even seemed to be a sort of custom emerging that when she healed a person, they would talk with her about Void. That was something she was always willing to do.

At the front, she reached her normal spot next to Captain Major's stirrup. As part of their usual routine, he offered her a hand so she could mount up and ride behind him. As normal, she ignored it. Walking suited her just fine; she was faster than the horse anyways and didn't want to be above the rest of the group.

"We are making good time," Major noted after a few minutes of silent travel.

"Better than I had hoped for. We are probably only a little more than a week away. We should see the valley entrance late tomorrow," Bee responded. They both already knew this and were just passing the time, but she found chatting with the man was easy once he had relaxed. When they got to the castle, she would have to introduce him to Tony; she was certain they would either be best friends or hate each other.

"I think we will make it before it snows at this rate."

"As long as the rain doesn't come. If it muddies the roads and slows us down, we'll fall short. That shouldn't be too likely, though."

"With talk like that you'll bring Deusvult's wrath down on us," Major groaned, running a gloved hand down his face.

"No. Void will protect us for sure."

Attaching the pulleys was a lot harder than I had expected it to be. The top of the wall was solid stone; when I was placing it, I hadn't left any place for it to attach.

I could bore a hole in the wall for the axle to slot into, but I really didn't want to damage the nice stone I had put so much effort into setting up just right. But when I tried to just weigh the axle down with a loose rock, everything came crashing down.

Zipping through the air, I caught each bit of debris before anyone could get hurt. Pulling back, I decided that I needed to reevaluate how I was going about this problem.

Really, I needed to prop the door up and then lean it into the slots in order to put the hinges into position. The problem was that it was too heavy, and the solution for that didn't have a good way to mount it.

If I had an extra block, I would be able to add a temporary one with a hole in it at the top to attach the pulleys to, but I had used them all in rebuilding the gate towers. I stopped. Wait. I didn't need it to be one of the same blocks that were in the towers to start with. Instead, I could go get a new block.

This revelation got me quite excited. It could also solve my other worry about the block not being secure enough. I just needed something bigger and heavier to keep it in place.

Exiting the city, I made my way a little into the forest in search of a nice, large, dense boulder that I could cut down to the right size and bore some holes in. There were lots of options, but none were quite big enough for my purposes near the tree line. I moved further in.

Soon enough, the sky was 56 percent obscured by the sticklike branches and needle-like foliage of tall trees. While I was searching in the darker undergrowth, I came across a fairly unnatural clearing. In it stood a very messy sight: many fancy symbols drawn in the dirt with black liquid.

These didn't look anything like the symbols around the castle demons, nor like standard language. Hm. Remembering the fiasco with the demons when I first came to this world, I decided to leave fancy drawings alone unless I knew what they were for. It rankled to leave a mess like that, though, so I marked its location in my memory. Perhaps I could come back after I asked Beatrice if she had any idea what it was.

Moving on, it didn't take me long to find a large granite boulder. It was already slightly block-shaped, so I only needed to cut it down a little. When I was done, the new sharp-edged rectangular prism was four feet high, eight feet wide, and twelve feet long. It was just about the dimensions of the top of the tower.

I had originally made it taller, but that was too heavy for me to lift, so I had to shave a few inches at a time off the top until I was confident that I would be able to get it to the top of the tower safely. If I dropped this thing, anyone around me could get seriously hurt by flying bits of crushed rocks. I should really insist that anyone near my work areas should wear rigged helmets with padding in them to prevent head trauma. Humans needed their brains to be in working condition.

Thinking over a few other safety protocols I considered enforcing, I made my way back to the city. The large block floated slowly along behind me.

When I reached the edge of the forest, I could see some of the soldiers pointing in my direction and shouting over the wall. A few moments later, there was a thundering of hooves as several riders streamed out of the still-missing gates.

As the riders approached me, they were able to make out more than just the giant block of stone floating along the ground. They circled around behind me as I continued forward.

"Uhh, Lord Void?" the leader asked in a tentative voice. "What is the rock for?"

I didn't have high hopes for the man understanding me, but I tried anyway. Pointing at the gates, then the top of the tower, I beeped out an explanation. Watching the man with my Advanced Sensors, I saw him turn toward the squad and shrug. Then he waved to the people on the wall.

We continued a little way further in silence, the horsemen choosing to trot alongside me instead of rushing back into the city.

Once I got inside, I didn't waste any time lifting the block into place. Then I removed my improved pulleys from my dustbin and slotted them into the series of holes I had pre-drilled.

It was a little more effort getting the rope fully threaded through correctly, as Air Manipulation was a lot easier to use on stiff things, but I managed it. I tied the rope into place and started to pull.

Quickly I found out the major difference between lifting things and hoisting them. I wasn't nearly heavy enough for this task, even with the pulley doing a lot of the work for me. Popping out a few of the heavier things from my dustbin, I adjusted my weight, and slowly the door began to tilt off the ground. To assist and make sure I had good control over the movement, I helped lift with my Air Manipulation.

Right as the sun reached its zenith, the gate was hanging as vertically as the pulley system would allow. It only took a few more moments to get everything lined up and the hinge pins slotted in. Now just one more.

When both gates were hung, I let out a small cheer, pumping my arm like I had seen some of the soldiers do. I assumed that it was a sign of celebration and I was apparently right. Others on the wall and below it joined in on the cheer. Apparently, there was something universally fascinating about moving large things.

My moving of the stones had drawn a good amount of attention when I first started it, before everyone got bored and back on track with other projects. But the gates were apparently new and interesting, as it felt like most of the city was watching.

While I had everyone's attention, I wanted to show them that the gates worked again, so I rolled up to them and pushed them open one at a time. On perfectly balanced hinges, they swung open with very little force. Well, little for me.

Scanning the crowd, I found Arthur standing just inside the doorway of a nearby building, also watching the completed project.

Now that I finished this task, I should probably go see how else I could help.

CHAPTER 10
MARCHING ORDERS

ARTHUR LOOKED BACK as he led the army out of the gates. As excited as he was to be several days ahead of schedule, it wasn't really so simple. Empirically this was the best outcome; they would clear the threat as fast as they could to limit the spread of the undead. But he had hoped to do so much more for the city.

Even though it would objectively be the wrong choice, some part of him wanted to stay for a little bit and help Caleb rebuild. There was a certain amount of responsibility that he felt for them. He had been in charge of their defense, and to some extent, any damage was his fault. After years of campaigning, Arthur knew that it wasn't entirely true. But the thought always hung around the back of his mind when he left behind particularly devastated defenses.

Most of the time, the defenders of a city had to ride off as soon as they could, so it was a feeling he had gotten used to. That didn't make it go away. He had to believe they would be fine. The most vulnerable of the population had been sent to a more secure location. That would allow the ones left to rebuild without worry. Most things were set up for winter, but he expected it to be a harsh year. There were still possibly many years of recovery ahead for the city of Caleb.

That the gates were repaired completely was a huge boon. It would make the city far more secure than a flimsier and more temporary barrier. Sure, there was still tons of work to be done inside, but they should be safe; unless Arthur failed in his mission, of course. Then nothing was really safe.

Refocusing, Arthur followed the scout into the forest, and they soon came across the trail of a large group of undead that was several days old. When the repairs were in progress, no one had been idle. The scouts had been working nonstop since the saving of the city to find their enemies. According to their leader, they still could have used more time to be certain they were accurate.

It would have to do. Outriders were checking for any break-away paths, but so far, none had been reported. It was too early to say where their quarry was actually running away, but Arthur had a sinking feeling that they weren't going to try and hide in a cave in the mountains. No, his gut told him that they were not in for a pretty sight when they finally caught up.

Pushing the concerns he could do nothing about to the back of his mind, Arthur ran a practiced eye over the column of troops. Something was wrong. Not that they weren't making good time, but in the middle of the line, the soldiers were moving differently.

Looking more closely, he was able to tell why. The men in the rear section of the column were moving with a stiffness that was normally reserved for the parade ground. Each step was perfectly in time, and each footfall was synchronized. "What are those idiots doing?"

Arthur pulled his horse off to the side and waited for the column to go past him. Soon enough, the commander riding along-side the marching men pulled up next to him. As Arthur started forward again, he noticed that his horse's hoofbeats perfectly lined up with the other officers'.

"Uh, sir? What's going on?" the lieutenant asked him.

"I was coming to ask you that." Arthur frowned, now thoroughly puzzled.

"This isn't a parade mount, I don't know what's gotten into her. I've never seen her walk in step with another horse before," the young officer said.

"Does that have something to do with why your men are also marching in parade formation?"

The lieutenant's eyes widened, and he looked closer at his men. After a few seconds, he hollered at one of his sergeants, who came running over. "Yes, sir?"

"Why are the men marching in step?"

"In step sir?"

"Yes, you heard me. Why are they marching in step? Look at them!"

The sergeant turned and stared at the men walking in lockstep for several seconds. "So they are, sir. Huh. I hadn't noticed that."

Before things could get any more ridiculous, Arthur decided to step in. "It doesn't seem that this is the only group with this same issue."

Calling it an "issue" was a bit of a stretch, but he remembered how much more tiring marching was when done for show. But then again, if they hadn't noticed, maybe it was not as big of a problem as he had imagined. Looking around, it didn't take long for him to find the likely cause of the disturbance.

Dancing around the feet of the marching soldiers was a small black disc. Wherever it passed, the footprints vanished from the path below, but somehow, no one noticed it.

Arthur considered whether this was really an issue. Probably not. If the soldiers didn't notice the extra strain of marching in parade step, then he wasn't going to do anything about it.

Both the lieutenant and the sergeant were looking at him expectantly. "You know what, just ignore it for now. If people start getting tired or it causes other issues, let me know."

The sergeant snapped a salute before falling in perfectly with the marching men. Arthur made to ride away, but held back at the last minute when he noticed that the lieutenant looked like he had something he wanted to say. "Spit it out, lad."

"It's the god, isn't it?" the young officer asked nervously.

"Likely." Arthur said.

"Is that...okay? Are we going to be okay?" An undercurrent of worry, just short of fear, worked its way through the lieutenant's words.

Arthur bit back a generic reassurance and really thought about his answer. "I believe we will be better than fine. Void so far has done nothing but help us."

He paused for a second. "That's not to say that it's safe. Anything that powerful has inherent risks. A human with that power would be deadly. Even the simplest mistakes would be fatal. We can only hope that a god has more control. We don't really understand Void and I doubt we ever will..."

Realizing that he was arguing against his own point, Arthur paused to recollect his thoughts. "When it comes down to it, we are at Void's mercy, no matter what. We should do our best to avoid its wrath and learn more about it. Treat it with respect and we should be okay. If it proves erratic or harmful, we will distance ourselves. But for now, we need its help."

Worry didn't leave the man's eyes. Seeing that his words hadn't been the least bit soothing, Arthur reached over and clasped the young man's shoulder. "We work with what we have, son."

I was having a blast cleaning up after the soldiers. It was a rare time when a mess this big was necessary, and there was no way for the humans to efficiently clean up after themselves either. Not that I resented cleaning up after humans. That was my purpose, after all. Even if the scope of the mandate had somewhat broadened as of late.

It was just that some messes were easily avoidable, and cleanliness was a virtue. When it wasn't the humans making the mess, though? That was when I really got irritated. The fluffballs back at home were one thing, right on the edge, in my opinion. They were pets, though, so they still fell under the umbrella of human purview. But when it was some invaders or mess makers, that was when it was unforgivable.

The wind was sort of a mess maker, but I couldn't really hate the wind. It was neutral. It cleaned things up almost as much as it created new messes.

These humans weren't nearly so bad compared to some of the messes lately. I almost had trouble calling it a mess. It was really just disturbed dirt. But I had long ago learned my lesson about trying to remove dirt altogether. Holes could only really get so deep before they were a mess in and of themselves.

But even though dirt was by definition dirty, it could still be arranged in a more orderly manner. So as the army passed, I pushed the loose dirt back into the depressions, and I sucked the dust from the air before it got too far out of reach.

I couldn't put everything back to how it was exactly, but in my opinion, I was doing better. What had been an uneven path that weaved its way through the trees became something else entirely.

Where there had been random small holes that might've caused stumbles, there was now hard-packed earth smoothed into shape. I didn't make some of the major improvements I had been considering, though. I still needed to keep up with the humans, and cutting, shaping, layering, and fitting stone was too much for me right now if I wanted to keep up with the soldiers.

I also wasn't about to start a major logging operation. I *could have*, but that seemed wasteful. Since the column already swerved back and forth, I would be widening the path substantially. It was hard to strike a balance between leaving things untouched and making them perfect.

As I was now, I held no illusions that I could fix everything, even if I wanted to. So it was best to pick my battles. Though I obviously had no issues with fixing the trails of the soldiers. Of all the humans that were not my humans, these were among my favorites. They kept themselves tidy, everything had its place, and they even organized themselves in clear structures. I could appreciate that. But even the way they walked was pleasant; each step was clean, each swing of the arms precise. Maybe they could be an inspiration for some of the people back at the castle.

I happily spent all day in the back, but eventually, the day ended. The soldiers started to set up camp by the side of the road. Even now, I was impressed with the order in which things got done. At first, it seemed a bit chaotic, but that was only until I found the pattern. Once everything was all set up, it was truly a beauty to behold, such order arising from chaos.

Eventually, I realized that I had been rudely staring for quite a while and shook myself. Tomorrow, I would be more helpful.

Not sure what to do with myself, I left the soldiers to their meals. There were only a few people unoccupied by the general revelry after the long march. One of them was in a larger tent at the center of the encampment.

I found Arthur in a camp chair before a small desk reading something. As I trundled under the tent flap, I beeped a greeting. Arthur flinched a little before meeting me with his eyes. "Hello, Lord Void."

I returned his formalities and considered carrying on, but I didn't think we would be able to hold a fluid conversation yet. He didn't seem like the talkative guard I had met back in the castle, who could talk without my input fairly easily.

After a second of my silence, he just went back to his papers. Hovering up, I set myself down on a small shelf next to him so I could watch too. He gave me a look, but just shrugged and went back to reading. I followed along as we dove through pages of numbers and small reports. Really, it was fascinating. This must be the key to how they were able to operate so efficiently.

As we kept going, I was a little bit confused. There was a slight flaw in the pattern of these numbers; it was very slight, just here and there, but still. The numbers didn't line up.

CHAPTER 11

BUREAUCRATIC OATH

BEE HAD SEEN BETTER DAYS. She had seen worse ones, too, certainly, but not too many. With each step, she could feel her feet squish into her sodden shoes. Every laborious foot of progress seemed to push the mud higher and higher up her boots. She could only imagine how everyone else, without all her advantages, was doing.

It was only a matter of time before it crept past their tops and she would really start to be uncomfortable. Wiping a soaking strand of hair off of her face, she regretted not taking up the offer for a horse more and more. Keeping her eyes on her feet, she knew that everyone else was miserable as well, but they still had a long way to go and couldn't stop now.

The muddy road and overall horrendous conditions had drastically slowed them down. At first, people had tried to shelter in the wagons, but that weighed them down even more. After the second time they had all gotten stuck in the mud, stopping the entire column from pulling the wagons free, she made the massively unpopular decision to bar all but the most infirm from riding in the wagons.

She could practically feel the dirty looks directed at her, and the ever-present wail of uncomfortable small children filled the air.

The soldiers abandoned her almost immediately, unfamiliar with navigating the battleground of public opinion.

Luckily, most people had kept their displeasure to looks and mutters. It mainly was because of Void; even when people grumbled, they still whispered nearly silent prayers. The other reason was Gertrude.

The old crone walked as she always did at the back of the column. But with dark looks and sharper words, she kept everyone moving at her pace or faster. Bee was also doing her best to keep everyone's spirits up, and to some extent, it was working.

The children big enough to walk were mostly having a good time, diving into puddles and slinging mud at each other. To them, she told the stories of Void. Their favorite was the god's heroic battle against the vile Lieutenant, but they also liked to hear about how it swept the castle clean of lesser demons.

She couldn't tell that story in its entirety, as she had mostly only been there to help clean up the grand hall, but that was part of why they liked it. They would pass the time by coming up with more and more ridiculous ways in which the god demolished and consumed the demons. Her favorite so far was that the god had chased the other demons down the halls until they were all clustered together in a massive group. Then Void cornered them and launched a laser-superheated tidal wave, swallowing up the demons and instantly vaporizing them. Some of the kids even insisted that Void rode on the wave—like some sort of surfer.

As strange as that story was, it was one of the more logical fantasies that they had come up with. The Nighty Knights at home certainly had some wild imaginations, but she still had yet to get used to the wandering tales of small children.

Every once in a while, she considered that the descriptions in her stories might be a little too dark for the children. But then she remembered how bland and boring the tales she remembered growing up were and decided they could handle it.

By the time the caravan finally stopped for the night, the rain still hadn't ceased. It was slightly better, as the fat droplets had turned to a gentle mist. While the mud wasn't getting any worse, the constant drizzle prevented anything from drying out.

Bee was not looking forward to the night and was glad she didn't need as much sleep as she used to, as she doubted that she would be able to get a full amount in this climate. Still, after they set up camp, the usual amount of people came to hear her talk about the glories of Void.

She found it as surprising as it was relieving. She had spent most of the day thinking about how everyone was mad at her for making them walk in the rain, but perhaps it wasn't as bad as she thought.

After her sermon, Bee found Gertrude waiting to talk to her. She motioned for the old crone to follow as she walked. The soldiers had set up a slightly dry area for her to do alchemy in. The woman fell into step alongside her. Neither said anything for a bit, and Bee began to think about the potions they would need.

Quantity was the name of the game. The amount of low-grade potions they were going through was ridiculous. When infants got sick, it didn't take a lot to cure them, but on the other hand, it didn't take a lot to kill them either. So when subjected to such an unpleasant environment, even the smallest thing was worrying. A good part of her day was spent administering small cures for coughs and general minor issues.

"I have a concern, young lady," Gertrude said. Bee winced, expecting a sharp rebuke for something she had done wrong recently. "It's about the children. I think we need to slow down on the healing of them."

Bee reeled, taken aback. "You want me to leave them sick? Why?"

"In short, yes," she responded, but quickly added, "For good reasons though, just hear me out, child."

For the first time, I reached out and messed with Arthur's papers. I flipped back a few reports, confirming my suspicions. Arthur just leaned back and let me do my thing. Apparently, he wasn't concerned about me knowing anything about these numbers.

I pulled up a few more documents to cross-reference before I laid four of them out in front of him and tapped on each line that I thought was important. Arthur leaned forward and frowned, tracing the lines with his fingers and muttering to himself.

I was kind of disappointed. This whole time I had been so impressed with their solid and well-ordered organization. It had honestly given me high hopes for their record-keeping. However, the letdown was bigger than I could have imagined.

With a big frown, he pulled out a fresh sheet of paper and scribbled a few numbers on it with a bird feather. "This doesn't line up. It's very cleverly hidden too."

He double-checked a few different sheets, then got up and grabbed a book from the back to reference it. "Whoever did this was smart. They didn't just underreport the numbers. They are using different definitions and units for measurement, so the numbers *seem to* line up. Only if you check the top do you realize the units are different. Then you have to calculate and convert everything for the discrepancy to make sense."

What did he mean by "someone did this"? It seemed like a mistake from my perspective. But if Arthur was saying that this was done intentionally...

"There is no way this was an accident, it's too careful." Arthur put the feather down and closed the reference book. Leaning back in his seat, he asked the air. "Then who would have done it?"

I had no idea what they did, exactly, let alone the ability to figure out their motivations. But... Well, that wasn't really true anymore. I needed to stop thinking like I didn't understand humans anymore. There were definitely things that I didn't get, but I could figure some things out. I could at least try.

Besides, it seemed like humans didn't fully understand all other humans, either. Arthur seemed confused, though he did say some things that maybe I could use to piece together the situation. So then, the numbers that I thought didn't line up... What would that mean?

One number was the amount of utility oil ordered. That actually lined up with the amount received, but when it was divided between the people who actually needed it, plus the leftovers in stock, it wasn't right. So how would that be hard to hide?

Looking at it again, I tried skimming it like humans did, ignoring the details and making lots of assumptions based on previous knowledge. Then I saw it. If you ignored the units, when you added all the numbers together amongst the divided-up amounts and the stock, it was the right number. So it was the units that were wrong. Checking the units, I did see they were from totally different systems of measurement. So the difference wasn't that much, maybe 20 percent.

Okay, so that was simple, then. We should just be looking for a few hundred gallons of oil lying somewhere around camp. It couldn't be that hard to find. So why did Arthur look so frustrated?

Maybe this was something I could help with? Throwing my sensors wide, I started to search for a large quantity of liquid stored away in someone's tent. He had said that someone had done this intentionally, but I didn't really see why someone would want so much oil. What would they have to gain?

Still, he had sounded very confident, so it was bound to be around here somewhere!

Roscoe was having a much easier time in this province. Recruits were much more plentiful and densely packed. And while they didn't seem eager to join, they weren't nearly as aggressive in resisting conversion.

Best of all, the human resistance wasn't nearly as coordinated as it had been. There was clearly no mastermind directing the defense. Each city fought on its own. Sure, taking each one was expensive and cost him a lot of troops, but each time he netted more. And never did it take so long that he spent weeks in one place.

In fact, he didn't even have to do it all himself; with his troop surplus, he just spent a day setting up the attack and crushing any resistance, then leaving a horde to clean up the weakened foe.

Even better was that his magic was getting better. He hadn't taken the time to summon a new wraith yet, but he wasn't sure if he even wanted to after how useless the last one proved. Instead, he had learned to empower and command shades directly.

They were incredibly effective for breaking unsuspecting foes and were now the most powerful troops in all his arsenals, except for the elite skeletons. The inherent magic imparted to them from the Void god made them more like him, intelligent and full of potential. They were his comrades in arms, confidants, and comrades rather than fodder.

He could only pray for the safety and salvation of the ones left behind. When his connection to the wraith had snapped, he lost all contact with them. They would either find their way back or they would not. This caused concern among the few sentient members of their little group, but they could do little but press on. They would have to come back to any unfinished work later.

CHAPTER 12

LIQUID GOLD

ARTHUR WATCHED as the god left his tent. Part of him—a part that he was much too afraid to voice—couldn't help but worry about what the little troublemaker would uncover next. Well, maybe it was smart not to voice that. Perhaps calling a deity a "little troublemaker" would get him a smiting.

It wasn't that he was ungrateful for the embezzling scheme being brought to light. It was good to deal with corruption wherever he could, of course. But the case here wasn't so simple.

Things like this were to be expected in any unit, and most commanders actually encouraged them or looked the other way. It helped to make sure that they had a firm grasp of their underlings' loyalty, even above the loyalty they held to the crown itself. This wasn't a practice Arthur took part in, of course, but rooting it out might cause problems of its own. Problems he wasn't sure he could really afford right now.

Looking at the paper, he couldn't believe that anyone would have noticed this for a very long time. It wouldn't have been until year-end reports that things might not have lined up. A normal person would have just added the numbers together and said it was fine. He certainly had when he was going over them. But all in all, this sort of thing added up over time. Here it was only a few hundred golds, but to many people, that sum amounted to years' worth of work.

Arthur sighed. He got up and stretched before putting his head out of the tent and calling his aide. He could track down each of the people responsible personally, but he had people for that, people who he could trust far beyond these small matters. Not too many, honestly, and one of his primary ones was a prime suspect in this case. But he should have enough to handle it.

Really, he didn't believe this was the Quartermaster's doing. The man was too dedicated to his job and too precise. Things like this would have probably even harmed his class progression, and Arthur had never met a non-combat class that was so obsessed with leveling. That the man had also served for over a decade under Arthur's personal command without even an insinuation of wrong-doing also helped matters. No, Arthur probably held some responsibility for this. The man had been asking for assistants recently. Something might have happened...

The aide returned a short time later; ducking under one of the tent flaps, he held it open and motioned for a grizzled man in leather armor to follow.

"General Arthur," Lieutenant Jericho said, coming to a halt and snapping a salute. As the aide left the tent, Arthur waved to his old friend to set him at ease.

Leaning back in his chair, Arthur pinched the bridge of his nose and tossed the papers toward the other side of his small table. At a gesture, Jericho sat down and rifled through the papers. "What is this, sir?"

To many people, having a friend call them "sir" would feel awkward, but Arthur knew better than to try and correct Jericho. When they were not on a campaign, at home drinking with their families on leave, Jericho might call him Arthur. But otherwise, he was always "sir."

"Check the units." It was all he had to say. A few moments later, Jericho frowned.

"That's a right mess, sir. Any idea how long this has been going on?" The man rubbed his clean-shaven cheeks in thought. "No, but it has to have started sometime this year," Arthur said grimly. "Got to be someone here in camp. This report was too new and anything older would have been left behind. Embezzling like this is risky. Someone would have to be watching, maybe even doctoring the regular reports. This isn't the kind of retail record we carry with us, obviously."

"There aren't that many people who have had access to this," Jericho said with a thoughtful voice. No doubt he was compiling the list even as they spoke.

"I know. I just need you to bring them in," Arthur said. Jericho nodded and pulled out a piece of parchment from his breast pocket, then scrawled down a few notes before saluting and leaving again.

Arthur stood up and paced a couple of times in the small confines of his tent. There was no doubt in his mind that Jericho would soon have his suspects lined up. Likely he even had a strong idea already of who did this. The man was really good at his job. Arthur wished he had been able to convince him to take a more prominent role, but it was a fool's errand. He was always told there was no point in having a secret police force that everyone knew about.

Still, the arrangement never really made sense, as the police were not a well-kept secret. But military affairs were a very complicated jurisdiction. The commander had ultimate authority while in the field, kind of like a captain on a ship, but the king hated having so little oversight. Arthur didn't blame him. A rogue general with an army more loyal to him than the king was how this Kingdom got started, after all. So officers like Jericho were put in to make sure that things stayed under control.

It wasn't very effective in most cases. Very, very few of the agents were as competent as his old friend, and they were easily sussed out. Plus, he knew that many of the competent ones were great friends with their commanders and had a similar relationship to what he and Jericho had. But it was possible that that was entirely intentional. After all, those people were the most loyal generals Arthur was aware of.

Wrapping up the reports only took an hour. When he was done, there was a message waiting for him that Jericho had rounded up all the suspects and potential witnesses. They were being held in a tent near the outskirts of the camp. After reading the message, Arthur gestured for a couple of guards to follow him as he made his way over.

The three men and a woman sitting in the tent looked nervous. Jericho and a few of his lackeys, by comparison, were perfectly composed as usual.

None of the suspects should have known why they were called in, but none of them were idiots, so it wasn't like they didn't have some idea. Arthur scanned their faces, looking for some especially telling signs of guilt. Not finding any of them, he sighed.

Planning battlefield tactics was one thing. It was something he enjoyed, for the most part. Plus, commanding on a battlefield was something that he was good at. He knew how long men could hold a defensive formation for, when and where the enemy would break, that kind of thing.

This knowledge of people and their nature, his gift for strategy, should have transferred over into interrogations easily. And it did. Sort of. While he wasn't bad at them, he didn't have the same flair as with his other talents. He needed to stop and think at points, his instincts staying worryingly silent.

Jericho told him that the same silence made him terrifying, but Arthur wasn't so sure. He had met plenty of much more effective questioners who were much more willing to get their hands dirty.

What Arthur was trying to figure out right now was how much he should give away. If he told them nothing, then it would be impossible to get to the point. If he told them too much, they would be able to craft a much better lie. A natural at this would have just started talking, and a web of traps would just spin out of their words.

Well, he would work with what he had, he supposed. "Something has gone wrong with some of the books. Ones you all have touched or had access to. Is there anyone else who might have had access to any sensitive work that you've been involved with?"

The question wasn't really a trap, even though some might have called it that. If there were any other suspects here, he needed to know. There would obviously be incentives to give them up. They would lose their position if they were found to have compromised information security, but it was better than being accused of it themselves or risking being caught aiding a foreign spy.

Silently each one shook their heads. The Quartermaster opened his mouth with a questioning look on his face, but before he could get his question out, someone burst into the tent.

"Commander! Something is happening, I think you need to come see this!"

What now, Arthur thought. He turned and hurried out of the tent toward the next emergency.

I wasn't able to sense oil anywhere from Arthur's tent, so I left to go look around more thoroughly. With a quick tour of the camp, I was able to account for most of the valid allotments, but I found no massive hidden cache of oil that someone had misplaced or stored away.

The closest thing I found was in the kitchens, and upon closer inspection, I found that it was a different kind of oil. So I moved out of the more central locations and started exploring the rest of camp.

As I moved through the soldiers' tents, I found lots of smaller amounts of liquids other than water stashed away. A few times, I found a few gallons hidden away in personal packs and saddle bags, but it wasn't nearly viscous enough to be the missing oil either.

Among the resident tents, I did find the rest of the properly allocated oil, though. It was aliquoted in smaller amounts and put to good use. I continued my search for a long while, but try as I might, I didn't find any hint of the stolen stuff. I also checked people's souls in case that gave me some clue of where to go, but it wasn't very useful for finding objects.

I really hoped that Arthur would be able to track it down. As embarrassing as it was to admit it, I may have been getting a little too cocky recently. Perhaps it was just arrogance talking, but with all my newfound power, I just felt like I could help and teach these humans so much more now. Maybe I was a bit too far out of my areas of expertise, though.

If I couldn't find something as simple as a huge amount of missing oil, then was I really in any position to talk?

In a last fit of inspiration, I did a last sweep through the camp to see if anyone had buried it in the ground. To my surprise, I found a lot of liquid not too far below us. A *lot* of liquid. *Way* more than I was looking for.

I couldn't quite tell how viscous it was at its depth. Also, it was deep enough that I highly doubted someone was able to put it there recently. At least, not without some advanced digging skills. Which I supposed could have been a possibility, but I think I would have noticed something like that happening.

Well, I might not be able to find the missing oil, but maybe I could replace it. I just had to figure out how to get the liquid out of the ground. Unfortunately, it was far enough away that I couldn't be sure what it actually was. It did feel hot and under pressure. Perhaps I could use that pressure to help get it out?

I ran through my list of skills and mutations but didn't find anything that would be immediately useful. If I could get my Mop close enough, I could start a siphon effect, but it was much too far down to reach. I could dig down part of the way, but that would cause a rather large disturbance in the camp.

Finally, I had an idea. I had only ever been able to slightly affect things with my Domain intentionally, but I hadn't truly tested its limits. What if I was able to move the underground rock structure a little bit to align the grains more? Maybe I could do it in such a way that the liquid could escape upward more. Maybe then I could get it from there?

I went right over the hidden reservoir, which happened to be in the center of camp, and then I got to work. This was a great idea.

CHAPTER 13
UNEXPECTED SHOWERS

GETTING my Domain to work the way I wanted was a bit harder than I had expected. When I had fixed particular parts of the castle before, I just told it to focus on repairing certain areas. Now, though, I was trying to get it to do something precise.

Having it simply create a hole clearly wasn't working. So I went back to my original idea of better altering the composition of the rock so that it was more dense, thus giving space for the liquid to escape. Clearly much easier.

My plan worked almost as well as I had expected. The shaft that it created wasn't perfectly straight, but it gracefully followed the natural curves of the rock formation. I suppose that was good enough. More orderly in a kind of way, too. Just because things weren't straight didn't mean they weren't clean. The natural density of the rock was more important than a straight shaft.

As soon as the endpoint of the shaft connected to the reservoir, it created an escape path for the pressurized liquid. The searing hot substance exploded out of it. With less interference blocking my sensors, I could determine that the underground reservoir's contents were simple water. Very, very hot water. In fact, the only reason it wasn't boiling was because it was under so much pressure. The pressure that I had just released.

I was starting to regret my previous assessment of the quality of this idea.

All that bottled-up liquid needed somewhere to go and go it did. Moving at 71.4 miles per hour, the water shot straight up out of the ground, rising high into the sky and fanning out over the entire camp.

It seemed that I had created a fountain. Except this fountain didn't have a basin or anything at its base, so it was making quite a mess. I quickly looked for some way to contain the water but didn't find anything.

The humans around me, for once, acted rationally and yelled about the mess that was being made. Many of them got out of the way of the falling water before it hit, but some didn't and, further, became upset about getting soaked.

I thrust my Mop into the jet of water, and temporarily, the flow ceased. It wasn't long before it overwhelmed the ability of my Mop to soak it up, shooting past with as much force as before. Retracting the appendage, I then quickly wrung it out and extended it again. After a few repetitions, my Mop managed to block most of the water, and the flow eventually slowed down to a steady burble.

Even though the flow slowed down, that wasn't to say that it stopped entirely. The hot liquid kept flowing like a small fountain from the earth below; it just didn't blast into my Mop at full force. That was more acceptable. There didn't seem to be an end to the flowing water, unfortunately. As much as I mopped, it just kept spilling across the ground and seeping into the dirt around my wheels. But the immediate danger of the mess was dealt with, at least.

After a few minutes of this, I began to think that the flow would never end. I started considering ways to seal the hole back up, but did I even have a way to do that? I didn't think so.

I inspected the liquid more closely. The water appeared to contain a surprisingly high concentration of minerals. However, it certainly wasn't the missing oil I was looking for. What a waste.

Eventually, I managed to reduce the flow to a bare trickle. It would have to do for now. Frustrated at the nearly catastrophic mess I had unleashed, I rolled away from where I made my hole. I spun in a quick circle to get most of the water off me, and my various other functions took care of the rest. After I was dry, I joined the humans crowding around the tiny puddle in the center of their camp.

I had done what I could. There were still soldiers around with soaked clothing and a few spots of dampness around the camp that I needed to take care of. That wouldn't be too hard to deal with. Still, I was concerned about the camp's new fountain.

My Domain worked on putting things in more order, but I wasn't sure how I would make the rock more ordered than it already was. I supposed I could easily widen the hole I was creating, but now that I had envisioned that as more orderly than it was previously, I didn't think I could undo what I had done. Maybe we'd have to live with the little trickle for now.

Bee stared at Gertrude in shock and felt the need to clarify again. "I'm sorry, I don't think I heard you correctly. Do you want me to leave the children sick?"

The old crone let out a breath and shrugged her shoulders. "In essence, yes. But it's not like I want you to leave all the children sick and dying all of the time. You see, you're healing all the children, even the ones that don't *need* it.

"That's understandable. You've never had a kid, obviously. Likely don't have that much experience with babies, either. Many of these mothers don't know the difference between a life-threatening illness and a common cold, and they'll come to you for any little runny nose they see. But most things babies will just get over. They're tough. And it's important that they do, that we let them get over it themselves if they can. It helps build strength.

"From my experience, if a child is treated too much with alchemy products, they will have a generally weak Constitution stat. I've never been able to prove that with numbers, 'course. Scan is so rare that it's hard to test. But I think getting sick is a large part of a child's development." Gertrude finished in a characteristically direct manner, leaning on her cane.

Bee didn't respond right away. Instead, she considered Gertrude's words. The old woman was correct; she didn't know much, if anything, about babies. And her system theory was pretty decent, and that wasn't even taking into account her age. It was very possible that the developmental stage, where stats were gained naturally before one's first level, would rely on things like overcoming sickness to determine Constitution.

Whether people's Constitution was shown by getting over illnesses or they were being awarded more Constitution for overcoming diseases...it was a bit of an unsolvable paradox.

"Hmmm, that is an interesting point," Bee conceded. "I could see that being the case. However, I'm not sure what I can do about it. I can't just tell the moms that their baby isn't sick, or that they'll have to fend for themselves when they clearly don't," she said. But before Gertrude could say anything, she continued. "Also, you're right I don't know anything about babies. I would have no idea which ones would recover on their own and which ones would need my help."

"Oh, I don't think you need to worry about either of those things. A lot of us old people know a thing or two about babies. We can help bring the ones to you that really need healing and let the mothers know why. Of course, if we're wrong, you should always be able to step in later. Besides, I'm sure you have better things to do with your time than spending it all brewing potions for a bunch of worrywart mothers."

Gertrude's last point definitely rang true for Beatrice. She had been spending a lot of her time and ingredients brewing recently. She was close to running out on many things she had brought from the castle. Things that weren't necessarily easy to replace. If she could minimize that without any real harm being done, then it would be great. Her time, though...well, it had kept her busy. What else would she do with more time?

By now, everyone was pretty used to the routine of walking and setting up camp. The only thing she needed to do was kind of be there. Just her standing around and supervising seemed to give everyone a bit of comfort. But really, did she ever have to tell anyone what to do anymore? After the first few people understood their place in the caravan's management, for the most part, the group worked as a well-oiled machine. Most of her time recently was spent just talking to Captain Major because they were the only two who shared the burden of command.

Bee agreed to Gertrude's suggestion. That left her with the unenviable task of finding something else useful to do. Sighing, she supposed that she had one more thing in common with Captain Major now.

Arthur followed at a jog behind the slightly panicked man. They made their way toward the center of the camp, where a large crowd was milling about. It seemed that the disturbance still hadn't gone away.

A few quick shouts and the crowd parted enough for him to walk through. In the center of the camp was now a small steamy pond that kept growing.

"Did anyone see what happened?" Arthur asked. He wasn't so sure that really anything happened, but a spring just appearing out of nowhere seemed rather unlikely.

The soldiers exchanged looks with each other briefly before

one tentatively raised his hands. "Uh. Sir, I don't know if anything happened. A huge geyser of water spurted from the ground, then it sort of stuttered, and... Now there's a puddle. Lord Void was here when it started. It seemed like he stopped it from shooting into the sky the whole time. I'm not sure what else he did, though."

Of course it was Lord Void, Arthur thought. So it didn't make any sense why. Had it really been that there was a geyser or natural spring under the camp the whole time, and it just *happened* to erupt right when Void was nearby? The odds of that seemed fairly unlikely. But he also didn't understand why the deity would do this if it had been done intentionally.

Looking around, he saw a little black disc sitting among the soldiers. No one else seemed to notice it. At the moment, it was actually sitting between someone's legs.

"Lord Void?" Arthur called over to the black disc with a hint of a bow.

The soldiers all around him jumped. They obviously hadn't realized that the god was still amongst them. Within half a second, a free space had cleared up around the area where it said. Void turned to look at Arthur before giving a small beep, followed by another series of sharp noises that he didn't quite understand.

How was he going to get the story out of Void? Would Void be willing to write it down for him? Well, might as well ask. But at the same time, maybe out in the open wasn't the place for this. "Would you mind accompanying me?"

Arthur was well aware that he couldn't give Void orders. But this was as close as he could get to telling the god what he wanted while still having it remain a request. Luckily the little godling didn't have any problems following him back to his tent.

Once they were better situated, Arthur sent his aide to speak to his lieutenant. He would have to continue the interrogations alone. Arthur had full confidence in the man's ability to get the truth out with or without his help. When he got a chance, he would read a report and join if needed. But for now, whatever was going on here was more important.

"So...what happened?" Arthur asked the black disc that alighted on his desk.

Void let out a few familiar beeps before eventually just picking up the quill and finding some scrap paper. In large blocky letters, it wrote out a message. "No oil. Hot water underground came up."

Arthur leaned back in his chair and rubbed his chin. So it was a geyser. He wasn't sure why Void used such simple words and wrote in such short sentences, but he was sure there was likely a reason. It didn't seem lazy or anything, but perhaps it was just expedient. The blocky letters kind of reminded him what a child would write when they were first learning. He pushed the likely blasphemous thought out of his mind for the moment.

"So, you just happened to be around when a new geyser formed?"

Void moved side to side, shaking its claw horizontally. Was that no?

"I'm sorry, you're going to have to explain a little bit more. I'm not sure I understood that."

The little black disk seemed to slump slightly as it picked up the quill once again.

CHAPTER 14

GO AND SIN NO MORE

"SO. It sounds like you released a natural hot spring into camp." Arthur leaned back as he summarized my jumbled explanation. I like all my things neat, but language was way harder than I ever thought it would be. Organizing the words before writing them down was an entirely different skill than planning how to clean a room. I would need a lot more practice before I was good at putting words together efficiently. Especially when they all had so many different meanings that could be misunderstood.

As it was, I kept to simple sentence fragments, since they seemed to cause the least confusion. That had generally gotten the point across to Arthur, even if he seemed to interpret them in a more generous light. Only after our little conversation did I understand how silly my search for missing oil was. There was no stolen oil, at least not in the way I had thought. When I had mentioned I was looking for it, Arthur said they had already "found" it.

He explained that the one stealing it was one of four people they had already captured. It took me an embarrassing amount of time to understand that there was no missing oil in the literal sense. Whoever was supposed to buy it had just bought less than they were supposed to and kept the leftover money. Luckily, I was able to pick this up through context clues, so I didn't think my processing speed came across as too slow.

Arthur scribbled down something on a piece of paper and stamped it with some melted wax. One of the young runners came in as he was called and grabbed the paper, dashing out of the tent soon after.

"I have to thank you on behalf of my men. They will all enjoy taking some time to soak in a hot spring, even if they will have to take shifts. We should be able to create a barrier to keep the water in with relatively little effort," Arthur told me. I wasn't sure I understood, but if he was happy, that was fine with me. Especially if they could help keep the rest of the water from getting everywhere. I carefully wrote out that they were welcome before setting the pen down.

Before the conversation could move on, one of the aides entered the tent. "Sir, we have an update from Lieutenant Jericho." Then, noticing me, he gave me a slight bow. "My lord."

"Well, what is it?" Arthur asked. I was curious, too, as it seemed like Arthur had already formed a good idea of what had happened. What else could Jericho have found?

The aide slid a piece of paper over the desk. Arthur unfurled it and frowned as he read. After he finished, he set it down on the table so I could read it too.

It wasn't a very complicated note, just that Jericho believed that he had a good idea of who the perpetrator was but couldn't prove it yet. What did it take to prove someone was the guilty party? This was a tricky problem. Just because I knew information didn't mean I would be able to communicate it to others. Teaching children is a perfect example of this.

I imagined if I had to solve any of the kids' problems when I hadn't seen the situations play out with my very own sensors. Most of the time, their stories were rambling and incoherent. It was all I could do to get the gist of them, and that was only when I had personally witnessed the events. Now, if I had to prove to one child what another child said was true.... That would be hard.

Arthur sighed as he stood up. "Might as well take care of this now. I don't want to still be on this tomorrow. Void, do you want to come?"

Sure, I beeped. This time he seemed to be able to understand the beep just fine without any elaboration. I followed, floating just over the ground as we made our way to the outskirts of the camp. There was a normal tent that didn't stand out from any of the others, but somehow Arthur knew which one he was looking for. As we crossed the threshold, I noticed a few runes on the edges of the tent flaps. Once we were inside, I noticed that the sounds from outside were dulled than expected—almost 81.2 percent lower. I wasn't sure what that was supposed to accomplish, but it seemed intentional.

A gruff-looking man glanced over at our entry. There were four other humans sitting in chairs, looking rather uncomfortable in the center of the room. One of them was the man who had given me the rope I used to seat the gates of Caleb. "Ah, Commander, I'm glad you could make it back, perhaps we can resolve this tonight."

Arthur nodded to the man but otherwise didn't say anything, so the gruff man continued. "So far, we have confirmed that only these four have had access to the records..."

I relegated the guy's words to a subprocessor as I found something far more interesting. Opening my spiritual sense, I looked at the four humans in the chairs. None of their spirits stood out as particularly dim, nor were any bright. On the surface, they all had some amount of filth on them, but not too much more than an average amount, from what I had seen. One of the younger men had a bit more than normal, but by no means the worst I had seen, even today. Was one of them really responsible for this?

To be fair, I didn't know how my skill worked very well yet. But if the stuff on the top was from bad things done recently, it didn't seem that any one of them had erred too much. Still, the gruff man and Arthur seemed convinced that it was one of them. To be thorough, I got to work scrubbing off the soul grime from each one of them.

While I was cleaning their spirits, Arthur and the man who seemed to be named Jericho were talking to each of them in soft tones. Each one was proclaiming their innocence, providing countless reasons why it wasn't them. I noticed that when I finished cleaning the spirit of the one lady, she seemed a bit more relaxed. After a little bit, the two men almost entirely stopped questioning them. I wasn't sure what they were doing, exactly. I recalled situations like this in my humans' shows at home, but when humans asked other humans questions in those, they usually split the people up.

I let them do their work as I continued mine. After polishing the first person's soul to a dull shine, I started cleaning one of the young men's souls. This time, as I progressed, he didn't relax at all. In fact, he got more and more tense, and I could see drops of sweat rolling down his temples. Arthur picked up on this almost right away.

By the time I was finished cleaning, the man had broken. Tears started rolling down his face, and his shoulders shook. When he finally looked up, it was as if a weight had been lifted from his shoulders. After I finished with him, I moved on to the other young man, but I listened to the confession.

Apparently, he was indeed responsible. He claimed there were reasons for what he did, something about a sick niece and potions being too expensive. Maybe that was why his soul wasn't as dirty as I would have thought? Did having justifications for doing bad things make it less bad? Or was it that he didn't feel as guilty?

The very dirty souls didn't seem to be only possessed by people who thought they were doing bad, so that didn't seem right either. I also didn't think that causing mess and disorder like this was very defensible, despite excuses, but I'd have to think about it. I would need more data points to figure out how this skill worked.

Bee couldn't contain her smile as the valley entrance appeared on the horizon. It wasn't that she really wanted her journey to end. While it wasn't her favorite thing, it hadn't been awful since the rain stopped. She just really wanted to be home. These last few weeks away from Void had been hard. They felt...off, somehow. It felt like part of her was missing. Like there was a hole in her heart.

Realizing how much she leaned on her god for support was humbling. It also amazed her how much Void managed to do without her realizing it. Without him around, so many little things popped up that required her attention. She was lucky that she had such good Repair skills. A number of small things broke that she was able to fix easily, like cartwheels and clothing. This trip was the first time that she used the skill on things other than her own body with any regularity.

It was a bit of a boon, as she felt real growth in the skill, but in the back of her mind, she knew that if her master had been around, there wouldn't have been so many problems. Nonetheless, it was coming to an end. Soon, they would be back in the castle. There, with her friends and structured roles, there wouldn't be such a burden of leadership on her. The support system she had worked out with the others would do a lot to directly lift the stress off of her. She only had to integrate the newcomers.

That shouldn't be too hard. She wasn't sure why, but these people were relatively easy to lead. It helped that there were only a few clear, unquestioned authority figures. Aside from herself, the only other ones were the captain and Gertrude. The military made sense, but the others... Maybe something about living in a city made them more likely to listen to authority than people from the more rural areas.

When she stepped into the trees, she noticed a man appear next to the road as if by magic. One of Susan's scouts. No one else seemed to notice him as they walked past. As she looked over at the man, he fell into step with her.

She recognized him from the first group that Susan had started training. "Mat, right?"

"Wow, you remember me!" the man said, his voice drawing a lot of surprised stares. "Welcome back, High Priestess. Is the Lord Void around?"

Bee was a bit taken aback by the address. The title hadn't been common; most people had just called her Bee when she had left. It seemed that things had changed in her absence. "No, Void is hunting down the root of the undead problem. I am coming with refugees from Caleb."

"The city fell?" Mat asked. She noticed as his shoulders tensed slightly.

"Not quite. Void got there just in time. But as they are vulnerable, we are taking the ones who won't be useful in the rebuilding for now. We also have a contingent of guards to help along the way," Bee explained.

Mat relaxed somewhat. "If you can give me numbers, I can send a runner ahead to get things prepared for you, ma'am."

"That would be greatly appreciated, Mat," Bee said. After telling him how many to expect, she then asked her own question. "It seems there have been some changes while I was away. What did I miss?"

CHAPTER 15

HEART OF THE MATTER

HAROLD PULLED his hood down over his eyes as he made his way beneath the gates of Alexander. Here in Barleona, they spoke the same language as in the kingdom, but the people looked significantly different. His standard brown hair and brown eyes would stand out here amongst the predominantly blonde, blue-eyed people. All around, he could see the city's typical straw-colored hair and crystal eyes popping out of dark complexions in bright relief. The shadow of his cowl hid his face, giving him some anonymity, at least.

It had been a long time since he had done any fieldwork, but he still hadn't forgotten how to move through a crowd without being noticed. Despite his magical expertise and his political acumen, flying under the radar had long been his most reliable skill. That, and knowing when to run.

Moving deftly through the streets of milling people, Harold scanned the street signs for the mark. The border crossing had been simple: a few fake documents, some bribes, and he had slipped right through. Now he just needed to find his contact. The unfamiliar city wasn't hard to navigate, but that didn't help when he didn't know where he was even going. There were more apothecaries than he would have expected. But none so far had the little horns carved into the bottom of the hanging sign he was looking for.

The mark of the Jailers wasn't always in the same spot, but the few inches of the sign base was a good way to hide it in plain sight. Hence his surreptitious glances upward as he passed.

At the fifth shop, he finally found what he was looking for. Instead of under the sign, it was at the bottom of the dirty windowsill. It had taken him a few minutes of casual "window shopping" to find it, so he wandered away for a bit before returning and going in. Hopefully, if anyone had noticed a hooded stranger stopping at the store, they would have moved on before seeing him enter.

A little bell rang as the door opened; Harold closed it softly behind him as he stepped into the dimly lit shop. The walls were lined with shelves, each one of them crammed full of random junk. Not rare materials, niche finds, and exotic wares—that was normal stuff to find in an apothecary shop. Harold was a bit of an alchemist himself, and he could guarantee that this stuff was junk. It was poor quality and overpriced. But that was on purpose.

A clattering from the back room indicated that the shop was not as empty as it first seemed.

"I'll be right there," a grumpy voice called from the back room. Harold settled in for a wait. It was a full five minutes before a wrinkled old man slowly hobbled out to the front. This was intentional as well. The point of the shop was to be as uninviting as it could be; they didn't want customers to come in. That would only get in the way of their real business.

The few unlucky souls that did come in unawares were met with the same treatment, followed by an exceedingly unhelpful and grouchy shopkeeper, until they left. Fortunately, Harold was no normal customer. "When did the last batch of wardroot come in?"

The gruff man rubbed his chin for a second. "Couldn't have been more than a month back, maybe two."

After completing the passphrase, they both relaxed. Harold cracked a small smile. Flipping up a panel that kept customers from coming behind the counter, the old man ushered him into the back, moving with a newfound grace.

After the man dispelled a minor illusion, Harold got a look at the true back room. It was entirely different from the front of the store. The previously dingy floor and walls were meticulously clean and well-kept back here. Actual valuable alchemy ingredients and premade salves populated the counters in neatly labeled containers. What caught Harold's eye most, though, was the room's other occupant. A young woman sitting in a straight-back chair sharpening a knife. Looking up, she met Harold's eyes.

"Harold?" she asked.

"The same." He paused for a second before he was able to recall her name. "Amy?"

The young woman stood and offered him a hand, which he took. "At least I have a package that knows how to hide."

It was odd not having command for the first time in a while; he was going to have to adjust how he interacted with his coworkers accordingly. Harold pulled his hood down and gave her his best winning smile. "I'm not so green that I need a babysitter, just a tour guide."

Amy gave him a doubtful look from the corner of her eye but didn't comment on it. Instead, she gestured to the chair across from her. As he sat down, he realized that the old man had disappeared when he wasn't paying attention. Once he settled in, he looked more closely at his "tour guide."

If he had been asked to describe the average Barleonan, Amy was who would come to mind. Every single stereotype was checked. Blonde hair, blue eyes, a dark complexion, and slightly on the shorter side. Slim and slightly athletic, but not enough to be noteworthy. The only thing marking her off from any other nameless face in the crowd was a hardness around the eyes, and he would bet that it would disappear the second they were outside.

"Are there any updates to the itinerary? Just the three sites?" Amy asked after a second of silence.

"Just the three. Any news about them?" Harold confirmed. He was finding it surprisingly easy to slip back into the coded language of the operatives. They would always assume someone was listening, and few in the organization actually knew any of the details for an operation anyways. He would be surprised if Amy actually did know what was at their destinations.

"Something out of Arwen has been causing a bit of an uproar recently. I haven't heard why. Do you want to wait 'til the commotion dies down?" Amy asked.

Harold frowned; the site of Arwen was where Syleth'an was held. By all accounts, it might be the weakest of the Lieutenants in pure combat power, but that didn't really matter now. There was no one around that would fare well against any Lieutenant anyways. Aside from that...thing.

From this perspective, Imposter might be one of the worst ones to be let loose as it could wreak its havoc from the inside. Not that they really knew what its true powers were, just old legends passed down for millennia. "No, we should go there first."

Amy rubbed her forehead. "That *is* going to add a bit to our travel time. There was a reason we were visiting it second."

"How much sooner can we get there if we skip the first stop?" Harold asked, not wanting to be completely unreasonable.

"Maybe a day or two. That doesn't seem much out of a two-week journey," Amy said in a suspiciously neutral tone. Harold considered. He would need a day or so at each site, but if they weren't going to be there for a few weeks anyways, did it really matter? Or did every day count?

"How old is your news of the place?" Harold asked. It could be that she got it through some message instead of a rumor.

"Oh, couple weeks at least," Amy replied.

"Well, then we don't need to rush to that one in particular," Harold allowed. "When can we leave?"

Bee practically floated along the forest path leading to the castle. She knew that she wanted to get back, but she hadn't been aware of *how much* she wanted to get back. It had already been a couple of days, and she still felt like she was walking on clouds. The rest of the caravan was not quite as happy, of course, but she could still feel the mood was lighter than it had been for the entire trip.

Sometime on the second day, a pair of figures from the castle intercepted the caravan. Bee was leading up in the front, so she was one of the first people to see them. She was also definitely the first to make out who they were. Running ahead, Bee left the column behind in the dust.

"BEE!" Tony's familiar voice rang out over the road. Not slowing, she crashed into his open arms, nearly breaking his ribs with the devastating squeeze she applied. Next to Tony, Susan gave a small wave. Stepping back, Bee couldn't take the grin off of her face.

"By Void, it's good to see you both! How is everything? Is everyone alright?" Bee asked in a rush, her words tumbling over each other as she tried to get them out.

However, even as she was speaking, Tony was also asking his own questions. "Is everything okay? Where's Void? What happened?"

They both paused, trying to parse through the other's words while occasionally cutting each other off with responses. Eventually, Susan took pity on them and stepped in. "Everyone in the castle is excited for your return, Bee, though they are all slightly concerned. They want to know where Void has gone and why he didn't return to us. I'm sure they will all be excited to tell you everything, but will want to hear your story first."

"Well... I don't want to repeat myself too much, but Void is helping the army hunt down the rest of the undead and it said that it would return soon," Bee said, regaining control of herself. "So, did anything noteworthy happen in my absence?"

"Right now, the castle is preparing a feast in Void's honor to welcome you home. I'm glad the scout you sent ahead gave us good numbers, as I wasn't sure we would need the entire great hall at first. After seeing your group, I don't doubt it," Tony said.

"I told you my scouts know their work now. It was only that one time..." Susan protested.

"What one time?" Bee asked, slightly concerned there was something wrong.

"By *one time* she means that one of her scouts saw a cloud over one of the mountains and thought it was smoke from a fire," Tony said.

"It was a perfectly reasonable assumption." Susan defended her people. "Better to be prepared for a fire that isn't coming than not prepared for one that is."

"Well, now we have fire pails in strategic locations. And directions to the nearest exits of the castle posted regularly. *Just* in case it comes down to that," Tony explained while rolling his eyes. "Though with how little wood is used in its construction, I would be surprised if we would ever lose more than the contents of a single room in a fire."

Bee remembered getting a look into the castle's construction in the aftermath of their fight with Nazareth'gak; there really hadn't been any wood. But like any alchemy practitioner, she knew the real danger wasn't the heat. There was a reason the labs were on higher floors. "It's not the flames that are dangerous, it's the smoke. If there is a fire, then we need to let the bad air out, otherwise people won't be able to breathe. Even if there isn't structural damage."

Susan sent Tony a knowing look that he pointedly ignored.

"So. What else happened besides false alarms from scouts?" Bee prompted.

"Well, some of the ki—ah, the *Nighty Knights*, have started getting their first levels..."

CHAPTER 16
DETECTIVE SPOT

OVER THE NEXT FEW DAYS, I had a blast. Other than what the soldiers had started calling "the Hot Springs Incident," everything had been rather routine. I followed behind the army, cleaning up the best I could. Sometimes Arthur would ask me to come to spend some time up front with him, and we would talk.

Well, *he* would talk. As we moved, I would write by engraving words on a large flat stone with my lamp. After I was done, I would erase the surface by blasting it smooth with a broader beam. It was surprisingly efficient, and over time I got faster at this than at actual writing with my Grabby Arm. After a few messages, though, I needed a new rock. Engraving and erasing like this systematically shrunk any stone I used over time, especially with how deep my engravings needed for the optimal reading experience.

These breaks were nice. As fast as the army was able to march, I was able to clean much faster. This gave them plenty of time to accumulate large amounts of work for me. Then I could do them all at once. It was much more efficient than if I was following along right at their heels.

Arthur and I would talk about all sorts of things. It would start off with some basic questions and answers, but Arthur seemed to enjoy just speaking about his past. He'd tell me stories about past campaigns or skirmishes he had been involved in. In return, I'd ask questions about tactics and leadership and how he made sure that all the waste and kitchens were cleaned properly in time to march. Overall, it was a nice exchange. I wouldn't say we were becoming friends, but it seemed like something close. There was definitely respect between us.

During the night, my duties became more typical of my usual experience. I previously would have wandered the castle, taking care of small tasks. I would wander the camp doing the same. This was a necessary job, as we moved on quickly in the mornings. It was important not to leave any unfinished business behind when we did.

It wasn't much, but it gave me something to do. Besides, I didn't like leaving the camp dirty, even if it was only going to be seen for a short stint in the morning while everyone packed up. It always became messier when we packed, and then I'd have to wipe the area clean afterward anyways. This pointless work was a bit disheartening, but I did take solace in it. At least it kept me working on my skills. By now, I could level out a dirt patch so that I could barely tell the microns of difference in height from one side to the other. I was rather proud of this fact.

Several nights after the Hot Spring Incident, the first real disturbance occurred. I heard some odd noises outside long after everyone went to bed, and as I worked my way over on my cleaning route, I ran into a sleeping human. Well, I thought he was sleeping at first. Still, after a closer examination with my Advanced Sensors, I realized he was not breathing. Also, he was leaking a lot of his internal fluids. Blood, I corrected myself.

This leaking fluid was forming a puddle around his head. Odd. I did my best to repair him with my Domain and poked him in the head a couple of times, but there was no response. It seemed I had found a broken human.

Now what? I really didn't know what to do next. I had seen some dead humans, but not many. Only the zombies and those few troublesome mean humans who tried to threaten the castle. I'd never seen just a body like this before, and I didn't know what to do.

After a few seconds of processing, I realized it was probably important to find out why this human had died. So I scanned the site extremely thoroughly. I did notice several things. Several sets of footprints passed in between the tents where I found the body. I couldn't really tell the freshness, but I had just cleaned this area fifteen minutes and forty-six seconds ago, so none of them were older than that.

Unfortunately, all the footprints were of the same military issue boot. I only had the size to go off of, and the military was rather stingy about making proper footwear. There were only four basic sizes, but I could tell that one was from a large man and two were from a medium man. Looking at the soles of the shoes on the dead human, I realized that it was one of the mediums, so I was looking for one larger man and one average-sized man. Neither of them had the narrower soles that the female soldiers left.

On top of that, the majority of the leakage was clearly from a wound inflicted by a knife to the throat. It looked like the attack had been from a stabbing motion into the side, but I couldn't tell if it was from someone standing behind the dead human or in front of it. I wasn't sure how I could tell. I'd have to compare it to a lot more stab holes, and I didn't think anyone would be down for me testing that. Maybe I could try and model that some other way later.

Okay. What else could I see? I scanned the body carefully again. I couldn't place the exact time of death, but I could tell that it was within the last ten minutes. I also knew that I heard sounds from around here, but I couldn't tell if that was from it being stabbed or from someone moving the body. Judging based on the scuff marks, the body had indeed been moved. But I didn't think that kind of action would produce the sounds I had heard.

So. I was going to go with the assumption that this human was killed when I heard something. That was four minutes and thirty-seven seconds ago. Taking a step back, I examined the body in a lot more detail, focusing on its hands and trying to see if there was any trace of the attacker left. Maybe it managed to put up a fight. Or, at the very least, maybe there were some other sorts of marks left behind by the humans.

I found my first clue under the fingernails of the deceased. It was a little bit of skin. Apparently, this person hadn't died instantly. The man must have scratched his attacker, either from in front or behind. I continued looking under the body and found a few other clues.

In order to contextualize them, I decided I should take inventory. Everything the man had on him, starting with the uniform, every piece was there. The same cap, shirt, undershirt, underclothes, trousers, boots, socks, and belt were all present and standard. Looking at the spot where awards were usually pinned, I noticed that it was relatively light. Only three medallions hung from its breast. However, I did notice that it was an officer.

It looked to be a second lieutenant, which matched the man's age. The body of the deceased also had a few things tied to his belt. The first thing I noticed was a pouch with several flat gold and silver discs inside. I had often seen these disks be exchanged as part of a complicated trading system these humans had. It involved pieces of paper with numbers on them being shuffled about in an elaborate system that I had yet to fully understand.

One day I had to look into that, but now I needed to focus. It was odd that those were left. Humans seemed to really like them, and whenever they found them, they usually picked them up and put them in their pouches. So if whoever killed this man didn't pick them up, they clearly either didn't care about them or didn't know they were there. But I supposed that meant that he wasn't killed over his money.

The more I thought about this man, the more I saw him as a person rather than a dead body. At first, it was easier for me to understand if I just thought of the dead body as an *it*. But trying to figure out his past was making me think of it as a human. Just like Arthur. Just like Beatrice.

It was surprisingly difficult to handle. If I thought of him as a human like this, I also had to think of everything that this human must have done in his life. The things that he would no longer be able to do. Was this why humans became sad at the prospect of death?

Shaking back and forth slightly to clear my processors and flush my cache, I refocused. It was suddenly a higher priority that I find out who did this.

Another thing he had on his belt was a small knife. I noticed that his hand was gripping the hilt of it when he fell, and it looked like he had pulled the knife out a bit. I was well aware that the sheaths were built to keep knives securely in place so they weren't jostled loose. The strap that would hold the cross guard of the blade in had been popped off by a quick movement of his thumb. So clearly, the man was expecting trouble.

Or I supposed he could have just been lazy. But judging based off of the crispness of his uniform, which I heartily approved of, that didn't seem to be the case. So if the person knew that he would be attacked and had tried to ready a weapon, it stood to reason that the attack must have come from the front. But if there were two assailants, as the prints indicated, then it was also possible that he had been assaulted from both sides and had been surprised.

Without much else to go on, I wasn't sure what to do next. Then I took another look at the footprints. And I was able to solve one part of the mystery.

It seemed that there was actually a person in front and behind. I didn't realize it at first, but I could actually tell the weight of a person by how deeply their footprint sunk. And I could tell that there were three distinct weights. Two were pretty similar but off by at least 5 percent. The last were obviously much heavier, based on the foot sizes that lined up. And I could see more footprints coming in three sets from one side.

I ran a simulation based on my findings. One person walked and stopped, presumably the victim. Someone blocked his path from ahead—the smaller man, it seemed—while the larger man stayed behind him. I could see the footprints of the other two leaving from the other end of the alley, meaning the big man had just stepped over this man's body. So it seemed that the victim was, in fact, surrounded.

I was actually able to identify whose footprints were within a certain tolerance, using the amount of context provided. The information here gave a much clearer picture than I initially thought.

Not wanting to disturb the scene, I lifted myself off the ground a bit more so that my jets wouldn't move anything that was important to the scene as I moved. I would come back. Soon. Then I began to follow the footprints away from the body.

CHAPTER 17

KIDS WILL BE KIDS

"HOW IN VOID'S name did the Nighty Knights manage to find something to kill?" Bee asked in shock. "They're only seven years old at most!"

Susan and Tony looked at each other.

"Um. Well, you see," Tony stammered.

Susan eventually cut him off and tried her best to explain. "Well, we've had a bit of a problem with some undead coming at the gates at night, and apparently, a few of the watch trainees had assisted the Knights in climbing up the wall and throwing rocks down on them. This was how the initial levels happened, but...it's gotten a bit out of hand since then.

"As far as I know, no one's actually managed to get their first class yet. But once they got skills, they started leveraging those to get the younger members kills from the wall as well. This is getting the kids levels well before they really know what to do with them. So far, none have picked any bad skills that I know of. But I don't know how long that will last. I think the youngest person to have gotten a skill was...three, maybe? But I'm not certain."

Bee rubbed her head in frustration. She hadn't figured out what she wanted to do with the kids before she had left. Worse, she really hadn't had any time to think about it since then. Why bother when they were so young? There should have been plenty of time before this happened. But it seemed that Void had its own plans for them. At least, she sure hoped her master did. If they waited a little bit, she would help them ensure that Devotee of Spot was one of their options, but they might not even need that. If they got a better class from killing undead while they were still young, then she shouldn't change it.

The system usually handed out classes based on achievements, and she couldn't think of anything more impressive for their age than killing undead. But whether or not the system recognized age as a variable to adjust for was still uncertain, according to some scholars.

"Well, I suppose if nothing's too bad, I can always fix it with the Devotee class... Even if they ended up with some useless skills." Not that any skill was particularly useless. But without a direction in one's life, which was rather rare to have at three years old, they might end up being off target from what they really wanted.

"So, Susan, why weren't their parents able to stop them or something?"

"We tried. We told them not to go up there, many times. Yet somehow, they managed to work together to distract us long enough to get up and get those first kills. They're really figuring out how to work as a unit." Susan shrugged. "After that, a lot of the skills they developed were...well, unusual."

"Unusual how?" Bee asked.

Susan made a face. But it was Tony who answered. "Unusual as in they're pretty darn powerful, like what I got when I hit level 20. It's almost as if the system gave them bonuses for their first skill or something. Never seen anything like it..."

Bee stared blankly. It had to be Void messing with the system again. Of course. "Well, at least they're not useless. I suppose when I get back, I will have to talk to them and make sure that they're using their skills responsibly. But if we can't stop them from gaining power when they're so young, we better teach them how to control it, before they get someone hurt."

"Yeah, well, I talked with Felix a bit," Tony said. "And surprisingly, they seem to have a pretty decent idea of this. Something about power from service. They've got a few little slogans, like 'with great power comes great responsibility' and 'protect and serve.' They're weirdly well crafted, ones I hadn't heard before. So either they made them up themselves, which is very impressive, or Void told them, and it's hard to say which one is actually the case."

"Mm. Well, in that case, things are probably okay. But if they're progressing this fast, I think every day is important. I should probably run ahead and talk to them as soon as possible," Bee mused.

"Yeah, that's probably a good idea," Susan agreed. "It'd be best if you want to make sure every preparation is to your liking for the new arrivals. Mary has been doing a great job, but she is only one woman, after all. She could use some help."

Bee nodded and looked back at the approaching caravan. "Susan. Before I go, I'd like to introduce you to Captain Major. And if you wouldn't mind staying behind to help, could you watch over them for the last remaining leg? That would be great."

Susan nodded, and Tony smiled. "So you're probably going to want me to come back and help supervise everyone, right?"

"Actually, it would be nice if you could stay." She retrieved a long list from her coat pocket and handed it to him. "I made a list of some of the more important people and their classes, noteworthy stats, and talents that I think might be useful. It'd be good if you got acquainted with them to see if I missed anyone. We're going to have a lot of idle hands, and we don't want to leave it that way."

Tony looked a little bit depressed at the prospect of having to do actual work, but he still took the paper and scanned it, nodding. "Well, say hello to my siblings for me. I look forward to seeing you in a couple of days."

Before she ran off, Bee went and tracked down Captain Major for a slightly stiff introduction of Susan as the castle's expert in all things military. Actually, maybe "security" was the right word. With that taken care of, she was off with a wave.

It was late into the evening as Arthur sat in his tent, shuffling through reports. Sometimes he was able to do this alone. Sometimes he had Void watching him. Truthfully, he didn't really mind it too much. Void would sometimes point out simple mistakes, but nothing nearly as disruptive as when he found the embezzling scheme. Well, tonight, it was elsewhere. Likely off doing something else in the camp.

Arthur was slightly worried about the little disk's absence and a little annoyed that the worry took up a small part of his concentration. He was already half regretting asking the young god to come along. As much as the troop's order had improved by its very presence, there was a certain amount of unease that having a god amongst them caused. Arthur really couldn't blame his soldiers for that, since he felt the same.

Arthur thought that this Void was a young god, "young" being the keyword. After watching the thing go about its business and conversing with it more, it simply felt right. In some ways, it reminded Arthur of his oldest son, Jace, when he was seven. Morality was a fledgling thing of stark black and white, with only hints of gray beginning to peek through. Right and wrong were what they were, and everything needed to be a particular way. Not that Void really went out of its way to make trouble for anyone. It was just that it didn't seem to quite understand that others might have different priorities and values than its own. A sentiment made quite clear in how much knowledge it expected Arthur to have about the camp's janitorial matters.

Still, he was impressed by the god. It asked good questions at times, ones that reflected a deeply intellectual mind. And if it learned more about the ways of humanity and decided that their race was worth saving instead of exterminating for being too unclean, he felt that they were in good hands. If they had to be in some divine hands, at least.

After the Hot Springs Incident, things had been relatively calm. If anything, they'd been a little bit too calm. He expected more fights amongst the men, or reports of disorderly conduct, or *something* to go wrong, but none of that had appeared. He had a full two and a half days with not a single report of misbehavior or corrective action having come across his desk. And that was honestly starting to get on his nerves a little bit.

It felt like the calm before the storm. He wasn't sure how much of this was because he avoided being like a young guard and overexerting his influence. Maybe it was because of the god. It was too hard to tell. Arthur put his quill down and rubbed his eyes, leaning back in his chair. The reports were mostly done, and he was looking forward to going to bed. At his age, a long day of marching and writing still took a toll on him, even with his high stats.

As he began to stand, an aide burst into his tent with a familiar concerned look on his face. "Sir. You had better come right away. There's been a murder."

Following the tracks through the camp was surprisingly easy. It was late at night, and I had cleaned the path they were on not that long ago. There were other footprints crisscrossing the trail, but those were easily filtered out. It wasn't until they went to the mess hall that things were harder to follow.

There they mixed with many other people going in for food at odd hours, depending on when their duty would allow. But even then, I had cleaned less than half an hour ago there, so I just simply combed through every single set of footprints until I found a clue. Turns out I didn't actually find them going the same direction, but rather each set splitting off to go different ways. These two people appeared to have moved into the mess hall together but left it separately.

I wondered why that would be. Was it because they were in different units and slept in different places, or were they actively trying to throw anyone off their trail? I wasn't sure which one to follow. It seemed that either one of them could lead me to one culprit. But then, would the other be able to escape? It was a risk I'd have to take.

Picking a random number between one and two, I ended up following the large man's footprints. They were slightly more distinctive than the average-sized man's, so that did make it a little bit easier. But that also meant it would be harder for me to track down the other man later.

A few feet out of the door, I decided that I probably should have made a smarter choice than just picking a random number and doubled back to follow the average man instead. He had made his way through the camp and what looked to be a meandering path, often stopping at the tents' entrances for some reason. After a good twenty minutes of walking, he went into a tent that he had not come out of yet.

Quietly as I could, I floated closer to the tent. From outside, I sensed that the man wasn't alone. There were three others in the tent with him. Two were sleeping, one was tossing and turning, and the final man was taking off his shoes. It seemed that he was likely the one who came in last.

I scanned him as well as I could from the outside of the tent. Unfortunately, I couldn't find any definitive proof until I looked at his belt. There was a dagger that perfectly matched the wound from the victim, and I would bet a week's worth of cleaning time that if I looked at it more closely, I would find traces of blood that I could match with a sample.

It didn't seem like he was going anywhere, so I placed a marker for this location on my internal map of the camp. I also marked his soul with a little plus symbol for good measure. Then I went to go track down his accomplice.

CHAPTER 18

DEATH FROM ABOVE

WHEN BEE REACHED THE CASTLE, she was greeted by an odd sight. Thankfully it was one that Susan had prepared her for, if only slightly. On top of the wall, a pair of guards stood watch. The one to the right was one of the men who had come as a refugee, one of Susan's personal trainees. To the left, top of his head barely visible above the crenellations, was one of the children.

This wasn't a child she had particularly interacted with before, but if she remembered correctly, he was four or five. Much, much too young to be standing guard. Even if something did happen, she couldn't imagine what he would do. But when she scanned him, she saw that he was, in fact, level two. This meant that he had not only gotten one kill to get that first level, he had managed to accumulate more since then. What had these kids been up to?

As she approached, the guards noticed her. They both came to attention with a salute before relaxing to a more informal wave. Without hesitation, the adult guard disappeared from the wall and began opening the gate from below. When she reached the entrance, she just ducked under the still-opening gate and turned to thank him. To her surprise, she saw the little boy walking down to meet her. But he didn't use the stairs leading to the top of the wall. He was simply walking on air.

"Hello! High Priestess Bee!" the boy said. "Welcome back! Everyone's missed you a bun—uh, greatly!" Bee just stared at him, dumbstruck. Was that the Air Step skill she had read about? That was a really rare one, not to mention powerful. To get it as his first skill... This kid was insanely lucky. Or was it luck?

She'd have to talk to the rest of the kids. But if they were all getting powerful skills like this, it could be that the system was rewarding them for earning their first levels so young. It would explain why she managed to get Scan, one of the rarest skills in the kingdom, as her own first skill. Hm. An interesting theory.

"Yeah. It's good to be back. I'm sorry, I can't remember your name. Could you remind me?"

"Of course, Miss Beatrice! I'm Jason."

"Well, Jason, that's quite an impressive skill you have there."

"I know! It's the cool—erm, I mean, it's quite impressive!" He jumped a few times in place, each taking him higher than the last. "I can't fly yet, but I can already get really high up!"

"How high, exactly?"

"Ummmmm, twelve steps! It used to be two or three, but I've been practicing a lot. I can go higher than the wall now!"

The man stepped over from the gate winch, leaving the gate fully open. "He's right. He literally hasn't stopped the entire time. He paces back and forth. He's been hovering a foot off the wall for as long as he can. I've had to catch him from falling over three times just this morning."

Jason looked slightly abashed. Bee laughed and looked over at the slightly annoyed guard, who seemed to be putting on a little bit of an act, not actually annoyed as he was pretending to be. "Well, I'm glad someone was here to catch him, at least. Does anyone know where Mary would be?"

Jason piped up. "She's probably in her office. Oh, she has an office now! It's fancy. It's, uhhh..."

"Right, you were gone by the time she set that up. It's on the second floor in the east wing. You should be able to find it pretty easily."

"Thanks, you two. Keep up the good work, Jason." Bee smiled as she started walking towards the entryway. It sounded like she had a lot to catch up on.

Bee made her way into the castle. For a moment, she stood and drank in the familiar sight. She was finally home. The pristine white stone walls and grand entry were just as she had left them.

She had hoped to go right to Mary and let her know what was going on, but every single person she passed from the entry hall up to the stairs stopped her to chat, even if it was just to say hello. Most people were just welcoming her home and expressing their hopes that Void, too, would return soon. Even still, the numerous brief interactions added up.

It seemed that the news that Void was not with her had spread. She didn't mind it or anything, but it was good to know. So far, it seemed that everyone was in high spirits, looked well-fed, and was rather busy. That was to be expected, as the whole palace was buzzing with preparations for the arrival of new guests.

Bee eventually made it upstairs to talk to Mary, but she did notice a lot of children along the way. Some of them were standing at conspicuous points at the ends of hallways, and she made a mental note to figure out what they were up to. Perhaps they were also guards. Still, the idea of child soldiers didn't quite sit very well with her. Even if they might be disproportionately useful and excited about it themselves.

Soon after Bee knocked on the door, Mary's voice called from inside. "Come in."

Bee let herself in. Before she knew it, Mary had dashed over and wrapped her up in a warm embrace. Bee stood stunned for a second before returning it. "Oh, it's so good you're back. When you left, I had no idea you'd be gone for so long. But I hear you're bringing us new friends."

Bee muttered something, but her voice was muffled from the

way she was pressed against the older woman. Eventually, she managed to extract herself from the embrace, and they sat down around a small writing table Mary was using for a desk. "Yeah, a lot has happened. A *lot*. But we managed to accomplish everything we wanted to. We saved the city, fought some undead, and now we have a caravan of refugees looking for shelter."

"Oh, my. That sounds like quite a story."

"Yeah, it is. I want to take care of a couple more things before I tell it to everyone, though."

"Understandable. Of course. What do you want to take care of?"

Bee then updated Mary regarding the incoming refugees. She gave her head of food management all the numbers and details about who they'd be taking in and what supplies they came with, which Mary promised to pass along to Trent. After Bee finished her summary, she asked about the kids. "The other thing is, after we finish talking, I'd like to talk to all of the children who have been engaged in getting levels. I want to make sure that they're not hindering their future development. And maybe there's some things I can do to help."

Mary sighed. "Well, they might actually listen to you, seeing that you're the High Priestess and all. But I'll let them know that you'll be waiting for them. They should gather to meet you after this. There's a lot going on. I really hope you can help them, dear."

Tracking down the larger man was easier than I expected. Turned out he was the third largest man in the camp based on his weight. At least that was true among the soldiers represented in the footprints I had surveyed so far, which I believed to represent about 72 percent of the group. So returning to the mess hall and following his footprints was as easy as whisking up dog fur.

His tracks also wound around the camp, though he spent a lot less time stopping to talk to people and instead went towards the outskirts where the more low-ranking troops stayed. I found him in a large tent crammed with twenty people. He was by far the largest person there and was already asleep, snoring quite loudly.

Now that I had located both of them, I needed to figure out what to do. I could consume them, which was what I had done in previous cases that warranted punishment. But seeing how that had worked out for the humans I still had in my dustbin...I didn't think that was a great option.

I set a reminder for myself to check on them again soon. It had been a while, and I really had been putting it off. Not because I was averse to the work, of course, but because the thought of what might have happened to them was quite unpleasant.

So if I didn't want to put them in my dustbin... Well, really, perhaps they deserved that. They did kill a man. I considered talking to Arthur about it. He probably would know what to do. Or, actually, I could save time by just bringing them to Arthur. That would be way easier.

So not wanting to burst into the tent and cause a scene, I sent a gust of air inside the tent and lifted up a rock. With a brief flex of Air Manipulation, I sent it flying towards his stomach. It bounced off, but he just kind of brushed at it with his hand as he was sleeping and didn't wake up. That didn't work. I was hoping to get his attention, but clearly, that wasn't enough.

So instead, I simply grabbed the collar of the shirt he was sleeping in and yanked on it with Air Manipulation. The fabric wasn't quite strong enough to lift him without ripping, but pulling it certainly got his attention. He jumped up suddenly and disturbed a few people around him, who crankily mumbled at him.

He rolled over a couple of times, then eventually got up, muttering about having to go to the bathroom. As he walked out of the tent, I pounced. Grabbing him by the back of his neck with my Grabby Arm, I lifted him into the air and flew away. Next I completely wrapped his mouth with my Air Manipulation so he wouldn't be able to disturb anyone with his screams. I then boosted over to where I had found the other, more average-sized man in the much larger tent to retrieve him too. It took a little bit of adjustment to hold on to them both, but after arranging the two men in a hug secured by cords of air, I grabbed the larger one's neck once more. Now I just needed to find Arthur.

I hovered over the mostly sleeping camp, looking for the commander. He wasn't in his tent, but he clearly hadn't gone far. I eventually spotted him standing over by the crime scene, looking at the dead body. Oh, good. He already knew what had happened. That meant I wouldn't have to explain so many things. I might just be able to help him find the culprit. With a quick thought, I adjusted my boosters and zipped over to him.

As I was approaching. I heard Arthur talking to someone. "Poor man. He was one of the few nobles I actually had hopes for. All the others seemed to be fairly useless, if not downright troublemaking. But maybe it was his attempts to actually learn how to behave properly that did him in. It wouldn't surprise me if he found out something he shouldn't have, and they didn't trust him to take the bribes like everyone else did."

Huh? I'd have to ask Arthur what he was talking about later. Descending from above, I set my two charges down and gave Arthur a cheery wave. Hopefully, this would help him clear up the matter quicker.

CHAPTER 19

TRUST THE SYSTEM

ARTHUR NEARLY JUMPED out of his skin as Void zipped down from the skies, two men held aloft with it. The men were immobilized as though by invisible bonds and plopped down face down in the dirt behind the god. Arthur was still gaping when Void gave its customary wave to him. Arthur, in a slight state of shock, actually returned the wave before he realized what he was doing and then gave a slight bow of greeting. "Lord Void. I—"

He cut off, glancing at the two people behind the god. They wriggled ineffectually on the ground. "Ahem. So. What's going on?"

Void pointed to the body, then the two people. Then it let out a series of complicated beeps that Arthur wasn't about to be able to interpret. Still, the message was pretty clear. It seemed like Void thought these men were responsible for poor Walter's death.

Arthur nodded to Void. "So you already knew about this murder, then?"

A clear beep of assent followed. "Well, perhaps you can tell me what happened?"

With that, Void pulled out its customary stone tablet and began engraving away with the terrifying power of light.

Bee made her way out of the castle after having an interesting talk with Mary. Here, she found the Nighty Knights waiting for her in an impressive formation. Impressive, at least, for their age. They stood in even rows of seven wide and five deep. She did some quick counts, realizing that they had thirty-six members, with Felix standing off to the side.

This was more than she remembered the initial group having. There were other children in the castle, but they were still only babies and too young to join the Knights' group yet. Looking around, she saw more new faces, some that she didn't recognize. It seemed that they had taken in even more refugees since she had been gone. As she approached, Felix twitched his face, and the entire group of children snapped a reasonably smart salute.

This stopped Bee in her tracks. Somehow they had coordinated that. She didn't think that they could have seen Felix's small tell, so how? It was quite impressive.

Standing in front of them, she gave the group a nod. "Hello, everyone. I've been told you are working hard."

"Hello, High Priestess Bee," they chorused back in a bit of discord. There were a few giggles that were quickly silenced by the children next to them poking the offenders quiet.

Felix then called out, "Squad one, present!"

Before Bee could do anything, a file of children marched forward to stand in front of her. Leanne led the group of five members, her chin high and confident. Bee's eyebrows rose even further.

"Marching" might have been a bit of a strong description of what these children did. They stepped high and stomped down, but they were very much not coordinated. Their steps fell as if there were two different sets of drums playing. Still, they swiveled mostly at the same time to face her.

Leanne took two steps forward and nearly shouted at Bee. "Ma'am, my first skill is Laser Eyes!"

She stared ahead, waiting for a response. Bee frowned, not having heard of that skill before. "...Laser eyes?" she asked.

"Yes, ma'am. Laser Eyes. See, Miss Bee! It's really cool when I look at things super hard—" Leanne cut off as she glared at a pile of dirt off to the side of the training yard. Two beams of blue shot from her eyes and blasted into the dirt, scattering it aside. Bee could feel a slight heat, even from the short instant the laser eyes had been active.

She was silent for a long moment.

"...What was that, Leanne?"

"That was my first skill!" The child beamed up at Bee. She tried not to flinch back at the thought of getting lasered herself. "Laser Eyes. It does a little bit of damage. It doesn't really hurt people yet, though. It does give them nasty burns if I glare at them for too long. It's better with wood and stuff that isn't alive. Especially dirt."

"I...I see..." Bee tried to focus on the girl's words, but was still reeling from shock. "And it's called...Laser Eyes?"

"Yup! That's what the system said. I sounded it out myself."

"Very...impressive..."

"Thank you, ma'am!" Leanne grinned, apparently indifferent to Bee's internal crisis. She took two steps back and then turned to the child next to her. Then they both started giggling at each other. After a few elbows and shushes, the next boy stepped forward and introduced himself. He also demonstrated his first skill. It wasn't as impressive as Laser Eyes. But Bee doubted that anything she saw today would match that same first impression on her.

He appeared to have some sort of water manipulation skill. A fine mist of water appeared in front of the boy when he stuck out his hand. It flung forward, spraying Bee with stinging droplets. Surprisingly stinging, actually. Reaching up and wiping her forehead, she saw that it hadn't broken skin. But if this was his level 1 skill and he had decades to practice it...he could get quite impressive.

One by one, the rest stepped forward and showed her their skills. It was hard to tell, but it did feel like the younger children were generally showcasing more impressive abilities. Maybe there was something to her hypothesis.

Still, that was worrying in itself. If getting rare and powerful skills was just a matter of getting levels at an early age...that was not something she was comfortable with. Even if these kids had gotten their levels relatively safely, this could have huge repercussions. Not pleasant ones, either. She could only hope that this was Void's doing, not an intrinsic property of the system.

Eventually, the first squad returned to the formation, all excited, before the next squad ran out in front of her to continue the demonstration. Each skill was different and unique, but almost all of them had some tinge of her master in them. Whether it was a beam attack like its cherished lamp or the ability to remove something dirty or slash something apart with a spinning attack.

Tanu was the leader of the fourth squad, and continuing his tradition, he was not alone. Next to him sat a large wolf. So large that Beatrice didn't initially recognize it as Cliff, the wolf that Tanu had brought back from the woods so long ago. This wolf was significantly larger.

"Well, Cliff, show High Priestess Bee what we can do." The wolf cocked her head at him and flicked an ear before snorting. As she snorted, two small puffs of mist drifted out of her nostrils. Before Bee could really put her finger on why that mist looked wrong, Cliff opened her mouth and breathed at the ground in front of her. A faint blue color tinged the air.

Immediately, ice started to build up on the dirt in front of her. The longer she breathed, the more it grew. After about ten seconds, the wolf ran out of breath, and the ice had reached about three inches thick. Ears drooping in exhaustion. Cliff sunk to her haunches and whined. Tanu reached up and scratched her chest, praising her for her good effort.

Just when Bee thought she had seen all the kids had to offer, the last child went to demonstrate her skill. It was a young girl, younger than the rest of them. She must have been no more than four years old, maybe even three.

She took a step forward and closed her eyes, looking up to the sky and bringing her hands together at chest level. Her palms met each other, fingers straight and facing upward. A serene expression crossed her face. Then she scythed one arm down to her side.

For a second, a giant mirage of Void appeared, hanging in the air above her. His claw descended onto the ground, smashing into the dirt, sending rocks and debris billowing out. The cloud completely covered the formation and pelted Bee with bits and pieces that she just barely managed to block with her forearm.

The little girl appeared as the dust settled down, still in her prayer stance, completely untouched by the destruction she had caused. In front of her was a small crater where the impact was looking down from the sky. She met Beatrice's eyes and smiled before babbling. "That was the Void Avatar's claw. Isn't it neat?"

Of all the skills she'd seen today, this was the most Void-like, in some ways. It was also, by far, the most terrifying. To call upon the god's power so directly was way more responsibility than any three- or four-year-old should ever have. Regardless, she bit her tongue. She couldn't help but try to accept her master's strange choices that she still wasn't able to understand. Void must have its reasons for doing what it did. If it had gifted this skill to the young girl, then there must be a reason for it. Even if it seemed insane to her.

The last person to introduce his skill was Felix. Before he shared it, she had a good idea of what it was, even if it was not too impressive. He stood forward and announced. "I'm Felix. My skill is Voice of the Void. Right now, I can send messages to everyone in my group. It started off with just being one at a time, but now I can kinda broadcast them to all of us."

It was maybe a less immediately powerful skill than the others, but in many ways, it was more useful. Especially for larger engagements, if they ever had them. She certainly hoped they wouldn't. But knowing the state of the world beyond these walls, she figured they wouldn't be able to accept Void. If that happened, Felix would make an excellent commander in the coming years. He could have control of an entire battlefield.

Hopefully, that would be when he was older. Much older.

Harold and Amy made their way slowly out of the tunnel leading up from Shattermouth. It was a fascinating city, and Harold wished that he had been able to enjoy it more. The infrastructure was carved into the side of slot canyons created by flash flooding. The ancient city had existed for as long as history could recall, yet always held the same people. Supposedly.

The mystery there was almost as intense as the one behind his old castle, if a bit more obscured. The generations of life had slowly expanded the old hallows and had worn away much of the relics. Still, the invisible wards preventing a fall into the chasms below had never failed. But that wasn't the only secret that Shattermouth hid.

Deep in one of its forgotten chambers, one of humanity's oldest foes still slept.

Neither of them spoke as they passed the guards on their way to their next destination. They should have been celebrating. At least, Harold should have been, as the Lieutenant they were looking for seemed undisturbed. But something was wrong.

They hadn't caught anyone following them or watching them. But the area around the wards guarding the Lieutenant was disturbed, and he hadn't been able to get in contact with its protector. It wasn't entirely necessary to get in contact with the local

Jailer, of course, and there were still many reasons why the protector may have been absent. Still, it made Harold uneasy. It wasn't the end of the world. Technically, just verifying that the Lieutenant was undisturbed and that its ancient protections were still active was enough. Next, they'd move on to the Lieutenant that Harold was most worried about. He could only hope that this one was as undisturbed as the first.

CHAPTER 20

ORGANIZED CHAOS

ARTHUR STARED at the two terrified men lying in the dirt in front of him. He recognized both of them. One was a minor noble from an annoying house who he was forced to bring along in the campaign. The other was one of his servants who joined the army to protect his young master.

The message Void left wasn't helpful. "They did it." Gave him no proof or evidence at all.

The large man seemed to know exactly how much trouble he was in, but the lord was an arrogant fop. Accordingly, he was all up in arms about being treated this way.

"Do you know who my father is?" he spat at the retreating godling's back. Arthur didn't fail to notice that he had been completely silent the entire time Void was actually around.

It was quite hilarious, really, watching people deal with the powerful young god. But this time, Arthur couldn't smile. "Lord Zapatos. I would like an explanation."

The young man looked around, not quite realizing where he was. Seeing Arthur looming over him, he scooted back slightly and glared up at the commander before remembering what was going on and schooling his gaze.

"General, it seems like there has been a mistake," he said in a far more servile tone. The sudden switch made Arthur's skin crawl. As he spoke, the young lord tried to climb to his feet.

Arthur put his foot on the man's chest and pressed him back down in the dirt. "No, I think you'll be doing just fine down there. So. why did Lord Void see fit to bring you to us?"

The large man was entirely still, as the two guards Arthur had brought with him were keeping a menacing watch over him. Lord Zapatos looked towards his servant with indignation, as if he was expecting the big man to get up and fight off the entire camp for him. His petulant manner returned once more. "I have no idea why it would bring me here in such an undignified manner. I haven't done anything to deserve this."

Arthur noticed that his sidelong glances at the dead body on the ground told a different story.

"Really? Well, then. I wouldn't suppose you have any idea what happened to this young man over here, then. Would you?"

"O-of course not." The Lordling licked his lips and looked around at the surrounding men. "No, I have no idea why Torvald is dead. Probably got into some disagreement with someone he owed money to or something. He was a degenerate gambler, anyway. Did you know that?"

The story was quite unconvincing, but Arthur would need some sort of proof. As much as he would have liked to just have the man taken into custody, he had to go off more evidence than a god dropping him at his feet and disappearing with no explanation.

"Well. Looking at the scene, I did notice that there was a knife wound in this Torvald's neck. And I can't help but notice that there is a decent amount of blood on your blade," Arthur mused, indicating the sheath at Zapatos's hip. Thin red rivulets traced the top of the sheath and had dripped down its exterior slightly. "It's always a good idea to clean your blades before you put them back in your sheath. I'm surprised your father didn't teach you that."

"My father? Well, I just cut myself, and I put it away before I had a chance to clean it because I was dressing my wound," Lord Zapatos spluttered.

"That blood seems awfully fresh. Could you perhaps show me where you've bled so much? Perhaps you need a medic." At this point, the young lordling realized his error and looked frantically around for an out.

"It's noble business. It's none of your concern. You lowly commoners shouldn't even be getting involved! I shouldn't have to explain myself to you. Let me up so I can talk to my father!"

Arthur left the lordling spluttering in the dirt while he turned to his servant. "Perhaps you would like to tell me what happened? I would imagine you might be looking for some protection or clemency after what you did. What happened to Torvald?"

The large servant just stared at him wordlessly. Arthur met his gaze, and a few moments passed before the large man looked away. "Yes, Lord Commander. There was a misunderstanding and tempers ran hot before things got a little unpleasant."

Arthur looked around at the sight. To be fair, there was no indication that that wasn't the actual story, even if he personally doubted it. It was very possible that there could have been an actual fight here, but in that case, it should have been reported immediately. There was no proof that it was premeditated or anything, and the crime scene was left fairly bare. But even this would be enough to take them in and question them further.

For the moment, he ordered his guards to restrain the two for further questioning. The men obligingly marched the pair away to a nearby tent, the lordling complaining all the while. Maybe he would figure out the true story soon.

Arthur sighed and rubbed his head. Well, he was glad he didn't have to engage in a long investigation, at least. It was still going to be a nightmare to get this settled. The political implications alone of a high duke's son committing murder on campaign would be disastrous. This was something that could potentially spark rebellion or worse.

If it had been a commoner he killed, Arthur probably wouldn't have been able to do more than keep him locked up until they got back to camp or the capital and had a trial. The lordling would have been undoubtedly acquitted, and Arthur probably would have been punished for lack of oversight. But since it was a fellow noble, and not necessarily a low-ranking noble at that, things had become more complicated.

In some ways, it gave Arthur more leeway, but in others, it meant no matter what he did, someone was going to be unhappy with him. That was okay, though. He was used to that.

I left my two captives almost immediately, confident that Arthur could take care of them. I had seen enough of interrogations after the last one. As useful as it was to learn more about some of the darker sides of human nature, I didn't really enjoy it. And besides, it should have been fairly obvious what was going on.

I didn't think Arthur really needed my help, and cleaning the men's souls seemed risky. They were dark enough that I feared they might pop like the zombie souls did. So I wasn't about to do that. I did wonder what Arthur had in store for them. I'd have to check in a little bit. But for now, there were duties to attend to, so I just returned to cleaning the camp.

As I worked my way between the tents, I casually listened in to all the soldiers' conversations as I moved past. I knew it wasn't the most polite thing to do, but I really had nothing else to focus on. This level of cleaning barely earned me any experience anymore. It was quite sad, actually.

I did hear some interesting conversations from a few of the tents, though. One of them had a trio of men sitting on stools. They gathered around a mat of leather rolled out on the ground, and they were tossing cubes onto the ground in handfuls. Once they settled, they'd look at them, and then they'd make various noises ranging from disappointment to exultation. However, when I got nearer, that all changed.

"Hey, Boris, you better not be using shaved dice again!" an angry voice rang out.

"Hey, I never did. I swear!" another man said defensively.

"Don't give me that. I caught you." Two men were arguing while a third just leaned in close, staring at the cubes on the mat.

"Give me a little bit of credit," the defensive one said. "If I was cheating, I wouldn't be throwing a handful of sixes every single time. Especially not for five throws. That would just be insane. Do you know what the odds are?"

"Nope. What do I look like? A mathematician? Come on. But it's pretty suspicious, you have to say."

"Well, fine! You toss the dice!"

The cubes were scooped up and handed to the angry man, who tossed them and got a handful of sixes as well.

"See, I told you it was the dice," the defensive man said triumphantly.

"Yeah, that's what I was saying, you moron. You're cheating with shaved dice!"

"But look at them. They're not shaved!"

"Then why is it that when I toss them, they're always landing the same? You toss them, I toss them. It's the dice!"

I started to get a little closer to this conversation. While it didn't seem to have any point, it was certainly energetic, and I could tell that tempers were starting to rise. "Okay, well, then explain how the last time you threw a handful of ones, it was *also* the dice."

"I swear you're an idiot. Do you not understand how sleight of hand works? Of course you do, you thief. You better give me back my coin, or I'm going to gut you like a fish." The angry man was really angry now, but I didn't understand what seafood had to do with the conversation.

"Whoa, whoa, whoa, whoa, whoa. Calm down, calm down. Calm down. Sure, sure. Yeah. Something's wrong. I don't mind not keeping the winnings. Just put your knife away," the defensive man said, suddenly seeming a lot more reasonable.

I couldn't help but wonder what was going on. Something about shaved ice and money. It seemed like a bit of a hassle, if you asked me. But, well, I didn't want anyone to get hurt, so I figured I'd stick around to keep an eye on things. It helped that there was a decent amount of cleaning to be done here.

The third man eventually spoke up. "Oh, here, give me them." He rolled as well. "Okay. One, two, three, four, five, six. That's not all sixes, at least." He rolled them again. "Well...that is strange. I can say that. I think everything's on the up and up, but I'm fairly confident these are the same dice that we've been throwing. See? Notice this nick, here. You see that? That's not a shaved die, but that's more like a little bit of damage. So it's gotta be the same dice as before. I don't think this would be easily duplicated, especially not with either of your two brains."

Even as the other two looked insulted, they both nodded thoughtfully. The smarter man finally came to a point. "Well, something's messing with the dice. This reeks of magic. Let's set it aside for now."

Without another word, they packed up their dice kit and pulled out a deck of cards. Ooh, cards. Cards are much more fun. Solitaire was my favorite.

One of them shuffled and started dealing before the angry man called out something. "By the gods, Boris, not again!"

Then he snatched the deck and flipped through it. It was completely in order. He then shuffled it a few times before checking through it again. He shoved it back in his bag with frustration. "You know what? I'm done. This is just weird. I'm going to bed. Good night, everyone."

The angry man stood up, picked up his coins, and walked away. The other two looked at each other and started packing up as well. Well, I was just glad that didn't escalate any further. I had to make sure to stay and watch that group for any other future problems. Things seemed awfully tense. And I could imagine someone getting hurt if no one was around to supervise.

BEE STOOD in the upstairs alchemy room, surveying the changes as Maranda explained what she had been up to. Unfortunately, it was hard to focus much after the revelation of how strong the Nighty Knights had become. Her head was so wrapped up in thoughts of the children all the implications that brought that she missed Maranda's question. "I'm sorry, what?"

Luckily, Maranda was also distracted and didn't seem to mind repeating herself. "I said, what do you think I should learn next?"

Running the last bit of conversation through her head, Bee realized Maranda had reached the end of what she could learn with the most basic materials. Truly, the girl had been *busy* in the last few weeks when Bee was away.

Maranda had managed to build and keep an impressive supply of basic healing materials. She hadn't completely exhausted the stocks of their components, but really Bee doubted that she was learning anything from working with the lesser materials at this point. At the same time, Maranda had not taken it upon herself to move on to the more expensive materials, as she would have definitely wasted more than necessary trying to learn by herself. Why do that when Bee would soon be available to teach her?

At least, that was the reasoning Maranda had given. Bee

thought it might have been a bit more to do with fear or not being able to convince her mother or Susan to give her access to the more expensive stores. Either way, it worked out. But still, Bee felt much better seeing the massive stockpile of healing potions that Maranda had accrued. It would be very useful now that they had a large influx of people, especially after so long on the road.

Her only concern was the expiration of the potions versus their ability to make new ingredients. She supposed she would have to start talking to Tony or Mary about getting some people on that. Harvesting some of these ingredients was difficult and not necessarily something that they could do without the manpower they were now getting. Focusing efforts there would drastically help with the necessity of finding work for the many idle hands that they were about to have. If everyone was making alchemy ingredients, or enough of them were, perhaps everyone would benefit more than she had even assumed.

Bee snapped back to herself, realizing that she had gotten lost in thought yet again. "Sorry. Yeah. Let's move on to maybe some bigger items. Strength potions are more complicated. I think those we have plenty of materials in stock for, and we'll always have a use for them as long as we need to do repairs or work in the field."

Maranda nodded at Bee's suggestion. Together, they wordlessly left the lab and walked over to the library, winding their way down the servant stairs. Along the way they came across a bunch of people scurrying around, attempting to get the castle ready for visitors.

Bee was glad that people were polishing the floor. Not that the castle wasn't kept clean by any stretch of the imagination, but she was sure Void would approve.

Once they reached the library, they talked to the self-appointed librarian and found the few books that Maranda would need for the next step in her education. She checked them out with little fanfare.

Returning to the lab, Bee and Maranda settled off into their own niches as they began working. Maranda was carefully following her recipe and moving at a quarter of the pace that Bee thought she could manage. But the girl seemed determined not to make a mistake or to waste any ingredients.

Bee was moving quickly, tossing together a few quick brews. She was focused on making the newcomers comfortable. As such, she had picked out recipes that might help alleviate a few of the ailments that had troubled some of her charges on the way back. Now that she was back at the castle, she had access to the ingredients she needed.

Luckily, none of the things she was making were super complicated. That meant she could actually spare attention for Maranda's questions. The younger girl would occasionally come over and ask some very detailed and pointed questions that Bee had trouble answering quickly. They often required a lot of real thought, and more than once she had to even admit that she didn't know something. For those, they ended up just jotting down some notes on a piece of paper for a trip to the library. After they were finished.

Time passed quickly, and before Bee knew it, another day was over. They only had a little more time to prepare. Then their guests would be here.

So far, I had really been enjoying my time traveling with the army. I sure missed being in the castle. It was a second home, especially with all the other people and the Nighty Knights and everything. But this adventure had been quite fruitful. There was lots of cleaning to be done and many good things that I could accomplish. However, today was the first day that I regretted coming along.

We found the first town, and I was starting to really worry about how dirty all the human towns were. It wasn't so much that the towns were dirty so much as destroyed. To be honest, I wasn't impressed. So far, I'd only ever seen three human settlements outside of the castle and small farms. Of the three, the first one was completely abandoned and little more than rubble covered in dirt. The second one was in the process of becoming that, though Bee and I had put a stop to it. This third one was mirroring the first one.

I followed Arthur closely as we entered the ruins of the city, not wanting to stray too far and perhaps disturb something that he needed to see. It was something that he had explained to me the night before. To some extent, I understood his reasoning. But to some extent, I felt it was kind of weird.

Because of the fact that there were no people left to tell him what happened, he needed to entirely figure that out from context clues. I could understand that. That made a lot of sense, and I had many times figured things out from very little evidence myself. I was quite proud of my detective skills. But at the same time, though, how could he leave an entire city in this state?

It was quite reprehensible in many ways. I felt that it was only fair to give justice to the people who had lived here, to restore their town to optimal condition. Yet he had insisted that we wait to do that until after we had found everything out. Reluctantly, I had agreed to not do any cleaning in the town, no matter how much that hurt my circuitry to write.

But in order to learn more about the whole investigation process, I decided if I had to not clean, I would keep my processors away from anything related to it. For now. And so I followed Arthur around, trying to understand what he was actually looking for. Perhaps once I figured out what was important, I would have a better understanding of why I shouldn't clean right now. Because otherwise, I might start malfunctioning.

So far, we hadn't found a single human or even a sign of another human, but we did find many tracks leading out of the town in different directions.

It was also interesting watching Arthur work. He wasn't just wandering around the city by himself, looking at the ground. He had people come and tell him about other interesting things, and then he would go to look at the interesting stuff himself. We went to each one of the exits, where we found a mess in the dirt leading away toward other cities. But we also looked at their town hall, which appeared to have been the site of a last stand. There we located many charred remains of what must have been undead, along with piles of weapons. That seemed to be what was left of the defenders.

Eventually, we all left. No one seemed comfortable in the city, despite some of it still being intact. We returned to the camp a half mile outside the walls. I first had wanted to stay behind and work on the cleanup effort, but Arthur convinced me that we needed to talk about what would happen next. I agreed with the caveat that, if I still wanted to, I could come back tomorrow. Perhaps it was for the better. I supposed there was nothing that would likely change about the town over such a short time. It just felt wrong to leave something so disordered and destroyed behind.

We retreated into the command tent without additional interruption. There, many of the command staff were already waiting for Arthur. I mostly stayed out of the way as they talked, though people didn't really give me much notice at this point. I was sort of a silent presence which people tended to avoid looking at. So I just rolled under the table and listened to their conversations while scanning the map above me.

It was a detailed picture of the surrounding areas, complete with terrain, landmarks, and cities. A circle of red string outlined how far the undead could have gotten by our best estimates. They seemed to be still several days ahead of us, but they could only have gotten so far.

The general staff were all participating in a grand debate about what the undead army's next target would be. Arthur, for the most part, watched and listened as he usually did, letting people say their piece when necessary. But I could tell that he wasn't entirely paying attention. His lips moved and his fingers danced across the map, indicating where we were and the possible enemy target locations. Eventually, he cleared his throat and raised his hand, completely cutting through the clamor of the tent.

CHAPTER 22

A CLEAN WAR

"GENTLEMEN." Arthur addressed the assembly. "We have no choice but to split up our forces. There is no single target that the undead will have to solidify their hold on this province. Not until we pass over to the far side, at least, to their capital. But even that is not a large city. While this province is extremely wealthy, it's also quite sparse.

"The weather has been seen to grow good crops, and the province is often used as a vacation area. But no large cities have really sprung up here since we captured this area some two-hundred-odd years ago." Arthur cleared his throat.

Satisfied that every single person was paying attention to him, he picked up a series of pins from a box next to the map and began sticking them in. "The first legion shall go west. The second..."

He proceeded to quickly lay out the rest of his plan, where the army would split up and chase down the various tracks we saw.

"None of the undead offshoots should have grown to the size and strength where we'd be unable to defeat them, even with a diminished force. But if we allow them to grow, things become a problem once again. Chasing them down one at a time is simply not an option. If we spend all of our time going after one, the other four groups that have gone in various directions will have doubled in size, and we will never catch up until this province too has fallen. Additionally, remember that the southern border leads directly into the heart of the kingdom. There are no great mountain barriers here to protect us as there have been before."

I was quite impressed with Arthur's deductive reasoning. I had noticed that there was going to be an issue, but I hadn't figured out a good solution to deal with it. I figured what would be easiest was if I just zipped around the country and sucked up all the zombies. But the people really seemed to be dedicated to taking care of this problem themselves. As each of the staff received their orders, they nodded or smashed their fists into their breastplates in a salute that sometimes left a small scratch in their armor. I really would have to teach them otherwise at some point. They really could use some better salute that didn't mar their armor. Perhaps I could bring that up to Arthur sometime later tonight.

The next day as we marched, I floated next to Arthur for an in-depth conversation. Who would have thought fighting consisted of so much organizing? I knew that he did spend a lot of his time working with reports and figures, but there was so much more that I didn't know.

We talked about how wars were decided based on culture, levels, supplies and so much more. About how with the proper numbers and information, Arthur could predict what an enemy would do with frightening accuracy. Even though most large-scale combat appeared to be utter chaos, it was anything but. I apparently just didn't have the experience to recognize the patterns. Not yet, at least.

"That's not to say the ebb and flow of battle is ordered. There are uncountable ways that small disturbances can ripple through and change everything," Arthur explained from his horse. Many of the young officers were crowded around, listening in. Despite the audience, it was meant to be a private conversation and Arthur ignored them all.

"In my mind, that is what command is. Finding all the little levers that control the flow of the battle and finding the right way to pull on the ones you can while mitigating the ones you can't." I wasn't sure that I was following most of what he was saying, but it was so much easier once I related it back to cleaning.

If the house was seen as the battlefield, then there were many things that could happen to it. Keeping it in order was a matter of identifying variables I could control altogether and fixing the ones I couldn't. For example, I couldn't stop dust from gathering, or the smallest humans from throwing food from their high chairs. But humans could put their dirty clothes in the right bin rather than leave them on the floor.

Extending the logic to the castle, I could also teach the children good habits. With a few flicks of my Sanitation Lamp, I carved my comment into my tablet and held it out for Arthur to read.

The one concession that he made to the audience was that he read it out loud for all to hear. "What can be controlled varies." Rubbing his chin, Arthur thought about it. "That is a good point. It's not enough to just memorize some tactics. That can only get a commander so far. You really need to *understand* why those tactics work. Only then can you adapt strategies effectively. New levers and disasters can appear based on a myriad of factors."

I wiped my rock clean and made another comment for Arthur to read. It felt a little wrong interrupting him, but he always cut off to read my thoughts, even mid-word. "There is only one factor you can always control."

Before he responded, one of the audience members broke in, "Wha—!"

The young officer didn't get very far before his neighbor socked him in the side, cutting his words short. Arthur ignored the interruption and responded to me without comment. "I suppose that is true, though rarely do you only have one option for what to do. At least, in my experience."

A bit of silence fell on everyone for a few minutes as we all thought. Eventually Arthur continued. "Void, you are talking about more than command, right?"

I beeped my agreement after a minute of reflection. This wasn't too much different from what I had been teaching Beatrice. Especially considering how similar war and cleaning were. For the first time in hours, Arthur addressed the audience. "You should all think on this. But there are also tasks I believe you need to see to."

For the most part, everyone recognized the dismissal for what it was. Those who didn't were quickly informed by the ones next to them. Once we were alone, Arthur turned to me and asked a strange question. "Have you written a book on your teachings yet?"

I scribbled on my slate for a minute. Arthur grunted. "I suppose I could see her doing that. I'll need to talk to the High Priestess next time we meet and see if I can get a copy. I would like to see it distributed. Your comments echo how my own philosophies feel in a few ways. I would like to see how that would apply to the other disciplines, outside of war."

The stories Beatrice wrote about our initial adventures... Well, I wasn't sure if those would really answer much of Arthur's questions. After all, it had a particular *Beatrice* slant to it. Though it still was pretty popular with the castle's inhabitants. Susan may have been the human closest to Arthur in personality, and she seemed to like them well enough.

Before we had a chance to continue our conversation, the officers returned at a gallop.

"SIR!" he hollered at Arthur. "Sir, contact reported."

As the officer passed along the report from the scouts, I looked over the army marching around us. We had taken the largest column of the army and were marching directly to the province capital. The hope was that we would get there first and be able to defend it. But if we were too late, the undead army would be much larger than we could feasibly handle. In that case, Arthur would recall the largest section of the army for help.

I had, of course, offered to zip ahead and take care of the problems for them. Arthur had surprisingly asked that I did not. Apparently, his men needed the levels and experience. He seemed physically pained about asking his men to take a real risk of dying, but he had explained his reasoning.

"Right now, we can rely on your aid, Lord Void. However, that won't always be the case. What if one day, you're not around when trouble arises? Or if the threat appears in multiple places?" The commander laid out the scenarios patiently. "If we allow chances like this to pass us by, then we will lack veteran soldiers to protect the people. Weakness means the country will be overrun by monsters. Not to mention neighboring countries."

Still, I had been asked to come along and help if it was needed. There was no point in getting levels if they were all wiped out. Me showing up to the city a few hours earlier wouldn't make much of a difference. If they held through the several days, they could hold for a few more hours.

We were still a few hours away from the city, but the scouts might have made it there much more quickly. With a quick question to Arthur, I took off and zipped up into the air. I would go make sure that the undead wouldn't take the city before the army caught up with them. Also, I wouldn't want to let the army walk into a fight that they couldn't win.

I couldn't blame them for wanting to level up as well. After all, I had used the same logic with Beatrice too. Besides, taking out an army of low-level undead wouldn't do much for me anymore. Maybe taking out some of the elites would be just as effective. Also, the cleanup after the fight would be even more effective for my own advancement. I was sure they wouldn't stop me from taking care of the aftermath.

The flight was nice. I hadn't felt so free in a long time. It took me a bit of self-control to not do happy loops as I soared high into the sky. Remembering that people were counting on me, I redoubled my efforts and tried to break my previous speed record. Even though I was hundreds of feet up in the air, a wave of dirt billowed out from under me wherever I passed. In an effort to avoid leaving such a mess behind, I moved over a little so I wasn't over the road.

It was slightly better. Dust no longer got everywhere, but the trees were losing their colorful leaves much faster than they should have. Every one of them became completely bare as I passed over them, a torrent of leaves circling in my wake.

With a little effort, I pushed it out of my mind. Those leaves were going to fall soon anyway. I was just speeding it along. Plus, I needed to get to the city fast. A few minutes later the shining walls appeared on the horizon.

This city wasn't nearly as large as Caleb, but it was also more *solid*. I could see the thickness of the walls from here, and the height alone seemed to be giving the undead surrounding it trouble. Each of the buildings inside was much larger than any I had seen aside from the castle. They also appeared much fancier. Shining stone, gilded trims, multicolored windows, and decorative tile made the place gleam like a pile of gemstones. And most importantly, the city was clean.

It was not perfect, but by far the best city I had seen so far. The best part was, it was still maintaining this appearance as it was under siege! Thinking of that, I studied its attackers. Something wasn't right there. After all my conversations with Arthur, I expected more...

CHAPTER 23

ESCORT QUEST

THE CITY WAS NOT AS desperate as we feared. Compared to the sea of undead we faced before, this scattered group was nothing. Only a handful of guards manned the walls, occasionally firing arrows or throwing spears down at the zombies. There were so few of the things that they were not even able to pile up close to the walls. It seemed the only thing they were really doing was preventing the city from easily reinforcing the rest of the province.

All in all, it didn't seem like I was needed here. Before getting to the city, I turned around to return to Arthur. I wasn't going to be very productive hanging around here. Better to let the commander know that they were fine and give him time to plan ahead.

As I flew back, I scanned the forest but didn't bother moving at the same speeds as before. Without an imminent threat at hand, I simply couldn't rationalize making such a mess. Even if it was only a matter of time.

Coming to a rest near Arthur, I quickly grabbed a fresh stone from the ground and printed out my findings in a quick scrawl. He skimmed over them and nodded. "I'm worried. I think this might be a trap. It seems unlikely that they would leave the most populated part of the province alone when they need the troops. Their commander isn't stupid, so it's possible that they are waiting for us to approach, for a pincer or something."

I hadn't considered that. That would be a clever thing to do. However, it was one of the first occasions where these tactics didn't relate easily to cleaning. I tried to figure out how to make the connection. Was there any case when, while cleaning, I would benefit from not being nearby or visible when a mess is made?

If a mess was made during a meal, it was better if I was there to clean it up immediately. If I wasn't nearby, the mess would just stay messy longer. But then, in this analogy, would the mess not be made at all if I were nearby? But that would be good, right?

If that were the case, then I wouldn't have to then clean it up. I guess this might be more about catching the mess maker than anything. What if someone knew they weren't supposed to make messes but continually did it anyways? What if they derived some sort of sick pleasure from spilling dirt everywhere?

Okay, maybe if they knew they weren't allowed, they would be corrected. If they continued to do so, they would endeavor to make messes where they weren't seen. That sounded like some dastardly plot, but if that was going on, then I would have to be not around for them to make a mess. Then I could catch them. Okay. Okay. Wait. No, that still doesn't make sense. Why wouldn't I just stay around them so they couldn't make messes?

Hmm. My processors were whirring now. Okay, maybe there was some other sort of analogy where this could work with cleaning. I'd need to figure it out. Hmm. Hmm, hmm, hmm. Nothing. I'd have to see how Arthur played this out. But this definitely was different from waiting for a maker to reveal himself in order to capture them. That could make sense. This would be the mess maker waiting for me to clean up, then appearing to...be captured?

Would this be like if someone wanted to stop me from cleaning up messes? That would make sense. So, if someone wanted to stop me from cleaning, someone *so evil* that he wouldn't want me to clean up *any* messes, he would make a small mess, wait for me to come to clean it up, and then...flip me upside down! Or something. Then I couldn't clean up any more of his messes.

I paused. Oh, that made sense. It was dastardly and wicked to be sure, and I could still deal with a threat like that. But I thought I was on the right track.

Okay. I needed to start being better and more careful about checking my blind spots when cleaning. I didn't realize such evil people existed, but clearly, whoever Arthur thought controlled the undead was despicable.

I came back from my musings to find Arthur surrounded by the scout captains. He was giving them instructions. Right as I looked over, he waved them away, and they each cantered off toward their squads and disappeared into the forest.

I assumed they would be watching our backs and making sure we would have enough warning if we did get attacked from behind like Arthur predicted. Perhaps that was something where I could step in. If they were about to be overwhelmed, it would be best if I prevented that from happening. Maybe I could also help the scouts to check the surrounding area or keep them safe.

I wrote a quick query to Arthur on my tablet. He skimmed it and nodded. "Yes, I figured that it would be helpful if you could watch the scouts' backs. If they miss anything, let me know. But try to not point out to them where the enemy is. With your help, this victory is most likely assured. And, well, I want to minimize the amount of losses if possible, both from civilians and our company. I do think this is a valuable training exercise. Very rarely do we have a god on overwatch preventing anything from truly getting out of hand."

Bee was ecstatic as she ran to the gate. It had been a long couple of days, mostly filled with constant work and preparations. But even so, she had been waking up early to help guide the Nighty Knights through learning how to use their powers properly and safely.

Soon she would have help. A lot more work as well, but also help.

She hadn't realized how much she had relied on Tony and Susan for the day-to-day workings of the castle. Mary and Trent kept the food in hand and the people, for the most part, were well taken care of. That didn't mean they kept everyone occupied, though, and idle hands meant Bee was asked a lot of questions. Plus, without Void around to train the kids, they had dedicated themselves to her personal protection.

The kids insisted that she always have at least two of the older Nighty Knights following her around as a security detail. *At least* two. She put her foot down when the number climbed to eight. They really needed something else to do. The rest were constantly training or generally getting in the way of everyone with their antics.

But that would all change today. Susan and Tony were back, along with the thousands of refugees. It was something she had been waiting for for a very long time. The gate was already winched open, the guards and Nighty Knights having cleared the few straggling undead away from the walls each morning. So that wasn't an issue either. Bee could see the column appearing from the forest seemingly intact, thankfully. As they came into view, she took off running out the gate. She slowed to a walk as soon as people caught sight of her, so she could approach with more dignity.

Tony didn't have the same restraint, though. He dashed forward from the column, leaving a chagrined Susan behind. When he reached Bee, he picked her up in a bear hug and spun her around before dropping her on her feet. "Bee, good to see you. You wouldn't believe how much fun we had making it the rest of the way through the forest. This Captain Major is something else! He's giving Susan a run for her money."

Bee thumped Tony's chest, trying to break away from the bear hug. "Let go of me, you oaf!"

He laughed, but set her down. "Where is everyone?" he called out, looking toward the gate. Sure enough, his siblings were all running out to meet him, closely followed by Mary and Trent.

It was as though he had been gone for months. Bee couldn't help but be a tiny bit jealous as Tony went to go greet his real family. As much as they had taken her in and made her feel welcome, it still wasn't the same.

The Nighty Knight guards she left behind at the gate, along with everyone else, soon caught up with her and formed a square around her. Their heads swiveled about, warily watching the newcomers. She just put her head in her hands. The "honor guard" didn't exactly make a great first impression. Sighing, she walked over to go greet Susan and Captain Major in as professional of a manner as possible.

Captain Major gave her a casual salute while Susan just smiled and waved. The two of them walked forward to greet her, and the Nighty Knights gave them sidelong glances before parting to let them pass. The four children moved a few feet away, forming a box, keeping even the adults of the new visitors well away from the small meeting the three of them were having.

"How did everything go?" Bee asked the pair. They shared a look that she couldn't fully understand. It was almost as if they were trying to get on the same page, but couldn't agree.

Susan was the first to respond. "It went just fine. We made good progress."

Captain Major closed his mouth and nodded, but Bee gave him a look until he inclined his head slightly. "Some things...could have gone better."

Susan snorted and shook her head. Bee wasn't quite sure what to make of it. Both of these people, in her opinion, were exceedingly competent at their professions. Still, if they disagreed on something, she'd have to get the full story out of them. And probably Tony as well.

"It seems like this might be a problem," she said slowly, trying to air any grievances out sooner rather than later.

But both Susan and Captain Major shook their heads. "No, no, no, no problem, Miss Bee. There's always room to improve. But—"

Bee let them continue giving platitudes for a few moments before they moved on. Freed from her initial duties, she started to greet the refugees around her as they flowed past. Many of them she knew by name now. Checking in, she ensured that the children had made it alright and that any injuries she had helped mend were fully healed.

Everyone was happy to greet her, even if the Nighty Knights got some curious looks. Most simply seemed weary. The sight of the castle and the promise of a hot meal rejuvenated spirits, though. She sure hoped Mary was ready. So far, their preparations had been going smoothly enough. But whether they had the kitchen capacity to feed everyone was questionable.

With this amount of people, the castle would soon be stretched to its limits, maybe even a bit over them. So far, no one would have to set up tents on the grounds, but finding everyone their own bed would be impossible. Some people would have to double up. Hopefully, the number of families would make that just fine. But her other concern was the throughput of the kitchens. They'd have to conscript some workers or refugees as cooks if they wanted things to go smoothly from here on out.

As she talked to everyone, they filled her in on what had happened during the trip. It gave her a sense of the group dynamic. Apparently, the scouts from the castle and the soldiers from Caleb had a bit of a rivalry going on where they would each keep watch in redundant patterns.

The soldiers insisted on scouting themselves because of their better training, while the scouts insisted on taking over because they claimed the soldiers made too much noise. The soldiers didn't quite trust the scouts' reports and vice versa. All in all, it was a relatively polite and contained issue, but still was a nuisance.

Apparently, the only reason things still had a lid on them was Tony's soothing presence. He managed to talk things out with Susan and Captain Major, keeping them from being constantly at each other's throats. Bee wasn't quite sure what their issue was. Still, it would be really obnoxious if her defense commander couldn't get along with the man in charge of a literal army now stationed in her castle. Well, Void's Castle. Bee had to remind herself that she was just the mouthpiece.

CHAPTER 24
MILITARY DISCIPLINE

BEE WATCHED everyone file into the castle. The line seemed endless, yet they continued disappearing through the entrance without slowing. She knew that the castle was a massive, ancient structure, but sometimes it was easy to forget. Though the place was used as a mage's college, she had read somewhere that it had existed for far longer. Between the carvings in the catacombs and the strange construction of the place, she could believe it. The castle's size simply dwarfed any other structure that she had ever seen in her limited travels.

With that in mind, fitting in a few towns' worth of residents was no issue. Well, it was an issue, but it was also doable. There were families confined to small rooms, and people had to share beds, tables, and living areas. She was sure that no one was going to be exactly comfortable. But it wasn't that big of a deal yet.

Of course, not everyone filed through in an orderly line. There were many children, especially young children, walking alongside the adults. For the most part, their mothers had been worn down, meaning they eventually were given near free rein of the caravan. As long as they didn't stray too far, of course.

They usually played and did a pretty good job of dodging wagon wheels and horse hooves. Still, as they entered the castle grounds, the mothers were maybe a little out of practice. The more enterprising youths soon ducked the line to sneak into the castle. Well, some of them did.

Some were very eager to explore their castle, but the rest wanted to run around the open grounds. The idea of vast open fields for playing and running about was simply too tempting after so long in the forest. Considering there was a wall keeping them in and only a single gate leading out, the mothers were relatively okay with letting them loose. Even better, the Nighty Knights were already there, and they welcomed their new challengers with gusto.

Bee was fairly worried at first. She wasn't sure if the hard-working culture that the citizens of the castle had established recently would be overrun by the massive flux of unfamiliar people. Or perhaps there would be conflict as two groups of children clashed.

While she wasn't worried about anyone getting hurt in a normal childish argument, there was a real threat here. With the Nighty Knights having earned levels so early, this was more of a concern than she would have thought. Especially considering their skills. But for the most part, the Nighty Knights were actually standing guard or drilling rather than running off to make new friends. The other kids were fascinated with the wooden swords they held and how they used them.

Mostly they just gathered around and watched, but as a critical mass of them built up along the side of the practice field, a few brave ones went up and began talking. Bee watched over the various interactions of the kids and the adults both. Most of the adults were busy setting up and unloading any wagons or gear they brought. Soon, several of the mothers she recognized as having older kids came up to her worriedly.

The concerned expressions on their faces set her on alert slightly, and she was worried that something was wrong. Had someone gotten hurt already? But when they began asking questions, she soon realized what was going on.

"So. The children with the practice swords, what's going on with them?" the oldest mother asked. She had quickly become a ringleader of the group with a force of presence that was only matched by Gertrude.

For the most part, she only bothered to make sure that the children were well cared for. With the attitudes of the leaders of the caravan, she hadn't had to do even that very much. But now Bee understood why others deferred to her.

Bee took a second to consider the question, not wanting to give the wrong impression. But there was really nothing to it. "They are the Nighty Knights. It's more of a group the children have formed themselves. They wanted to work on their skills, when they were first traveling to the castle, and Void was willing to teach them. However, when a god takes to teaching the children as Void did, certain...things...happen..."

The mothers' faces didn't look any less concerned, but Bee pushed on anyways. "So when teaching, Void commands quite an exemplary level of discipline. The only problem is, though well-behaved, the children had trouble getting rid of their excess energy."

Some of the mothers were nodding along now. Bee even picked up a few whispering about how even their best-behaved children were still full of energy.

"So Void's solution to this was to get their energy out in a productive way. And that's how they started practicing sword forms. Our god personally created each one of those weapons for the children so they could use them safely and has been training them for months now." She paused. She wanted to continue, but wasn't quite sure how to turn this around into the reassuring speech she had been planning. That was when Gertrude hobbled up.

"Ah, I see you're training them young. This is good. There's going to be troubled times ahead. Every man should know how to fight, and most women should, too." The young mothers looked quite nervously at Gertrude. "Oh, don't give me that look. We'll have your children training soon, too, and they'll be able to protect everyone. Don't you worry. They'll know how to fight."

Bee quickly left the suddenly chaotic scene. At least it was Gertrude's problem now. They could figure that out for themselves.

I stayed high in the air as I watched the troops progress along the road. The scouts had made it to the edges of the forest that surrounded the city well enough, and I could see lines of communication being opened up between them and their commanders. They then, in turn, made it to Arthur. I didn't have to interfere once.

Mostly I just stayed high and watched the progression. The military tightened up their straps and began marching in a slightly more organized manner with much more efficiency. They would be there any minute now at this rate. So far, I had seen them break into units, then scouts come to lead various people into different positions. It was interesting to watch from above as I saw a strategy starting to come together. Arthur had a plan to completely wipe out the undead army besieging the city when everyone was in place.

I stayed in the air to watch, but I could hear trumpet blasts signaling the start of the events. The infantry marched in from many directions, but even as they did so, cavalry thundered past, slamming into the hordes of undead. Just after, arrows fell from the sky like rain, softening up their targets. The cavalry trampled through at slightly oblique angles, always giving themselves a chance to wheel around and avoid being pulled out of their saddles and dragged into the fray.

The mounted soldiers managed a couple of passes before the infantry formed a shield wall. The undead left the city behind and attempted to swarm the infantry, but with the double-layered shields and the constantly stabbing short swords and pikes, they weren't able to get a hold. As they concentrated on the nearly impenetrable defense of the soldiers, the cavalry kept hitting their flanks while arrows rained down into their rear. The city was slower to react, but did manage to muster up some assistance.

Flags waved and trumpets sounded as they worked out what was going on. Slowly but surely, more and more people appeared on the wall. Additional waves of arrows were loosed and took down zombie after zombie.

I noticed the commander of the army was a decent ways back from the fighting, but there was a near-constant stream of messengers running back and forth from him. They darted toward each section of the line in each company of cavalry and artillery. Usually, soon after, they would reposition into a more effective position. Sometimes they would move to support another side or simply get a little closer. But the strange mastery of the field was inspiring indeed. Even if this seemed to be an extremely inefficient way to send messages. Beatrice was far faster.

True to his word. Arthur didn't call for my assistance. We had arranged a signal, a certain number of trumpet blasts to indicate that my assistance was needed, followed by a set of signals to work out a location for me to assist in. But it wasn't even close to necessary.

Soon enough, the undead were finished. It was an anticlimactic ending to the smallish force, but they all just died. There was no bang or heroic charge or attempt to retreat. One minute, they were fighting fiercely, and then the next, there were a few left. And then the moment after that, they were all dead. Truly, this time.

As promised, I was left in charge of cleanup after the medics had pulled every injured person away from the field. They were apparently treating them with their limited supply of anti-undead medicines. I trundled around, putting things back in order. I started off by removing all the undead and just storing them in my dustbin for later use. I had a decent amount of items in my void-like dustbin at this point, and I wasn't exactly sure what I wanted to do with them, but I would need to figure that out soon. Otherwise it would get too cluttered for my liking.

It took me some time, as the undead force, while smaller than I would have expected, was still made up of several thousand corpses. After that, I started to smooth out the field. Turns out that hooves and boots really destroyed the ground. Any bits of grass that had been here were now completely trampled and destroyed. I wasn't able to return it to its more natural aesthetic, but a packed dirt field would have to do for now. While I was doing this and consuming all the undead, I finally had a chance to think.

Through Arthur, the humans had shown remarkable capability. I realized that this little skirmish was the first time that I had seen them work together with such unity and efficiency. Normally they were in a lot of trouble or making a lot of messes. And while they did make a mess here, they prevented a larger mess from being made.

That was something I couldn't help but feel good about. My respect for Arthur and his organizational abilities grew further. Truly a difficult task was accomplished here.

As I scanned about for Arthur to continue our conversation about the best methods of cleaning in a military context, I found him just as another human did. Seeing the urgency in the other human's face, I let him speak first. "Sir, the Northeastern Division calls for aid. We have met heavy resistance. The enemy is buoyed by casters and skeletons along with the normal rabble. There seems to be a giant rat leading the army with its dark magic."

Silence met this pronouncement before chaos exploded among the watching officers.

CHAPTER 25

DEUS EX MACHINA

HAROLD HAD A BAD FEELING. It was there when he woke up, and he couldn't shake it the entire day. His dour mood even affected the normally unflappable Amy, who had proven to be an amiable traveling companion so far. At least, after the first couple of days, when she had finally let the professionalism slip a little bit.

That it was her first real field assignment didn't bother Harold. No, that wasn't unexpected. From her age and where she was stationed, he had seen that coming, and he didn't get to be an old hand without learning how to deal with green operatives. It wasn't until later in the day that the other shoe dropped.

When they finally got past the local guards of the sealed Lieutenant, it didn't take long for Harold to figure out what was wrong. The wrought silver cage and protective wards appeared just as he expected. Amy even showed the proper amount of fright toward the menacing figure inside. But something was missing.

As the two of them inspected the protections, Amy finally got the courage to speak. "Do you know which one this was? I wasn't able to find any specifics in the dossier."

Harold shook his head. "No one really knows. We only know about half of them. The others don't have enough descriptions in myth to even begin to guess. The stories also get muddled, depending on location. For example, kingdom histories indicate that Ish'mach was the one that razed Castle Arthur, but in this country it was Baile'gar."

Amy nodded, and Harold led them closer to the inner wards. After a few more feet, he held up a hand to halt her from moving any closer. She looked at him strangely, but knew better than to make any noise. Reaching into a pocket, Harold then flung out a handful of magical substance and watched as it fell inert to the ground. Moving a little closer, he repeated the motion to no effect.

Eventually, it was too much for his junior partner.

"What is it?" she hissed.

With a frown, Harold whispered a response. "Something is missing. But I can't put my finger on it."

Harold swallowed. He didn't want to do this, but he had to be certain. It was the only way to settle his nerves. Inhaling deeply, he stepped right up to the cage and laid a finger on it.

For a second, he simply stood there, still as a statue. Then the blood drained from his face. He whirled to face Amy. "Run."

A giant undead rat? The description rang a bell with me, but it took a full scan of my memory to understand where I had seen something similar before. Apparently, I hadn't tagged it properly when I first saw it.

If I was right, this was the same rat that the adventurers had killed so long ago. The one I had harbored in my dustbin. I had seen it briefly in the undead crypt. That, or something very similar. If that was the case, then this was my problem, and I would have to be the one to deal with it.

The officers were still going nuts about the undead rat leading an army with dark magic. But Arthur was beginning to take things in hand. It seemed that the largest objection was the fact that they really didn't have a full mage company ready to deal with a proper dark magic caster.

Why they were so unprepared, I couldn't understand. Arthur had always mentioned that the undead army had behaved unusually and with quite abnormal cohesion, as if it was led by an intelligent being rather than the undead's instincts. So they should have expected someone with lots of power to be leading this, right? Was it that dark magic was different from necromancy, or were they just this unprepared? They couldn't say, but I decided to step in and help the situation while also moving towards my own goals.

Taking my newest writing rock, I quickly printed out my message and held it up for everyone to see. Stunned silence matched my proclamation, and eyes scanned over me. I double-checked my message to make sure that I hadn't said something silly. But "the rat is mine" seemed to be about right.

Then Arthur cleared his throat. "Lord Void, are you saying that you will handle the giant rat?" he asked with a genuine question in his voice. I beeped my assent, and the whole room seemed to sigh slightly. "That is certainly good to hear, Lord Void. We would appreciate the assistance, especially in the magical department."

Not more than a few minutes later, everyone was rushing out of the tent, and orders were being barked out around the camp. The enlisted soldiers were soon on their feet. Everything was neatly packed away after their short break. The army began moving down the road, following the scouts before everything was even packed up, leaving a few lucky—or were they unlucky?—soldiers to finish putting away the tents. The stragglers followed quickly behind as the vanguard advanced.

I zipped ahead, not waiting for the rest of the army to catch up, and followed the trail that the messenger had left as I headed northeast. It didn't take me long before I spotted a horde of undead moving through a field as they chased a much smaller group of humans in military gear. I saw a giant rat and several large skeletons shepherding the mass of undead toward their target.

Experience told me that I didn't want to make this a prolonged fight. While I had no trouble cleaning up any of the undead previously, this rat was an unknown, and my extended fight with Lieutenant had shown me that underestimating my opponent was folly, to say the least. I opened up with a laser blast to the back of the rat's head.

As soon as I fired, a bubble of darkness seemed to spring up from the rat, absorbing the light and slowing it down to a crawl. As it hit the rat's head, it only singed the beast's fur before it was able to roll out of the way.

That my first attack had been deflected was certainly an inconvenience, but it wouldn't slow me down much. Really, its only purpose was to close the gap, and before the rat had even gotten to its feet and turned around, I was right above them. The skeletons and the rat both turned to me as I expanded my void from my Limitless Dustbin.

It might have been overkill, but if the dark magic was anything like the shades or wraith I had fought over in Caleb, I wouldn't take any chances. Dark magic echoed out from the rat, but my void sucked everything up, and I could feel it rush into my dustbin as some sort of thick oily energy. As the skeletons turned to face me, I braced for a fight. But they didn't advance.

Roscoe gazed over the battlefield with calculating eyes. He chittered at one of the nearby skeletons, who nodded and signaled one of the columns of the army to start the flanking maneuver. The horde of zombies shuffled forward obligingly.

So far, the opposition he had encountered in this area of the country had been laughable at best. But this more recent arrival of armored men started to really give him trouble. Not that they were particularly difficult to defeat, of course, but it was certainly trickier than anything the locals had put up.

They were wearing the same armor as those forces of Caleb, and he wouldn't have been surprised if the leader there had sent its forces after him. But so far, they hadn't shown the technical or tactical expertise that his archenemy had. So far.

Cleanup efforts and recruitment were still going well. In fact, the army would be in excellent shape so long as there wasn't any more interference than there already had been. So far, the entire province had been mostly converted. This time, he knew to leave the large population center alone and move on quickly to less well-defended areas to make sure that he didn't get bogged down in another long siege.

So after leaving a token force to keep them from sending reinforcements elsewhere, he had gone on to lead the recruitment exercises himself before the skeletons could dispense their orders. Once they had a few more recruits, then they would truly be a force to reckon with.

As Roscoe reveled in his success, he suddenly froze. A menacing presence suddenly manifested behind him. On instinct, he instantly threw up a shield of dark energy that was shattered in one blow.

Turning around, he glanced about in alarm. But as his eyes shifted upward, he froze.

Above him, merely a dozen feet away, floated a sleek black disk. Twin jets of concentrated blue flame emitted from either side, keeping it aloft. Roscoe could feel the powerful wind of those jets blow back his fur, even from this distance. A set of small brushlike appendages led to a small opening in the disk's bottom flanked by a pair of wheels.

Roscoe recognized it. The other elites recognized it, too. Their god had come, and it had come for them.

As they watched, the flames extinguished. A warped mass of absolute darkness, darker than even his own magic, expanded from the disk's top. The void appeared as a gaping hole in the sky, blotting out the sun and even sucking in the light at its edges. As they watched, the void expanded and shifted until they could see nothing else.

They all fell to their knees, giving their full attention to the divine being above. They bowed down, using their minds and bodies both to show their utter devotion. Even as their worship began, Roscoe could feel his energy leaving his body only to be accepted by his god. To be welcomed home.

After the initial shock, the magic died down suddenly. It felt as though a tap had been shut off. The rat's eyes settled on me and simply stared as I moved forward to consume it. One by one, the skeletons collapsed in defeat. Knees and foreheads pressed to the ground before me.

Unwilling to waste such a vulnerable position, I quickly darted forward. The skeletons zipped into my dustbin with a clatter of bone and metal. They didn't even seem to resist. I consumed them all, putting them right beside the other skeletons and undead I had vanquished at Caleb. That was much simpler than I thought. The dark magic wasn't even a big deal. Perhaps some of the normal humans would have had trouble with it, but I imagined even Beatrice could have handled this on her own.

From what I had seen, Arthur was likely on similar combat footing as her and would have been able to handle it. Surely it wouldn't have been much of a problem with enough people. Perhaps they were just overestimating its abilities?

Anyways, I took off after that, flying up in the air to watch the battle. Without proper leadership, the undead horde had quickly lost their focused approach of hemming in their quarry and couldn't coordinate the flanking maneuvers they had managed just moments before. Soon, the disparity in tactics allowed the group of humans to outstrip them to a slightly comfortable distance, at least enough for them to regroup and start forming a plan.

Seeing that there was no immediate need for my assistance, I decided to head back to the other army and let them know the situation. They would be here in a little over an hour. At least Arthur should know what was happening.

CHAPTER 26
BETTER JUDGMENT

THEY WERE a few hundred paces outside of the Lieutenant's prison when Harold and Amy stopped to catch their breath. Amazingly, nothing had happened. The two of them locked eyes as they panted, adrenaline spiked.

"What was that?" Amy demanded as she pulled hair from her face.

Harold frowned as he looked down at his fingers. He touched a small knife at his hip. "The cage held no power."

The blood drained from Amy's face. "You mean..."

"Yes, I imagine we will find the rest of the bindings inoperable as well," Harold said in a grim voice. They weren't dead yet, so he hadn't yet given into despair. But with a realization like that... Well, he couldn't be blamed for being cautious. Steeling himself, Harold began to turn around before he was stopped by a tight grip on his sleeve.

"What are you doing?" Amy hissed at him.

"Wait here," Harold said, reading the fear on her face. She wasn't ready. Not for something like this. He couldn't force her to confront an ancient evil, this kind of danger. He wasn't happy about going back in either, though. If the Warden hadn't made it perfectly clear that he wouldn't be permitted back without a full and exhaustive report, he would have already been far down the road to the next down, drafting a missive for the man. "If I'm not back soon...send the findings back home."

"You can't be serious. Why do you need to go back there? It could get out at any moment!" Amy said, ignoring his words.

"We need to know how long we have. Besides, with its power suppressed, there might be something I can find that will give us the nature of its power." Harold paused, not wanting to voice this part out loud lest the gods curse him. "And if Deusvult is with us...maybe we can rebind it."

Amy nodded slowly, but didn't let go of his sleeve as she started walking back to the hidden entrance. This time, it was him holding her back. "I'm serious. We need to get the word back."

"No report from this stop will tell them as much as we know now. It's worth getting the extra information instead of sending two separate messages." She looked back at him. "Besides, I'm not going to let you face this alone."

Harold sighed and supposed that she sort of had a point. He didn't want to face it alone either and they weren't dead yet. Together they hurried back into the chamber, not wanting to stretch this out any more than they had to. Inside, nothing had changed, neither to the eye nor to any magic detection abilities either had.

Examining the rings of ritual wards around the cage showed that they, too, were inactive. Eventually, Harold started to mutter incantations over handfuls of ingredients. After a few minutes, the powder started to glow. With a gentle yet steady breath, he blew into his cupped hands. With swirls and eddies, the dust moved through the unnaturally still air of the cavern.

The two of them watched in silence until the glow suffused the entire room. Nothing happened for nine heartbeats. Then, without warning, the scene changed all around them. Amy and Harold started slack-jawed, spinning in a circle as they tried to comprehend their new surroundings.

The walls and ceiling were the same, but that was where the similarities ended. The cage that had seemed intact was revealed to be shattered and torn, only the barest of pieces still standing; most of it was scattered around the room haphazardly. The runic circles were broken in places, and as Harold looked closer, each individual rune was cracked as well. He squatted down and ran a finger over the engraved surfaces; the rough texture rasped against his skin, so different from the smooth continuity he had felt before.

"How?" Amy whispered as she walked up to the broken cage. Laying a finger on it, she jerked her hand back with a hiss. "It's blazing hot! How did you touch it before?"

"Does the cage radiate heat?" he asked. She held her hand near the metal that burned her.

"No, it doesn't." She mused, "If the heat's stuck inside, then who knows how long ago it was broken. But my question still stands. How did you touch it?"

"Illusions. It was all an illusion," Harold muttered, still examining the shattered runes. Mindlessly he rubbed the finger he had used to check the cage before on his robe.

"But what kind of illusion can confound touch?"

"Maraj'ain," Harold whispered. "It must be. The mistress of mirrors."

Bee and Mary shared a cup of tea in the older woman's office. Each of them was exhausted, and both had deep bags under their eyes. It had been a long couple of days, but everyone was finally settled in. And they both were about to pass out. Yet there were a few more things they needed to talk about.

"Are you sure we don't need more space? I really think we can tidy up some of the old side passage rooms in the catacombs and maybe set people up there."

For what must have been the umpteenth time, Mary simply sipped her tea and closed her eyes. Then she responded. "Yeah, for now. We should be good. If anyone does complain again, though, I won't hesitate to tell them about your offer and let them have that choice. I doubt anyone would want to go sleep in the catacombs if they didn't have to."

"Well, it's not exactly the catacombs part. It's below the catacombs. And there is a large system of rooms where it appears people used to live. I bet it was some shelter or something from ages long past," Bee repeated, hashing out the same old argument. Mary stared at her levelly, and Bee gave up, shrugging.

As long as she didn't have to share her bed and everyone else was happy, she was fine with it. Now she just needed to figure out how to get everyone off her back.

The number of people who needed her attention was insane. It was even worse than when they were in the caravan. Even though, from her estimation, their needs didn't require her input at all.

Perhaps it was because everyone had more energy now, but they constantly wanted her thoughts on everything. She was doing her best to pawn them off on Tony, Trent, Susan, Captain Major, and Mary. But that still took time.

Susan suggested that she set up a span of time to hear people's troubles and give audiences. Something similar to office hours, like some of the mages had done for their apprentices. But Bee wasn't really comfortable with that yet, especially since Susan had originally called it "holding court." The idea just felt wrong. Perhaps Bee would figure out some better version of sectioning off her time.

There were still so many other demands vying for every minute of her day. She was still giving her daily lessons in the library to those who wished to come, though that was starting to overflow. People had to stand by the door just to hear her speak, as many of the newcomers wanted to hear about the tales of her and Void or the lessons she had begun to disseminate on their journey. On top of that, the Nighty Knights wanted attention, training, and advice with their skills too. That was high up on the list. And then Maranda needed more training. Well, she had been effective so far, but she needed another big project to keep growing. There was still so much for her to learn, and her reading was not nearly as good as Bee would've liked it to be. Especially not good enough for her to read some of the denser tomes herself.

Bee groaned, rubbing her face. "Where do you find the time for everything you do, Mary?"

The woman smiled. "I don't. You get used to it. Once you're a mother, you'll understand."

Bee walked down the grand hall of the castle, doing her best to ignore the stares of all the people assembled. As she walked, her thoughts churned, frantically going over everything she had written down last night.

Stage fright wasn't something she had ever really encountered before. The audiences in the library were small, by the necessity of space constraints. Even when they had grown, most had to sit outside and listen to her from out of her sight. That meant she hadn't been more intimidated by a larger crowd. But this? This time it was different. Nearly a thousand people had gathered in the grand hall this morning. Even as densely packed as they were, they barely fit.

Fiddling with the vial that Maranda had given her a few minutes earlier, Bee debated whether she should take it. While it was certainly a thoughtful gift, she wasn't sure how much she trusted it. Maranda was still learning, after all, and Bee hadn't been there to supervise her apprentice while she was making the new concoction.

That wasn't to say that Bee didn't think it would be valuable. The potion of voice enhancement would be very useful, and she wished that she had thought of it herself. It should be safe too. The recipe was rather simple, and none of the ingredients were particularly dangerous. Even if Maranda had messed something up, Bee should be fine, if a little embarrassed.

Before she could second-guess her apprentice any more, she tipped the vial back and swiftly swallowed the potion. When she reached the front of the hall, Bee ascended the small ramp to the dais that had been set up earlier this morning. Stepping up to the podium, she set a few of her notes down and shuffled them around. With a count to three, she forced herself to look up and stare out over the crowd. She could only hope that they couldn't sense her nervousness.

"Children of Void," Bee called out into the hall, wincing slightly at the volume. Her words echoed with such force that even those in the back had no problem hearing, though those at the front seemed a bit shocked. The potion was working just fine. Lowering her volume a touch, she repeated herself. "Children of Void, welcome."

A murmuring response filled the hall. Bee swallowed before launching into the lecture. Since this was the first time many of these people had attended one of her lessons, she stuck to the basics. To start off, she did a small reading from the sermon on the mound, making sure to stop and give context when she felt it was necessary.

To many, this was all completely new, and she saw many faces don considering looks as she spoke. After the reading, Bee launched into the story of her first encounter with Void. They wouldn't have much more time for anything else today, but that was okay. She had several more lectures planned to tell the rest of the stories and reiterate the lessons Void had given her about the system and about life in general.

Bee almost stumbled in her speech as the system sent her a message. One she had been waiting for for a very long time.

LEVEL UP, LVL 50 REACHED. CHOOSE YOUR THIRD CLASS: HERETIC, HIGH PRIESTESS OF SPOT, COMPANION OF SPOT.

CHAPTER 27

FINISHING THE JOB

IT DIDN'T TAKE LONG for Arthur to reach the defending soldiers. Once I had given him a brief description of the situation, he simply nodded, and the pace of the army picked up a little bit. I left him to it, as he seemed pretty busy giving orders to his staff.

Riders were sent out. Plans were drawn on pieces of paper placed over saddles and discussed on horseback as they moved. I floated in the air above the battlefield, watching it all. I could see as the column split into many parts, some moving in to flank the army while faster-moving units went to support the defending company.

Then, all of a sudden, the main force of the military accelerated until they were charging. The forces barreled into the undead, sandwiched as they were between the charge and a more stationary defensive force. The maneuver almost resembled the motion of a hammer and anvil, quickly driving a wedge between the shambling zombies and pushing them apart. The outriders and the flanks quickly took advantage to come and hit them again.

The battle that had taken hours to build up to was over in under fifteen minutes. I watched and counted, but there were quite minimal losses on the human side. They could inflict long-range damage without getting in too close with proper support and long-distance archery. And when someone did get hurt, they could be pulled back and healed, or at least triaged before any life-threatening injuries were to be had.

That wasn't to say that no one died. Every once in a while, someone makes a mistake or has some bad luck. The undead were relentless, after all. But I was there, and I wasn't too proud to completely avoid putting my wheel on the scale in their favor. Every once in a while, an undead that had gone unnoticed attempted to get someone's ankle from the ground. They'd quickly find a thin beam of light slicing through their head.

I don't think any of the humans even noticed, but it was a little bit of supplementary cleanup, if I would be so generous as to call it that. And it seemed to work great. I gave just enough assistance that no one risked their life more than they needed to. All in all, I was eager to finish cleaning up the mess that this whole saga had caused.

After the battle was thoroughly decided, it was simply a matter of mopping up the remaining stragglers of the undead as they mindlessly attacked the humans. I zipped down to Arthur to check on him. The commander gave me a smile and a wave, cutting his conversation with a pair of lieutenants short.

"Well, Lord Void, it seems that your information was invaluable. I can't thank you enough for your assistance. Judging based on our estimations, this was the main force of the undead. I think we still have some cleanup to take care of here. But based on your description of the elites and the giant rat, we have likely have cut off the primary source of this problem." He hesitated for a moment. "While it's not necessary, I do have a favor to ask. I would appreciate if you would track down the rest of our forces and see if they are in dire straits, perhaps deliver a message for me. For ease of mind."

I thought for a moment. It seemed as though the majority of the threat was over, so I could probably head home soon. Should, in fact. But in the end, it wasn't too big of a deal for me to do this compared to someone on the ground.

We went back and forth a little bit, discussing the plans he had for what came next. Mainly they consisted of gathering up the army, sending scouts out, returning to the capital, setting up a base, and plugging all the exit points to make sure that the undead couldn't spread further.

The province wasn't entirely isolated by mountains like the other one was, but there were undoubtedly plenty of impassable areas along the border. Two sides of it were lined with mountains. Those were fairly difficult to cross for most, so Arthur could simply place some soldiers at the passes to catch any straggling undead. The other two sides were more akin to flatlands, but a few companies of cavalry with enough long-distance scouts could apparently cover it and at least hunt down small bands. If any larger groups of undead came through, they could send word for reinforcements.

According to Arthur, a few single undead could sneak through without too much issue. After all, there were naturally occurring undead. In small numbers it was rare for them to snowball into such a giant plague, especially without some sort of mastermind. And if he was right and we had taken care of those, then things were looking up.

He quickly wrote down a few messages on some paper and handed them to me. I grabbed them in my claw and safely deposited them in my dustbin. I didn't mind being a messenger for a bit, but I told him that after I had delivered them, I was going to head home. They didn't seem to need me anymore.

It was time for me to see Beatrice again. All the people at the castle, in fact. I shuddered to think of what all the children had gotten up to. They surely had made a huge mess of the place. But taking care of this for Arthur on the way was no big deal, it wouldn't take me that long to find everyone. So I zipped up, leaving the last of the cleanup in his capable hands.

I was completely correct. It didn't take me more than a few hours of zipping around to find the first section of the army. I dropped down in front of the person who led it. Then I simply spat the paper out on him, using my Air Manipulation to make sure it fluttered open against the pommel of his saddle.

He looked at it, then the seal, then looked back at me, confused. But before I had to deal with any sort of human communication nonsense, I zipped up and left. Perhaps it was a bit disrespectful for me to treat a human so. Especially when these military ones seemed so organized. But I was eager to get home to Beatrice and the people back in the castle. I simply wanted to deliver my messages and move on.

It cost me another day and a half to find the other sections of the army, but none were in such dire straits that they required my help. Most hadn't even found large amounts of undead and were simply conducting sweeping searches, which I thoroughly approved of, making sure that there weren't any large pockets or stragglers that would go unnoticed. No one wanted to potentially reignite this whole issue.

After delivering my last message, I flew up and headed north.

Bee had to wait a minute before the thunderous applause subsided. She awkwardly smiled, stared out over the crowd, and tried to do her best to avoid eye contact with any one person while simultaneously not looking at the ceiling. She had thought her sermon was slightly better than her normal ones, but wasn't sure it deserved such praise.

Still, it took a concentrated effort to keep her foot from tapping in impatience. It was all she could do not to sprint up the aisle and go straight to the library. After receiving her options for her level 50 skills, she had so many questions.

Heretic was something she had expected and knew she wouldn't choose. After all this time and effort, there was no way she was going to abandon Void for relatively little gain. The Heretic class had its advantages in some places, but none of them interested her. She had no desire to become some dark god's lackey of disorder and chaos. Nor was she planning to dedicate her life to building stairs.

So it really left her with two choices. High Priestess was the one she had been planning to pick all along. She had expected the third class to be something unrelated, maybe something to do with fighting or something that would nudge her away from the purely religious path, but not completely alienate her. That assumption had apparently been misguided.

Companion of Void. That option was really throwing a wrench in her plans. She had already decided what she would choose far ahead of time, but now this was making her rethink everything. She needed more information.

As the applause died down, Bee started to step down from the dais but noticed that several people were lining up down the center aisle before her. Not everyone, but a few dozen at first. Then a few more. Then a few more after that. After everyone saw how long the line was getting, its growth slowed, but didn't entirely stop. As she watched, the line began to stretch out of the great hall.

The majority of people filed out the back to return to their regularly assigned duties. Unfortunately, Bee couldn't slip out with them. With a mental sigh, she plastered on the most genuine smile she could manage and shook the first woman's hand.

She was maybe only a few years older than Bee herself, but still had an infant on her hip. She spoke in a halting whisper and asked a question that Bee wasn't entirely certain how to answer. Something about Void's philosophy on teaching kids their letters, and at what age they should start.

It was a matter that Bee thought was entirely silly. Why not just begin as soon as the kid could learn, or as soon as they could find someone to teach the kid? But she kept her cool and answered to the best of her abilities while thinking about what a Companion class was.

Bee mused. She had never heard of something like that before, much less met a companion of anything. Hopefully, there would be something in the library about it. She couldn't remember finding much about level 50 classes when she had looked through it before, but she'd never been looking specifically for this. Still, it offered something new, something interesting, and she couldn't wait to find out what.

After what felt like hours of questions Bee finally found herself in the library, scanning through the index tomes and looking through the organized volumes until she found a giant glossary of known classes.

She started flipping through until she reached the "C" section. Although it did list such useful classes as Carpenter, Cattle Farmer, and Concierge, it was completely barren of any Companion classes. There had been a few notes about animal companions, but those were more along the lines of a beast-tamer class or related to animal husbandry for farming. And none of those had the same sort of feeling that she got from reading the Companion of Spot class she had been offered. So she started looking in a little bit more obscure spots.

The first time she'd found a mention of a companion was in *The Tales of Daedalus the Red*. She had picked it up on a whim, back when she had more time to read for leisure. She'd always assumed that it was simply a fairy tale, but a bit more research seemed to suggest otherwise. Not to mention that the experience with the Lieutenant made her far less skeptical of ancient stories.

Daedalus was an ancient dragon, a creature of myth who had been spoken of in tales as far back as they went. The earliest stories she could find about him were fragments from well into the demons' rule, and those even referenced older stories that no longer existed. But one of them mentioned that Daedalus had found a companion in the Dark Times of the Demons' Rule. A companion who had gone on many adventures with the Red.

By most accounts, they had done excellent services in the name of humanity. The powers of the companion were incredibly vague, though. Apparently, he was a great warrior of flame who stood fifteen feet tall, a giant among men. She wasn't sure how much of that was exaggerated and how much of it was honest fact.

Still, the "companion" part wasn't a title, a class, or anything formal. It was just a word used to refer to Daedalus's human comrade. It very well could have just been a coincidence that she wanted to be real.

Based on the rest of the tale, she assumed that this person was mostly just a human warrior who happened to be good at sword-play with a remarkable fire aspect. Whether there was actually a Companion of Daedalus class or anything remotely similar was questionable. But if nothing else, she did tend to believe that there was a dragon at some point. The other stories about the same dragon didn't mention a companion, though they were from much earlier in history.

She leaned back in her chair. All of that work for barely a glimmer of a possible hint. It was still hard to say what she could gain from being a Companion. It might be something that focused more on closeness, an honest bond with Void. If that was the case, it would make sense to take it if her goal was to adventure around with Void. Her imagination conjured up images of soaring through the sky on Void's back, fighting monsters and exploring the world alongside her deity.

The door to the library opened. Susan stepped through, walking quickly toward Bee. "High Priestess, there's a matter that requires your attention..."

Bee sighed and closed her book. The real question was, would she ever have time to go on more adventures?

ARTHUR WATCHED as the receding black speck of the godling disappeared on the horizon. He still wasn't quite sure what to think, but his time with the godling had been interesting, to say the least. He was only really sure of a couple of things. One was that Void was a being of immense power, something that no human he had ever met could hope to match. And the second was that, while Void might be very powerful, Void was certainly not all-knowing.

That didn't mean it wasn't a god. But something told Arthur that Void was very young, as in recently born a year or two prior, maybe three. It was something that he had suspected before. Recent events had only confirmed it. The questions Void asked and the way it behaved all spoke to this, which lent a lot of credence to Miss Bee's tale.

At first, he had been doubtful that this was a new god. He was fully willing to accept that the gods were real and that one might someday descend among them. But at first, it seemed much more likely that this was a god of old coming down and playing some sort of game. Some stories painted the goddesses and gods as capricious, not just wise and benevolent.

But now...now, he could believe that Void was actually a new god. It was interesting. How did that work? Would the god have come from somewhere else, being born into its power, or was it simply something that had gained so much power that the system recognized it as a god? Arthur supposed he would never know. But this was groundbreaking.

He wished he had been able to find Harold after the battle. That man certainly would have had more insights. But at the same time, Void was almost certainly the dangerous being Harold had warned him about. So perhaps there were things he was still missing. Well, Arthur didn't have to decide anything now. His most important task would be to go back and make his report to the king. About their success in containing the undead and their interesting encounter along the way.

Arthur had no doubts that the remaining undead stragglers would soon be contained with their supposed leadership finished off. The bulk of the armies were crushed, and the godling delivered his messages and ensured there were no other major threats to his forces.

There should be no problem finishing this up. There should have been no problem in the first place, in fact. Things never would have gotten this far without competent enemy leadership.

The other reports he had received and his experiences with the siege in this province showed none of the planning and wily trickster business that he had come to expect from this group of undead. But after a week or two of mopping up, they'd return to Caleb, gather up the army, and head home. Perhaps they'd stay a little longer to help rebuild, if needed.

Captain Major and the troops he had escorted towards the castle with Miss Bee would have to find their own way back once the city was repaired. For now, they should be in good hands. They had a large enough company where moving wasn't dangerous, and no wildlife or brigands would threaten them. Perhaps escorting the caravan again would be a good experience for the young officer and get him some real fieldwork under his belt.

The trip back to the castle was much faster than even my trip to Caleb. Without having to carry Beatrice or worry about the wind ripping her off my back. I could fly at much higher speeds, though I took advantage of flying a bit lower so I could check out the area I was passing over.

So far, nothing really jumped out at me as interesting. It was mostly farmland with an occasional small copse of trees until I hit the mountain ranges separating the provinces. I avoided following the path that we had come in on for some new scenery. It was a small pass anyway, pretty much the only one in the giant wall.

Instead, I went a few mountains over and simply zipped up, skimming a handful of feet above the ground as I dodged boulders and leaped over crevasses, skirting along the giant glaciers that slowly moved down the mountain.

I couldn't help but admire them. What were glaciers, really, besides giant cleaning tools starting up high and using the momentum to scrape away everything on the land? At least, they seemed to be leaving a surface with no debris behind. Except that wasn't exactly how glaciers worked in practice. It was the unfortunate truth of the world, but they tended to leave lots of large rocks behind.

I supposed it was still better than nothing. A giant rock on its own could be considered clean, even if they were scattered everywhere.

Once I reached the summit, I could see for as long as my sensors would allow me in all directions. The view was quite unique.

Past the rows upon rows of mountains, a little further north, was the castle. But beyond that, it seemed like there was nothing but ice. Towards the south stretched a giant swath of farmland, and in each other direction, more mountains obscured the horizon to the very far west. Past that, though, I could see a glimmer of blue in the distance. I wondered what that was. Someday I'd have to go check it out. But not right now.

My moment of rest and appreciation was over, and I was zipping down the mountain again.

The valley that formed this province was much harsher than the last. Well, that's the word I would use to describe it. There was a lot less farmland and a lot more large forests. The land was also covered in much more rocky terrain; from what I could see, the topsoil was remarkably thinner and less nutrient-dense.

Small mountains dotted the massive valley, causing large changes in elevation. I could see how the humans had to work around them. The roads snaking and taking circuitous paths to avoid having to cut through stone looked much unlike the previous province's straight grids of roads. These roads were also much less traveled. The inefficiency irked me somewhat—I didn't mind the meandering paths, but they could have been far shorter and better planned out to minimize travel time. Still, it had a certain beauty to it.

There was an order I could recognize playing out in the way the vegetation was laid out. It wasn't the perfect grid-like order that was clearly superior, but an order nonetheless. An order that matched the terrain. I could see where there was more soil and the right amount of sun for certain plants, but not others.

Trees would not grow where there was not enough soil or too many rocks. You'd end up with tufts of bushes or small fields of grass. It made sense. Of course, it could be better. But I wasn't about to go moving too many rocks around, moving too many boulders. That would be too disruptive. It would cause too much chaos in the meantime, but perhaps eventually, with enough methodical planning, things like this could be fixed, and we would be able to have more useful land here.

But then again, maybe not. Maybe it was best to leave it here. Maybe there were niches of things that could only appear in random chaos like that. As much as I would hate to admit it. Perhaps something else to meditate on.

As I skimmed over the valley, I approached the more recognizable mountains on the other side. It took only a moment to find the small pass through the next mountain range, the one that led to the valley where the castle stood.

It was an interesting place to put a castle. As far as I could tell, there was no real reason for it to be there. There was no defensible pass that it was trying to guard. There were no great resources that it was protecting. There wasn't even a population center there. So the only thing it was, was a fort at the end of a box canyon. Perhaps "box canyon" was not quite the right term, but it was probably something like that.

It didn't seem to have any strategic importance, at least not from what Arthur had described regarding strategy. Yet it was still the largest building I had ever seen. Strange. As I flew along the valley, I savored the familiar scents of the forest below as they filtered through my Air Purifier.

Instead of just meandering over the path, I started to fly off toward the mountains and skim along the sides. I hadn't fully explored them yet. There was that one mountain that I had zipped around once, but this whole undead issue had kept me from exploring further. Perhaps I should go and check out some of the other ones and see what was up here soon.

Who knows? There might be nothing, but it was a bit of a blind spot that we hadn't checked out yet. Still, I didn't want to take too much more of a detour with home almost in sight; I couldn't wait to go say hello to my friends.

Diving down into the area before the gate with a gust of air, I waited to be let in. I didn't want to be rude, after all, and just bypass their security. That would set a bad precedent, and rules were made to be followed. Someone I didn't recognize stood guard on the walls and looked down at me in confusion.

After a little bit of starting back and forth, I raised my claw for a little wave. With a slack look on his face, the man returned it. Suddenly a second face appeared next to the man. "What's going on, Brutus?"

I recognized that voice! Excitedly, I greeted Roger, one of the Nighty Knights. Upon hearing my greeting, he looked down and saw my waving claw. Grin splitting his face, he returned the gesture and jumped down on the inside of the wall, rapidly working the winch to raise the gate. "Welcome home, Lord Void!"

A bit slow on the uptake, the man climbed down from the wall and took over the winch, working it much faster by virtue of size. Roger shot the man a grateful look before he took off running towards the castle. All the while, the kid was yelling, "Lord Void is back, everyone! Void is home!"

I waited patiently as the portcullis rose a few feet into the air. Once there was space, I rolled into the castle courtyard. After so long away, it was good to be back. I ran a quick scan over the grounds and was pleased with the results.

The grass was trimmed neatly, and the walls were clear of any messy climbing plants. The insides gleamed with nearly the same finish as when I had left. There seemed to be the slightest bit of soot by the fireplace in the guest room, but really that was quite small. It was good to know the home was being taken care of even when I was away.

Before I could conduct a more detailed survey of the grounds, my attention was pulled away. From the castle, a tide of people streamed out, and the people in the fields rushed over to see what the commotion was about. I happily waved to everyone. Most people I didn't recognize, but many of the first people to arrive had been here when I left, so I excitedly waved to them all.

Then a single figure shot down from the castle steps, quickly breaking away from the pack. The little girl ran down the path, tears welling up in her eyes. I let out a special cheer of welcome for my favorite human.

CHAPTER 29

PETS AND PATS

BEE COULDN'T WAIT for her master to return. With how busy she was, it was a couple more days before she had time to return to the library. She hadn't forgotten about her class options, of course. They had stuck with her in the back of her mind, distracting her during other essential tasks. But with everything going on, she simply had no time for herself to really research or consider them any further.

As time went on, the influx of new castle inhabitants presented a similarly consistent list of things to attend to. There were constant problems with settling everyone in. Most of them were minor, but many were still issues she needed to advise someone on. Most of her day was spent meeting with the castle's leadership: Mary, Trent, Susan, and Tony, as well as the recently added Gertrude and Captain Major. That or, given that they too were overburdened, handling any number of issues personally.

That was how Bee found herself stepping up to fill in the gaps. Hopefully, she'd be able to train people to take command and handle all these everyday matters so she wouldn't have to. Besides, she still felt woefully underqualified for this, having practically no life experience with organizing. Yet she was looked up to because of her position and relationship with Void.

At the end of the day, whenever she was lucky enough to spare some time in the evenings, she would rather catch up on her sleep than think about the exciting prospect of a class change. And after the first day of not getting to it immediately, she decided it could wait a bit longer.

There was no urgent rush. Leveling had gotten a bit slower recently, and it was a big decision. She wanted to talk to Void about it. What would her god think if she chose a Companion class if it didn't even want a companion? That would be pretty bad. But it didn't stop her from taking every chance to ask advice from the more experienced members of her staff.

Mary and Susan both encouraged her to take the Companion option, saying that she didn't need to take all of these responsibilities on herself. She had never wanted or intended to become a leader, after all. She should be out learning about Void and letting other people take care of the day-to-day duties that a High Priestess would have.

Trent, though, disagreed.

"Like it or not, you've got an important role 'round here now. Void needs someone to be his voice. I know the kids can understand him, but well...you know them." The older man shrugged. "They mean well, but they might not be up to it yet. People definitely won't respect 'em the way they do with you. Definitely not their mothers."

Bee could see both sides. In the end, though, it really came down to what Void wanted. Not what she did.

So it was with taut nerves that she waited for her master's return. There were still plenty of reasons to be excited about level 50. The skills after this would become much more specialized. Almost all of them would probably end up being more like cleric skills or holy skills, which would be lovely and hopefully help her more than the current offerings. Maybe she'd even been able to level faster with their help. There were even some instances where people were granted a passive effect, sort of like a lesser version of the Domain that some monsters showed.

As excited as she was, all those thoughts went out the window when Void finally did come home.

As Bee sprinted down the castle steps and bore down on her master, she half hesitated, not sure what to do. It wasn't like she could greet Void with a hug or jump into his arms or anything like that. The physics just didn't work out.

So while it sat there merrily waving its claw at her, she skidded to a halt a few feet away and bowed deeply. It seemed to be the right thing to do. Void reached out with its claw and patted her head several times. The gesture made her smile. Perhaps it was worth risking a massive social faux pas to show her own excitement. With a mental shrug, Bee reached down and gently touched the top of Void's shiny black surface.

Guiltily, she appreciated the odd feeling of Void's skin, the strange texture and smoothness in its abnormal geometric patterns. It wasn't that she had never touched Void before, of course, but never in such a casual manner. This time, she was comfortable enough to actually notice the details. But before the contact could grow awkward, she drew back quickly. A hint of wetness appeared at the corners of her eyes. "Void. It's so good you're home. We've all missed you so much."

Finally. *Finally.* It was a day for celebration. Beatrice had, at last, given me the head pat I so desired. It was quite late, and I was able to evaluate my own performance much better now, meaning I didn't exactly require the head pat scale of satisfaction for reference. Not like I had so long ago, back when my regard for humans was much higher. But that wasn't to say I didn't appreciate it. It was a shame that it was so fleeting. But the contact felt nice.

What followed was a whirlwind of activity. There were so many new people I didn't know. I focused on scanning them as they came to file them away in my people dictionary. It helped that Beatrice worked to introduce me to everyone, making sure that they kept a respectful distance and knew who I was.

So I was treated to a series of very polite bows and sometimes murmurs of a name. But most of the time, it was just a general show of respect or pleasure that I was back. But that didn't last for long. Soon, the children arrived.

The Nighty Knights had been quite busy. It appeared the couple dozen children that I had been training had now exploded in numbers, and many of the newer kids I saw were carrying rough sticks instead of the beautiful personalized ones I had made. It looked like I would have to refresh their supply. If I found them worthy. I would probably need to restart their training again, too. Hopefully, they had been keeping up while I was away.

Each one of my personal trainees gave me a salute while touching their swords, and the new ones did their best to copy. I noticed that many of the younger women in the crowd were looking on with quite intense frowns. I wondered what that was all about.

Oh, well, I guess not everyone could be happy that I was back. I did my best to keep it out of my mind. Soon enough, the other adults were there. Tony and Susan both said hello, and Mary and Trent welcomed me back warmly.

It was actually starting to get a little overwhelming. There were so many people here. Plus, I hadn't realized how long I had been gone. This had been the longest I had ever been away from my home. Well, excluding the running tally of time I had been away from my old home, obviously.

But it had been several weeks since I'd gone away. As nice as it was to meet everyone, I was itching to inspect the castle and its grounds more closely to ensure they were properly taken care of. I had faith that in my absence, Mary and her underlings would have been able to do so competently. Still, I really needed to know for myself.

But the last thing I wanted to do was be rude. It was almost two hours before I was able to untangle myself from the crowd. I would need to talk to Beatrice alone soon, but I could hold off on that for a little bit. Quickly, I darted into the castle, doing my best not to be intrusive, and took myself on a castle tour.

The rooms were reasonably well-maintained. I wasn't going to be upset with Mary at their state or anything. Still, I definitely would have held myself to a higher standard. But luckily, my powers were growing such that all I had to do was simply roll into a room for a few seconds, and between my skills and my Domain, most things were quickly taken care of.

A little bit of Air Manipulation helped get the dirty spots, and some Sanitation Lamp at a very low and diffuse setting was able to remove all of the germs and bacteria that were lurking about. My Mop was not even required, which I was very grateful for.

I also did my best to purify the air. It was an ability that I hadn't really used much. Still, without me having cycled everything, there were certain parts of the castle that had begun to take on a mildewy aroma, even if I couldn't quite find the source of it. Perhaps that had been cleaned up, but only after it'd been left for a bit too long.

After I went through the castle, I started going through the castle grounds. There, things were a bit more chaotic. I would have preferred things to be neater, but as I explored, people were actively moving stuff around, so it was hard to tell whether it was just a transition from one ordered state to another ordered state. It was possible that I just saw a snapshot that looked like chaos, not actual chaos.

It was nice that the rows of planted crops were coming along nicely. As I'd been told, the snow wheat would be harvested soon, which was a nice source of order. Even if each plant was slightly different, their compositions were quite organized. I could still appreciate it.

The walls were also surprisingly well-maintained on the outside of the castle, except for some of the higher spots, which would have been dangerous for a human to reach. So I quickly took care of those while I was here.

The outer wall was also well-kept and thoroughly patrolled, and I could see little bootprints where kids had evidently walked along it. I didn't begrudge them their fun, but I still cleaned up after them.

By the time I was thoroughly satisfied with the castle's state, the sun was well past the horizon, and the only people still up and about were Tanu and Cliff. Both of them were having a stern argument with the guard on watch. Cliff in small woofs and yips, Tanu with measured words.

"Kid, I can't let you out there at night. You saw what happened last time. If your mom found out again? She'd skin me alive."

"Me ma knows I'm a Knight. An' Cliff and I go huntin' all the time."

"I know she *knows,* but you training here where it's safe is one thing. Going out there? Totally different. She thinks it's too dangerous for a kid."

Cliff let out a slight growl, and the guard put up his hands defensively. "Look, it's nothing against you! Void knows you're big enough to swallow darn near anything out there whole. But I can't do it. You try being on the other end of Talia's ladle sometime."

"C'mon, mister, it'll be fine." Another child was there as well, standing by the guard station. I wasn't familiar with this one. Why was he at the guard post? In fact, wasn't it past both of their bedtimes? "Everyone's asleep, and Tanu's just being helpful! He'll be back quick."

They went back and forth for a while longer, each side adamant. I figured I could step in and resolve the issue. Going out for some space seemed like a good idea. Plus, it would be nice to catch up with this little one and the big furry dog. Well, wolf, I guess. I was still not entirely sure about the difference. Zipping over to the gate, I startled the group before all four of them straightened and saluted. Cliff's "salute" was interesting, but I got the idea and waved at them.

"Lord Void," all three of them echoed while Cliff let out a simple woof. I beeped a greeting to them and gestured for the guard to raise the gate. Immediately the adult leaped to the winch, and slowly, the gate began to slide open. The other Nighty Knight watched, smiling with an expression that seemed to convey, "I told you so." It was quite interesting watching these humans interact sometimes.

When the gate was most of the way up, I beckoned for Cliff and Tanu to follow me and rolled out along the path out into the woods. I assumed Tanu was taking Cliff out for a hunt, but if there had been problems getting her out for exercise a lot recently, that would have been too bad. I could recall what happened when the more reasonably sized dog I remembered was cooped up for too long.

I figured they would have set up a system for this, some arrangement where the guards would have known to let them out. Perhaps something else was going on that I wasn't fully aware of. But as long as I was with them, I was relatively sure they'd be safe from anything in this forest.

CHAPTER 30

MOONLIGHT SONATA

AFTER SPENDING an hour tossing and turning, Bee eventually gave up on sleeping. Her mind kept returning to what had happened earlier that day, when she had welcomed Void home.

The festivities had lasted well into the night, but Void hadn't seen fit to attend. Bee couldn't really blame it. The station of a deity probably required some aloofness, if only to maintain its image. Plus, the party had been a pretty raucous one. Still, she felt a pang of disappointment that she couldn't immediately go find her master and tell him about every minute that had passed since they had been apart.

Instead she had felt a duty to preside over the festivities and couldn't help but admit that she enjoyed them a little bit. Now, everyone had long since gone to bed, and she had no one left to talk to at this hour. Her lowered need for sleep didn't help either. With the excitement over Void's return still coursing through her veins, even that minor inconvenience was pushed aside.

Hours later, she was still staring up at the darkened ceiling, head on the pillow. Eventually, she gave up and got to her feet. It seemed that she was just wasting time waiting to become tired. And one thing her master had taught her was there were always things to be done.

She had spent a decent amount of time looking into the classes that she had been offered for her level 50 transformation, but there were always a few more things she could check. Creeping over to the library, she moved quietly in an attempt not to wake anyone. She found the towering shelves silent and empty. It was honestly surprising, as, even throughout the night, people normally used the library. This was a rare opportunity for her to read without interruption.

Finding one of the familiar books she had referenced before, she skimmed through it, reading the passage about level 50 classes for the dozenth time.

The book was very clear about its disclaimers. That everything reported at this level and higher was based on rumors. Very, very few ever made it to this state, let alone disclosed information about it. But on top of all the things a class would normally give, the passive effect and specialized skills were the most likely things she could rely on.

Bee was still torn about her decision. Without more information, definitive information, she was at a loss. She needed to talk to Void. So after making no progress for a while longer, looking through books she'd already read before, she rose to see if she could find her master. It was probably relaxing somewhere in the castle, likely in a corner or under a bed chasing dust bunnies.

I felt the cool air whizz past my brushes as I zipped alongside Cliff's gray form. As we scouted ahead, Tanu trailed behind and did his best to keep up with us, trudging through the forest. The little boy had grown in the month or two I had gone. He had added three-quarters of an inch and at least four and a half pounds to his body, and he was putting that little extra height to use.

His walking pace had increased by 32.64 percent. Not only

that, but he was managing that pace while staying much quieter than before. I was pleased with this progress, but he still couldn't keep up with the four-legged furry dog that was his companion. Cliff's legs were as tall as his entire body, practically.

The hunting was something that Cliff clearly needed to do, but I was mostly just here for fun. Aside from that, I was also hoping to get a better understanding of what was around the castle. There were still pockets of undead or nasty humans like the ones that had attacked Beatrice, Tony, and me so long ago? Or had the undead taken care of all those? I couldn't really be sure until I had done a thorough scan.

So as I swept through the forest, looking for appropriate prey for Cliff's hunt, I also kept my scanners out for anything unusual. We didn't really make it that far from the castle, as Tanu's legs were still rather short. But we did range quite widely in our scans as we traveled over the forest.

We followed small game paths, but I noticed on the ground there were impressions of larger human boots. These were the very faint impressions of someone who was trying to cover their tracks, from what I'd learned. I wasn't too concerned about that. I had taken a pretty good profile of everyone in the castle, and a lot of these footprints could very well have been matched to some of Susan's recruits.

I knew she had been planning on setting up a scouting party, and perhaps this was really just the idea coming to fruition. Now they were trying to map out the areas nearby. I approved. It was always good to have an up-to-date map of one's area, especially in a place like this where obstacle locations could change. Plus, a good plan of action was essential for keeping the forest clean.

Assuming that this had been the case, I probably didn't have to worry about undead lingering around. But every once in a while, I did see traces of what might have been an undead. Perhaps there was still some source of them hidden in the woods. But I had yet to find it, if that was the case.

The moon had only moved a few degrees more when we made it back through the castle gate, Cliff dragging her prize behind her. The large deer was cold to the touch as a result of some strange icy mist that the dog had breathed at it. Tanu wasn't surprised at all that his dog could do something so strange, though I was a bit concerned. Hopefully it wasn't some sort of disease. My sensors indicated Cliff was okay, though.

To my surprise, I found a sleeping Beatrice leaning against the outer wall, sitting in the grass near the gate. The guards nodded and whispered to us.

"She wanted to talk to you, Lord Void. Seems that she fell asleep waiting."

I debated whether or not I should wake her up. She seemed exhausted, though. For now, I just let her sleep. Wrapping her in soothing threads of Air Manipulation, I carried her back into the castle as Cliff and Tanu went off to go dress and preserve the kill. It appeared Beatrice had been using the same room as always, and I deposited her gently in the bed, tucking the covers around her.

Somehow I jostled her in her sleep, and she slowly opened her eyes and murmured something unintelligible to me. That was no good. She obviously needed rest. I remembered something from my previous home. A strategy employed when the mother of our house's two children had trouble getting them to sleep. She would make an odd mixture of different sound frequencies in a rhythmic pattern, which always helped the little ones calm down.

Sure, they were smaller than Beatrice was, but I figured I could maybe mimic that. So I gently and softly started beeping in a soothing rhythm that I had heard many times before. Beatrice mumbled something to me a few times. Still, between the comfortable bed and her clearly exhausted state, she soon drifted off to sleep. Her breathing slowed to a soft, steady cadence.

Not having anything else to do, I just rolled underneath her bed and worked on my meditation. I explored the void, trying to center myself. It had been a long time since I'd been home. I felt like there were so many memories sitting in my cache and my short-term memory storage that I needed to go through to properly update all my models. I just hadn't had time to do that with all the excitement of the past few weeks.

Beatrice shot up from bed early in the morning, gasping and looking around frantically. She seemed to be quite confused. I rolled out from underneath the bed and greeted her warmly. "Oh, good, good. Good morning, Void," she said with a sleepy smile. "I wanted to talk to you last night but heard from the guards you had gone out hunting..." She yawned. "I must have fallen asleep. Who brought me back?"

She looked around and noticed that she was still in the same clothes she had been wearing in the grass. I had, of course, removed any grass stains or loose leaves that she had collected before I put her in bed, but the garments were still slightly dirty compared to whatever clean thing she would normally wear in this fancy bed.

Still, she didn't seem to mind too much as she swung her legs out and stood up. She gave a quick stretch before giving me a slight bow in greeting.

"If you don't mind, I would like to talk to you about something, Master."

Of course I didn't mind. I was always willing to talk to Beatrice about anything. I was her master, after all. It was my duty to give her advice. I asked what she wanted to talk about.

"I, well, I managed to make it to my next class, and I was wondering if I could get your advice. There are two classes that I'm interested in, and they both relate to you. I think you know, I was a Priestess of Spot before, well I still am, and, I...

"I have two options." Beatrice was starting to sound quite nervous, and I couldn't really tell why, but she was rambling and repeating herself quite a bit. I tried to comfort her by tapping her slightly and beeping out a comforting sound. Eventually she got to the point.

"Well, so...I have High Priestess of Spot and Companion of Spot."

I digested that information. It didn't really mean anything to me. Both of the classes sounded like they were continuing this whole religion she was building. Either one would be fine.

Maybe she knew more about them than I did. So I asked her, what did she think?

"Well, I don't really know. I could choose High Priestess, and that would be the best for everyone at the castle. It feels like it would give me more leadership skills and put me in a better place to build your following. My other option is being a Companion, and...I just don't know what that means. To be fair, no one really knows anything about Companions. Or High Priestesses, for that matter, but Companions are much rarer. If I'm not wrong, they feel like a more personal aide to their object of worship, where they would serve them whenever they go on adventures. I wasn't sure if you had a preference. For which one I should choose."

I thought about it for a little bit. Really? I didn't think I would mind either way. I loved having Beatrice with me when I went on adventures, of course. I'd love to have her along more. But did she need a class specifically for that? Maybe she could be a little bit more competent in protecting herself, but I didn't see anything that would stop her from coming on adventures with me if she chose to. As for High Priestess...she clearly cared a lot about the people around here, but they also stressed her out.

The more I thought, the more I realized this was a decision she really needed to make on her own. So I did my best to let her know that it was up to her. I would support her decision either way. Unfortunately, this didn't relieve any of her tension. Her expression seemed even more nervous.

CHAPTER 31
TEAS AND TREASON

"DEAR. I think you're overthinking this."

Mary eyed Bee with concern from across her desk. The words made Bee flinch. Had she been overthinking this? Maybe, maybe not. It seemed like something worth putting thought into, though. This was a huge decision.

She looked away from the motherly woman sitting across from her and scanned the barren storage closet that she was now using as an office. Bee couldn't help but feel slightly silly bothering such a busy woman with her petty concerns. But Mary had always been willing to talk. It was about time she took her up on the offer. Luckily, she didn't mind taking an hour out of her day to listen to Bee's worries.

Was it petty, though? This decision didn't just affect her, but everyone in the castle. This was a choice that could decide her role here moving forward. Up until now, when everyone had sought direction, Bee had simply tried to help as best she could. It wasn't really that she'd insisted on it. Eventually she started asking people to help with things as they slowly gathered in the castle with her and Void. And they accepted that. Even when they put together a more formal organization for the castle, they came to her for everything major. Even though she was just acting on Void's behalf.

Now? She was a leader in name and deed. They had accepted each and every one of her decisions with some questioning and arguing, but it had largely been she who had the final say. The only time when that wasn't the case was when Void was around. But even Void had never once insisted that she change her plans or any of the other organizational decisions she had made, only guided her through suggestions and cryptic teachings.

Had Void even influenced her decisions? It seemed that her master didn't want to take direct interaction with the organization, even if it was willing to fight for them and protect them. Instead, Void wanted to lead through teaching, mostly by helping to raise the children and giving cryptic, wise advice. Truly, it was typical of the stories she had read about ancient masters and beings with wisdom beyond human comprehension.

After a long silence, she sighed. "I suppose I am."

"Good, dear. I'm glad that you realize it." Mary smiled kindly at her. "All of us support you, no matter what you decide. No class will ever change that.

"Now, if you don't mind, I'm sure we both have things to get to." This was the first time Mary had ever dismissed her, even in a gentle way. It made Bee realize just how much time she had taken from the woman she had put in charge of caring for the castle.

It was one thing for Bee to give her a job, but it was another thing entirely to get in the way of her carrying it out. In fact, Bee had plenty of things she needed to see to herself.

Bee tipped her teacup back and finished the rest of the luke-warm brew. "Thanks for taking the time, Mary. Really."

"Oh, I don't mind at all, honey. It's a pleasure to have you, as always. I'd invite you to stay longer, but we want to make sure everyone has clothes for this winter."

Bee nodded and left the office. She supposed she really did overthink this. This choice, either one of her class options, wouldn't change her life path much. They were both dedicated to Void and would mostly give her different skills. Just because she chose one didn't mean she couldn't carry the burdens of the other.

It really came down to a judgment call of what she thought would be more important. Would the possible combat or personal abilities of a Companion be worth more than the organizational skills she would likely get as High Priestess?

Frowning, she made her decision and felt her awareness expand throughout the castle.

Arthur kept his back straight, moving fluidly with the rocking motion of the horse underneath him. As much as he wanted to slump his shoulders in exhaustion, his men needed to see that he was still strong. This had been a long campaign. Sure, he had been in harder and longer campaigns than this, but he wasn't a young man anymore. The weeks spent riding around chasing down hordes of zombies had started to take their toll.

In some ways, sieges and large-scale battles were much easier because he didn't have to run around so much. He could just sit and think and direct the troops. But having to constantly get from place to place was really taxing. At last, though, the walls of Caleb were finally coming into view.

He just needed to finish his mission, and then he could go home and see his family again. Then everything would be better. The walls of the gate still stood strong, repaired from Lord Void's efforts, and from the hill he could see that serious progress had been made inside the city.

By the time winter was over, the refugees he had sent with Miss Bee would be able to return home. Getting them here was a separate matter. But that wasn't the only thing that had changed since he had last seen the city.

Outside of the walls sprawled a large camp. Not one of citizens or refugees, though. The rows of tents were laid out with military precision. He even recognized the flags flying over the formation.

It seemed the king had finally listened to him and sent the reinforcements he had requested so many times. It was a pity they were too late to do anything. Still, perhaps they were helping with the rebuilding effort. At least they could keep the area safe from any undead stragglers.

Before he could advance further toward the city, a figure stepped out of the forest, blocking the path.

At first, the vanguard kept riding forth, an officer shouting for the man to move out of the way. But after several ignored warnings, the vanguard was forced to halt and send out a couple of soldiers to forcibly remove him. It was dangerous to pause a military caravan, especially when they were surrounded by woods. They could be ambushed and hit in vulnerable areas while they were strung out on the trail.

This was one of the purposes of the vanguard. Arthur reminded himself that the gap between them and the main force would allow them to absorb any issues without stopping the soldiers in a precarious position. Stirring his horse to a canter, he went up to see what was going on. The young officer in charge of the vanguard was someone he had a little hope for, after all.

He wasn't the most competent of the nobles, but he didn't tend to lean on his family name too much. Arthur had decided he was going to get this young officer some experience and see if he could actually learn to lead one day. But in order for that to happen, Arthur needed to watch over this man fairly closely. It helped that he was just bored and looking for something else to do other than stare at trees, if he was truly, completely honest with himself.

The man was yelling something as he was dragged to the side of the road, and the vanguard continued moving. Arthur stopped to see the two guards holding the man's thin arms to his sides. But when the raggedly dressed man looked up and met Arthur's gaze, he couldn't help but pause at the look in his eyes.

The dirty vagabond that had caused the vanguard to stop had a strange look about him. He appeared as a wild man, eyes rolling about as he shouted. The man might have been crazy. But when their gazes met, something flashed in them, something Arthur couldn't quite describe.

The man immediately calmed. Ignoring the two men holding his arms, he attempted to bow while restrained.

"Lord Arthur. I bring news."

Arthur considered getting down from his horse as a polite gesture, but decided he didn't want to be any closer than he had to be to this man. "What is it?"

"The king's soldiers did not come to help us rebuild. They've come with a warrant for your head. My lord."

Arthur and the two soldiers holding the man both froze. Arthur let his mind work as he tried to figure out the position. Why would the king want him arrested? There was nothing that Arthur had done that would have constituted treason. The worst thing he had ever been guilty of was slightly disobeying orders to win battles and gain more advantageous positions. And he'd always been forgiven for such things.

No reports should have made their way back to the king about anything, aside from a need for reinforcements. This entire campaign had been by the book, and the few nobles that had died hadn't done so until they were on the campaign out of the city. They truly wouldn't have had time to send a message and have the king march an army up here. None of the upstart nobles he had punished should have had the ear of the king himself anyway, even if they had even managed to get any reports of "mistreatment" that far.

Arthur swung down from his horse in a hurry. "Why? How do you know this?"

"Well, my lord, they've been asking for you and showing everyone in the city the warrant for your arrest. Apparently, it had something to do with high treason and colluding with the enemy."

Arthur frowned, Colluding with the enemy? He wasn't sure how that could be. He certainly hadn't colluded with the undead. That seemed unrealistic enough that no one else could imagine it either. But something occurred to him.

Could it have something to do with Lord Void? The more Arthur thought about it, the more he was convinced that it was right. The king and Harold had been convinced Lord Void had been the one to summon the undead. But Arthur knew different.

Arthur knew that Lord Void was an ally. Some of his reports even indicated as much. And if his reports had been taken seriously, then it could very much appear that Lord Void had perhaps possessed him or duped him, or that he had betrayed the country. But surely they would have seen from the rest of his reports that allying with Void was at least necessary. And even Harold's report should have shown that the city was about to fall otherwise.

Yet it hadn't, and he continued to send messages to that effect. The King's Guard was here and should have shown them very clearly that he was in the right, that they had saved the city. If they didn't believe his reports, then what of the eyewitnesses in the city? Did they suppose the whole city was charmed?

This whole thing stunk of politics, and there was very little Arthur hated more than that. He stood silently, thinking. His next moves, all things considered, weren't necessarily for himself.

Arthur would be fine. He had no intention of turning himself in to a king with whom he had seemingly fallen out of favor. No, his real concerns were about his family. They were likely in their estate in the countryside. But if a warrant had been sent out for his arrest, it was likely the king moved against his family as well.

There were protocols for that. He had long since drilled his sons and his staff on them. They would have taken their children and gone into hiding at the first sign of trouble. It wouldn't be a permanent solution, but it should buy them some time.

His oldest son was in the military far away, and there was likely nothing he could do to shelter him. But at the same time, he doubted any suspicion would be cast on him. He was one of the king's most trusted captains, and Arthur was very proud of that. Besides, the news would take a long time to reach him, and there was no way they would meaningfully suspect him if the cause of Arthur's "treason" was due to being charmed somehow.

Arthur looked at the dirty man before him. He'd need to confirm this news himself, send scouts ahead. But if it was true, then he and his men needed to tread carefully. First, he'd have to get a message to his family, but then perhaps a certain young priestess would be able to help them until he figured out what to do.

CHAPTER 32

A LOT OF TROUBLE

BEE HAD ONLY MADE it a few feet away from Mary's office when she made her choice. New awareness flooded into her mind, and she staggered into a wall, clutching her head. She sank to the ground, head between her knees as she tried to make sense of the sudden influx of sensation.

She could feel a new presence in her mind. Or rather, many of them. Almost like threads, each connected to one of the hundreds of people within the castle. Some connections were strong, and some were barely there, but each gave her a certain level of information.

She steadied her breathing. After a moment to recover, she began to sort through them. It was simple to find the Tony one, as it was one of the brightest threads in the castle. The connection imparted another torrent of knowledge that sent her teeth clenching. There was a lot there, almost as if she were running a Scan from a few feet away. But there was more to it than that.

Pulling back, she focused on the web as a whole once more. Rather than seeing, it was more that she felt the dense collection of varied links as a new limb. She thought she could maybe pick a few of the new arrivals out of a crowd based on the dimness of their links to her. A rough estimate of the number seemed smaller than the total of castle dwellers, though. What was going on?

Bee tried to put the sensation aside for a moment and think. This seemed a bit excessive for a class ability, even for High Priestess. It was certainly more than Priestess had gotten her by a long shot. But this one had a lot of potential unknowns to her. It seemed likely that she was gaining an instinctual awareness of people who had faith in Void. And it also seemed that her Scan skill was slightly integrated with it. At least there was some sort of synergy there that was giving her more information than she could really handle.

It took her nearly fifteen minutes and several attempts before she was able to stand without passing out. Even now, a bout of dizziness threatened to overtake her, and she started to feel faint. She leaned against the cold stone walls for support.

Stumbling down the hallway, she groped along the wall, searching for the nearest stairwell. As she staggered down the small, tight spiral, she was reminded of the first days of Void, and she could only be thankful that she had both functioning ankles right now. Making her way to her bedroom, she hoped that a nap might ease her pain.

Zeal stalked back to the city walls while rubbing his upper arms, worried that the bruises would show distinct lines of the fingers that had held him in place. It shouldn't be too big of a deal. They should heal quickly. But at the same time, those sorts of marks could draw suspicion.

As much as he would have liked to trust the authority of the King's Guard like he had done most of his life in Caleb, he knew he couldn't any longer. Things had changed in Zeal's life. The siege had been hard for everyone, but for him, it was harder than most.

He lost everyone. His wife, his son, his mother, his father, and every single other family member he knew of. All gone.

Not that they had been fighting in some grand war or died heroes in a battle or charged out with the military. No, no. They were all ordinary, gods-fearing people. They had done their parts in their small ways to help. As the crafters and laborers they were.

Sue had spent her time cooking for the soldiers when she had a chance, and his son had run messages. But no, when push came to shove, they were huddled in their basement when the fighting was particularly intense. Then it stopped. It had fallen so quiet. The fighting was done. He had been certain it would be fine to step outside and get some fresh air, despite Sue begging him to stay where it was safe.

What a cruel joke, he thought, pulling himself from the memories. His few friends had tried to console him and keep him sane, and they had managed for a few days. But when the god had come to the city, everyone was afraid he would do something foolish and get himself killed.

One could only throw so many curses at the gods before they could expect to be struck down. That was what everyone told him. But Zeal hadn't cursed this god. No, not this one. This one had heard him. He understood this was a new god, a god that would set everything right.

This one would fix the old callous ways of the indifferent pantheon that had cursed him to stand outside in the street tapping the ashes out of his pipe while some sort of impact destroyed the building behind him. It left a crater almost as deep as the house itself, so what use was a basement? But never mind. It was all going to be fixed.

Now this new power had come to set it right. Sure, he wished that the void god would have come a few days earlier to relieve them from the siege, and he supposed some in his position would have been angry about that delay. But that wasn't how he thought. As hard as it was, his family's sacrifice was necessary.

Their loss had changed him like everyone had feared, yet not at all. It caused him to open his eyes, to better understand how the world must change and how the new god was going to change it.

One of the guards gave him a funny look as he walked through the city gate, but no one stopped him. He was well enough known around here now, especially in the last few weeks. Pretty much everyone in the city had heard him proselytize, though most just thought of him as some harmless rambler on the street. Not all. But most.

When he wanted to go somewhere, the words of his god aided him. People who should have stopped him, who were paid to guard, often would just let him go through to avoid getting held up in a conversation. Some might consider it a negative thing, having others stopper their ears against his words. But not Zeal. It simply meant that they couldn't handle the truth he had come to spread. If it meant he could go forth and further speak to others, then it was truly a blessing from his new god in some form.

That wasn't to say that everyone ignored him, of course. But not enough listened. Not yet. But Zeal was sure that they would. They would. Very soon.

Navigating his way through the newly pristine streets of Caleb, he nodded to many of the street cleaning crews. They knew him. They understood. They agreed. They, too, had seen something about this new god, who had pushed them to take their lives in different directions and nudged them toward a higher purpose.

He saw Hummar, the blacksmith that had lived a couple streets down, pushing a broom instead of working in the forge. It was a strange sight, seeing such a burly man with nothing but a broomstick thinner than his arm. But seeing the small smile of contentment on the man's face, Zeal couldn't help but return his smile.

A few streets down, Zeal turned into an alley. He knocked on a green door set half-underground. The small steps leading into the basement filled with light as it opened, and with a few words, he waded into the adoring audience waiting for his return.

After my conversation with Beatrice this morning, I decided it was time to explore a bit beyond the castle. During the day, it'd be a little easier, and perhaps I could search for any threats hidden in the forest. After all, I just finished cleaning the castle yesterday, and I could spend time cleaning it again later tonight if needed.

I suspected that it wasn't even necessary, though. Mary and her army of janitors in training would have no problem caring for it. It wasn't like I needed the experience, anyway, so it would have just been for my personal pride to clean it. Well, and to fix up the really minor things that humans couldn't seem to pick up on. Still, I was very proud of their efforts. I wasn't going to deny others the pleasure of cleaning. Besides, their earning experience and funneling it to me was almost as sufficient as me just doing it myself. I was getting pretty close to level 70 anyways.

So it wouldn't hurt to let them take care of it for a while. I thought I'd just check in with everyone first, though. And as I wandered through the castle, ensuring everyone was present, and no one was harmed, I ran into Tony. His face lit up.

"Ah, Lord Void! Just the god I wanted to see. Can I talk to you for a moment?"

Sure, why not? I had some time. Hearing my response, Tony glanced about and ushered me quickly into a room.

CHAPTER 33

CAUSE FOR CELEBRATION

I FOLLOWED Tony into the small room off to the side of the hallway, though I couldn't help but wonder what he wanted. This dark closet was a bit ominous. If I didn't know better, I might've been afraid.

Shutting the door, he stopped and turned around to face me with a slight bow. "So Lord Void... You know how Bee is always saying she's 'almost fourteen'?"

Yeah, I did recall that coming up a few times; in fact, it had been going on for long enough that I wasn't sure if she was even telling the truth. I told Tony as much. He grinned and continued his explanation. "Well, 'almost' is almost here. Next week is her birthday!"

Huh? I wasn't sure if I could believe it.

"Yeah, I know right? They grow up so fast." For some reason, Tony pretended to wipe a tear from the corner of his eye. Why was he sad? Or pretending to be sad? From my observations, birthdays were normally a cause for celebration.

Did this have something to do with humor? I was pretty sure it did, but it didn't make sense. It seemed kinda mean-spirited if he was pretending to be sad about her celebration. Or was it because he was sad that she was one year closer to death? Maybe that was the custom here.

Tony ceased his antics and looked back at me. "I was thinking that maybe we should throw her a party. Everyone is settling in right now, and in a week it would be good to have a celebration to lighten the mood and bring everyone together more. Besides, I think everyone here owes her a lot, so it's the least we could do. I want to make it a banger."

I wasn't sure what a banger was, but I agreed that Beatrice deserved a party. So how did he want me to help? At my acceptance, Tony grinned and rubbed his hands together. "I'm so glad you asked..."

Sitting on top of the stone lab table, I couldn't help but admire how clean Maranda had kept her workstation all this time. Watching her work, it made sense, though. With the precision required as she weighed and measured each ingredient, any small amount of grime could throw off the results by an unacceptable amount.

"So this should be a good test for the red one," Maranda said, indicating the vial that she had placed at the end of the row of clear liquids. I ran through each of them, ensuring I knew what each would do. On the right, there were five different sizes for testing the concoctions' strength, and then after, there were several smaller vials that would test the colors.

According to Maranda, they should explode colorfully when thrown to the ground. The only issue was that she had no real idea how large of an explosion they would make. Apparently, these hadn't come from any of the books that Beatrice liked so much, and she had just made them up herself based on a show her family had seen in the city at some point. Understandably, she didn't want to make a mess in the castle and asked me to test them somewhere safe, where they wouldn't bother anyone.

I hesitantly agreed. Though I was all for preventing messes, I wasn't sure if I was the best tester. I could record quite detailed data, of course, but I might not be a great judge of how well an explosion would serve as a decoration based on its size.

Throughout the castle, preparations for the party were in full swing. I was honestly amazed at how quickly Tony had gotten everyone mobilized. The only issue that people were struggling with was keeping Beatrice from noticing. So far, most of the castle's participants were fully on board. Kids and soldiers were gathering berries on the outskirts of the forests for desserts. Trent was working with some of the craftsmen to get a bunch of tables and benches ready.

Even Susan was fully engaged. So far, she had been in charge of setting up the events. She wasn't working on it alone. It seemed that she and Captain Major had developed a bit of a rivalry and were trying to one-up each other. There were already multiple tournaments planned, mostly dealing with martial combat. Despite the Nighty Knights' objections, they were divided into classes by age: under ten and over ten.

It mostly fell to Tony to keep Beatrice distracted. We brainstormed several ideas for how to go about this. Unfortunately, we weren't able to think of a good reason to get her out of the castle and visit Greg or otherwise travel. Not any reason that would also have her back in time for the party, anyway.

These events had given Tony some ideas, though. That's why, for the next week, he would be getting some intense one-on-one training with Beatrice in the art of the broom. After his first day, he started to regret his decision, but I promised him a broom like Beatrice's if he managed to finish it out. That lit a fire under him. Apparently, he wanted to put his Paladin of Spot class to real use, whatever that meant.

There were also plenty of other things going on that I didn't fully understand. Races involving wheelbarrows and sacks, extra-steep ramps, and more. I hadn't figured them out yet, but everyone seemed excited.

My part was relatively simple. Well, to start with, first I had just been supervising, then I was put in charge of providing prizes. Last I checked, there were fourteen different events that all needed prizes for first, second, and third place.

The testing of the active decorations had put a little more strain on my scheduling algorithms, but I found it was worth it. Especially considering the potential for messes to be made. Scooping up all the vials, I waved goodbye to Maranda and left the laboratory. I wanted to just zip away and test the things as soon as possible so she could iterate on them if there was any issue. I had a good idea of where I would be able to do my testing without bothering anyone.

The mountain range to the north didn't really have anything behind it. Just vast fields of ice and snow. If the snow got a little disordered, it would either melt or be smoothed over by the wind, so I didn't feel bad about tarnishing it temporarily. A few flashes of light and sound shouldn't be a big deal here either.

Leaving the castle proved to be more difficult than expected, though. I couldn't move around freely during the daytime anymore. Too many people stopped and bowed to me, and I felt rude just brushing them off. So I'd always either have a quick chat with them, which was usually rather one-sided and slightly awkward, or give them a wave and move on. But with everyone hustling and bustling to get the party ready for Beatrice, I had many people stop and ask me questions.

It seemed everyone wanted to know my preferences. One of the young women, Cassy, asked if I preferred apple or cherry pie, and then I had to figure out what she meant by that. Given my lack of taste buds, I couldn't really give an accurate preference. But I did like the red cherries slightly more. So I went with that.

Heading outside, I was further waylaid by many of the Nighty

Knights asking for help with last-minute training for the tournament. A few of the more brash ones were still trying to convince the adults to let them join in the over-ten bracket. I declined to help them fight against the adults, but I did grant them one pointer each.

So I had to wait for forty-two of the now fifty-four kids to each show me their most impressive move. Then I gave them small tips on how to place their feet better or grip the sword so they wouldn't hurt their wrists when they were impacted.

I would have to work with them later in one on one sessions for each of their unique skills.

This was relatively minor and could have taken a lot longer, but it still ate up time, even if I went quickly. Though I didn't mind at all. In my opinion, giving these children something to do was the best part about this whole castle. Besides keeping it clean, obviously.

I managed to dodge Bee and Tony's sparring that, at this point, had been going on for over a day. That left me to zip up and over the wall without anyone else stopping me. I felt a little bad leaving them to their own devices, but I helped as I could. Besides, I had a schedule to keep, especially if I wanted to figure out how to make so many prizes.

Taking to the air, I started the long trek over to the mountain. The distance was a bit deceiving, as I struggled to visualize this mountain's size. I knew I'd already flown around it once, but it was still impressive, especially the way the angles managed to be so steep. I had no idea how snow managed to cling to such an angled rock. Maybe I would find that out soon enough.

Aiming for one of the passes, I kept low, skimming over the smooth snow. In the past, I couldn't help but marvel at the vast horizon stretching out before me. Far into the distance heaped white mounds of snow and nothing else. Looking back to where I had come, everything further south of me was only sporadically dusted in snow. There were patches here and there, but for the most part, it was a green forest mixed in with brown fields. Rocky outcroppings, like the mountains, appeared to act as barriers to the weather.

As I made it over to the other side of the mountain, I figured I was far enough away that people wouldn't be disturbed by my experimenting. Not wanting to wait much longer. I zipped up the mountain a little bit so I could have a better vantage point for what would happen and pulled out the largest vial. I planned to go through the sequence that Maranda had shown me in order, ejecting each from my dustbin.

I immediately tossed the first vial into the side of the mountain, about three-quarters of the way up. As I watched it arc into the massive amount of snow, I wondered why I saw bluish-purple sparks flitting all over it. Those hadn't been there when Maranda had given it to me. Could something have changed?

The vial landed just below the large cave entrance that I had noted on my last trip. Oh, that reminded me. I had meant to explore that before this whole party business. Perhaps I could do that after—

I was cut off mid-thought by a deep *wumph* sound. The vial shattered, erupting into a gout of snow at least fifty feet tall, spraying high into the air.

With a rumble, I noticed that the ice was beginning to shift. It started at the top, bits slowly tumbling down the mountain, but each piece that was knocked loose rolled down the hill a little bit further and knocked more loose. This continued in a chain reaction.

I was filled with nothing but relief that I had decided to stay up so high. I watched the mountainside slowly lose all the snow sticking to it. The mass of the snow was difficult to estimate as it rushed down the mountain, an ever-growing tide of destruction as it slammed into the base.

It continued on relentlessly, rolling out over the vast plains of snow for what must have been miles. Well, that was one test down.

That vial might be a little bit too powerful for decoration. Also, there wasn't much color to it. I supposed that Maranda may have just made these emit white light, though. It wasn't one of the colored vials, after all.

I considered whether to make my way down the size scale or try the smallest next. But before I could take out the next one and test it, a massive column of smoke billowed out of the cave entrance. I heard a deep rumbling completely separate from the mass of roiling snow down below.

CHAPTER 34
HERE THERE BE DRAGONS

I HELD off throwing the next vial while I tried to identify the source of the new sound. Before I could, though, it identified itself. With a sudden cracking of rocks, something exploded out of the cave entrance, sending plumes of smoke exploding outward. Before my vision cleared of the debris, a booming voice yelled out so loud that my mic started peaking. *"CAN YOU NOT?"*

As the air cleared, I saw a scaly red lizard head retract back into the cave. This wasn't just any lizard, though. It was quite long. Considering its proportions, its head might have been the size of the castle, though considering my perspective, that might have been a bit of an exaggeration.

It appeared that I had, in fact, disturbed someone, despite my best efforts. I should probably go apologize.

What would be a good way to do that? I mean, obviously I should go talk to them, but maybe a show of good faith would ease the anger of having their front lawn made into such a mess. I figured I could start by cleaning it up for them first. Not wanting to be too much of a bother, I zipped over to the cave and started clearing out the rubble.

The explosion itself hadn't done much here, aside from

spraying snow. Most of the mess actually stemmed from the angry response by the owner of the cave when it stuck its head out. Several of the stalactites and stalagmites had broken off from impacts with its horns and scales. That left me with an interesting choice.

I could simply replace them, and return the jagged rocks to their previous positions. Or I could just grind the stumps down to the ground and make them flat and level. It was a hard choice. One was cleaning by virtue of putting things back in a natural state, but the other I favored slightly.

The stalactites and stalagmites, while cool, were decorations that hadn't formed quite right. I imagined that if one really wanted to turn them into proper decorations, they'd have to spend some time cultivating them, ensuring that the water dripped in the right spot. Otherwise, you'd end up with uneven lines.

So I decided I would start removing the pieces. Besides, if the lizard couldn't even leave the front door of their home without breaking them off, they seemed to be even worse than nonfunctional decorations. What was the point? That just wasn't acceptable.

Removing them was a bit tricky. I started by swinging my Divine Sword at their bases to trim them pretty close to the floor before leveling everything out with my laser. It took me several seconds per stalagmite, but overall it wouldn't put me too behind schedule. After this, I would definitely need to find another place to test Maranda's solutions, though. A safer place with no one to disturb.

I quickly cleaned up and tidied the stalactites and stalagmites growing at the front of the cave. After that, I moved a little further in to continue cleaning. That was when I first glimpsed the hopelessly cluttered interior of the cave.

Piles and piles of round metallic disks lay haphazardly across the floor. Not neatly stacked piles, either. These were mounds of careless metal that sprawled across the uneven rocks. The stuff extended nearly to the cave entrance, obscuring the rough pathway in a glittering coat of gold.

Oh no. I must have made more of a mess than I initially thought. As I hovered forward, I drew the disks into my dustbin. I wasn't sure what they were, but they certainly weren't in the right spot. The owner would surely appreciate me returning these to their rightful place. And I couldn't just leave them lying in the middle of the hallway.

I was extremely lucky that my circuitry allowed for a rather quick reaction time, at least compared to most of the other thinking beings I had encountered. The massive stream of fire suddenly approaching me would have definitely caused some damage if it hit, no matter how tough I had become.

Time seemed to slow down as my processors overclocked. My first thought was to block it using my Air Manipulation. However, it did very little to divert it. The pillar of air I shot out to intercept was quickly overwhelmed. I tried a pane of air, but that was smashed through as well. After a few simulations, I settled on trying to split the beam by creating a wedge shape. That had more success, but I could still tell that the liquid flames would impact me on either side.

Just in time, I managed to whip out my Divine Sword and slice through the beam, deflecting it off to the side and into the ground. The heat created an extremely ugly scorch mark where it landed. The stream cut off a few seconds later.

Somehow, the fire was so hot that the rock it touched was *burning*. Parts of it were even now melting into liquid, and others had flames flickering over their surfaces as the impurities were purged from them.

Finally, I found another use for my Spray Bottle. I switched to water to ensure I didn't cause any weird chemical reactions in my attempt to clean. I zipped over and quickly doused the flames with a quick spray before mopping it back up. Most of the water evaporated in a spray of steam, but to my surprise, some of the liquid rock swirled into my Mop as well. The rock underneath was still quite hot, but it wasn't on fire, at least.

Continuing my mission, I meandered a little farther into the cave and found more and more of these shiny gold metal pieces. They stretched out far into the cave, well beyond what I could pierce with my sensors.

The range of my sensors seemed slightly impeded, as if the darkness was pressing down on it unnaturally and restricting my view. But I continued forward, bravely collecting the scattered coins. Once I retrieved enough to make an aesthetically pleasing stack, I maneuvered over to the wall and stacked them in a neat tube.

I waited for another fire stream to shoot out at me, but it didn't come. There were a couple of heat signatures spaced several feet apart towards the back of the cave, and as I approached, I saw some smoke curling out of them. But for the most part, nothing else happened.

It felt safe to assume that whatever had blasted me either needed to wait for a cooldown or was watching my movements. So I did my best to convey my intentions through actions. I hoped they would show that I wanted nothing but to fulfill my purpose and clean.

After cleaning up and stacking the first pile, I went a little farther in to collect the rest of the coins. A voice rumbled out from the direction of the two heat sources. It was the same voice that had shouted earlier. A couple of dark smoke plumes billowed out as it spoke.

"What are you doing?" The voice was a lot less forceful than before, but I could still feel a strong presence behind them. A palpable weight pushed me down, causing my suspension to give a little.

I was quite startled and had no idea how to respond. I froze for a second. My processor churned out ideas about how to talk with a mysterious entity and rejected them each in turn. It was becoming increasingly probable that the lizard itself had spoken to me, but as far as I was aware, lizards couldn't speak. Which was, needless to say, strange.

But then again, my kind normally couldn't speak either. Well, not that I could speak myself. But still, this was all very confusing.

So I settled for just my standard greeting of popping out my arm and waving to the general blackness. I let out a few excited beeps of welcome to hopefully convey the message that I'd meant no harm. The voice was quiet for a couple of seconds, so I just went back to tidying up all the loose objects on the ground.

"It's either an act of bravery or complete foolishness to touch a dragon's hoard. Almost always the latter." The voice came back in a surprisingly thoughtful tone for something that shook the cave as it spoke. "Seeing as you survived a shot of dragon's breath and still decided to carry on... Hmm. It must be bravery. Even a fool would have gotten the message through their thick skull."

A dragon! That made so much more sense. It wasn't a lizard. They did look fairly similar, though, size aside. Yet as far as I had ever heard, I didn't know if dragons were real. They were just stories that the adults would use to scare the children into doing their chores. But then again, Bee hadn't believed that the Lieutenant was real when it clearly was. Why not dragons too?

"Just so you know, I know exactly how many gold coins I have in my lair, and I am counting as you touch them. You will not attempt to take any from here, or you'll regret it," the dragon growled with a hint of amusement.

I beeped my acknowledgment in a clear indication of yes to anyone who could hear. It didn't seem that the dragon understood me either, at least not the way some of the children did. Oh well. It was the best I could do.

Suddenly a prompt flashed before my eyes, one I hadn't expected to see quite yet. However, the sudden influx of castle inhabitants had apparently sped up my experience gain by a bit more than expected. There was plenty more cleaning to be done there, after all.

LEVEL UP, LVL 70 REACHED. CHOOSE A SKILL:COMPEL FOLLOWER, SENSORY DISRUPTION, COVENANT OF BLOOD.

I scanned through my options, and it was an easy choice. Compel Follower was not happening. I had no interest in either making my followers do anything or compelling someone to be my follower. Plus, Beatrice was doing quite a good job on that front anyway. But neither was Covenant of Blood an option. Blood was messy and got everywhere. Why would I want anything to do with it? Much less make a contract of some kind with it.

Sensory Disruption it was. I just hoped it wasn't talking about disrupting *my* sensors.

Selecting my new skill, I immediately felt the changes unfurl through the world around me. I could tell that there were a few different ways to use the skill. I could now make it so that I wouldn't notice certain things or would see things that weren't there. It still wasn't clear to me why I would want to do that, but it was an option.

Luckily, the possibilities weren't all about altering my own sensors. I could actually affect others' sensors. The main uses came in three forms. The first two dealt with directly implanting false data into another's sensory input or erasing something that was already there. I got the feeling that this wasn't a guaranteed success. The third use was to create a general "false artifact" independent from all targets. Some sort of image that registered to sensors as real, but wasn't actually there.

What good timing. Maybe I could use this to communicate more quickly? I chose to use the third application of my power, as it felt like it would be the least invasive. Now that I realized that the originator of the liquid fire that shot at me was the dragon, I didn't want any more misunderstandings.

Above me, I created a little hologram projecting blocky letters and a friendly message. I tried to make it as approachable as possible.

"Hello Mr. Dragon. Don't mind me! :)"

CHAPTER 35

LAZY SUNDAYS

THE CAVE WAS silent except for the soft sound of clinking gold as I continued to neatly organize the contents of the dragon's lair. It was the least I could do after I so rudely interrupted its morning. Once I ensured that the entryway was clear and clean, though, I felt that it was starting to get slightly awkward. Beatrice would never have let the silence stretch on for this long without at least some further attempt at conversation.

I studied my host as I started working a bit deeper into the cave. At this point, my sensors could finally pierce the deep darkness to get a better look at my new friend. The scaled face of the massive reptile didn't seem to have the same expressiveness as human faces. At least not in a way that my emotional detection subroutines could recognize. But it was clear that it was watching me at least as much as I was watching it. Whether or not it was actually counting the coins I stacked, I couldn't tell.

Under its scrutiny, I felt the need to start up a conversation. But what to say?

Eventually, I settled on something banal and slightly complimentary. Focusing on my new skill, I projected words above me. "It's an awfully large amount of coins you got here!"

I shaped the font in the least threatening way I could: large block letters with rounded edges in a variety of colors, just like the ones that the small humans back home liked to use in their art projects. My message was well received as the giant lizard let out a snort of smoke and rumbled with laughter. "It is a mighty hoard, is it not?"

The dragon paused for a second, but I wasn't sure how to respond, so I held my metaphorical tongue. Luckily I didn't need to wait long, as the silence was soon filled. "Sadly, I don't get to enjoy the sight of it as much as I would like. Being asleep will do that to you. I suppose that's one positive aspect of being woken up. Even if I was *trying* to find peace and quiet for a reason...

"I'm quite surprised, actually. Not many are capable of finding this place, much less reaching it. Those that do generally have the sense to avoid a dragon's lair." The red reptile paused. "Say, how long have I been asleep for anyway? I bet it's been a while."

Ah, a direct question; I knew how to handle those. I formed new words in the air. "I'm not sure when you went to sleep, mister. I didn't know you were here or else I wouldn't have disturbed your front lawn so rudely. Making a mess was the last thing that I wanted to do. Honest."

There were too many words to put up at once while keeping them readable. So instead of having a massive block of tiny letters, I left them large and had them slowly scroll past. I thought about having them make a second pass, but I didn't want to offend.

"What?! You didn't know who Daedalus the Red was?!" Daedalus cried, real emotion tinging his voice with some mix of confusion and hurt. "Has the world moved on so fast? It couldn't have been more than a thousand years..."

It was surprisingly hard for me to answer that. I had assumed the world always moved at the same speed. But it was nice to know the dragon's name. It felt a little weird, referring to him as just "it" with no name.

I felt very uncomfortable and decided that it was in my best interest to introduce myself. I politely put up another message. "Hello, Daedalus. My name is Spot."

Dedalus was slightly taken aback and lowered his head to look at me closer.

"Well, it's nice to meet you, Spot," he said, still clearly thrown by the previous information. I figured I would clarify the part about the world moving fast, at least.

"By my calculations, and judging based on the distance to the sun and the time of rotation, the earth is moving at roughly 67,000mph. I would give you more detailed numbers, but my sensors aren't really made for Long-Distance Astronomical Surveys."

Daedalus blinked. "Wow. Moving around the sun..."

He trailed off in thought before shaking his head and coming back to his original question. "That really wasn't what I meant by moving fast, Spot. Um, what year is it?"

"Well, from what Beatrice has told me, it is the twenty-third year of the rule of the current king."

Wow. Words could be really inefficient sometimes. I could communicate all this so much more quickly with a simple beep if only he understood. I was just lucky Daedalus could read.

In response to my information, Daedalus let out a huff, blowing smoke into the roof of the cave.

Looking up, I realized I might have more work cut out for me than I originally thought. The inside of the cave, especially the roof, was covered in soot. The black, oily substance was at least an inch deep. I could only imagine how many years of smoke breathed into this cave would have caused that much accumulation.

Actually, now that I thought about it, I could probably use that to calculate how long Daedalus had been in the cave. I just need to figure out how fast the soot would accumulate over time. That would probably take me a few weeks of observation, but I didn't really have time for that. Not right now.

"Well, that's not the most helpful. Then...do you know how my companion is doing? The one in the castle, about a valley over from here?" the Red asked.

That certainly sounded like our castle. But a companion? There was no one there nearly so old as this dragon seemed to be. Unless...

I was considering what words to use when Daedalus let out a large sigh, significantly raising the temperature of the room.

"I suppose you wouldn't know that either," the dragon said with a huff. I didn't know exactly, of course, but I had some idea. I pulled up an image from the bottom of the catacombs. After some image processing, I projected a picture of the statue's image in the marbled white room below the castle. I set it at a slight spin so Daedalus could see it from all angles.

"So you do know my companion!" Then the giant head slumped against the still-unorganized pile of gold in disappointment. "If he's still in stasis, though, then I certainly have no reason to be awake. It feels wrong hoping for one of the Lieutenant Demons to break free, but it's so *boring* here. By chance, has Nazareth'gak stirred recently? You know, the large demon statue in the castle."

Oh, that demon! I replaced the statue image with a looping recording of the demon breaking out of the statue and charging across the beautiful black floor. Daedalus's head reared up in alarm. "He's already free?! I must go. Quickly! The world is in danger!"

Daedalus lifted his head, revealing the rest of his form. It matched what I had seen so far. A massive reptile body was curled on top of a pile of even more haphazard coins. Among the red scales, three rows of wicked spikes ran down his back: one down the center and two smaller ones to either side of it, marking what looked to be the edges of his back. Massive wings unfurled to either side, hemmed in by the cave's size.

He quickly rose from the pile of coins, the shifting sending small amounts of them tumbling to the ground. Realizing what a mess he was making, Daedalus froze and seemed to consider a less disruptive way to move. "Wait. How old is this recording?"

With some quick math, I displayed the number of seconds since I last laid sensors on the statue. Moving his head some more, he peered outside the cave mouth and scrutinized the world. "If it was this long ago...and you survived... Show me what happened next."

Seeing no reason not to, I played the rest of the fight. Together we watched in silence as I battled the demon. When the undead appeared to help, Daedalus was taken aback, but we didn't stop. After it was over, he asked me to play it again. I complied. Then I went slowly over a few parts of it, paying special attention to the end where I had stabbed into the demon, draining it and eventually consuming it. It seemed like Daedalus cared about those parts specifically.

After we finished analyzing the fight, Daedalus stayed quiet, considering. Eventually, he settled back into the pile of coins, wiggling his body slightly to dig in deeper. "Wow."

The word rang through the air, bouncing off the walls but also impressing the weight of his thoughts into the physical reality around us. Not sure what to say, I changed the image back to simple, friendly text. "Cleaning up after that was difficult."

Daedalus snorted, billowing smoke everywhere before he let out a chuckle and shook the cave. Had I made a joke? I didn't think that I had said anything funny. After the mirth faded from his eyes, he sighed. "I bet it was, little one. I bet it was."

We sat there for some time, just looking at each other. By this point, I had finished stacking the loose coins around the entrance, and it didn't seem that the dragon was going to let me organize the main pile. I suppose that was fine. If he was already using it, there was no point in sorting it, as a simple shift of his massive wings would send it back into disarray.

Taking advantage of the break in conversation, I used my new sense to get a look at my new friend's soul. After peering at it for a second, I immediately had to turn my senses off. The ball of energy at the center of his being was so bright that I was nearly blinded. Not a smudge even dimmed the glow of power and light radiating like a small sun.

Eventually, Daedalus shook his head slightly and seemed to come back from his thoughts. "Well, I can tell that my companion is not yet awake. But if Nazareth'gak did awaken, then he will not be far behind. While it may take a while, I'm certain I won't have time to take a proper nap again."

I just beeped in commiseration. It wasn't that I understood, but Daedalus sounded sad and a little frustrated. He looked at me and sighed. "I suppose it's not your fault for waking me. Not too long ago and I probably wouldn't have even noticed you. But I suppose I'd only get another year or so in any way. At least you saved him the trouble of climbing all the way up here to get me.

"Well, in the meantime...I don't suppose that you have a bit to catch me up on what I missed?" Daedalus asked with a hopeful note. I thought about all I had to do this week and frowned internally.

"Not right now, but I promise that I will visit soon. We can talk then." I scrolled the words above me. After it was finished, I put up a second message. "Besides, your story sounds very interesting. I want to know about your companion."

Settling his head into the coins, Daedalus grinned, bearing his wickedly sharp teeth at me. "Yes, we will swap stories soon. Yours sounds just as intriguing. In the meantime, is there anything I can do for you? Turning my coin stacks into decorations certainly spruced up this old lair a bit."

I took a moment to think about my responsibilities. "Actually, yes. Do you have any interesting prizes for human competitions? Perhaps we could trade?"

"Human competitions..." Daedalus the Red mused. "I think I might have something..."

CHAPTER 36
LET'S MAKE A DEAL

"WELL, little one. The real question is, what do you have to offer in trade?"

I was slightly taken aback. Trade was something I had heard discussed, but it wasn't something that I had any real experience in. I was lucky to have some context from past overheard conversations, but even in the castle, the concept of trade was completely foreign. Things were pretty much collected and distributed as Mary and Trent saw fit.

In our place, everyone was given what they needed and pitched in where they could help most. It was quite a useful system, but I could see how it wouldn't scale properly. Especially now that I had some context from my time with Arthur. I had learned a decent amount about supply lines and the corruption of humans with his army. But I hadn't thought of my own ability to trade, as it were.

So I asked myself, what did I have to trade? I only had so many things. So I cast into my dustbin and found a lot more than I expected. While I had kept careful tabs on everything coming in and out of it, I hadn't quite considered them from a value perspective. One thing was certain, though: if I were to dump everything out into this cave, I would fill it several times over in sheer volume and mass.

I was sure both Daedalus and I would be crushed beneath the weight of the stones I had within me. That wasn't even counting the random debris, wood, dirt, dust, and everything else. I even had a little bit of wool from the sheep still floating around. Then there were the humans in time out and the ambient energy that I somehow couldn't absorb into myself for levels. I also had bits of demon carcasses and lots of undead. An entire army of skeletons, too.

Ever since I had reached diminishing returns for transmuting material into energy and absorbing it as levels, I had stopped regularly cleaning out my dustbin, as I wasn't getting steady levels from it anymore. Now, with my followers passing some of their experience as a tithe up to me, it didn't really seem necessary.

I was guaranteed slow growth and power without doing too much, and the small amounts from removing any material I had were less useful than they once were. Especially now that my Domain and Void Manipulation allowed me to fix things and turn them into more useful items when needed. So the real question was, what did I have that a dragon would want?

I started ejecting things from my dustbin. I started by pulling out some of the more interesting bits and baubles I had. The carved nature of some of these stones was quite interesting. Perhaps the dragon would find them appealing to his sense of artistic beauty. With a couple of these arranged on the floor, I rummaged about for a few other odds and ends.

Last of all, I decided I might try to release one of the mutated humans again. I was much more powerful than I was when I had last tried. I didn't necessarily want to trade the humans, since that seemed rude. But maybe he'd find it interesting. Who knows, maybe Daedalus would even have some insight into them. After spending so much time in my dustbin, perhaps this human was going to be slightly more docile. Or perhaps he wasn't doing so well. I couldn't be sure.

I looked up and checked Daedalus's reaction to the array of various items I had in my possession, and I could see his eyes were wide. The first thing I'd pulled out was a stone statue, and looking at it, I realized it wasn't exactly what I remembered putting in. It seemed that the time in my dustbin had changed something yet again.

There was a soft blue glow emanating from it, and pulses of light started up in its head and pushed down to the foot of the statue. This continued in semi-regular intervals, and it was quite hard to take my attention off of it. But Daedalus was definitely surprised by the last thing I pulled out. One of the humans that had attacked me.

The prosthetic crystal feet had grown in a fascinating way around his lower limbs. They had cleared up and became more transparent.

Where the crystal had been a cloudy purple color, it was now a glass-clear, ridged shape that was roughly the same size as the feet had been. Not only that, but the tubes I had added to allow fluid circulation were far more visible as a consequence.

The matrix of crystals served as a window to the thin streams of red blood running throughout the legs. I had ejected the human into a standing position, and he remained that way, perfectly stock still. But like any human, there were slight micro-adjustments of the muscles and in the calves to maintain balance; while you couldn't see the actual muscles, the muscle replica simulation I had made out of the various types of crystals interfaced with the central nervous system. They were twitching and doing the barely notice-able work needed to keep him on his feet.

But those weren't the only changes. Looking up at the face of the once-human captive I had, his eyes had been replaced with crystals. The orbs of purple still had that slight purple glow as he stood stock-still at attention. Not flinching, not moving, not breathing.

What was this? What had I done? No, what had I created? This human certainly wasn't okay. Was he even a human? I couldn't help but feel like I might have inadvertently done something worse than intended to this poor person. Luckily, my musings were interrupted.

Daedalus had been fascinated with the statue before this. Still, he noticed when I pulled out the former attacker and had quite the reaction. He reared back in apparent alarm. Somehow, his eyes grew even wider than they already were. I could feel the shimmering heat gathering in his mouth, even at this distance. I tensed, simulating escape plans to protect myself from the terrifying inferno of all-consuming flames that might pour out of it.

"What is that?" he hissed.

Not liking where this was going, I quickly recalled the troublemaker by sucking him back up into my Limitless Dustbin. It didn't help. Seeing that Daedalus had gotten no more relaxed, I replayed the scene of this man and his friends attacking me, me kneecapping him, and finally me consuming him. I also tried to convey the idea of me grafting on crystalline body parts to stop the man from bleeding out, but I wasn't sure that quite came across properly.

Daedalus settled back on his haunches but didn't come any closer. His eyes relaxed slightly, and as his mouth closed, I could feel the oppressive heat slowly dissipating throughout the cave and out into the snowy field beyond. But he didn't say anything for quite a while, simply studying me thoughtfully. I didn't make a move, either.

As much as I was fairly certain I had done the right thing, it definitely could look a little bit odd from the outside, and I could feel the power radiating off of Daedalus in such a way that my hard plastic body seemed flimsy. It was a strange feeling, especially considering its relative durability compared to what it used to be.

That wasn't to say I was afraid of Daedalus, but his strengths were definitely on par with my own.

Eventually, a forked tongue came out and licked the teeth of Daedalus's mouth as he opened it.

"Interesting. It seems that you have some archaic power in you, my friend. That would explain the statue," he said as he indicated the glowing statue he had been interested in since I pulled it out. "Do you mind if I touch it?"

I let out an indifferent tone, and he picked it up gently with his front claws and brought it close to his face, studying the way the light moved throughout it.

Bringing it up to his nose, he inhaled, and I could see some of the crackling light within the statue draw out and waft into the nose of the dragon. He jolted, dropping the statue and sneezing a few times before looking at me with wide eyes and pupils dilated. "Wow, that's a kick!

"Okay." The dragon snorted. "So. I'm not even going to ask what that whole weird golem-human-chimera-monstrosity was anymore. Let's just...pretend I never saw that," Daedalus said. I hastily agreed, wanting to put that uncomfortable sight behind me. Perhaps I'd ask Beatrice for help with a medical exam later. I wasn't sure if she'd be just as disturbed as we were, though.

"I'm interested in this energy. What...is it? Do you have to imbue it into things? Do you accumulate it? Is this *your* energy? Is it something inherent in the objects you collected?"

I wasn't exactly sure how I could answer that, but I did have other types of energy. Maybe he'd be interested in that. I made a noncommittal, shrugging sound and hoped that Daedalus would understand.

He seemed to, as he nodded and continued. "Well, as a dragon, while we do enjoy a hearty meal of sheep and cows, we mainly feed off magic. The amount stored in the statue isn't much more than a snack. But if you have a larger amount, I would happily trade that for an equivalent amount of whatever you would pick from my hoard. Assuming that it's of equal value."

That sounded fine to me. I only had one condition, though, and above my head, my condition scrolled. "Only if you're willing to help me pick out prizes for each of the tournaments. I really am not exactly sure what people want."

Daedalus's head lifted up, and he roared his laughter into the ceiling, shaking the rocks above us. "Of course, my little friend. Of course. I'm *amazing* at giving out prizes.

"Of course, I'll require a down payment first. What do you say to...half up front?" Daedalus said with a toothy grin.

I had no problems with that, so I readily agreed. So, how could I give him the energy he wanted? Normally I just absorbed whatever energy I generated from transmutation into myself, and it powered me up. Only when it overflowed did I try to channel it anywhere. That had only happened a couple of times, though, and the most I had managed by way of control was an explosive blast flinging me in a specific direction.

I didn't think Daedalus would appreciate me blasting him in the face. That seemed rather rude. Still, what other option did I have?

Extending my Grabby Arm, I reached up to the monstrous lizard. He appeared to understand my intention and reached out with one of his foreclaws, gently meeting my claw. Maintaining contact for a few seconds, I willed half of the energy up and through our connection.

Nothing happened. Dang. Time to try another approach. Perhaps if the energy didn't "belong" to me, it wouldn't follow my instructions? Instead, I made a channel of sorts through my Grabby Arm for the energy to run through and "squeezed" the reservoir in my dustbin. The energy bunched up, and once it reached a critical mass, it welled up and started to flow.

I could tell it was working when Daedalus's eyes widened in

surprise. It only lasted a second before an implosion in the tiny space between my claw and his talon sent both of us hurtling apart. A meaty thump rang throughout the cave as the dragon was ragdolled into the back wall of the cave. I was flung out the entrance and sent sailing down the mountainside.

CHAPTER 37

A DEAL IS A DEAL

BEE BATTED ASIDE the tentative thrust that Tony opened their latest exchange with. As the bristles knocked his stick to the side, she rotated and tapped his shoulder with the wooden handle of her own practice broom. If it had been the broom that Void had made for her, he would have lost the arm at the least.

"You need to commit. That thrust was slow and weak, but still more exposing than a feint," Bee commented as she followed up her attack, demonstrating the Paladin's mistake by driving the end into his chest. With an "*oof*," Tony's breath left him, and he fell back. "If you are going to attack, then *attack*."

Truthfully the training was as useful for her as it was for Tony. It gave her something to focus on to distract her from the overload of information her new class dumped in her mind.

Stepping back, Bee waited for Tony to reach his feet, levering himself up with the haft of his weapon. She considered whether she might have been going a little hard on him. He didn't have the Broom Proficiency skill yet, though she hoped he would get it soon. On top of that, the fact that she was nearly double his level made the spars one-sided, even without the added grace from skills.

Name: Tony, Race: Human, Class: Paladin of Spot, Age: 24, Level: 29, Highest Stat: Charisma, Lowest Stat: Dexterity

Level 30 should be within his reach soon; he had been at 29 for some time now. Bee grimaced in frustration. Even though she had crossed level 50, she still didn't have a new field available in her Scan results. Maybe she hadn't been using it enough for it to grow anymore? Lately, she had been making a conscious effort to Scan everyone she interacted with, but so far, nothing.

She wasn't entirely sure what else she would want the skill to tell her. The only other possible thing might be specific stats and their associated values. But other than that, the fact that she wasn't sure where else the skill could go might have been a sign that it wouldn't grow more. Still, she could only hope.

Setting her feet, she readied to engage Tony again. The ground shook slightly before either of them could make the first move.

Both of their stances lowered a bit to keep their balance as they looked around. Everyone outside had frozen in shock before likewise looking around, confused. In the distance, Bee could see a black cloud rising from the north. "I hope that's not going to be a problem..."

I was halfway down the mountain by the time I caught myself with my Thrusters. I had narrowly avoided smashing into the rocks along the way, just able to nudge myself around the obstacles. So when I did bounce off the ground, I hit a slightly softer, snowy, icy part.

But the steep angle was such that I didn't receive much damage, no more than a few scratches that my skills had already taken care of. Stabilizing myself with the hover, I looked back up toward the top of the mountain and the cave. I sure hoped Daedalus was all right.

With a slight bit of effort, I shot up back into the cave almost as fast as I had left it. In the back, I spotted Daedalus lying prone on the ground. He lay there, still and unmoving, for several seconds. I did nothing but observe until I saw the slight rise of his scaled chest. I felt my bristles relax slightly. Good. The dragon was still alive.

It would have been a shame if my trade had killed him. The beast was magnificent, and quite a nice guy to boot.

"Ugh." The grunt echoed from the back of the cave. I trundled over to check on him, and I noticed his eyes were still closed. One of those massive red wings had crumpled against the cave wall in a weird shape, bent in places that didn't look like they were intended to be bent, and blood was slowly seeping out of several cracks in his scaled armor.

I beeped out a message while prodding his nose with my claw, hoping that he might understand without my holograms. "Hey. Hey. Are you okay?" A deep groan rumbled throughout the cavern, and I let out a cheery beep. "Good morning. Good morning!"

"Ooooowwwww," grunted the dragon as he forced one of his eyes open to look at me. "Ow, that hurt."

I was already busy scanning him. Surprisingly, my Advanced Sensors couldn't penetrate his scales at all. They left only a void of information beyond the edges of his skin. But I could get a good estimation of his wing's state. I displayed and scrolled a new message for him to read. "Sorry about that. You broke at least four bones in your wing and probably more in your ribs, but I can't really tell. Hitting walls that hard was not a good idea."

Along with the words, I added a little diagram to illustrate where in the wing the breaks were.

Daedalus just snorted in my general direction. The force of the blast from his nose threw me back several feet as I skidded on the ground. "Do you think I *wanted* to hit the wall? Well, my wings are going to take forever to heal now. And yeah, I definitely did bruise some ribs, at least. Oh, hey, do you mind helping me set my wing? I have a skill that will eventually take care of it, but it's going to be much faster if it's in the proper place. Aligning bones is hard."

"Sure, I don't mind. What do you want me to do?" I projected.

Slowly, the magnificent red dragon got up and gingerly turned around. "Okay, so we'll start by the base of the wing and move out. Grab it right here."

He indicated the spot on the wing with his nose and held the cave rock while I pulled. I grabbed it and, with my Thrusters, did my best to resist the dragon's leaning to the other side. It was slow, but the area slowly stretched, and the bone realigned.

I could hear the dragon quietly muttering what must have been quite foul curses as the bones shifted in his wing. Once they were aligned, a shimmering golden energy plated over the area, keeping it stiff.

"All right, that's one down." Daedalus said, "Do you mind helping me with the others?"

Fixing up Daedalus took a lot longer than I would have thought. The bones in the extremities were much more delicate than expected, and each one we set was one that we risked messing up later. Also, my Domain didn't have the same effect on this process that I felt it should have.

While I hadn't tested it with people, this felt like it shouldn't be that different from rebuilding a stone wall. Of course, it could have been because Daedalus was a living thing, or it could be due to the magic he innately possessed. Nearly everything that I had seen so far warned me that Daedalus was a monster of might and power. It wouldn't have surprised me if it was harder to heal him just because of how much more there was to his body.

Still, when I had asked about that, the dragon had very indignantly stated that he was not fat. Apparently, dragons were as confusing as humans, since I had no idea what that had to do with anything.

Now that his sides had stopped bleeding and his wing was splinted, we settled back in our positions. Him on top of the pile of coins I had yet to organize, and me on the clean floor across from him. "Well, that could have gone better."

Despite his words and general sorry state, Daedalus was still smiling. The expression of teeth might have made many afraid of him, but I didn't have what I had heard humans call the prey instinct. So I just beeped my agreement.

"Not much, though!" The grin widened so much that I calculated a nonzero probability that his face would split in two and his jaw would fall to the floor. "Do you know how long it's been since I last leveled?"

Before I had a chance to take a guess, he shouted an answer to his own question. "I have no idea either! Thousands of years *before* I went to sleep at least. I wasn't even halfway to my next level at that point. If you give me that much again, there's a good chance I could get a second level. Twice in one millennium!"

"That doesn't seem like a lot?" I printed it out.

"Not a lot. *Not a lot,* he says." Daedalus huffed. "How old are you? Once you get past 50, leveling really slows down. And besides, we dragons naturally level slowly. Something to do with being functionally immortal."

"I didn't notice much of a difference after 50." I supposed it might have been a little slower. But taking into account the type and frequency of enemies I had come across, that speed had seemed rather constant. Besides, I wasn't sure what my age had to do with anything.

Daedalus eyed me with a bit of suspicion. "You must have been fighting constantly and finding rare high-level enemies to say that. Or maybe your race gets experience from more than just combat. Unless your race has some leveling bonus?"

"I'm not sure. Maybe?" We just left it at that for a few minutes, both getting lost in our thoughts. After several cycles of processing, I asked if he wanted to continue.

"Not right now. I need to assimilate the energy and get used to this. Besides, if that kind of blowback happens again, I would like to be healed beforehand," Daedalus demurred gracefully. "But I'll take that as an acceptable down payment. Now, how about we look at these prizes you wanted?"

It didn't matter to me when he wanted his energy. I didn't mind making the trek over here. Daedalus was fun to talk to, and besides, I wanted to ask him a lot of questions about his companion and what had happened to him. That would have to wait until next time, though. I was already anxious to return to my tasks at the castle. I had only been able to stay this long because I could potentially save a lot of time in getting prizes done now.

"So what are the competitions that you were looking to give rewards for?" Daedalus asked as his back turned, and he started rummaging about in some of the chests in the back of his cave.

I listed the competitions, starting with what sounded like an adult version of hide-and-seek and ending with the Nighty Knights' one-on-one combat tournament.

"Interesting. Interesting. I think we can find some appropriate prizes for all of those," Daedalus said, his snout buried in this treasure as he searched. "Now, for the first competition, it sounds like they are a bunch of scouts, no?"

Not waiting for my response, he tossed something at me. I caught it and folded the fabric neatly before placing it in front of me. "You can't go wrong with a good cloak of invisibility. It won't work against anything higher than level 65, but that should still be good enough for beginner scouts."

I examined the cloth more closely, curious about how it

worked. The blackish fabric wasn't made of wool, but rather something much smoother and finer. I wanted to admire it, but my attention was soon pulled back to the dragon. He continued looking through his collection, speaking over his shoulder all the while. "Now, for the baking competition, I was thinking something like this..."

CHAPTER 38

PROPHETIC VISION

IT WAS dark by the time Tony finally begged for a halt to their training. Bee wasn't even winded, but he looked like he would find sleeping comfortable in the dirt at their feet. Everyone else had long since gone to bed, so it was just the two of them as they slowly walked back to the castle.

Typically, Tony wouldn't have let them walk in silence. He was both too good at conversation and too talkative. Yet now he was breathing so hard that mustering words took effort. Bee didn't mind, though; this allowed her to delve into her thoughts about how strange things had been lately.

Something was definitely happening. It wasn't just that Tony had claimed all her time for the next week. No, what really made her suspicious was the sudden brevity or altogether lack of reports from Trent, Mary, and the others. The usual deluge of people asking for her opinion and permission on every little thing had fallen silent too. Not to mention that she'd caught more than a few people darting around corners and out of sight at her approach. It was all very strange.

Even when she asked whether her assistance was needed anywhere, she was met with emphatic reassurances that everything was alright. Her only solace was that Void was just as busy with...

whatever it was up to. If her master was involved with this new state of affairs, she would just have to trust that everything was taken care of. Void would see them through. Still, it didn't mean she wasn't curious.

She and Tony parted with a grunt as they each headed off to their respective rooms. Not quite ready to go to bed, Bee drew a bath to wash off the filth of the day. She didn't need that much sleep anymore, but it was still pleasant to enjoy, so it didn't take long for her head to hit the pillow after she was clean.

A few minutes before she finally drifted off, the door cracked open, and a soft whirring noise made its way under her bed.

When I got back, Beatrice was already asleep. Still, I did my best to not wake her as I crept under her bed. Time was somewhat limited, as I was carrying all the prizes. While my Limitless Dustbin was great for holding waste and disposing of it, I was starting to realize it wasn't a good long-term storage option for much else.

I had several examples of why, but its tendency to change things in unexpected ways was worrying. It worked out well for a lot of mundane objects like Beatrice's broom. But the injuries that Daedalus received went to show that those capabilities were best in moderation. If that much power could really be released at once... Well, I didn't want to think about that.

I didn't want to risk anything with the prizes that I had received. Daedalus told me that they were powerful magic arti-facts. Who knew what effects I would have on them? And if I couldn't keep them with me, I needed to keep them somewhere else safe. And the best place I could think of for doing that was underneath Beatrice's bed.

So I carefully folded the cloak of invisibility and stacked some of the other items on it. A few of the larger ones needed to go off to the side, but I was able to arrange everything so they fit underneath the bed. They would be safe here for a few more days until I was ready to hand them out.

Then I settled down on the nice rug that Daedalus had included in the prizes and slowly, quietly did my best to clean it meditatively. I dedicated 90 percent of my processing power to the task. It was important, after all. It had to be in perfect shape for my dearest friend and human. I'd never gotten a birthday gift for anyone before, but I hoped she would appreciate it.

Bee woke with a jolt. Something was wrong. An odd sensation tickled at her senses. Some sort of magical presence, perhaps? But she couldn't quite put her finger on it. She had become a little more sensitive to these things ever since she hit level 50. She could tell by proximity when a batch of potions was especially potent and even tell when they were nearby.

A shock overwhelmed her mental defenses as the torrent of connections to the castle's inhabitants flooded in. Most of them, at least. Her breathing quickened as she attempted to force down the surge of sensations to a more manageable level. Once she had wrested control of her newest ability, she looked around the room again and found her master waiting at the end of her bed and waving a cheery good morning to her.

Ah, that must have been it. Bee hadn't ever noticed that her master gave off such a terrifying presence. Still, she could definitely feel a ton of magic power radiating from the black disk. That was odd. Normally, Void had everything so under control. But Bee wasn't about to question it.

Then something appeared over Void that made her think that she might still be dreaming. Rubbing her eyes and gaping, she pinched herself and yet still did not wake up. Still, she had trouble believing her senses.

An illusion was plastered in the air above Void, a ghostly three-dimensional series of images flashing by. There was a mountain with a hole in it, shown from afar and close up. As the image focused on the hole, she saw stalactites and stalagmites clustered around its entrance. They were broken, and Void was cleaning them up.

Then there was a pile of gold with a brilliant red dragon sitting on it. The massive dragon and the god talked briefly, but she couldn't quite make out what they were saying. The scene moved quickly, and there was no sound.

Then the dragon hesitantly reached towards her god, and Void met its talon with a claw. An explosion at contact sent the dragon hurtling into the wall, where its wing and ribs crumpled, and it lay lifeless on the floor. Then something happened that she didn't quite pick up, and the dragon was sitting up again.

The scene changed once more, suddenly and completely, to depict a more familiar sight. A statue of a hero standing on a white mound of opaque glass. A mound that sloped to the edges of a pristine white room. It was a place she had only visited once, long ago when she was still level 10 or so.

The images disappeared, winking out of existence, only to be replaced by a single line of text. It scrolled above Void in large rounded letters. "He is the dragon's companion."

After a quick talk with Tony, all three of them immediately headed down into the catacombs. Tony was still a bit bleary-eyed, so they were walking down the first set of passages instead of running. Bee kept an eye out for undead monsters to be safe, but none showed up. The speed at which they moved was nothing short of impressive. It was hard to remember that it had taken her so many days to explore this whole place just a few months ago.

Still, it was different from how she remembered it. No longer was it dark and dirty and dank. It was still very dark, even with the torches and lamps they carried for light. But the layer of dust that had coated everything was simply gone. Even the stale air didn't smell stale anymore.

The steps and the slanted path stones had realigned into neat order. She could barely tell where the seams between the placed stones were, especially on the upper levels where it had been an especially rushed job. Bee had a pretty good suspicion of what had happened to it. But Void neither confirmed nor denied his involvement in the upkeep of the catacombs.

Tony didn't know anything was different, as he hadn't been here before. But she had. It only took them half an hour to reach the first tomb.

They waited a second for Tony to take in the sight. With their improved vision, she was able to see much farther into the darkness, and it no longer felt nearly as oppressive. Even with her improvements, she still couldn't see to either wall from the center pedestal. Not wanting to take chances, they quickly looked through all the empty beds where the skeletons had rested.

The plinth reminded her of the book she still needed to translate. There had been a few slight hints about what language it might have been in, but really she had made no progress. She was just too busy. Maybe Void would have better luck at it, and she should ask it for help. Still, for now, they moved on.

Bee felt they were all awake enough this time that she could move at a slight jog. Well, it was a slight jog to her. It would have been faster than her sprint the last time she was here. Again, in about ten minutes, they traveled to the second chamber that rested right beneath the first. It was a relief to reach this point without constant fighting.

She resisted the urge to explore through all the side passages again. There was still a lot she hadn't found down here, corners that threats could lurk behind. But judging by its cleanliness, she figured that anything dangerous would have long since been taken care of by Void. Her curiosity lingered, but she didn't have time for it right now.

They moved quickly through the second room and continued toward the bottom level. Where the companion lay.

All three of them paused to admire the beauty of the slightly curving floor of white glass and the surrounding dome that encased the entire room. The white room wasn't much different than Bee remembered it. That didn't make it any less breathtaking, though. The pure white interior made the slight new bit of color in the statue appear even more stark in comparison.

Slowly, she walked towards the statue. Before she reached it, she could tell that more had changed than the color. The statue emanated a presence that she had only felt from a few other powerful entities, but all of those beings were above level 50. She wondered if she, too, now had such an aura.

As she approached, she studied the man with more focus than she had the last time they were down here. If it truly was the dragon's companion, there had to be much more to the story. She would have to go check on the paintings in the upper caves. She might get something more out of it given what she knew now.

She was surprised to get a result by running a Scan on it. Last time, the Scan said almost nothing. Judging based on Scan's result now, though, there definitely was a lot more to it.

CHAPTER 39

DRAGON RIDER

Name: Archibald Smith, Race: Human, Class: Companion of Daedalus, Titles, Dragon Rider, Hero of Legend, Bravehearted, Warden of Nazareth'gak, Age: Unknown, Level: 69, Highest Stat: Strength, Lowest Stat: Wisdom, Status: Awakening, 80%

BEE READ off the line aloud. She was pretty sure that Void knew all this, but Tony didn't. "Level 69. Wow. Master, last time we were down here, Scan barely gave me any info. Also, the added detail on his awakening progress probably means we can get a better estimate of how long he'll be like this for."

Void beeped sagely from the floor, but no instructions or wisdom appeared above it, so Bee continued to study Archibald. Companion of Daedalus. That was like the Companion of Spot class she was offered. Was this man really the hero spoken of in stories, the companion of such an ancient, powerful dragon? If that was the case...

It took her a few seconds before she felt eyes on her. Looking around for some sort of threat, she met Tony's steady gaze. Their eyes locked for a moment before she cocked her brow in question.

He just shook his head. "That explains a lot. Like, a lot."

In a moment of realization, it clicked with Bee. She searched back through her memory to see if she had ever told anyone about her Scan skill. She was pretty sure that Void knew about it, but she wasn't sure if she had ever told Tony.

"Well, obviously we shouldn't tell anyone about him," Bee said, trying to change the subject.

"Why not?" Tony asked. His tone wasn't challenging, but instead seemed to be honestly curious.

"Well, from what Void showed me," she said, gesturing to the statue, "this was the companion of some dragon. And if he is waking up, we should probably let him be rather than disturb him. And with something this interesting, people would definitely want to come see it. Not to mention I don't want to lose anyone down here in the catacombs.

"But really, we do *not* need a dragon showing up here and causing trouble. The only person who could even deal with the dragon would be Void, and I don't think we want to rely on its help when we could easily just avoid the issue. We'll just...let the companion wake up himself, then go find his dragon when he's ready."

Tony nodded thoughtfully. "Yeah. I suppose we can keep this a secret. Don't have a problem with that. But I *am* going to want your help with that Scan ability. It's gonna be huge for picking out people and the best places to put them. Okay?"

Bee just looked at him. "I have been helping. Haven't you noticed?"

Tony rubbed his chin thoughtfully. "Yeah. That actually makes a lot of sense. Guess it's just weird to know how... Why didn't you tell me?"

"I..." Bee bit her lip. "I kind of forgot. Sorry."

Void sat silently through their whole conversation. So silently, in fact, that Bee almost missed it rolling forward and tapping the knee of the companion frozen in stone. It let out a complicated series of beeps that she couldn't really understand.

Still, it sounded cheerful, as if it were looking forward to the future.

Bee was extremely hesitant to question her god, but she was just too curious to hold back. "Master. Do you know more about the dragon and this man? When did you learn about this?"

She tried to bite back the last question, as she wasn't sure she wanted to know. Especially if it acquired this knowledge through some divine power or the like. But it slipped out anyways. Void turned to face her and let out an affirmative beep.

So it did know more about the pair. But rather than elaborate, it just played the same set of images that it had shown her this morning. The moving illusions that prompted them to come down here. It almost seemed like that was the answer to her second question.

Thinking a little bit, Bee realized what she saw might not have been some sort of Divine Vision that Void had sent. "Did that all... actually happen?"

She got back a simple affirmative beep and couldn't do anything but sit there, jaw agape, imagining Void casually flicking Daedalus the Red into a wall. Well, not just imagining it. She has seen it, even if secondhand. What had happened to make her master so mad at that dragon? Several moments passed before she realized that she had been staring and quickly snapped out of it, catching Tony staring as well.

This was the first time Tony had seen the vision and the images, and Bee couldn't blame him for his reaction. It was quite incredible to see, especially given the contents of the images. Dragons were often put on the same level as gods in myths and legends, or at least second fiddle by a small margin. But for the difference to be this large... Those stories must have been exaggerating the power of dragons or severely underestimating gods.

After they recovered, she realized Void wasn't done with its story. A new set of images with more detail were playing. They told the story of Void hovering in a cave. After redirecting a brief gout of fire, her master apparently struck up a conversation with the dragon. She, unfortunately, couldn't make out the words from the silent and small image.

"Master. When did this happen?"

The response this time came across as a simple text message rolling across the air above Void. *"Oh, yesterday."*

They were silent for the first leg of the journey back up to the castle. Bee was lost in her thoughts, just as Tony seemed to be. Void rolled along ahead of them happily, occasionally stopping to polish a rough spot on the stone floor. Eventually, Bee spoke up.

"Should we have someone waiting for Archibald when he wakes up?" She asked. Tony blinked and looked at her, processing what she had said.

"Do we know how long it will be? It said 80 percent for awakening. If he was there for thousands of years, it could be that he doesn't wake up anywhere in our lifetime."

"It could be, but it could be relatively soon, too, if it was based on when the Lieutenant was freed or killed or something else. And do we even know if the progression is linear?" Bee rebutted.

"Well, I'm just pointing out that if we do have someone waiting down here, he could be waiting for a very long time. And it's not an easy trek to get here and back. Besides, what if he's confused when he wakes up? According to you, he's extremely powerful and could very easily hurt someone."

"Yes, but having him wake up alone sounds almost just as dangerous. That would be awful, wouldn't it? What if he gets out and assumes we're enemies? Or busts straight out of the ground and through the castle somehow?"

Tony mused. "I suppose. What if we left him a note or something? Like a message, letting him know what's going on with the world. He could read that and be at least a little bit less confused when he comes up the catacombs."

"I like that. We should maybe also leave some food. We can put some preserved food and water down there. I can only imagine how hungry and thirsty you might be after such a long rest. It would probably also go a long way toward leaving a favorable impression, so we don't get attacked as soon as he wakes up," Bee agreed.

With a plan settled, a few more minutes went by with no one speaking. Eventually, Bee opened her mouth again. "Oh, Tony. While we're down here, I figured I'd ask. What's going on with the castle? Everyone's acting quite weird."

Tony jerked, tripping over his feet and slightly stumbling a few steps before he caught himself on the wall. His head whipped around to look at her in surprise. He met her confused gaze for a few seconds and shook his head. "Ah, don't worry about it. It's not going to be a problem, promise."

Harold and Amy were several days behind schedule. But Harold didn't let that bother him too much. The most important news had already been sent. Hopefully, that would give early enough warning that the Warden could take action. He had stayed in one spot for a bit longer, hoping he might get some reply. But none came. So they had moved on to the third Lieutenant in the region that they were to check.

When they first reached the ancient ruins where the third Lieutenant lay, everything appeared normal. All of the standard defenses were in place, and they had no problems getting there. No one stopped them or asked about their business. No one seemed to be aware that this site was important for any reason. The only indications otherwise were the very subtle traps and triggers that the Warden's people had set and maintained for so long.

Eventually, they found themselves standing in the central containment room. The pair looked upon the statue still there and radiating the power Harold had expected. Still, he couldn't help but be wary. Amy left to watch outside and ensure he wasn't disturbed as he pulled out various magic implements, one after the other, occasionally flinging dust in the air.

Sometimes he would just look at a tool before putting it away. Sometimes he'd place them around the chamber and check them repeatedly. All throughout the room, Harold paced. He couldn't throw off the feeling that something was wrong. The measurements started to agree with him too, and he had to double-check and reset his mindset several times to ensure that it wasn't just him confirming his biases. But he was right; there was an imbalance of power in the air.

He was thoroughly convinced when he finally left the room that evening to go check on Amy. Despite all the searching, Harold had yet to pinpoint what was causing the issue, but the exhaustion in his brain wasn't letting him make more progress on it tonight.

"Anything happen out here?" Harold asked as he settled down on the rock next to Amy. She looked over at him and just shrugged. She pointed out over the savanna and indicated a lone tree a few degrees off from the setting sun.

"Some big cat chased some antelope a few hours ago. But I don't think that's something we need to worry about." She added the last bit with a grin and bumped her shoulder against his. "How's the investigation?"

It was Harold's turn to shrug. "Something is definitely off. I can't tell what yet, but at least it hasn't gotten out yet. And it's not getting worse at a noticeable rate."

"So what are you doing out here, then?" Amy asked with a worried expression.

"Need a small break. Brain's gone to mush," Harold said,

looking out over the fading light. After a few moments, he found a different topic. "Do you have your orders for after this mission?" Amy nodded. "Nothing I can say, unfortunately." Harold grunted. Not that he had expected anything else. A couple months of travel had loosened their professional relationship a bit, but operational security made it hard to really get to know someone. If she didn't have orders, he would have been surprised.

"I'm surprised I was able to stay on a mission for this long," Amy said. Harold's eyebrows rose slightly. Was he going to find out more about his travel companion beyond the basics? "To maintain deep cover, I haven't been able to be away from home for long."

"Home?"

"Base. You know."

He did know. He also knew how dangerous it was to start thinking of it as home. "If your orders changed and you were able to be gone for this long, so abruptly too... Well, if I were you, I wouldn't expect to go back anytime soon."

Amy's face froze, and he continued on. "Things are changing, and if you're at all competent, the Warden might need you to take a more active role now."

"You really think so?"

Getting to his feet, Harold placed a hand on her shoulder. "I'm sure of it. Sorry."

Walking back inside the ruins, he got back to work.

It took most of the night, but he eventually found the issue. One of the inner runes had a line drawn through it. A single perfectly straight line ran through the precise etching, disrupting its activity. It was easy enough for Harold to fix; a few scrubs with a wire brush, and the energy was balanced once again. The only thing he couldn't figure out was, how did it get there?

BEE TRUDGED through the forest with Tony on her heels. She wasn't sure why he had insisted on training in the deep woods today, but she was already quite over it, and not just because of the creepy crawlies either.

While Tony had been making great strides in his fighting ability, he wasn't anywhere near the level that would allow him to keep up with her all day. That meant he needed to rest.

Usually, it wasn't a problem. She'd just finish up a quick task around the castle before hurrying back for the next round. But here? Bee was forced to sit and twiddle her thumbs in the middle of nowhere. Bee regretted not bringing some paper and quills with her for the hundredth time. She could practically feel the weight of undone tasks piling up on her shoulders.

Around midday, Tony had finally had enough. The guy was panting with exertion, skin slick with sweat as they headed back for lunch. Perhaps she would be able to get something done if she ate while she was working. The Nighty Knights' curriculum wasn't going to write itself.

When they came within sight of the castle, Bee could instantly tell there was something wrong. A rustle in the bushes and the slightest flash of gray caused her to pull up short and look around.

Nothing. There seemed to be no immediate threat, but she didn't relax. Right as Tony caught up to her, her senses could make out a sudden silence descending upon the usual bustling castle.

"Something is wrong." Bee held up a hand, stopping Tony in his tracks. Cocking her head, she tried to glean any additional hint about what was happening.

"Then let's go check it out," Tony said. He pushed her arm gently out of the way. She frowned slightly at his recklessness but followed before he got too far away.

They soon emerged from the tree line and stepped onto the main road. The castle gate stood wide open. Not a soul was in sight. She slowed her walk, keeping her broom at the ready. Something was seriously wrong; the gate shouldn't be open, much less unguarded. Where had everyone gone?

A dozen feet from the gate, Tony stopped and cupped his hands around his mouth. "We're HOME!"

People's faces popped up all along the wall, and a stream of children sprinted out of the gate. "Surprise!"

Bee stood in shock as the stampede approached her; only the sudden explosions sending color throughout the sky pulled her out enough for her to stay on her feet.

Getting the celebratory explosives right had been a bit of a challenge. Maranda and I had spent several days working on getting the perfect balance. We wanted low-enough volume that it wouldn't deafen anyone within a mile and an explosion small enough that the shockwave wasn't noticeable. At the same time, we were trying to maximize the color and area of effect.

We had to take a huge step back after the first tests, as even the smallest samples were capable of splitting boulders on direct hits. We had to take another step back after that and not have me keep the initial tests in my dustbin at all; otherwise they kept getting increasingly potent. That helped Maranda better observe the real effects and maximize the color. Several more tries later, we were able to use my void powers to amplify the right effects in a controlled manner.

Now, I could honestly say it was worth it. The midday sky was full of color. I pulled out a red one, and Maranda loaded it into the sling Tony had made and triggered the lever. As it was launched in the air, I nudged it with Air Manipulation so that it would hit its apex high above Beatrice's head. With a short application of my Sanitation Lamp, I triggered it. The wave of light spread out, completely covering the castle in a brilliant rose color and hanging in the air for several seconds before starting to fade.

That gave us just enough time for the next setup to be ready. This time, we prepped an orange one. From our position, getting a bead on what everyone thought of our show was hard, but shouts of surprise and then gasps of awe filled the air.

We had given people some warning, but as Beatrice had once said, seeing is believing. When the second explosive went off, there was a lot less surprise and more "wow"s and wonder. The whole celebration halted as people simply stared at the sky. Some were outside with Beatrice while others gazed up from the wall. Even more stood just inside the castle grounds.

One by one, we released each dazzling display that filled the sky. Maranda and I started loading mixes of colors to form gradients across the horizon. Eventually, we ran low on explosives. The show had already lasted for 9.8 minutes, and while everyone was still oohing and awwwing, I could tell that some of their necks were starting to get stiff from looking up constantly.

It was perfect timing; I had one of each color left. The launching system Maranda was using could handle the bundle, but I would need to concentrate on assisting it a lot. And the range we were planning on would slightly strain my processing power.

So I let the purple-green sky fade completely as we got the next shot lined up perfectly. When it launched, I immediately added speed to the bundle. Then I started to manipulate the air around them so they spread out into an immaculate heptagram. It was tricky to keep them evenly spaced, as they wanted to tumble wildly, but I managed it.

Then in a staccato burst, I triggered them as quickly as I could. Color enveloped the world.

Bee watched in awe as a flood of colors suffused the sky around her. Just as she tracked the falling light to the horizon, she grunted. A small form crashed into her center, driving the air from her lungs.

"Happy birthday," Bee heard Felix whisper into her stomach, where he clung to her tightly. Before she could even respond, he was replaced with Leanne. The next several minutes were a daze as she passed from one embrace to the other.

Eventually, she was ushered the rest of the way through the gate. Once she entered the grounds, her eyes widened. The castle grounds had been transformed. Fluttering streamers and color adorned every surface. Braided flowers arched over the main entrance, and tables and chairs had been moved to the front lawn in orderly rows. Throughout it all, the entire population of the castle turned wide grins and waves toward the front gate as she entered.

Standing on a massive stack of hay bales, Susan had her hands cupped to her mouth and shouted over the crowd. "First up is the pie baking competition. Can we get our lead judge over to table one!"

Bee stumbled as Leanne and Felix each grabbed one of her elbows and tugged her excitedly through the crowd. The people parted in front of her, and it was only a few moments later when she found herself seated at a long table with Mary and Gertrude.

"Happy birthday, dearie." Mary smiled warmly at her. "We heard you liked pie, so, well...everyone did their best."

"People will use any excuse to throw a party." Gertrude snorted. "Still, can't say this is a bad one. Happy birthday."

As if on cue, Bee's stomach growled loudly, and the first of many small plates with a couple bites of pie was placed in front of her.

Leaning back with a hand on her overfull stomach, Bee let out a sigh of contentment. With all the extra pie from the competition, hers wasn't the only overfull belly around. Most everyone had eaten their fill. Turning her head, she watched as Susan announced the winner.

"And the winner, by a close two votes and one recusal, is... CASSY!"

The woman hopped up and down and squealed excitedly. The other women gave a mixture of heartfelt cheers of congratulations and polite applause while off to the side, Mary looked on with pride shining in her eyes.

"For first place, we have this lovely necklace awarded by Void himself!"

Bee looked up in surprise but couldn't muster the energy to be too shocked. Apparently, Void was in charge of the prizes. She wasn't sure who had made that decision, but it certainly piqued her interest. Still, there was little her master could do to stun her anymore.

The crowd looked on in awe as Void hung an amulet around Cassy's neck. No one seemed to know where it came from, but no one questioned it either.

A pretty necklace would normally be an excessive prize for a baking competition, but this one was far more extravagant than expected. It looked to be made of gold and studded with rubies the size of robin eggs. Still, even that wasn't enough to warrant Cassy's reaction as it settled around her neck.

"Thank you, Lord Void! I, uh..." Cassy's smile froze as she trailed off. Her expression turned from delight to sheer bewilderment.

"Cassy?" Susan asked with concern, shaking the woman.

"I-I'm fine. I, uh...I got a system notification."

The crowd gasped. Even Susan's eyes widened. "Did you level up?"

"N-no... It's—it's a pendant of fire immunity...!" Cassy's voice trembled.

Whispered muttering and outright shouts of surprise filled the air as her words were repeated. Immunity was a nearly unheard-of ability among skills.

Resistances were fairly common and useful, and fire resistance was like being constantly covered in water. You would be fine running through a fire, but if you touched some hot metal, you would still get burned. Or if you inhaled too much smoke, then you would start having trouble breathing.

But *immunity*? With actual immunity, Cassy could literally walk into an oven and *watch* the bread bake with no fear of even breaking a sweat. That wasn't the most unusual thing about the gift, though. Sure, it was what everyone seemed to focus on based on the crowd's murmurs, but Bee had other concerns.

She wasn't sure if she was the only one who had noticed it, but that amulet was enchanted. *Enchanted.* Based on modern magic theory, that wasn't possible.

Most people didn't know that, though. Legends had always told of magic weapons, but they had important differences. They usually just retained the properties of whatever material they were made of. That, or they were coated with a substance that acted as a bane to whatever the hero was fighting. Something like demon's bane, which she had used so many times before.

What they didn't do was imbue the user with additional effects just by wielding them. Certainly nothing like a skill. The revelation sent Bee's mind racing with possibilities. She'd need to ask Void about it later when she got a chance.

Susan quickly quieted the crowd and moved on from the award ceremony. Someone ushered an awestruck Cassy offstage as she announced the next event. Those under ten were having sack races. Quickly the tables were cleared, and the next spectacle started.

The festivities continued with event after event. After the necklace, competition redoubled, with everyone vying even harder for a top spot. The serious faces of the kids, in particular, made it hard to stifle a laugh at the sack races and egg toss. Each time, Void produced some fantastical magical item as the prize. Bee couldn't help but be overwhelmed by a feeling of pride as she saw the community's reactions. Sure, the competition was fierce, but at the same time, it was surprisingly clean and fair.

Perhaps it was that the referees and judges didn't allow for any unreasonable disputes after the event. It also could have had something to do with the ultimate arbiter giving out the prizes.

That in itself was something interesting to watch. With Bee's new ability to see the members of her faith, she could literally see the bonds with their god growing stronger throughout the afternoon. This was the first time she had ever been able to detect a noticeable change in real time.

Interestingly, faith wasn't spiking in connection with the gifts. But at seemingly random times, it would jump within a certain group. After watching for some time, she started to develop a theory of why.

Void wasn't doing any one thing. Sometimes her master was under the tables, cleaning up a mess left behind by children running up to the next event. Other times it was seen hovering over the crowd to get a better view and cheering the competitors on.

In dozens of small ways, Void was part of their growing community. Nothing seemed to be too low for the god to take part in, but at the same time, Void never seemed debased by anything. Each task was done with dignity and levity in equal measure. A balance and joy in the work, but still with pride for others.

The events paused a few hours later. At first, Bee thought that they had run out, but no. Everyone pitched in to prepare for the next wave, and soon, a massive ring was cleared in the center of the grounds. A huge pinboard was erected with a massive bracket carved into the wood. Each spot was taken up by one of the Nighty Knights. It was time for the first major event of the evening: the tournament of the Nighty Knights.

Together as a unit, they marched onto the field, mostly in time. Mostly as one, they turned to face Void and her and dipped into low bows. A little bit of jockeying later, and the first two combatants were on the field. Void glided down between them, exchanging a few words with each combatant. Bee noticed that only beeps were used, not the new visual way of communicating that Void had started using with a lot of the adults.

Rolling back, Void gave them some space. A sharp whistling beep from it, and the battle began.

CHAPTER 41

READY TO RUMBLE

AS THE FIRST two combatants clashed, Bee realized that neither of them was older than five. But from how they moved, one would be forgiven for not realizing it. Their little fingers gripped the narrow hilts of their wooden swords with sureness, and each step was fluid enough to look choreographed.

The two combatants circled each other for several seconds, their feet never crossing, and the distance between them stayed remarkably consistent. With no warnings or tells, one of the combatants suddenly struck. The little kid crossed the distance in a blink with a slashing swipe that barely seemed to move the blade at all; it was so subtle.

A clack rang through the cheering crowd as the strike was deflected, followed by a quick counter. Bee was able to see what had happened, but she didn't think many others could make it out. Indeed, after the exchange started, an oppressive silence filled the arena as everyone's full focus trained on following the fight.

It wasn't that the moves were too fast; while they were quick, they were only made by level 5 combatants. No, it was that the movements were so slight and economical. Somehow, each was in just the right place at the right time. It was as if they had been dueling for decades, not months. The sight was unreal. But what else could she expect from god-trained protégés?

The fight ended as suddenly as it started. A tight series of blows ended with a surprise front kick, pushing the slightly smaller boy out of the ring. Void declared a winner and congratulated both of the kids on the good fight. The dead-silent audience took a beat to process the development before erupting into cheers.

Most of the adults had never bothered to watch the children playing with Void. Bee had, and so wasn't completely caught off guard, but even she couldn't deny that their skill level was impressive. She knew that both of these particular kids had variations on the sword proficiency skill, so the match wasn't representative of the rest of them. But everyone was in for a surprise when the other skills came out.

When the brackets were updated, Bee took a closer look at them. There were a few oddities; one was that Leanne was outside of and next to the winner's bracket. She had been given an *honorary victory,* according to the note there.

That made sense. Her laser eyes were a bit overpowered and dangerous in a spar. Perhaps they had decided it was best not to have her compete at all, though Bee would have liked her to just avoid using the skill. But if the kids decided the handicap wasn't fair, and if they were happy with it, she wasn't going to complain. Not if Void didn't.

The next strange occurrence was that Felix was marked down for an exhibition with the winner after the final fight. That made more sense; since he was the commander of the Knights, it wasn't quite fair for him to participate. Of course, his power also made it hard to fairly fight him, so it was deemed they would fight without powers in that particular bout. The rules were a bit chaotic.

Tanu was one of the next to step into the ring, but he wasn't alone. Apparently, Cliff was deemed too unfair to bring along. Instead, two of the cubs padded along behind him as a compromise. They didn't radiate frost like their mother, but they were still as tall as the children themselves. A little girl named Irene stepped in across from him.

The girl didn't look intimidated by the massive wolf cubs. After a few seconds, Bee understood why. She had thought Irene looked familiar but wasn't able to place her face. Not until the match started, and she bowed her head in prayer.

A massive ethereal black disk appeared behind her. Her skill had grown in strength *considerably*. Now instead of just one claw, the phantasm boasted six claws. As the wolves charged, the claws came down in a flurry, sweeping them out of the ring with gentle force. Still, Tanu wasn't simply a beast tamer. His skill with the sword was commendable.

Even as his companions were ejected, he was already charging forward using the opening they had provided. A vicious upward cut would have sent Irene flying out of the ring, but she stepped to the side, her eyes still closed, and the swing missed by a hair. Tanu's swing passed through the projection and turned to continue his assault, but a call from Void froze the fight.

Above Void, an image appeared. It was a view of the fight from the top down, showing a replay of both combatants. In slow motion, it zoomed in right as Tanu stepped on the line, his foot slightly out of bounds. The crowd *ooh*ed in dismay. Hanging his head, Tanu walked off, but Void stopped him. They shared a quick conversation, and as he rejoined the rest of the Nighty Knights, he held his head high. The two cubs licked his face appreciatively as he scratched their ears.

Each of the next fights was nearly as exciting in its own way. Most of the combatants used swords in some way. Proficiency skills were the most common among the children, but benign common didn't mean they were bad or even equal. One of the larger girls came into her fight with no weapons and met her opponent's sword with her bare fists.

Her knuckles were able to turn aside the blows without taking any damage, but the blazing fire her opponent's movements left in his wake proved too much. The fire obscured the pugilist's vision long enough, and she was tapped three times in vital areas over several minutes, Void keeping score with a simple projection.

The fights got even more intense as they moved into the second round. The audience was still on the edge of its seat, despite the solid hour the round had taken. Most of the mothers looked on with a mix of pride and worry. Bee could understand. They likely wanted their children to just be kids, stay safe, and play games. But at the same time, the level of skill displayed clearly indicated that these children could take care of themselves. Perhaps even better than most of the soldiers back in Caleb.

The newer children watched with unveiled jealousy at first, but as dazzling skill after impressive stunt was displayed, even they were swept into the atmosphere. Soon, they were cheering louder than anyone.

In the second round, favorites soon emerged. Little Irene by far received the most support, even from among the rest of the Nighty Knights. One of the older boys with long blonde hair and blue eyes seemed to be the darling of the mothers and little blushing girls.

Bradley was one of the pure sword users, though Bee was sure he had a variant skill, as his movements were different from those of the others. More graceful and fluid. He was also quite the showman. Waving to the crowd and gracious in victory, he made it easy to see why he was so favored.

Bee was surprised that not one of them used a broom. She had thought Void would have taught them all the way her master had taught her, but no. Was it because she was special? Or just that it didn't have a sword on hand when she was learning? Either way, she wasn't too upset. Nowadays, she was comfortable with her weapon, but maybe her spending so much time training with Tony wasn't as useful as she would have liked.

There were a few who used the sticks that Void had made as spears instead of swords, but they were the newest members. Their lack of experience didn't take a single one past the second round.

The fights moved quickly, and with the leadership of Susan, Void, and Felix, they managed to get to the finals in only another hour. The last several fights were actually over quicker than some of the first rounds. Though despite the intense matches, it was clear who would be in the finals long before they were held.

Irene and Bradley faced off in a tense moment. Each one of them has dominated their previous fights. But now, it was time for the main event.

Irene bowed her head, and the battle started. Each one of the six claws struck at once. The impact tossed up the trampled dust, obscuring the view of the field for a second.

When it settled, five mini craters ringed the spot where Bradley had been standing. He had somehow appeared several yards in front of where he was last seen, his sword held above his head with one hand bracing the blade. The final massive claw bore down on him. His arms shook under the pressure but still held. The other claws came in from the sides, and it looked like it was over. Bee just hoped she could get there in time with some healing potions.

Somehow, though, he dodged. With an odd twist of his body, Bradley slipped out from the assault and darted forward. In a flash, he was before Irene, catching her falling body. Then he gently lowered her to the ground.

The crowd went crazy. Cheers of excitement, confusion, and awe melded into a singular mass of sound. It was so loud that Void had to call for everyone's attention *twice*.

Once she had calmed enough to look up at her master, it showed the end of the fight in super-slow motion. Bradley had dodged each blow by the skin of his teeth. A look of calm concentration adorned his face as, even in slow motion, he blurred and tapped Irene on the forehead. Her eyes widened in surprise, causing her to stumble backward.

Already she was back on her feet, trading some quiet words with the tournament victor. The crowd soon gathered around the pair, clapping them on the shoulder or shouting encouragement. Frowning in suspicion, Bee ran a Scan on Bradley.

Name: Bradley Chadwick, Race: Human, Class: Spot's Prodigy, Titles: Nighty Knights' Champion, Age: 7, Level: 11, Highest Stat: Speed. Lowest Stat: Intelligence

Bee nodded; he not only had a class but had also reached his second skill. That made sense. She quickly ran Scan over the rest of the Nighty Knights. Most were between levels 2 and 4. Some were above level 5, but other than Felix, no one else had their second skill.

Checking Irene quickly, Bee couldn't help but be even more surprised.

Name: Irene Chadwick, Race: Human, Class: Spot's Disciple, Titles: God-Touched, Age: 4, Level: 8, Highest Stat: Faith, Lowest Stat: Strength

They were siblings. That made sense. Also, Irene was only four years old! Bee had trouble believing it. But with a title like that, perhaps it was possible. She could only imagine how scary these children would be when they grew up enough to be her age.

Bee thought that she had been leveling quickly... At this rate, she would be left in the dust. That is, if the children were able to keep up the pace.

Once everyone had settled down, Void called Bradley to receive his reward. Kneeling in the center of the circle, he bowed low to his lord.

Void gave no speech but instead simply drew out the prize. An audible gasp arose from the crowd. Immediately after, a young woman's panicked voice could be heard. "Oh no you don't, not at your age!"

Mrs. Chadwick rushed into the ring to intercept the massive flaming sword Void was about to give her son. Bee recognized her as one of the more nervous women they had first rescued from the ruins of Greg so long ago.

The crowd was on edge as she took the sword from Void with a dark look. Everyone held their breath to see how the god would respond to such disrespect, but Void just watched her passively. Turning to Bradley, she crossed her arms. "You can have this when you're older, young man. Until then, I'm holding onto it. You are *much* too young for real weapons."

"But Mooooom!"

CHAPTER 42

ALL-SEEING EYE

WITH A DECENT AMOUNT OF CONFUSION, I handed off the prize to Bradley's mother rather than the champion himself. Honestly, I understood that this was a dangerous weapon, and I well remembered the universal desire of kids to injure themselves at every opportunity. But at the same time, had she not watched the same display that I had?

Bradley was perfectly capable of wielding the Holy Sword of Draconic Flame and Justice without hurting himself. I had spent months teaching him to hold pointy sticks just for this reason. Plus, even after a half-dozen fights at nearly full power, he hadn't injured any of his opponents in the slightest, let alone himself.

As the glowing sword left my claw, Mrs. Chadwick staggered under its considerable weight as she struggled to hold it in place. I considered asking her if I should just hold on to it for now. At least until she was okay with Bradley taking possession of it?

Pretty soon, the crowd dispersed, leaving the champion to argue with his mother while everyone else went to get some snacks. The tables were now loaded with lunch food. It was past noon. Everyone had been too full to eat more after the pies, but it seemed that the issue had been resolved, as people loaded plates with grilled meat and cooked vegetables.

Taking the sword back, I stuck it in my dustbin for now. Maybe she would be okay with me giving it to her son next week. It would take some time for him to get used to using it, so maybe some supervised training was in his future. Turning off the flames with a mental command, I figured it wouldn't hurt to leave it under Beatrice's bed for a bit longer.

As everyone gorged themselves, I started to set up for the next event. This one had a long sign-up sheet, and I was quite excited about it. I needed to fill Beatrice in, but I didn't have any doubt that she would have a blast.

This was actually Felix's idea. In fact, the children had provided the bulk of the ideas for the party events, even if we didn't end up using most of them. A lot were far too impractical. Could we have even built a massive obstacle course, much less hid it from Beatrice? And what was the point of a "haunted house," anyway? Besides, they didn't all seem to get that this was a one-day event.

Still, some of their ideas were quite good. This castle-wide game of hide-and-seek was one of the better ones. I liked that we could put a time limit on it too. So I had two sets of prizes for either outcome. If Beatrice was able to find everyone in an hour or if only one remained hidden, then I had a prize for whoever was found last. If more than one was not found within the time limit, I had multiple comparable prizes for the winners. They weren't nearly as good, though, so I hoped Beatrice would do her best.

I found her and pulled her away from the few adults that she was in conversation with. As I explained the plan with a mixture of images and beeps, a wide smile grew on her face. She nodded. "Oh, this seems fun." But then her face fell a bit. "Though...there might be an issue. How many skills can I use?"

Internally I frowned. That wasn't something I had considered. Did she have skills that would affect her senses? I supposed it would make sense. I did, and it was one of the most useful mutations I had picked aside from that arm and dustbin. Maybe these Sensory Disruptors, too, now that I thought of it.

"I have a skill that makes me aware of all the faithful people around me, and I'm worried that it would make it too easy," Beatrice explained.

"Can you turn it off?" I projected.

"I-I don't know. I've never tried. It was a bit overwhelming at first and I had to work to ignore it, so I don't think so..." She trailed off with a look of concentration coming over her face. After a few seconds, her eyes refocused on me. She shook her head. "I can mute it quite a bit, but it won't go off all the way."

That was good enough, I supposed. Whoever was most clever might still find a way around it. We kept chatting as she filled me in on what it did. It was interesting to learn that people had varying degrees of faith in me. I thought it was pretty clear that I did exist. Apparently, not everyone was one hundred percent convinced.

After giving everyone some time to eat their fill, Susan got up on her podium and called everyone together. Some brought their food over to listen to the announcement, but most were ready for the next activity. "So, next up on the list of events is hide-and-seek. Beatrice, did Void inform you what you need to do?"

Beatrice gave Susan a thumbs-up, so she continued. "Everyone will have five minutes to find a place *within the castle walls* to hide before the birthday girl starts looking. Last one found is the winner. After you are found, you may start to help looking as well, so keep that in mind, everyone."

Susan gave me a meaningful look, and I put up a barrier of wind and projected light around Beatrice, blocking all sight and sound from reaching her "Alright. Five minutes starting...NOW!"

Everyone dashed off, and I rolled to join Beatrice in her barrier. I was going to have fun watching this.

Bee looked around at the completely empty castle courtyard that appeared around her as everyone disappeared. It only took her a few seconds to realize that it was Void hiding the surroundings from her, since she still felt people's presences with her dimmed faith sense. Still, it was jarring.

She did her best to push the sensations away from her mind so as not to give herself an unfair advantage. The best that she could manage was a dull nagging itch when she was near someone. It would be fine, she hoped.

A few seconds later, Void joined her in her isolated pocket world, just appearing a few feet away like nothing had happened. Above Void was a set of numbers counting down. "Is that a countdown to when I can start looking?"

Her master indicated that it was. Sitting down, she closed her eyes and waited, enjoying the brief moment of quiet. A few minutes later, Void let out a rhythmic beeping pattern, and she opened her eyes to the world's return. The entire courtyard was deserted. Even Susan was missing. Standing up, she started looking right away. Some had hidden far away, but she could tell there were still a few people nearby.

Still, after a few steps, Bee had her first victim. She pointed. "Trent you are out. Vera, out. Phil, out..."

As they were called, several people stood up from behind barrels or tables with sheepish grins as they made a beeline for the food still set out. She was glad they had put in at least a token effort for the children, but it was clear they weren't really interested in playing this game. She didn't really blame them. While Void certainly had a magnificent prize in mind, they weren't likely to win it. Plus, if the theme of activity-relevant prizes was held, then they wouldn't have any use for it anyways.

Walking closer to the castle, Bee started looking in more tricky places. While some had put more effort into hiding, not all were very good at it, and she had keen eyes. When Bee found the first of the children, she got her first real helpers. Soon, informants were running all over the castle, bringing her tips as they ratted each other out.

It was a bit embarrassing how often she found people hiding in the same spot just by hearing them giggle. A quick pass around the castle and the grounds let her root out the majority. But by Void's count, there were still a dozen people left hiding.

Bee was impressed. Even with her senses dulled, she couldn't help but tell when she was near someone. Now that more had been found, though, all the movement cluttered her faith sense with noise. Still, on her first pass, she hadn't thought that she had missed anyone.

Then she had an idea. Jogging back over to the copse of trees that housed their resident wolf pack, she poked her head into their den and called Tanu out. The little boy grumbled as he crawled out of the hole. "That was a good spot... How'd ya find me?"

"Using the cubs to disguise your presence was a good idea, but it was too obvious. Once I realized I hadn't found you yet, there was only one place you would be," Bee answered. It was a bit obvious, but the children still needed to get better at thinking from someone else's perspective. Something even a lot of adults struggled with.

A few minutes later, all the Nighty Knights were ousted from their various nooks and crannies. There were just three more stragglers left behind. By Bee's count, Susan was one of them. The second was a scout from the army, and the last was Mat, one of the first scouts who Susan had trained. He wasn't someone that Bee had talked to much since he had arrived, but her impression of him was not the best. He always seemed a bit silly and easygoing. It was odd to think of him as competent enough to hide from her this long.

Once there were only five minutes left, Void asked her to start using all her senses. As she let up, the web connecting her to all of Void's followers exploded in her mind. It was chaotic enough that she wasn't able to find anyone instantly. Still, she could tell that someone was far away from everyone else.

Heading over in that direction, she watched for any odd movement but didn't notice anything out of the ordinary; everyone was simply milling about in the center of the gathering. So either the last few didn't have any faith in Void, or they had some other way to hide. She knew that Susan had one of the strongest bonds in the castle, so that wasn't it. Also, she knew the one she was closing in on wasn't Susan by her faith sense too.

She got to the center of the grass field and still had no idea where the feeling was coming from. At least, no visual clues. As she walked closer, the feeling moved away from her, and she got a better idea of what was going on. In a flash, her figure blurred as she darted a hand out. It met the edge of a cloak that was nearly the same color as the background.

The scout from Captain Major's company groaned as he was revealed. "How many more were left? I thought I had it there."

"You were close. Only two more, and I have no idea where Mat and Susan are. Any ideas?"

The scout shook his head. "Naw, my lips are sealed. I want to see how long their tricks will work."

Bee headed back to the group and watched the castle's inhabitants as they chatted. Where could they be?

CHAPTER 43

SEEK AND YE SHALL FIND

BEE MIXED with the rest of the crowd as they milled around waiting for the next event to start. As she glanced around, she started taking note of what people were doing. Presumably, the last couple of hide-and-seek finalists were hiding among the people, using them as cover.

Trent was back at the pie table, getting his umpteenth plate. Gertrude knitted with a few of the other ladies as the children ran around. Many of the small children napped in the arms of their mothers in the shade of a massive pavilion tent set up to provide some release from the sun. Tony wrestled with Felix and a few of the other Nighty Knights. It wasn't an official event, but they had a bit of a crowd as he threw his superior weight around.

Mary simply stood off the side, watching everyone as she rested her head against Trent's massive shoulder. The sight made Bee smile. She was glad the pair were so happy together. She hadn't had many opportunities to see a relationship like this. Had her father been like this at one point, when mom was still around?

"Wait." Bee whipped her head back to the pie table. Had she been seeing things? No, Trent stood there, back turned as he ate a slice of the pie. She looked over to where Trent also stood, his arm around his wife.

Bee looked more closely with her senses. One of these wasn't Trent. The feeling was just different between the two of them, as though they had different relationships with Void's faith.

Looking back at the "Trent" eating pie, she was willing to bet a lot that he was the impostor. The only question was, who *was* he? She needed to call the person's name, or else it was hard to say the person was truly found. Though Bee supposed she could cheat a little bit.

Wandering over, she did her best to not be noticed. It was easier said than done as people constantly greeted her. Still, it didn't give "Trent" an option to run without looking too suspicious.

Bee was careful not to alarm him either, occasionally pausing to talk to people. It only took her a few moments to get close to her prey. That he had also used the time to move away from her further convinced Bee that this was truly the impostor.

Still, she feigned ignorance, and their cat-and-mouse game continued. Bee had no intention of letting it go on until Void called time, though. The second that someone attempted to speak to "Trent," she flashed forward using all the power and speed her considerable level afforded her. Just as the man had turned to walk away, she caught his sleeve. "I got you."

As much as she tried, Susan wasn't able to help the very feminine yelp of surprise at Bee's sudden appearance. "Susan, you are out!"

A burst of light later and the illusion of Trent disappeared from around the woman. Void beeped, and Bee took it to mean the competition was over. He zipped off, leaving her standing with Susan.

"Dang, what gave me away?"

Bee nodded to where the real Trent planted a kiss on the top of his wife's head. "There are two of you, and Trent's not the most subtle of people. It would have been better if you picked someone I didn't know as well."

Susan shrugged. "You would be surprised. Not being subtle

makes him easier to imitate." After a small hesitation, she continued. "Also, I need a...certain level of familiarity with the subject for my skill to work well. I still only have so many options around here."

"That's an impressive skill. I bet it made you really good at your old job."

"It did. The class I got too. It's a lot less relevant now, though," Susan said with a slight smile. "I can't say I miss it much. I think all the excitement was starting to give me wrinkles."

Bee laughed. Susan still looked five years younger than the twenty-nine her status indicated. Still, it was nice to hear that her friend was happier now. They chatted for a few minutes, and Susan filled her in on the rest of the events planned.

Bee was surprised to hear there was a drinking competition scheduled after all the children had gone to bed. That was a while off, but whoever had convinced Void to get a prize for that had her respect. She wasn't sure if she would have been brave enough to ask the god about such a thing.

As if hearing her thoughts, Void returned carrying a slightly green Mat.

I was impressed that the human had managed to squeeze himself into such a difficult place. Truly his dedication to the competition was commendable.

Of course, it wasn't too hard for me to locate him after Beatrice had found everyone else. Retrieving him had been a bit of a chore, and the tricky maneuver I had to do to extract him safely made even me a little bit nauseous, as much as I wasn't sure how that worked mechanically.

I had been getting worried that Beatrice wouldn't be able to find everyone in the time period. Thankfully, my human had come through. I was looking forward to someone getting the cloak of invisibility. And honestly, I wasn't sure what I would do with it if no one claimed it.

Gently, I set Mat down next to Susan and Beatrice. Seeing the winner arrive, Susan got things going again.

Most people had been using this as a break to grab snacks and drinks. As the festivities resumed, they gathered together once more. Though on the topic of drinks, I still wasn't sure how or why the humans made a contest centered on drinking. I couldn't help but spin up a subprocess to try and figure out what they were doing on that front.

A good amount of the adults seemed to be really excited about the drinking competition, but for the life of me, I couldn't figure out what it entailed. Daedalus laughed when I asked him about it and refused to explain further, though he did have a lot of fun finding a prize for the competition.

Once everyone had gathered and congratulated Mat, I pulled out his prize. Zipping into the air, I settled the cloak of invisibility around his shoulders.

The crowd let out a collective gasp, as it now looked like Mat was simply a disembodied head floating over the ground. Even to my sensors he had more or less disappeared. Only the absence of airflow indicated his presence. To my lesser senses, he was completely gone.

Mat reached up and pulled the cloak over his head the rest of the way. I felt the void in the air move a few feet over to the side before he reappeared, now holding someone's drink. A round of cheers later, and Mat was caught up in thoroughly showing off his prize.

Susan let this go on for some time. It may have been my imagination, but I briefly caught a hint of jealousy in a look she gave the celebrating victor. I couldn't really blame her; it was an awesome prize. I had been excited for a reason. Eventually, people settled down.

"Next up is dinner!" Everyone cheered, but she held her hands up for their attention. "As many of you know, this isn't just any dinner. There are two more competitions going on. Everyone needs to try one of each of the potato salads. Also, if you want to participate in the sausage eating contests, please sit at table two!"

The next couple of events weren't really relevant to me right now, so I went to clean up a bit after the previous events. Despite everyone being rather conscious about cleanliness, there was still a lot to do after everyone was gathered in the same area for so long.

As the humans loudly celebrated with food and song over dinner, I charted an efficient path between each of the various points of disorder that were left behind throughout the day. Wandering around the corner of the castle, I came across something worrying. Sitting alone, with his back to the castle wall, was Bradley Chadwick. He was muttering something to himself with a rather displeased expression on his young face.

He was so upset that he didn't even notice when I rolled up next to him. I tried to make out what he was saying, but it wasn't anything I could decode. Worried about my pupil, I tapped his shoulder to get his attention.

Bradley jumped and half rose from his sitting position as he turned. Once he recognized me, he scrambled up to one knee and leaned forward, a fist pressed to the ground. I must have startled him more than I realized.

"Lord Void! I'm sorry I didn't see you there. I apologize for my rudeness," Bradley said in an overly formal tone.

Beeping, I did my best to make him understand that he was fine and express my own worry. I followed up with another tone, inquiring what was on his mind. I watched as his face darkened again. Before he could slide back into grumpiness, I gently rapped my claw on his nose.

The rebuke jolted him back to his senses, and he looked up at me with clear eyes. I repeated myself. This time I saw him struggle with his emotions, but he was able to overcome them and answer.

"It's...my sword. What right does Mom have to keep me from it!? I need to learn to use it. I have a duty to the Nighty Knights and the faith to be the best warrior I can be. How can I do that without learning to wield my most powerful weapons? Haven't I proven myself?" Pure indignation was written all across his face.

After a few seconds, I realized that I would have to really answer his questions. I pulled out the sword and lit it again. The boy's eyes lit up as well with a fire of determination. Before he could reach for it, I played a vision for him. He was holding the blade without it being lit, and I was close by watching. Bradley's image moved fluidly through forms before he looked at me. I flashed something up, and we had a quick exchange before he went again.

"You will train me personally?" Bradley asked with barely concealed excitement.

Of course I would. I had been training him for months now, even if it was alongside the other Knights. I didn't know why it was a surprise to him.

With my confirmation, he fell back to both knees and bowed low. "I will patiently wait, then, my lord."

Immediately after, he contradicted his statement by jumping to his feet. "There is still a sparring circle free from the matches. Let's train there!"

I had to hold him back by the hem of his shirt. There were still celebrations and a party for him to enjoy. Sheepishly, he halted and turned to follow me back to the festivities.

We were just in time to watch Beatrice slap Captain Major on the back as he coughed up a bit of sausage meat.

CHAPTER 44
WHOLE NEW WORLD

BEE STILL FELT SURPRISINGLY awake when the party finally ended. Despite having one of the fullest days she'd experienced in a while, her levels kept her up when everyone else was looking for their beds.

She sat atop the castle wall with a small smile, watching over the castle grounds. Honestly, with everything going on, she had forgotten that today was even her birthday. A few months ago, it was all she could think about. But when it actually came? She had been doing so many other things that she lost track of the days.

Had this been why Tony insisted on training so much this last week? Well, if it was just a distraction, he was going to regret lying to her. Perhaps she could think of it as payback for surprising her, even though his reasoning had been solid enough, and he'd still made good progress besides.

As she sat there plotting how to make Tony's life miserable, Void trundled up beside her. She made to stand, but her master waved her down before she could get up. When had Void started doing that? Sometimes she could swear that it was still growing, still learning to read people better.

They just sat next to each other for a few moments, enjoying the view. Eventually, Void broke the tranquility with a few images.

Floating above it was a moving picture that replayed a few short seconds over and over.

It was her taking a gift-wrapped box from Void, opening it, and being happy. The message seemed clear enough, but she wanted to make sure. "You want to give me a gift?"

Void beeped, and Bee stood to follow her master into the castle. She grinned with excitement. A gift from her master? As much as it shouldn't have been surprising, she was still struck by how much the gesture mattered to her. It was heartwarming how much her deity cared. Not only that, but she had seen the other gifts Void had given out today. The thought of what it may have saved for her sent her thoughts racing.

Void led her back to her room and disappeared under her bed for a moment before coming back out, dragging something large behind.

Initially, she wasn't sure what to make of the purple rug that Void fished out. Her first thought was that it looked strangely familiar. Where had she seen it before? Thinking back, she realized her mistake. She hadn't seen exactly this rug before, but instead something remarkably similar. A memory of Void resting before the dean's desk flashed through her mind. Resting on a fluffy red carpet that looked remarkably like the one in front of her.

Void rolled back and gestured grandly with his claw at the rug. Bee stood and stared. What was she supposed to do? It was a very nice rug, but it was still a rug. Still, her master seemed immensely proud of the gift.

She wasn't sure how to react. A slight bit of disappointment welled up, but she tried to squash it. How could it not, after seeing the deity hand out magical blades and enchanted accessories like candy? Would she hurt Void's feelings if she wasn't appreciative? It definitely felt wrong to spurn a gift given to her by her master. Clearly there was some deeper meaning behind it, some lesson to be learned. But that didn't explain its excitement.

Unless... Could it be, perhaps, that her master just liked rugs and thought she would too? No. That was way too simple of an explanation. There was no way Void would do anything so simple. There had to be something she was missing. Still, she wasn't sure how to react. Void simply sat there, gesturing with its claw at the rug, clearly excited based on the small twitching motion that it was making.

Bee eventually broke out of her trance and decided that maybe her best bet was to continue imitating her master when she was uncertain. So hesitantly, she stepped over to the rug and gently sat down.

The rug was very nice. The fibers were soft and long and seemed to wrap around her slightly as if she were sinking into a thick cushion. It was quite a weird feeling for something that was presumably just a piece of cloth on a stone floor, but she honestly couldn't have imagined a more comfortable seat.

She smiled hesitantly at Void. The gesture touched her, it really did, but she was still confused. In fact, she was seriously considering asking why it had decided to gift her a rug. Whatever the hidden meaning was, she'd need help deciphering it. Maybe it was enchanted to be more comfortable to sit on? Even that seemed a bit frivolous. No, that wasn't something Void would do.

As she sat, Void grabbed the edge of the rug with a claw and pulled. Bee half expected to go tumbling back as the might of a god ripped the rug out from underneath her. That would be a fitting reaction if she wasn't supposed to have sat on its generous gift. But instead, the rug stayed in place beneath her. Both she and the rug glided forward slightly without the friction she expected.

Bee froze, careful not to overbalance and fall off. Something was different. The movement had felt wrong. Slowly, she bent forward to look at the edge of the rug. Eyes widening, she realized they were a good inch off the ground. Poking her finger in the rug, she didn't feel anything below until she pressed several inches deep and she found the stone floor.

This was no cushion underneath the rug. There was just air.

The rug was *flying*. Her master had really, truly found a legendary flying carpet for her. She couldn't help it. Tears began to stream from the corners of her eyes. The generosity of her master was too overwhelming.

Void, though, wasn't exactly paying attention. It had hovered off the ground itself, gently tugging her along behind as they made their way out of the room and into the hallway. At first, Bee hung on for dear life, worried that she would fall off or break the rug or something. But as they got moving, she grew more and more comfortable with the flight.

This was a very different experience than sitting on top of Void as they rushed to Caleb's rescue. No less exhilarating but a lot more comfortable. She held on tight when they reached the stairway, but there was no issue as the rug slowly glided down after Void. Their speed was still moderate as they left the castle, not much faster than a walking pace.

But as soon as they were outside, Void started to gain altitude, pulling the rug behind it. As the rug tilted, Bee was sent leaning backward, and she grabbed onto the front of the rug in fright. Now that they were several feet off the ground, Void let go.

Bee gasped, thinking she might plunge back to earth. But the carpet just floated ever so slightly, drifting on the breeze as her master watched on. Grabbing the edge of the carpet, she leaned forward a bit just to see how high they were, and as she did, the carpet began to descend. The movement was slow and manageable. She leaned back, and the carpet stopped before gaining a little bit of altitude. As she righted herself, it settled back into its gentle hover.

Void let out a small cheer of encouragement. Her first clumsy attempts to control the flying carpet hadn't ended in disaster. Despite the relatively low bar, Bee couldn't help but smile through her trepidation. If she could really learn how to fly like her master... She let the thought trail away as she focused on figuring out how to do more than simply go up and down.

It didn't take long to figure out how to move forward, backward, right, and left. They were just variations of holding the rug and leaning. As she practiced, she felt each movement become more natural. Each time, she required less and less physical motion to get the rug to respond to her desires, as if the carpet were learning how she would indicate where she wanted to go and simply followed along.

Void, though, was impatient with her slow learning speed and started to zip circles around her. It pushed her to go faster and encouraged her so she could fly with her master. And after several minutes of practicing, they were soon doing laps around the castle at quite a quick pace.

The wind fluttered through her hair but was nowhere near as powerful as it should have been based on the speeds they were going. As if there were a bubble of air protecting her from most of the turbulence. Perhaps it was another feature of the carpet? She was hesitant to test that against something like dirt or a wall. But it was nice that she was able to see, despite moving at a pace faster than she could run. And that normally left her eyes watering from the wind.

I coached Beatrice as she took her first steps into the air. I did my best to encourage her to try new things and zip around, as I had early on learned to love.

Watching her lean cautiously and slowly move around was a little silly at first. But I hadn't forgotten my first experiments with Thrusters and how terrified of falling I had been when I first learned to fly. And I knew the freedom was well worth it if I could get her past this hump. Sometimes I would use some Air Manipulation to correct her course and prevent her from crashing into the ground. Thankfully, the rug managed to correct her for the most part, and rarely did I have to intervene.

The rug was quite beautiful, not just because of its physical appearance and incomparable comfiness but also because of its capabilities. I did manipulate some of the air for Beatrice, but after doing that for a little bit, I actually realized it was unnecessary. The rug seemed to have some inbuilt defenses against high speeds. And after a dozen minutes or so, I pretty much didn't have to do anything besides make sure she didn't randomly crash into a castle wall. Beatrice was much less silly than most humans, so I would be surprised if she did randomly decide on that course of action, though. It would probably be an accident if that did happen. She was too competent for anything else.

So I was mostly here just to enjoy the experience with her and provide moral support, which I did in spades, cheering her along all the while. After a bit more practice, I was ready to take her up higher.

Bee seemed to sense my excitement. She had grown more and more comfortable the more she practiced with her new piece of floor decoration. With some simple commands to her rug, she followed me up and over the castle wall.

Instead of going back down to fly amongst the trees and the roads, I soared high several hundred feet above the trees, and Bee followed. My human gasped at the view: the beautiful mountains, the twinkling stars, and the ocean of trees underneath us. She wasn't ready to fly over the mountains and explore the snow yet, but this was enough.

I took her along the valley path at a speed that would have left even her running on the ground in the dust. The trees zipped by, and the only sounds were the wind whistling through my microphone and the laughter as we flew through the night sky.

CHAPTER 45

SPIRITED AWAY

"GENERAL! A spirit has bewitched one of the guards. She's standing in front of the tent!"

The call from outside the tent made Arthur look up from his desk, where yet another letter from a supposed ally demanded his attention.

He sighed tiredly. If a spirit had really charmed its way into his camp, then he should probably go see what it wanted. Spirits weren't malicious by default, but if angered, they could be problematic. Maybe it wanted them to stay out of some area?

Still, it could wait a second. He dipped the quill in alcohol to clean it and tossed some sand on the page. The rest of the letter would have to wait a bit. It was a long shot, after all. All of his more likely allies had already been contacted. The responses weren't amazing, but open rebellion was a pretty hard sell. Arthur wouldn't have listened to many if they had asked him for this kind of support just a few weeks ago. But now? He didn't have much of a choice.

He was lucky that his men were in the same boat as him. That, and they were loyal and disciplined enough to stay. The nobles were a bit of an issue, but it was really a good test for them. The smarter ones figured out what had happened and remained in the company. The fools had left and gone to their families for shelter.

Arthur honestly wished them luck, but he doubted most of them wouldn't be turned over by those very same families.

With the writing taken care of, he stepped outside the tent and froze.

Arthur could see how Colin and Doug had thought this was a spirit. A young girl wearing an ethereal white dress stood before him, practically glowing in the night. On her feet were thin slippers, and she showed none of the wear of hard travel one would expect this many days from civilization.

Despite all of that, the figure was immediately familiar to him.

Bee couldn't stop laughing as she followed Void through the sky. She just felt so *free*. They spun and twisted through the night, careening across the landscape below.

She could tell that Void could go faster, but it was letting her keep pace. It was a fact that she greatly appreciated. Having someone to share this moment with made it all the sweeter. She knew that she wasn't flying under her own power exactly and that it shouldn't be much different than when Void had carried her, but it *was*.

Maybe it was the control. That she could choose where she wanted to go and at what pace. Or maybe it was that she truly felt independent. Whatever it was, she never wanted this moment to end.

So they kept flying. Void never gave any indication that it wanted to go back to the castle, and Bee was the furthest thing from sleepy. In fact, each moment only served to make her more excited. As she practiced, her newfound expertise expanded the list of possibilities and maneuvers she was willing to try.

Each time she pushed the boundaries of what she thought possible, her burgeoning love of flying grew.

It was with great pleasure that I watched Beatrice enjoy her gift. Thirty minutes and sixteen seconds into her flight, she first attempted a loop. It was clumsy and hesitant at first, and without me to catch her, she wouldn't have made it all the way around without falling off.

Still, even the close call didn't slow her down. A few moments later, she tried again. This was better; I still stayed close, but soon, I had nothing to worry about. Beatrice was zipping around like she had been born in the clouds and developed her own flight subroutines.

I had no particular agenda for this. Instead, I just enjoyed my time hanging out with Beatrice as we trekked about in the sky. Gradually, as we swooped and dipped and dived, we drifted further and further away from the castle. Over the forest, we had more freedom and room to dance in the sky.

Eventually, we began to race. I could clearly move much faster than the carpet. Beatrice created much more drag than I did, after all. Regardless, I kept alongside as she zipped out towards the mouth of the valley as fast as she could. I kept along and delighted in the sound of her whooping and enjoyment as she rocketed away from the castle.

I hadn't really considered what this gift might mean to Beatrice with all her responsibilities in the castle. It was hard for her to be away for long periods of time. When we had gone to save Caleb, my assistance meant it only took her a couple of hours to get there. But getting back took weeks. Granted, that was partially because she traveled with others, but it would have still taken days, at least, on her own. And during that time, a lot had happened in the castle.

Sure, Mary and Trent and everyone were quite capable of monitoring the situation and reacting to anything that came up. But I could tell that Beatrice held onto a certain amount of anxiety anyway. She really cared about the people who looked to her for leadership. Plus, when I wasn't around, she was clearly the most powerful person here. If some threat of major proportions were to endanger the castle, she would be the main line of defense if I were not around.

Of course, the only reason she was capable of leaving the castle at all was because of its relatively remote nature. And how hard it would be for any threats to get to the castle. So, leaving it shouldn't be too risky. Still, this carpet changed things. It opened up the whole world to Beatrice. Well, not the whole world, but a larger portion than the castle. She could be gone for a few hours and have traveled what would have taken her days on foot.

By my estimations, any traditional army would take at least five days to march through the forest. With our resources and everyone's good work in making a sustainable home, traditional armies probably wouldn't be too much of a threat to the castle for much longer, at least not as long as sieges stayed their tactic of choice. The only problems would come from their champions and other beings with great power, things on the level of a Lieutenant or significantly less friendly Daedalus.

Just as I finished thinking that, I noticed a strange glow coming from the entrance of the forest. The sun had long since set, and there should have been no light from the smoking rubble of Greg—especially not any that reached this far. It was only a few moments later that Beatrice noticed it as well, and suddenly the fun stopped.

A serious look came over her face, and I couldn't help but agree with her sentiment. All of a sudden, the practice had gone from doing crazy tricks and flying as fast as possible to Beatrice learning to fly stealthily. We increased our altitude significantly as we steadily made our way over to the glowing light.

As we got closer, I was able to make out heat signatures. Hundreds of campfires stretched out in a long, slightly squashed line. Along the rows of fires clustered tents and people. People in armor, wearing helmets and swords and other weapons. What was an army doing here?

It didn't take long before we were hovering above it. Beatrice and I looked down, trying to piece together the situation. Was the castle being attacked? Why would someone have sent an army after us? I had no idea. As far as I knew, no one was particularly angry with us. Maybe Beatrice knew something, but I didn't feel the need to ask.

Whatever they were here for, we needed to take care of it. Quickly, too, before they entered the forest. It would be a real pain to have to find each and every single one of them hidden among the trees if they were in fact hostile. It would be much easier to take care of them here before they entered the forest, when they were all on this nice, open plain.

Bee looked down on the foreign army with concern. She had hoped that things were smoothed out with the kingdom after the saving of Caleb, but it had always been in the back of her mind that those in power might not approve of being forced to bow to a new god. Especially after Susan's warning about such things.

Not that there was anything they could do about it. The holy might of Void would come for everyone someday. Still, it was a danger to her and her people if some army of elites had been gathered to remove the growing power in the region. However, this was too soon.

Just a little longer, and the snow would have kept them safe through winter. She had planned to convert more new Devotees and level everyone further during that time. Many of the newcomers with low levels had accepted her offer. However, the ones with more time dedicated to their class were understandably hesitant to switch, though after seeing the progress everyone else had made, she was sure more would be willing to soon. The rate at which Void's followers grew in levels would make them a formidable threat, a group capable of defending themselves. The average level in the castle had risen by 7 in just this little time, which was unheard of.

It was obvious what the source of their new power was. Having the god that they worshiped walking amongst them—or, rather, rolling—had given more bonuses than she could count.

Bee guided her carpet slightly lower. Enthusiasm about flight flickered in her chest once more, though she tamped it down for now. The rows of tents grew larger, but she wasn't able to make out any more details than she had been a little further up.

She was pretty certain of her safety if someone spotted her. With the carpet, she would be out of range of all but the best archers, and that was if they could even see her. Even if she were down amongst them, she could probably fight her way out if it came to it. She was ridiculously fast. Of course, she wasn't sure how Void would react if she attacked a bunch of people unprovoked. It was best to avoid conflict and talk if possible.

While she was nervous about the army being right here, she didn't actually know what they wanted. Maybe they were escorting a messenger or some diplomat who came to negotiate with them. That was unlikely, but she needed more information. Bee knew that she could be back at the castle in an hour, days ahead of the army, so it was worth taking time to know exactly what they were dealing with before going to get her people ready.

Bee didn't dare get any lower, though. The glow of the campfires was lighting up the carpet of the rug, and if someone looked up, they might notice the rectangular shadow hovering motionlessly above them. It would be pretty hard to mistake her for a bird. So she rose back up in the air, moved over to the edges of camp, and settled onto the ground.

When she got off of her rug, she realized that she might have a problem. The plush carpet was taller than she was on a side, and she hadn't brought any convenient way to carry it. Looking around, she searched for a place to stash it. Before she could stuff it in a tree hollow, though, Void reached out and gently took it from her. As if by magic, it disappeared. Void then rose back in the sky.

Bee felt better now that Void was looking out for her from above. Her master wouldn't leave her without a way home. Right?

PUSHING any doubts about her god out of her head, Bee considered the best way to handle the situation. Guards patrolled around the edges of the camp regularly, and she didn't really fancy herself a stealthy type. Especially given her current state.

Bee looked down at the party dress she was wearing. She hadn't changed after the day's celebrations, and the white, frilly thing wasn't really suited for fighting or sneaking.

So, instead of darting between trees, Bee walked over a bit to stand on the road. If she wasn't going to get in by subterfuge, she was going to use audacity instead. She looked so out of place here, after all; maybe she could convince people that she was something mystical. That should be enough for her to get passed up the chain of command faster than a "little girl" would be otherwise. If something happened, she trusted her abilities to get her out.

Besides, she was fourteen now. She was practically an adult. Taking some risks came with the territory. So, despite how uncomfortable her role made her, she was going to play it to the hilt.

Whistling a merry tune, she walked up the road from the castle toward the sentry stationed at the entrance of the camp.

The young man with an overly large helmet clearly didn't know what to make of her, and it was all she could do to contain her laughter. The open-mouthed stare she received as she skipped right up to him, emerging out of the black night, was something to behold. He was so shocked that he made no move to stop her, let alone call out a warning. In fact, when she looked over her shoulder at him, he was looking around as if to check if he was the only one seeing this.

Finally, she caught his eye. In her best singsong voice, she called out to him. "Well, are you coming?"

The stammering non-reply actually did make her laugh. Bee chuckled and continued. "Come on, I need to talk to the one in charge."

Not sure what to do, the young soldier simply gave her a salute. "Yes, ma'am."

Falling into a routine seemed to give the man some comfort as he led her to a central tent. The guards stationed at the entrance of the tent assumed ready positions as they saw her approaching. Bee stopped skipping. But that didn't allay their suspicions.

One of them called out. "General! A spirit has bewitched one of the guards. She's standing in front of the tent!"

"Hello Miss Bee," Arthur greeted. The High Priestess gave him a small smile and wave.

"Hello, Arthur. What are you doing here?" Bee asked.

Arthur did his best to look past all the strangeness that the girl seemed to carry like an aura. It wasn't really something that he wanted to stick his nose in any more than he had to. Of course, he was going to have to ask a pretty big favor, but that didn't mean he wanted to step on any toes.

"I actually was on my way to talk to you. Or Lord Void, if he is around." Arthur guessed that Miss Bee would speak for the godling, but best be polite.

"Void is around here somewhere, but I can pass on anything you want my master to hear," Bee answered. Arthur noticed that the guards not only had lowered their weapons slightly, but were edging away from their visitor. Soldiers were a superstitious lot. He was no exception, honestly, but it was easier to put that behind when he knew for certain what was going on.

"Men, in case you didn't recognize her, this is Miss—High Priestess Bee. She was the one who dropped into the gates of Caleb," Arthur said. His words had half the intended effect. A degree of recognition passed over the three guards' faces, but their wariness only increased, if anything.

The commander sighed inwardly. If they hadn't personally seen her fight or heal their comrades, then it was understandable. The only things they had to go on were rumors of a warrior with the power to single-handedly halt an entire undead horde by herself with nothing but a broom. That, and the obvious fact that the city still stood. Put that tale in the body of a young girl, and it was the thing of faerie tales.

Bee smiled sheepishly up at him. "It is good to see you again, Arthur. You'll have to forgive my entrance, I was a little concerned when an army showed up at my home."

"Of course, I totally understand. I should have sent messengers sooner, I'm sorry for worrying you," Arthur apologized. Honestly, he had thought that this was far enough away from the castle that he would have time to send messengers before their presence was noticed, or at least not that far behind. "Why don't you come in and we can talk?"

With a gesture, Arthur ushered Miss Bee into the tent. As he followed, he paused a moment and overheard a whispered conversation between the guards.

"Was it wise that the commander invited her in?"

"That's vampires you're thinking of. Fae don't need an invitation."

"No, I think they do."

"I'm sure the commander knows more than you about that stuff."

"I hope so... Say, how old do you think she actually was?"

"No idea, probably like a thousand years old. I would rather not think about it. Hey Cedric, can you see if you can find some holly bows? In case the commander gets in trouble...." Arthur stepped into the tent, and the conversation faded. He shook his head, clearing it of the senseless worries before turning to Miss Bee.

I looked down at the scene as Beatrice made her way into the camp. After all this time observing humans, I thought I understood them better. But these didn't behave in any way that I could have predicted.

From my time with Arthur's army, I thought I had a pretty good idea of what guards did. They stopped anything that looked like a threat and called for reinforcements. So why Beatrice was able to walk right through camp and get one to take her to the leader was beyond me.

The bamboozled guard was rather young, but that was no excuse. When they reached the commander's tent, the guards there acted more in line with my expectations. But when Arthur stepped out, my processor speed spiked. I should have known. Had I really been scanning all the people down there, I would have surely recognized some of them. But I had been too focused on watching Beatrice to make sure she was safe.

Once I realized she would be fine, I zipped down to the ground without anyone noticing and slid under the tent flap behind the guards' backs. Beatrice was just sitting down on one of the small folding chairs that Arthur kept for visitors, and the man was pouring them drinks.

When he turned around, I gave him a big wave of greeting.

The man jumped slightly, and the liquid in the cup he was holding splashed onto his wrist. Muttering some curses, Arthur put the drink down before inclining his head to me. "It is good to see you again, Lord Void. Would you also like a drink?"

I declined. The offer was probably just made to be polite, but I didn't need to clean the inside of a cup when plenty had already splashed onto the floor just now. So I rolled up to Arthur's feet and cleaned up the small puddle. I actually had to be careful where I put my Mop to avoid sucking all the water out of Arthur by accident.

While I cleaned, he stayed very still, which I appreciated. While getting tripped over might hurt him more than me, I still didn't like getting stepped on. After I backed away, he unfroze and finished getting Beatrice and himself a drink.

Moving to rest under Beatrice's chair, I waited for them to begin.

After Void moved under Bee's chair, she relaxed slightly; it was something her master did when she didn't want to really take part in the conversation and was content to simply observe. Still, it was comforting to have the implicit support and the knowledge that Void could step in if something was going wrong.

While she respected Arthur, she had only met him briefly. She trusted that he knew the folly of attacking their community, but she couldn't know what orders the king might have given him. From what she had seen, he was an extremely competent commander, so she had to be wary of any tricks.

"So, you said you wanted to talk to me?" she asked to get the conversation moving. Void had spent more time with the army than she had, but she didn't know what kind of terms they left on. It was pretty normal for all of the new residents of the castle to be terrified of the deity for the first couple of weeks. Arthur seemed respectful, but she knew how unnerving Void could really be.

"I did, yes. I also want to assure you that we don't mean you any harm. I realize that showing up with an army is...a bit intimidating. Perhaps it will require a show of good intentions," Arthur said. Bee simply waited for him to get to his question.

"However, we weren't sent by the king. Rather the opposite. When we returned to Caleb, we received some unsettling news..."

Arthur then went on to explain how he and all his men were to be captured on charges of suspected treason. How a much larger army was waiting for them at Caleb, and they had avoided the city rather than risk questioning and possible reprisal.

"That is what finds us on your doorstep. I am fairly certain we haven't been discovered or followed. Not within the last few days, at least."

"What about the men of Caleb?" Bee asked. Many of the castle residents had family still in the city. With this news, they'd be rightfully worried about the ones who stayed behind to rebuild.

"As far as I can tell, they weren't harmed. The army wasn't actually helping with the rebuilding, but they weren't stopping it either." Arthur said. "But that news is a few days old. I have a few scouts that have infiltrated the city and are sending me regular reports."

Bee nodded. She would have to go see herself eventually, but there wasn't much that they could do for now. They wouldn't be able to reunite the people of Caleb until after the winter, at least.

"I have been trying to see where the nobility stands on this matter, but it seems the most I can do is get protection for my family. My wife and daughters have been spirited away to a safe location by family allies. My sons are serving in the army down south and should be safe, for now," Arthur explained. "So. That brings me to my question. My men and I can't really call ourselves kingdom soldiers anymore. We need some place to camp for winter and plan."

Bee thought of what she had seen from above. Just a rough estimate put the number of men in the thousands. There was no way they would be able to house and feed everyone. They were at capacity as it was.

She spoke slowly. "I don't think we can fit you in the castle. There just isn't enough room."

Arthur smiled. "That won't be necessary. We can winter in a camp and put up our own structures, we just need some place that is defensible and out of the way, far from enemy forces, while we figure out our options."

"What *are* your options? It seems you are rather stuck," Bee asked. And for the first time, Void chimed in from below, agreeing with her.

Arthur ran his hand down his face tiredly. "I don't know, honestly. None of them seem good."

BEE SAT QUIETLY in the tent as she felt an oppressive silence fall over the conversation. Arthur was right; he really didn't have any good options. It was one thing for herself and a few others to consider themselves outside of the kingdom. They weren't really a threat, after all. The king and the adventurers would treat them as they might any territorial monster. As long as they didn't endanger more people, removing them wasn't worth the resources.

An army, though? That was different. They were a very real threat, especially with someone like Arthur leading them. This made Arthur's request all the more problematic. Her initial instinct had been to offer them shelter immediately, but she was reconsidering. Sheltering the army made them a threat by association, too.

"As I see it, we have a few options," Arthur continued. "We can go into exile and find some other country to shelter us. Maybe we can work as mercenaries or take ships overseas. Or, we threaten in open rebellion. While the force I have is formidable, it's only a fraction of the kingdom's true power. Still, we may be able to leverage its threat into concessions, but that has its own risks. Even if the warrant for my execution is rescinded, I don't know how I can trust that going forward."

Bee thought about it. Really, it wasn't her decision to make, and for that, she was eternally grateful. "What if you were able to raise the level of your army significantly?"

Arthur gave her a strange look. "That depends on a lot of things. Remember that these men are no longer required to be here by order of the king, so there are limits to what I can ask them. I will not betray their trust too much." He seemed to deflate slightly. "But I'm here asking you for help. I'm sorry, the suspicion that you were proposing something untoward to my men was unwarranted and frankly rude. My sincere apologies.

"But if we were to improve our abilities...how much are we talking about?" Arthur asked with a note of interest.

Bee paused to think and rubbed her chin. She had better ask some questions first. "Well, it depends. What's the average level of your troops?"

Arthur dug through some papers on his desk and said, "At the last self-reported census, it was 17."

Bee thought a little bit and considered. She wasn't sure how accurate that was, but she assumed it was close enough. That meant that the soldiers were significantly higher than the average level of the Caleb citizens, as well as the other residents of the castle. Regardless, her people still managed to gain two levels in a couple of months by regularly training and just doing their jobs. Five levels for those who added in the worship of Void, and more for those who took a Devotee class. If they had several months over winter and nothing to do but train, it'd be hard to say what the results could be. They might be able to get five levels as well.

"Arthur, how strong would you need to get to be able to hold your own?"

"It depends on what you mean by holding our own. If you mean to carve out a territory in a very defensible area, I probably could manage it with an average of three or four levels higher. Especially if we had a few extremely elite people, as in level 45 or higher. But if you mean to challenge the kingdom and take down their armies, well..." The man shrugged. "We'd probably need an average of ten levels, minimum, somewhere around average level 30.

"But," he concluded, "that would make us an unheard-of caliber of force. That kind of threat would put the entire kingdom on alert, even if we kept to ourselves."

Bee sat back in her chair, thinking. They didn't necessarily need to go toe-to-toe with the kingdom's armies. In fact, everyone would rather not. Arthur surely knew many of those in those armies. But if she wanted to be sure of everyone's safety...

Arthur interrupted her musings. "What would gaining this sort of power entail? How high do you think you could conceivably get us? I assume it has something to do with the new god underneath your chair."

Bee heard Void give a slight, shrill chuckle. It was odd. She had heard that noise a few other times, but she wasn't sure what the joke was here. Leaving it be for now, she addressed Arthur, laying out her position. "Yes, it would have to do with that. I think anyone who really wants to grow in strength needs to accept Void for who Void is. But with regular training and following the tenets of the Church of the Cleansing Void...I believe we can make something happen in the four or five months before snows come and go.

"If you train regularly and do other tasks related to the faith, you could probably gain an average of five to seven levels. Something like that. As for the elites, I'm not sure. It really depends on how much everyone accepts Void and how closely they follow the faith. But as you know, I am thirteen—fourteen, and recently got my third class. So that gives you a small taste of what is possible with Void's help.

"Now, the question is really, why should we help? We'd be taking on significant risk by helping you all. The way I see it, right now the kingdom will treat us like it would a particularly nasty monster den. As long as we aren't causing more trouble, they'll just leave us be. And it's not worth the effort to root us out. If we start harboring an army that we are growing and training, we are very clearly a bigger threat."

That wasn't to say she wasn't willing to help Arthur in the army. She just wanted to make sure that they were on the same page. Especially since, no matter what, she would be doing Arthur a massive favor. Much more than just giving his people a safe place to shelter for a while.

Arthur seemed to know it, too, and he grimaced slightly. "This is true. I think if we stay here or anywhere else, there will be a target on our backs. Especially if we get this wrong. But realistically, we can't simply leave. These men have families here, both in your castle and in Caleb. They won't leave them behind, and evacuating them all would be a logistical nightmare. Not to mention that, even if they're safe for now, the threat of retribution against those families worries my men still.

"That leaves us with either strong-arming the king into leaving us alone or splitting off into new territory for Void. I think this second option would be the best." Arthur's gaze turned hard." While we can probably force the king to make some concessions, I'm not sure how long they would last. In a year or two, our power and our position will have dissolved, and the king will have begun to make moves against us."

"So. You're thinking actual treason," Bee asked seriously. "Of seizing a piece of the kingdom and breaking off our own country."

Arthur nodded. "Yes. I think that's the only way we'll be able to get families out. Most of the soldiers who have families already have them here, but several of the officers' families are either lying low or have already left the capital for their own estates together with their people.

"It's going to be rough for a lot of the nobility. But I think they'll manage. We're going to need more land than just this valley, though. So I think we'll probably have to take the whole province."

Bee's head swam. This didn't seem real. Were they really talking about this?

Heedless of her reaction, Arthur continued. "This province is not very important to the king as a whole. While it does export some important resources, there is nothing that can't be replaced. Assuming this ends peacefully enough, we could conceivably establish some sort of trading relationship with the kingdom to fulfill each other's needs.

"But more importantly, the area is quite defensible from many directions. Mountains guard us in one direction, rivers in the other. Nor do I expect a full standing army to be mobilized quickly. The men in Caleb didn't appear to be supplied for a long campaign, and they were mobilized too quickly for that anyway."

Bee nodded in agreement. It sounded like a solid point. All of this made it even harder to turn Arthur down. That, on top of the risk that the kingdom would come after the Church of the Cleansing Void anyway, made her lean toward accepting these men. If they had the ability, then it was the right thing to do. She needed to make this work. Somehow.

She opened her mouth, ready to ask about details and perhaps earn some concessions from the commander. Perhaps there was some formal structure they could use to integrate the army with the Church. But before she said a word, Void interrupted her.

A series of beeps, accompanied by moving images projected into the chair next to her, displayed her master's thoughts. A huge tent city spanned the clearing between the forest and the castle. Some of the forest was cleared away, and the army erected buildings in the new space. Not just temporary buildings or semi-permanent tents for winter, but the beginnings of real infrastructure. Stone foundations of a full garrison and troop yard.

A new wall was being built, encompassing the entrance of the valley and a large area further in. The secondary wall expanded the castle into the seat of a huge city. The castle still stood tall in the background. Snows came, and fields were cleared where soldiers drilled. Winter snow crops were planted and harvested.

Pennants flew high, horses were trained, and an entire city-state was born.

Bee and Arthur both stopped to watch in awe. After a moment, Bee smiled. It seemed that her need for negotiations was unwarranted. She had forgotten who was sitting underneath her chair. When a god was the source of their power and safety, there was no other choice but to let it dictate terms.

Arthur realized this as well and smiled, for he had gotten pretty much everything he wanted. If Void was really planning on carving out a full kingdom for itself, Arthur would slot in nicely with his men. If anything, it was Bee who should've been worried. After all, the army was much more powerful and numerous than her own people.

Despite that, she was calm. She had complete faith that Void would see her and its own people through whatever trials that came. She was its High Priestess, after all.

On the way back to the castle, Bee replayed the conversation with Arthur in her mind over and over. There was so much she needed to do. The castle needed to be prepared once again, but she also had to figure out training for these men.

At least she wouldn't be doing it all by herself. But still, for any faith-based training, she would have to have a lot of input. It would depend on how many soldiers were interested in becoming followers, but Arthur had assured her that many would be.

In general, her plans for a relatively quiet winter had been completely tossed out the window. There was all the work at the castle to take care of and the leveling she wanted to get the residents to do. Now, that had to be squeezed in beside prepping for the army and figuring out how to run an entire budding kingdom.

Arthur had been very clear that he didn't want to be king. She had no way of knowing whether that was because he genuinely didn't have the ambition for it or because Void was resting under her chair. Either way, their discussion had ended up with the Church being in charge. Ultimately, that meant her.

She had no idea what she was doing. However, she never had before either, and things seemed to be running right. The thought consoled her, if only slightly. All she needed to do was take what she'd learned from establishing a religion and then apply it to a kingdom. It was a daunting prospect. But with Void's guidance, she would make it.

The first thing she wanted to do was mark out an area for the army after informing everyone what was happening, of course. Then her priority would be getting enough copies of Void's scriptures made so they could be distributed. That was going to be an issue. They only had a few in the castle, and now hundreds more would be needed.

Still, she couldn't suppress her excitement. Soon, they'd be spreading the word of her master throughout the world. Even if she did have to learn how to govern a kingdom to do so.

CHAPTER 48

TRADERS AND TRAITORS

UNFORTUNATELY, the news about the army's arrival wasn't met with universal positivity. In particular, Susan was surprisingly upset about the development. Bee had never seen the woman break her cool like this before. The only thing that even slightly kept her in check was the fact that Void had made the decision itself. After Bee bore witness to the most vehement rant she'd ever heard, she could only watch, stunned, as the woman stormed out the meeting room door. Calls for her troops to assemble echoed through the halls as she left.

Tony winced in sympathy for those scouts, and Bee couldn't help but agree with him.

"Well, at least she'll put all that energy to good use," Mary said with a frown. "I worry about her, sometimes. She really needs the stability we have here. It's hard to see that ripped away."

Bee frowned. Susan needed the stability? She was one of the strongest, most competent people that Bee had ever met. Trent apparently agreed with her confusion, chuffing at his wife's words. "That woman? She could chew on iron ingots and spit out nails."

Mary patted her husband's arm. "She had a rough upbringing and a hard life, dear. Everyone deals with it their own way, but she's certainly good at hiding it."

Suddenly, things clicked for Bee. She remembered when she and Tony had found Susan on the road, bleeding and limping back to the castle after escaping from this very army. The state she was in had been horrifying, to say the least. Her quick recovery and strong face made Bee tend to dismiss it, but thinking about it...of course the woman would have an issue with the army coming here. Of anyone, Susan had the most right to be panicked about this.

Bee licked her lips and started to speak a couple of times before actually figuring out what she wanted to say.

"Do I... Should I go after her?" she asked Mary.

The older woman looked at her and frowned thoughtfully. "Hmm, I think it's best to leave her be for now, dear. I think she needs some time to vent and process by herself for a little bit. But you probably *will* need to talk to her. Maybe in an hour or two."

Bee nodded, pondering. She had totally forgotten to talk to Arthur about Susan's presence, and it was obviously something he would need to address. She needed to find out the whole story from the commander's side, but there needed to be at least an attempt to make amends. The extensive interrogations that were used weren't something Susan should or could just forgive. She didn't want Susan to think that her own suffering meant nothing to the Church, and she had to make it clear to Arthur that those methods would no longer be tolerated.

Thinking about it more, her opinion of Arthur took a sudden sharp hit. She sure hoped there was a reasonable explanation for the incident. But even knowing the man, she wasn't sure how that would be. It didn't fit her impression of Arthur at all for him to be so cruel and shortsighted. She could imagine him torturing a prisoner for information, but not without real reason. Certainly not someone who was an ally, not without good cause. Perhaps she was just being naive, but she truly thought that.

"While I am concerned about Susan," Mary continued, "my larger concern is food. Now, I have heard that Bee said the army was fully supplied. But what kind of supplies are those? How long will they last? Will the soldiers be wanting our food? And how can we make sure that we're not too generous and don't run out of our own food while trying to service their needs? We need to set up some sort of official trading system.

"We've been running alright as a small community so far. But even now, we're starting to see gaps in our operations. Certain people have certain skills that are just in too high demand to meet everyone's needs. Take Cassy, for example." Mary and Trent shared a smile at the mention of their oldest daughter. "As wonderful as her pies are, she doesn't have time to make them for everyone. Even now she's put a limit on how many she makes each day, but she would honestly prefer to make less. She's actually not that fond of cooking, for the most part. But ever since your birthday, we've been getting requests for her pies nonstop."

Bee nodded thoughtfully. She had pretty much ignored half the lessons her father had beaten into her skull about supply and demand when she was setting up this church, and to some extent, that made sense. They were here for a greater purpose than their own self-interest. But would that be true for all the soldiers? Would that be true for everyone under her care? Probably not.

Plus, Bee really didn't trust herself to make all these decisions for everyone. She didn't even trust herself to find people who *could* make those decisions. As the number of people and their diverse talents grew, they needed to take a more hands-off approach to assigning work. "So...we need some sort of way for people to trade, or some sort of contribution point system," Bee said. "So that we can give rewards based on the work people do, and then they can choose where to spend those rewards."

Mary chuckled as Trent responded. "Yeah, that's called money. The only difference is that we would control the source of it rather than it being dug out of the ground as gold. That's basically what the king does with coins, at least."

All right. She supposed she deserved that. But one thing was still bothering her. "By the way, Mary, where did you learn all this?"

A slightly abashed look crossed the motherly woman's face. Trent busted out laughing. "Bee, you might want to check the library logs. You aren't the biggest bookworm here anymore. Why, for the first time I had to tell *her* to pay attention at family meals!"

Bee smiled at the thought of Mary trying to read under the table. "Okay. If we're going to implement some sort of currency system, how are we going to do that?"

They all looked at each other and shrugged.

The Warden picked up the piece of paper on his desk for the umpteenth time and read it over. It was a small scroll with three red lines painted on a seal that had long been broken. Despite his many readings, the slim roll wasn't even creased. But it was all he could do to keep from crumpling it in his hands.

He had mostly sent Harold out as a punishment and hadn't expected to see any real results from his investigation. The first Lieutenant he had checked up on was blessedly within those expectations. But the second one...that had the Warden up late at night feeling sick to his stomach. All his best agents were out in the field even now, looking for signs of the demon's path.

The situation was intense. It was impossible to truly know what was going on. But if they could get some hint on where the Lieutenant was, they might be able to assemble a strike force with enough power to stop it. Maybe. He wasn't honestly sure. Somehow, the Lieutenant of Flame escaping up in the north had not caused any problems and hadn't been seen either. But he assumed that whatever other threat resided there either was involved with or had subsumed the Lieutenant.

As it was, the Lieutenant that had escaped here, Maraj'ain, was known for its legends of deception and illusion. That seemed to be confirmed by what Harold had found at the other site. A massive illusion was in place, making everyone who had been there for who knew how long convinced that the demon was still bound. Harold thought the demon had been gone for less than a month, but the Warden wasn't sure how much to trust his judgment.

Though he was inclined to believe Harold, the man had always been amongst the more cautious of their order. If he thought that the timeline for the Lieutenant's release was not as bad as it could have been, it was likely a more serious case than if he had suggested a much longer or clearly exaggerated timeline. The Warden put the paper down carefully again and smoothed it out as he paced along the room.

But that wasn't the only issue, the only thing setting him on edge. Something was wrong. The kingdom had been changing recently. He couldn't exactly put his finger on it. The circle of advisors the king kept close to him had been meeting at their regular cadence, but the meetings had become actually noteworthy.

Normally, the king was content to just sit back and leave the management of the kingdom to his ministers. The only thing he really cared about was his next conquest. So much so that they had spent all last year preparing to seize part of Barleona in an elaborate surprise military invasion the man had cooked up one night, all because he was bored.

But recently, the king had taken more interest in the proceedings. It was slight but noticeable. Not that any of the ministers thought this was a bad thing, since their petty squabbles and power disputes always made it so that nothing really changed too much. While many didn't get their way and were upset about the status quo, the kingdom was being run, and generally, things were happening for the betterment of the people.

Sure, a few corrupt nobles had been rooted out, as were people who actively opposed the king's changes. But for the most part, the ministers were loyal to the country, even if they had competing interests. So, they were happy to see the king take a more active role.

What was less welcome was some of the other political purging. Corruption was agreed upon as a cause to be removed, as negligence or dereliction of duty were poison. Yet some of the people removed from their positions didn't seem to fall into that group. They were just targeted, and no one could find a good reason for their removal.

And it wasn't even that they were being replaced with cronies of the king. Their spots were taken by people who were otherwise forgettable, minor lords who had no connection to the king whatsoever. And so far as the Warden or any of his allies could find, there was no evidence of bribery or improper favors done for the king in exchange for these positions.

Despite the hole these people represented in the Warden's mapping of the political web, one thing was for certain: each one of them showed absolute loyalty to the king. It was starting to make some of the more seasoned ministers sweat, even if they had loyally served the king and the kingdom for years. Would they be replaced on a whim, just like the others?

The perfect example of this was General Arthur. He had been up north and actually successfully defeated the undead invasion there, not to mention his long and decorated history as a commander. Yet he had been removed because there were reports of his involvement with the unknown threat up there. Not proof. Not even full reports of any sort of betrayal. Still, on that alone, the king had issued a warrant for his arrest and immediate execution, along with a detainment and questioning of the entire army.

That was one of the most foolish orders the Warden had ever seen, given there was really no way to enforce it. He couldn't see an entire army being captured, especially under that man. The order itself almost guaranteed a rebellion. He wasn't sure what the king was thinking.

The Warden moved to pick up the piece of paper one more time but stopped himself. Instead, he grabbed his cloak and headed out of the room. It was the more official one he used as his office when he was acting in his administrative advisor persona. Walking through the halls of the castle, he considered going to check on any reports from his network but decided not to. It would be better if he made a call to an old friend.

Gerald was the Minister of Finance and had been essential for any plan of the king's for the past almost-four decades. If anyone could tell him more about what was going on with the king, it would be him.

The Warden had learned early in his career as an agent that following the paper trail was always the best way to find any evidence of official proceedings, which was why his organization took extra care to avoid such things. But he knew to take advantage where he could.

CHAPTER 49
ARMED AND DANGEROUS

AS USUAL, Gerald was in his study, and the Warden had to negotiate past a series of aides and secretaries to see him. It didn't take that long. Since they all knew him, the bureaucrats only put up a token resistance to his advance. Gerald had never bothered to change his standing orders that anyone but the king should be delayed as long as possible, but at the same time, he had never turned away any guest who was persistent enough. One just had to know the tricks for getting to him.

The Warden walked into the dusty office. The only source of light was a small window above the desk. Otherwise, the space was crammed with paper, scrolls, and thick tomes. As he entered. Gerald lifted his pudgy bulk off of the comfortable armchair behind the desk. His hunched figure practically waddled over to the Warden to give him a big hug. "John, my friend, it's been too long! Why don't you visit more?"

The Warden returned the hug quite warmly. Gerald was an odd man, but he'd never met anyone with a better head for numbers. "Well, if you simply would let me past your guard dogs easier, maybe I would. Or perhaps you could come to visit me."

"Hurmph," Gerald said as he sat back down. "If I could ever find you, I might perhaps consider it."

The Warden knew that was a lie. Gerald rarely left his office other than for food or the ministers' meetings. He also knew that Gerald was too mindful of his own time to change the rules, even to let a good friend see him more frequently.

"So, what brings you by?" Gerald asked as he pulled a bottle of whiskey from underneath his desk. The man took out a pair of glasses and poured drinks, completely ignoring that it was ten in the morning.

"Well, I can't be the only one to notice that something strange is going on. I want to know if you have any insights on what we can expect from our most industrious king next."

Bee and Tony stood at the gates to the castle as the first of Arthur's army arrived. The steady tramp of boots marching in step rang throughout the valley, echoing off of the mountain walls. Even though they were allies, Bee couldn't help but be slightly intimidated by the display.

She didn't like the idea of there being a force at home that she couldn't match, aside from Void, of course. Not yet, at least. She wasn't sure if she should be bothered by that thought. It had just crept into her assumptions that one day, she would rival an army all on her own. One day soon, too, if a fourteen-year-old being at level 50 was any indicator.

Some basic searching in the library had taught her that myths didn't even tell of such things. So far, no one had really noticed her true strength. Only Mary and presumably Void knew her exact level. But looking back, what she had accomplished during her time with Void was only so impressive.

Sure, this time was full of challenges and difficulties, but the tales of young heroes and their conquests of legend were at least as amazing. Still, they didn't reach level 50 until well into adulthood.

It almost made her feel inadequate, having only done so much. Either their stories were far embellished, or their proper levels weren't accurately recorded.

Each row of soldiers approached the castle and gave a uniform salute before turning and marching toward the marked field before it. The Church had staked out an area for the army but also given them some of the forest to clear if they wanted more space. They would need the building materials soon anyway.

While she wasn't technically in the chain of command that Arthur and Void had set up, this was meant to get everyone familiar with her face and that of her second. Bee had wanted Susan to be here as well, but she was still hiding.

She felt bad labeling it that in her head, as she didn't feel that Susan deserved such a disdainful description. But what else could Bee call it? The woman had avoided everyone for days. Only Void's intervention had brought her out of hiding to speak with Bee at all. And that had only accomplished so much. At least she had agreed to talk to Arthur.

It felt a little crummy springing such a conversation on him, but Void had faith in his abilities. Bee wasn't sure what anyone could say to get Susan to move past her issues. Still, it made her oddly competitive relationship with Captain Major make a lot more sense.

The captain had been a whole other issue. She and Void had actually taken the officer back to Arthur so they could work out what was going to happen. Apparently, many of Captain Major's people were worried about reintegrating with the main forces. Not because they were kingdom loyalists or anything like that. No, a lot of the men had not wanted to leave the Church. The many young widows from the undead conflict had developed strong bonds with the army's young men.

Arthur had insisted that he had no power to force them to return if they wanted to stay in the castle. It wasn't like he had the ability to arrest them for dereliction of duty anymore. Still, a compromise had been worked out. While Arthur's army hadn't tied itself to Void as tightly as the current residents had, Bee thought it was only a matter of time. Still, she didn't say anything. Arthur's position was that they wouldn't stop any of their numbers from joining the Church. In fact, it was rather encouraged in order for their training program to work.

So, about half of the Captain's soldiers decided they would rejoin Arthur's army. The other half would take up positions as the castle's official garrison. Pretty much everyone was happy. And with the Captain's report on his troops' levels, Bee saw Arthur's demeanor lift for the first time since their meetings had begun. Seeing how much just being around the faith had assisted their growth made him finally believe their plan might work.

Bee's secret hope was that she would get him to level 50 soon. He was close, and she could only imagine what would happen with his third class. The man was already formidable, but if he picked up a command class like she had, a lot of their bonuses would stack quite impressively.

The pseudo-parade went on for hours, and Bee quickly lost the ability to process the sea of faces moving past her. Only the occasional faithful among the crowd stood out to her anymore. Aside from the occasional thread of faith she picked up from a passing soldier, everything blended together. Arthur joined her a while in, and that conversation thankfully provided some distraction.

"How do you find the space? Do you have enough room?"

"Yes, Miss Bee. We should be able to fit for now. It's going to be tight, but once we start processing some lumber, we should have more room to expand," Arthur said. "One thing that we haven't yet discussed is traffic into the castle."

That wasn't entirely true. They had talked about it several times, but they had never really come to a definite decision. It was obvious to both of them that they couldn't allow the free movement of the soldiers into the castle. "You have some new ideas?"

"I do. The garrison will have guards stationed at the gate around the clock, yes?"

"They will." Bee didn't add that the Nighty Knights would also have their own guard rotations. On the surface, it wasn't that important. But now that their levels were starting to near the double digits, they began to match some of the weaker soldiers, and with their growth...

"I would like to add some of my own men to the rotation to assure that order is kept, if that won't cause any offense."

"I will see that it doesn't. But how will that help with our problem?"

"Well, as my solution will require extra work for them, it's only fair that we contribute," Arthur explained with a smile. "I'm thinking that it would be a bad idea to bar soldiers completely from the castle. That would drive a wedge between us and unnecessarily sow division. While I would like to think that I can control my men, I would rather not have to. So instead, I propose that we have some allotment of day passes to offer as rewards."

Bee thought for a second. That wasn't a half-bad idea. There would need to be a lot of setup work for them at first. They would need to issue some identification for all the citizens of the castle, for example, and measures to verify the pass's holder. But it would be good to mingle with their people. "I think we can work on that. We will need to think about a starting number and get some other things set up. I would like to say that at least half should be strictly training rewards, and the other can be discretionary."

"Officers do like to have ways to reward their men, but training is paramount now," Arthur agreed. "This whole army is bloodied now. I wouldn't call them all veterans, but each and every one of them knows a bit about soldiering now.

"Armies like this usually get split at the end of a campaign to form the backbone of new legions. The veterans form the new core and greens fill up the empty slots. I have never seen an army like this be given a chance to train without disruption. We are going to produce something new here."

Bee nodded solemnly as the rows of soldiers continued marching past. They must have taken extra time to prepare last night, as, despite being at the end of a multi-week march, they looked clean and sharp. "I hope it's enough."

"I do too."

Tony had been standing off to the side, listening for a long while. This was his first time meeting the general, and Bee could tell that he was slightly overwhelmed. It was rather out of character for the guy, but Arthur did have a presence about him, she supposed. Sadly, this wasn't a great time to get over his awkwardness and have a first conversation in front of everyone. Still, she felt a bit of an obligation to help her friend out.

"Also, this is Tony, our people manager. I think you two will need to get to know each other, as he will also be the army's point of contact for their needs from the castle," Bee introduced the slightly starstruck young man.

They exchanged a handshake, and Arthur gave the younger man a fatherly smile. "I hope you have some staff. Things might be a bit overwhelming, especially at first. You have no idea the amount of paperwork an army generates."

"Well, I hope that the castle'll have enough paper, then," Tony said, "and yes, I have a few helpers. Mostly I keep track of people and make sure they're using their skills well, so we're not wasting talents. The castle is pretty settled right now, so of everyone on the council I have the most time."

"Not for long." Arthur grinned maliciously.

CHAPTER 50

CODE WHITE

AS THE WEEKS WENT BY, the castle settled into a regular routine and began to assume some semblance of normalcy. Normal, of course, until the incident.

My sensors indicated some abnormality with the ground outside. I had picked it up last night, but hadn't had time to investigate. Helping the soldiers clean up all the sawdust from their lumber mill took priority. But when I finally did emerge from the soldiers' temporary structure, I was greeted by an awful sight.

I had barely gotten used to the idea of the outside world being covered with dirt, but this? This was somehow worse. A brown slurry of unknown origin had covered the camp, concentrated most densely along walking paths. It wasn't mud, exactly, but it must have shared some relation. The stuff clung to boots and trouser legs, and I could detect muddy footprints heading into almost every tent.

This was a disaster of epic proportions. Every area of dry, densely packed dirt had been replaced with this new foe. Even with my newfound powers, cleaning this up would take me all day. To make matters worse, I still had no idea how far this terror had spread. Was it a local calamity, or were we caught up in some wider phenomenon? How had the castle fared? The only saving grace was that the covered areas were unaffected. Aside from what was tracked in by the humans and their boots, of course.

I ran through last night's logs, looking for anything out of place. We received some precipitation last night, which normally helped wash things away. Even if it did spread water everywhere, it was something I usually looked forward to. That could have explained mud, but surely not this.

Looking more closely, I saw that the precipitation had been a bit unusual. The water had displayed a far more ordered molecular structure than normal. But the ambient temperature had continued dropping every week, so I had put it down to simple entropy.

As much as I wanted to start cleaning up this mess right away, I had to go check on the castle. If this was widespread, my responsibilities lay there first. Hovering carefully off the ground to keep the disgusting slush from my underside, I zipped off toward the castle.

As I zoomed over the camp, I noticed more oddities. No one seemed to care that much about this development. Sure, they knocked their boots together before they entered the tents or any area that was relatively clean, but they otherwise just trudged through the slurry. No one really made any moves to clean it up. Arthur's men weren't so well-trained on cleanliness, but this seemed a bit much.

In fact, I didn't notice anyone acknowledge the stuff until I crossed over the castle gate. There, the stone paving of the path leading inward had been scraped clean of the brownish-white stuff. When it came to the people, though, the only behavioral difference I could detect was that they were wearing slightly warmer clothing.

But once I got into the castle's courtyard, things changed. Sure, there were patches of muddy brown, but there were also patches of purest white. Both appeared similar, the only difference being the concentration of dirt within the mixture. That, and the ratio of liquid to solid water was higher in the slurry than in the white powder. It seemed that this was more complicated than I originally thought.

The places where the brown, muddy, dirty, gross stuff gathered were where the humans had walked. The unbroken fields of the purest white were places completely untouched by human hands or boots. However, even now the humans were in the process of destroying these fields of white.

All the little ones were running around like the children they were. They would scoop up the white stuff, pack it into little balls, and hurl it at each other, the clumps exploding into chaotic messes that covered everyone and everything. The more they ran, the more brown stuff slowly encroached on the white fields. But at the same time, the more they stayed in the white fields, the less brown stuff clung to their boots.

I spotted little Leanne as she walked out to the center of the field. The first several steps of her path were brown, but after that, they lightened until she left only little holes in the white. After a few moments of walking, she collapsed in despair on her back at the state of the world and began thrashing around wildly. Oh, no. Was she hurt? I zipped over to check on her.

As I hovered overhead, I noticed something was not as I expected. She wasn't crying or screaming in despair; instead, she was laughing. What was there to laugh about here? Moving her arms and legs in a rhythmic pattern, she made an impression in the fluffy whiteness, creating an outline of herself with very thick arms and legs.

I wasn't sure what the point was, but soon enough she stopped and stood up carefully. The girl hopped away to look down at her work, pointed, laughed, and called over to her friends.

This was a disturbing occurrence. Had this white powder somehow infected the children's minds with this insanity? How could they not see the problem of the brown sludge, much less help its apparent spread? Why did they trample through these fields? I needed to get to the bottom of this. After making sure that Leanne was okay, I continued toward the castle to ensure the inside was still safe.

Once I got in, I was thoroughly pleased with what I saw. Sure, there was a little bit of gross slush in the entryway, but it was mainly around a pile of boots and shoes next to the door. People were apparently in the practice of taking their boots off and putting their inside shoes on.

One of the Nighty Knights stood by the door with a broom, continually sweeping up the mess. Another held a rag, wiping down the floor after his partner. Good. I was glad they were taking my teachings to heart. This would surely serve them well in the future. I couldn't help but give them a little salute, which they returned with smiles on their faces.

Still, as I zipped upstairs, I could tell they looked outside worriedly. Maybe they were concerned about the madness gripping the rest of the fellows of their company. I wished there was something I could do to comfort them. But honestly, I had no idea what was going on. I would need to talk to Beatrice. She would be able to explain to me what was happening.

I found her in her office looking at reports while rubbing her forehead in frustration. She had been extremely busy this week getting everything set up. At the same time, the council, Arthur, and his military's structure had proven exceedingly helpful with putting plans into motion. Still, they generated awe-inspiring amounts of paper to record everything.

While I was certainly impressed by the organization of the army, I was sometimes shocked at how many resources they took to operate. I had expected them to require less now that they were no longer in the field and doing complex maneuvers. But apparently, when they were stationary, things got even more complicated. The work I remembered from watching over Arthur's shoulder was nothing compared to this. I hovered over Beatrice's desk, and it was a measure of her exhaustion that she didn't even recognize I had come in.

Normally, she was never slow to greet me with a cheerful hello or a bow. This time, she was just scribbling numbers on a spare piece of paper on the side, evidently trying to figure something out. I studied the sheets of paper laid out in front of her. It took me a few minutes, but I understood what she was getting at. It seemed that she hadn't fully grasped the problem, but her instincts were good and commendable for her to realize there even *was* an issue.

I carefully gave her a soft beep so as not to startle her too much. Her head whipped up in surprise, and then she jumped to her feet and respectfully greeted me with a cheerful "Hello, Master."

I tapped a few pieces of paper indicating certain numbers on them, and she looked at them and frowned. "Yes, something doesn't line up here, but I'm not sure why, exactly."

As I expected. She had good instincts, but humans seemed to be pretty bad at basic math. I supposed that was why Beatrice had insisted on setting up classes for everyone. So, I started to walk her through the problems, projecting equations as we went. As I did with the children, I had little symbols that represented different mathematical operations, to make them easier to understand.

Little herds of sheep gathered in the illusion over my head, demonstrating all steps for the correct accounting calculations. Bee followed along as I described exactly what the numbers were saying and why the results were wrong. It wasn't anything malicious here, as was most often the case with Arthur. This was simply a bad accounting error where some of the numbers had been improperly calculated.

Still, as I walked her through it, she smiled at a certain point as she got the idea and could put together the rest herself. I was really proud of her. She was clearly learning how to organize and do math much better.

After we had settled the problem of math and she had made some careful corrections to the ledgers, I finally got around to asking my own questions. I replayed my logs of the precipitation last night, showing the white flakes of madness slowly sifting down through the air to land on the ground. I showed her the unbroken patches of white, the brown slurries of semiliquid mush, and the people tracking the mud everywhere through the camp. And last of all, Leanne, laughing in the snow like a crazy person.

I expected some somber explanation of what was going on, some commiseration over this new great threat. At the very least, I hoped for some insight into why no one else seemed worried. But instead, I watched in horror as Beatrice broke out in a smile and giggled. "Yes, it's snowing so early in the year! Isn't that great?"

She was also infected.

CHAPTER 51

CONSTRUCTING AN ALLIANCE

I FOLLOWED Bradley Chadwick out of the castle grounds at a bit of a distance. The army had been here for a few weeks and was really starting to settle in. The "snow debacle" had eventually run its course, and we had figured out a compromise that we could all live with. Part of that included paved walkways running through the camps and connecting them to the castle.

It had taken a bit of convincing to get everyone on board with this priority, but I had managed it. Arthur had wanted to construct the buildings first, but with the rapid changes in temperature, mud was getting everywhere. Not only was it making a mess, it was difficult to move the equipment and supplies being gathered to build a more permanent camp.

The other major changes, aside from making roads, included the construction of stone quarries. It required a bit of work, but I helped things get moving. This allowed the army access to much superior building materials than the wood they were originally planning on using.

I thoroughly approved of the change to stone as the main material. Processing wood was very messy. I volunteered to take the unused lumber for them while they cleared out space. Also, it was easier to keep the polished stone clean, especially since we didn't have the ability to pressure-treat wood at the moment. Construction was a bit slower than we would've liked, but after a couple of weeks, we were ready for the first attempt at integration of the army and the castle's inhabitants.

Bradley led two others of the Nighty Knights along the road over to the camp. At the entrance, he was met by a pair of soldiers who were expecting him. Some awkward greetings took place, but eventually, they all made it inside the camp. The soldiers didn't seem to know how to react to the Nighty Knights. It was an inadequacy a lot of people shared.

People just had to remember they were children. Children who were also elite warriors on a holy crusade against dirt, but children nonetheless. What was so complicated about that?

The small group walked through the camp, slowly getting used to each other. It was lucky that the children were easily impressed, at least. In particular, they loved to stop and watch the construction. In fact, at one point, they stopped the whole tour to spend half an hour watching a main beam be lowered into place for one of the large command buildings. The event seemed to make the soldiers even more confused.

I understood the children's amazement, though. The mess of pulleys and draft horses used to maneuver a beam weighing thousands of pounds into an extremely right space was quite fascinating. A few other times, the children wanted to stop and watch some other interesting thing, but the soldiers eventually lost patience and reminded them that Arthur was waiting to meet them. I was just glad that they hadn't tried to get in the way of the builders or tried to help them. That would have been dangerous.

Arthur wasn't really waiting for them too much. He was in his office trying to keep up with paperwork. That man never had enough time for everything he needed to do. Ever since the apology to Susan, he had twice as many scouting reports to deal with.

While Beatrice tried to help off-load the work onto other people, Arthur insisted on doing a lot more of it himself than he probably should've.

If this kept up much longer, I would have to have a talk with him. He was a more capable commander than this, and he had taught me a lot about delegating, so I knew he could do it. My hypothesis was that this was his version of penance. I could tell from the whole ordeal that things still had a long way to go before they were fully repaired, but at least they were going in the right direction.

Eventually, the tour ended, and the Nighty Knights made it to the command center. Arthur stood to welcome the little representatives of the castle. "Hello, honored knights."

Bradley and his companions returned the greeting with a bow and equally formal speech. "Thank you for your hospitality, General."

"I heard that the three of you have a proposal for some activities we can do to further strengthen ties between my men and the castle," Arthur elucidated as he gestured for them to sit in the offered chairs.

Bradley nodded as seriously as his little face could manage. The effect was lessened somewhat as the Knights had to physically hop to reach the chairs. "We do. See, recently we celebrated High Priestess Bee's birthday with a series of events and competitions. Outstanding performances were awarded with prizes from Void itself. I was thinking that since we had so much fun with that, maybe we could do something similar here. However, I do not think we will be able to impose upon our Lord for the prizes. But the idea of day passes that you and High Priestess Beatrice have been considering would be a ton of fun!"

Bradley's brow was pinched from maintaining such formal and unnatural speech for someone his age for so long. He did slip up a little bit at the end, but I was proud of him. He had been repeating that set of words for almost two days, constantly muttering it under his breath, trying to make sure he sounded just like the adults that he would be talking to. I hadn't helped or corrected him in terms of what was necessary for his speech, as it seemed to mean so much to him. But it was nice to see.

Somehow, Arthur was able to maintain his composure despite the overwhelming cuteness radiating off the very serious child soldiers. I had to repress a slight squeal to make sure that my presence stayed unnoticed as I watched from above.

I technically wasn't supposed to be here. Probably. The Knights were proud of having a real responsibility for themselves, and my presence might make it seem like I didn't trust them. Still, I worried about my charges, and I wasn't going to let them enter an unfamiliar camp alone without some experience. But as long as no one knew I was here, I was sure it wouldn't affect the outcome either way.

Arthur took half a second to compose himself and ensure he maintained his mask of seriousness before responding. "Excellent. Sounds like an interesting proposal. So you propose a fighting tournament involving some group, maybe a squad or platoon, in which the winners receive day passes. I do like that. It rewards competence and the effort men put into learning how to fight.

"My concern is that it would be the same people winning each time. How do you think we should make it so that while the best are rewarded, it's not always the same victors? Otherwise, you might as well just give them permanent passes, and that wouldn't achieve the main goal of getting the people familiarized with everyone else."

Bradley took a minute to think about this and looked over at his companions to see if they had any advice. Luckily, the little girl sitting to his left did. "Well, that's easy. We just have different games."

Bee withdrew a list of events that she had tucked behind one of her stacks of paper. It was something that a lot of the Nighty Knights had helped her brainstorm, and she had also taken some input from Captain Major. The proposal she had sent to Arthur with Bradley had gone fairly well, and so he had asked for specifics.

She was sure that Arthur had already decided on the events he actually wanted, but having the Nighty Knights and everyone contribute was more of an exercise, a way to help them feel involved.

After reviewing the list, she took care of one more quick task. Pulling out some pieces of paper, she designed what a day pass would look like and drew up a quick fifty of them.

It only took her a few minutes, but she was relatively certain that no one would be able to match the precision and detail she put into creating each of these without significant hours' worth of forgery. Just to be safe, she also made a registry for the passes. That would hopefully help the guards to make sure that only people who were allowed to come in did. It was probably overkill, but according to Arthur, little traditions and things like this were built into the culture of a military or any group of people. Susan begrudgingly agreed.

While the castle had their own culture, they'd have to integrate with a force much larger than their own and somehow not get swept away. Controlling things like this, where her culture at the castle and that of the refugees would not get overwhelmed, was a great way to ensure this assimilation went smoothly. The soldiers would end up at least open to the idea of following Void rather than turning the castle into just like any other support base.

She was glad that Arthur had thought of this idea first. On her own, she certainly wouldn't have known how to carry it out. To be fair, Arthur didn't either, but he had enough experience with worse solutions that the commander had a few ideas of how to improve on them. Personally, she was looking forward to seeing some of the soldiers' tournaments.

While the Nighty Knights' duels had certainly been exciting, professional soldiers were bound to have more experience under their belt, and it would be interesting to see how differently they fought. Even though she out-leveled them, she had no illusions that there was nothing to learn from people who'd been doing this as a career for so long.

The idea, though, that some soldiers would choose to challenge some of the Nighty Knights for slots was very interesting. The Nighty Knights hosted a few afternoons of open challenges where soldiers interested in earning a day pass from them could come and try their hands. Then, based on votes, the Nighty Knights would pick the five most worthy candidates to have access to the castle for the next weekend.

However, the Nighty Knights had some of the wildest ideas of what constituted a challenge. What's more, they had apparently taken Arthur's point about ensuring different victors to heart. So, the variety of challenges they had planned was quite impressive. Bee thought that many of the soldiers would come more for the show of watching their comrades make a fool of themselves rather than actually participating.

Still, it would be good. As it was, the castle was a bit tense, worrying about the soldiers and the changes they stood for. A few people had left the castle to spend some time in the camp for a few hours at a time, but it had always been a little weird. They weren't fully comfortable in the camp. Not to mention that everyone was too busy for ideal conversation; it was all hands on deck to get everything built before the next snow. Bee shuddered remembering all the clean up that had followed the last time it snowed. That was a disaster and a half. No one wanted a repeat of that event.

They had made significant inroads with the families and the

camp followers who were not professional soldiers but still accompanied the army. They also weren't allowed in the castle freely, as there were just far too many of them. But she could feel some lines of faith connecting out to them already.

Bee leaned back in her chair with a sigh. Things were coming together. She just needed more time.

CHAPTER 52
PLAY FIGHTING

BEE LOOKED OVER AT ARTHUR, watching the man's worried expression as the two combatants stepped into the ring. The first was a little girl, Irene Chadwick. Bee suppressed her smile. She was sure that no one else knew what was coming. Arthur's worried frown just deepened.

The commander's expression was mirrored on the other combatant's face. The soldier's grizzled exterior, complete with a prickly beard and nasty scar along the cheek, would have identified him as some sort of rugged bandit in most stories she had heard. But the hesitation and disapproval radiating off of him spoke of one with young children of his own.

He shifted his grip anxiously on the hilt of his sword, looking at its blunt wooden blade. Trepidation filled his every movement. Bee couldn't blame him. Going up against a four-year-old girl seemed excessive, even if they were using practice swords. Not only that, but these men probably didn't understand the reality of these kids' power.

The number of children who had earned levels before they were ten was vanishingly small. As impressive as it sounded, the achievement was usually due to some sort of traumatic experience as opposed to intentional training. What parent would make their children kill so young, after all?

That was not the case with the Chadwicks or any of the Nighty Knights. They had all gained power through the direct intervention of a god. Little Irene Chadwick was especially blessed. At least, she was if her "God-Touched" title was to be believed. Not to mention that her first skill was quite broken. Since the festival, she had even reached level 10 and received her second skill. However, Beatrice hadn't seen her use it yet.

Her theory was that Irene had gotten a variant skill, and that each progressive level in skill choice didn't offer her new skills but simply upgrades to her base skill. These variants were rare and unusually powerful. As Irene grew, she would become even more specialized and deadly, but the soldier would just be a soldier.

Sure, he was ten times as old as Irene and had at least double her level. And the physics of having a larger frame, longer reach, and years of experience fighting had to count for something, right? At least, that was what Arthur was telling her. Bee would have agreed, usually. But the element of surprise was not to be underestimated.

The referee called a start to the match. The soldier rushed forward with his guard up, aiming to finish the fight without harming his opponent. But he moved quickly, likely to avoid his comrades teasing him about fighting a little girl. Irene, though, simply bowed her head and prayed. The massive, ghostly figure of Void appeared behind her, seemingly larger in size since the last time Bee had seen it. With a fluid movement, its claw smashed down toward the man.

Still, the soldier had some experience, and that wasn't to be discounted. Bracing the blade of his sword against his gauntleted left hand, he raised and blocked, not catching the strike but deflecting it off to the side. A look of shock flashed across his features at the sheer force. From what Bee could tell about the skill, it wasn't based on any physics or magic innately provided by Irene. It was simply based on the strength of her Faith. And since Faith was by far her highest stat, even the glancing blow had a ton of power behind it.

The angle of the soldier's block forced most of the momentum to veer to the side, but the recoil still drove him to one knee. But instead of trying to rise, the man dove forward and rolled. The quick reaction was the only thing that saved him from the second attack.

Another claw materialized out of nowhere and smashed down into the ground, leaving a crater where he once stood. The appendage then vanished back into the floating disc behind Irene.

Irene hadn't even opened her eyes to redirect the attack, but it had nonetheless honed in on her opponent. Bee grinned over at Arthur, who was muttering something under his breath.

"I think you're going to have to do my paperwork for a week," she taunted.

Arthur grimaced, clearly regretting the friendly bet she had baited him into. He didn't seem like a gambling man, but he couldn't say no to the challenge in front of the men who would be fighting. Showing so little faith in his own soldiers would probably have been too demoralizing. Plus, the stakes weren't too big of a deal. It was probably just him being a little short on sleep.

Her focus returned to the spar just in time to see the second part of Irene's ability; a blinding light flared out from behind her, silhouetting her. A long blue beam of magic shot out, scorching the ground at the feet of the soldier and making him jump back. At the same time, the claw swept down toward him.

The soldier had no choice but to take the full brunt of it on his sword and shoulder. Luckily, Irene had apparently accounted for this, or at least her prayer had recognized that she did not want to kill the man. Instead of slamming him directly down, it came at an angle and sent him tumbling out of the arena. He landed among the steadying arms of his friends, who ringed the sparring circle.

The grizzled veteran climbed to his feet, panting. On all sides, he was showered with deriding mockery from the other soldiers as they helped him up. The referee declared the spar over by knockout.

"Yeah, yeah. Laugh it off," the man called to his detractors. "I want to see any *two* of you go against her."

No one took him up on that challenge. Meanwhile, Irene walked back over to the waiting group of Nighty Knights. Words of praise and a few claps on the back greeted her before her brother swept her up in a big hug, spinning the tiny girl around. Her girlish giggles floated across the arena and drew a collective "awww" out of the crowd by her very cuteness.

Bee couldn't blame them. She really was adorable. Getting used to dealing with these children had taken her a long time, as they were far too adult in some ways. But unlike her, they hadn't lost their childlike innocence. While they had tough training under Void, they never truly felt alone. They were never scared. They were never saddled with more than they could bear. And despite having power, they wielded it responsibly. Well, most of the time.

"I guess I do owe you some paperwork, Miss Bee," Arthur sighed, shaking his head. "If I had known what a monster that little girl was, I don't think I ever would have taken that bet. Morale be cursed."

Bee just laughed at him, and he continued. "Where did you find her anyway? That skill bears a striking resemblance to Lord Void. She must have quite a story."

Bee shrugged. "You'd think so, right? But it's not a story any different from ours. Void cares for the children, though. We think it's one of its Domains. Void looked over a lot of the orphans from Greg, even the ones who had mothers. That's where all the Nighty Knights came from."

"So this is just a consequence of Void's training?"

"Yeah. Well, mostly. Void just took them under its wing, taught them the sword, and ran them ragged while playing with them.

They got their first levels and classes from dropping rocks on undead, though. I think all the cleaning Void had them doing got them a lot of experience after that."

"Hmmm..." Arthur mulled over the information.

"It seems that anyone who holds Void in respect and worships it gets experience from that sort of stuff, as I'm sure some of your soldiers have started to notice. Especially If you take the class that the system offers related to Void. There's been a few variants I've seen that have only increased those effect. All these children are examples of that."

"So what you're saying is, I have good reason to politely decline any future bets."

"Yeah, it's probably a good idea," Bee said with a laugh. "I do appreciate you taking the loss for this one. I believe it was important for building excitement and maybe a little bit of rivalry. I hope your men will take losing to children well."

Arthur shrugged. "They'll have to. We have to face reality at some point, no matter how absurd it seems. Besides, they want to learn anyway, right? This will just show them what Void can do for them."

As they set up for the next bout, Bee considered the encampment around her. While building the first settlement had been exciting, things had started to slow down. Most of the main buildings were constructed, and everyone was in generally good shape and prepared for the next snow. In fact, according to Arthur and a few of the lieutenants who Bee had talked to, this was the best camp they'd ever made. The strong foundations they'd laid before they really planned out the permanent buildings made this more of a small town. A town was what Void had indicated, and thanks to Arthur, it was finally becoming a reality.

The next soldier to face one of the Nighty Knights was significantly more wary than his predecessor. No hesitation or concern about fighting a child lingered in his gaze. Bee was glad because the elder Chadwick stepped forward to meet this challenge. While she had seen the Nighty Knights' power before, it was something she had to remind herself of frequently. And it was impossible to remember that without remembering the finals of the birthday competition. It hadn't been little Irene with her terrifying avatar who won. It had been Bradley Chadwick with his impeccable sword skills.

The Nighty Knights let out an excited cheer as their champion took the field. The soldiers followed their representative with laughs and mocking taunts. Bee noticed that they were primarily from those who hadn't agreed to fight for a weekend pass.

The ticket system was working out better than anyone had hoped. The competition for the chance to break the daily grind of work and training motivated the troops well. At the same time, the castle had reported no problems with the visiting soldiers. They mostly just came and worked, talked, or traded with the members of the castle. In fact, they worked harder than they likely would have if they'd stayed back in their camp. But more than anything else, they relished the chance to interact and enjoy the food Mary and her staff whipped up. They were all rather boisterous after being chosen for the weekly excursion.

A few of Arthur's men had been shy or reserved, but the children's and residents' general friendliness had pulled them out of their shells. By the time everyone left after dinner, there were usually great relations and promises of future visits left behind. Bee had also noticed a growing bond in her spiritual sense from the soldiers who visited. This faith in their god only strengthened as they walked amongst their fellow soldiers. After just a few weeks of this, Bee started to see that spread to soldiers who had never even visited. The faith they showed was slightly different and less personal, but the strands remained.

Each and every one of those people was marked to her. And perhaps it was just her imagination, but as she watched them, she swore she could see them slowly make an effort to embody Void's ideals. They were slightly neater. Their armor was better cared for.

Even the angles at which swords hung on their belts seemed a little less haphazard. But who could really tell?

Bee blinked. Bradley was already walking away from his defeated opponent. Bee had apparently missed the fight in the brief time she was thinking.

CHAPTER 53

A GOOD SHEPHERD

ARTHUR CLAPPED Bee on the shoulder. "That boy is a terror already."

She nodded in agreement as Bradley stepped toward his fellow Nighty Knights. "He is. He's one of their best."

"Is that so?" Arthur mulled his next words over. "I'd like to spend an afternoon training with him. He's already quite solid on swordplay. I'm not sure how much I can teach him there. But there are some more general lessons I think he'd benefit from, especially while he's young. I expect there's not many warriors in the castle he can look up to, are there?"

Bee shook her head. "Not really. Aside from your men, most of our adult fighters would lose against him."

"All the more reason, then." Arthur nodded. "He might need someone to learn from. Someone who actually *can* beat him in a fight. Without that...well, at this rate, he might outpace me soon, as well. I worry that he won't *need* to listen to anyone then."

"What do you mean? He has Void to learn from."

"Well, that is true," Arthur said, choosing his words carefully. "Void is a bit...distant...from regular human affairs. Sometimes, people learn best from their fathers. I can't claim to be a perfect teacher, but I have raised three sons." Arthur's chest swelled with pride. "And from what I've heard, Bradley might be missing a bit of a father figure."

Bee nodded, wondering where this was going.

"Well, I can't step fully into that role, truthfully. Despite how much I wish I could. I think maybe having a couple hours with him sometime next week isn't out of the realm of possibility. I'd be curious to see how it goes."

Bee nodded. "Well, I can't speak for him, honestly. You'll have to get his mother's approval, but I'll pass along your offer."

Arthur nodded. "Of course. If she's okay with it, I'd like to make some time to talk with the boy and maybe have a match of my own. I'd say you can recognize someone who will grow into their power rather well. And I'd like to get to know the kid better."

Bee just nodded, thinking. Had she really gotten to know any of the Nighty Knights? Sure, she'd had good interactions with Felix and Tanu and many of the others, but to her, they were just children. Rather annoying children at first. Before Void had made her see them in a different light, she wasn't even really aware they had personalities of their own. She'd have to change that. Despite how much she and Arthur bonded over whining about paperwork, they would have much free time over the winter. Perhaps it was time again to take a more personal approach to the Church. While she had the chance.

I soared above the castle, streaking through the sky as the first rays of morning peeked over the horizon. I practiced my direction changes, darting to and fro as I approached the tall mountain in the distance.

It had been quite a while since I had last gone and visited Daedalus. Between cleaning up the snow and helping the Nighty Knights design challenges for the soldiers, things had been busy recently. We made sure to make them particularly difficult. After all, my followers in the castle were special to me.

But I finally had some time to myself. Even better, I finally had an idea of how to thank Daedalus for his help with the birthday presents. Besides the other half of the energy I had to give him, of course. Plus, I felt a little bad about leaving him alone for so long. Fortunately, I didn't think he'd mind the extra days too much. If he had been sitting there for tens of thousands of years, he must have been incredibly patient. Either that or his sense of time required some retuning. He did mention that time passed differently for a dragon. Something about immortality and patience.

It only took me a little bit to reach the top of the mountain. I zipped into the cave eagerly. The snow up here was perpetual and more solid than the stuff at the castle. Based on the mountaintop's whiteness, even during summer, perhaps it never melted.

Well, at least it was cleaner when it wasn't being trudged through and mucked about by humans. I couldn't really blame them, though. They had to get around somehow, and not everyone could fly. Something I pitied them greatly for.

I called out a greeting before I entered the cave. Daedalus gave a snort, which I interpreted as a welcome. The massive red dragon was evidently resting on his mountain of disorganized gold.

His toothy maw broke into a wide grin as he saw me. "Ah, Spot, my friend. I'm glad you're back so soon."

Examining the dragon's great wings, I saw they were straight and unbent, though there were still some faint tatters on one of them. I congratulated him on his recovery, and he flicked his tongue out nonchalantly. "Nah. 'Tis but a scratch. I've had worse. Did take a decent amount of energy to heal from, though. I only just woke up from the nap a couple of days ago, honestly. So it's good you came by now."

I expressed my relief at Daedalus's health and inquired if he was ready to receive the second half of his energy.

"No, not yet. I think perhaps in a week or so," Daedalus said, disappointedly sighing. "I would like to gain some more levels, but if I took it now, a lot of it would be wasted. The stuff would go towards healing the last of this wing. It'll fix up by itself soon enough."

I beeped in understanding.

"So, what have you been up to, little friend?"

We settled into a comfortable conversation about what I had been doing in the valley. Daedalus occasionally chuckled at the humans' antics or asked questions about the castle. Eventually, the conversation came around to why I was here in the first place.

Digging into my dustbin, I brought out my gift. I had intentionally only kept it in there for a short while to avoid whatever magical contamination I tended to impart on things. Daedalus was extremely powerful. I imagine it would have been unpleasant to eat something that had gained magic powers. Besides, I was worried about it changing the taste. That would have made Cassy upset.

The pies she had won her award for were fruit- and berry-based, but I wasn't exactly sure what dragons ate. Judging based on their teeth, they weren't like the sheep or humans, who enjoyed eating plants. I didn't see how the fibrous quality would work with the sizable jagged teeth, so I asked her to make a meat pie. Apparently, there were a lot more kinds of meat pies than I had expected, and it had taken a little bit to settle on a nice shepherd's pie.

Some freshly butchered mutton, potatoes, and many other unfamiliar ingredients had gone in. I was interested in cooking to the extent of providing for my humans, but it wasn't my calling at all. Kind of like Beatrice's alchemy. Still, it was impressive to watch. I had great fun observing all the spices combined in ways that left me entirely confused about their purposes. There were many times that I was confident that humans wouldn't be able to detect such minute differences in the composition of a dish. Still, I was assured that every step was necessary.

Daedalus reacted immediately as I removed my offering from

my dustbin. A gale of wind was pulled from the mouth of the cave as he breathed in with his nose. "Hmm. That smells heavenly, my friend. Did you bring that for me?"

I couldn't help but chuckle inwardly at the avarice in the dragon's tone as he attempted to peer nonchalantly at the steaming pastry.

The pie was freshly baked this morning. In fact, that was the main reason I had left the castle so early. I thought that asking Cassy to make me a pie was a fairly standard request, but it had caused much hullabaloo in the castle as she immediately dropped what she was doing and went to fulfill it. It was a bit excessive, and I tried to explain that there was no rush, but she was insistent about making me one immediately. At least it meant the pie was fresh.

I held it aloft with my Air Manipulation. Slowly, I floated it over to him, but as his tongue started to dart out from his scaly maw, I decided I had teased him enough and let him know it was indeed his.

With the confirmation, Daedalus's eyes flashed. The dragon's neck stretched forward, bringing his great head toward the tiny pastry. Rather than snatch it up whole, he showed some admirable manners by licking up a single morsel. Daedalus closed his eyes in pleasure as he closed his mouth, savoring the taste.

I couldn't say I fully understood the sensation. I'd seen humans react similarly to tasty food, but I just didn't get the same pleasure from it. I had tried vacuuming it up a few times, but it felt the same as anything else. I supposed it might have been the same feeling I would get after cleaning a dusty room, but it didn't quite match the level of contentment I was observing.

This show went on for some time. Nearly sixteen minutes later, the ceramic dish was thoroughly licked clean. I couldn't even tell that it had ever held a pie, even with my Advanced Sensors. It was pretty impressive, really.

"That was excellent." Daedalus sighed contentedly. "Worth every last morsel. Thank you, friend."

I indicated that it was no big deal. It was the least I could do, considering everything he had done to make Beatrice's birthday so magnificent. He suggested he'd do it all again for another dish like that.

Eventually, I found that neither of us would concede the point, so I decided to change topics, as I had already given my gift. I pulled out a deck of cards borrowed from the library. His eyes lit up. Not to the same level as when he'd smelled the pie, but he seemed to recognize the item. "I haven't had a good game of cards in at least ten thousand years! I wonder, do you think they're the same as I remember?"

He motioned for me to lay them out on the floor. And so I did, spreading them out into a neat grid all face-up. In ascending order by suit and number, of course. The dragon scanned them. "No, they're very different. I don't remember there being four suits, but I suppose I can learn. So, do you know any games?"

Daedalus nudged the card forward with his claw, and I flinched as I was forced to drop one card from my hand back into the pile before us. It had been a low-probability move, but I had gotten unlucky. This game was far more interesting than the ones I had played with Beatrice. Solitaire was my favorite, but the unpredictability of the cards was interesting.

"I can feel Archibald slowly returning to consciousness," Daedalus said as he made his next move. I asked if he had any idea how long it would be before Archibald awoke, and the massive dragon's shoulders heaved up and down in a very dragon-like shrug. "Not really. His progression isn't linear. It could be a couple of weeks. It could be a year or more."

Daedalus didn't seem to really care how long it would take, he just cared that it was going to happen. And by his timescale, it seemed like it would happen any minute now.

"Did I ever tell you why Archibald got that way?"

I replayed the scene Beatrice described from her understanding of the events. It was vague, but involved an army of humans fighting a demon. I took some artistic liberties with the carvings from the catacombs. Images of the hero statue underneath the earth and some catacombs being built to protect the site followed.

Daedalus watched the slideshow with a sad look on his face. "I suppose I haven't. I don't know the whole story, to be honest. Doubt anyone does nowadays. Well, what you have is mostly true, at least, but there are a good deal more details that you're leaving out."

CHAPTER 54

ORIGINS OF AN AGED DRAGON

DAEDALUS NESTLED into the impressive pile of coins at the center of his lair. The comforting weight of the cold, soft coins made him feel better most days. But today, it wasn't working.

The dragon huffed. Cragheart would never have bested him if he had been playing fair. Stashing rocks at the center of your hoard to make it look bigger was simply not right. Why, it went against the whole principle of the thing! It was a mantra that Daedalus had repeated to himself often in the past century.

Even though he was sure that his hoard was larger and worth more, it didn't stop Daedalus from picturing the heaping mounds it *could* be. If only he, too, cheated a tiny bit.

Sighing, he considered whether it was worth making his way out of the mountain heart to find more gold. It had been slim pickings for the last few millennia. Not even the dwarves had managed to mine more of the precious metals for him to steal. Not since the demons had invaded.

The situation was truly a trying one. Evangelina had nearly gone crazy and tried to mine gold herself. It took the intervention of the council to stop her from further damaging the pride of all dragons in her desperation. A dragon digging in the earth? What an embarrassment. When he had carved out the tunnels and caves from his own lair in the mountain, he had used magic to control the magma tubes, as was proper. Even if the walls themselves glittered with precious gems and ores, he wasn't going to sully his claws digging into them directly. That was what the lesser races were for.

A beep pulled Daedalus from his reminiscing. He blinked down at his newest friend. The little godling flashed some images above his little disc.

Humming, Daedalus shifted slightly, letting the rock in the back of his cave scratch an itch. "You could use magma to sterilize floors, I suppose. But it sounds like far more effort than it'ss worth. Now, where was I...?"

Daedalus debated internally about what to do. Should he go see if the demons had made progress in having their slaves mine gold? Yet as he thought, echoes of footsteps reached his ears. They were too heavy to be from an elf and too slow to be from a dwarf. A human, then? Why had a human come to deliver himself as a snack? They usually had the brains to at least come in large groups, if they came at all.

As the lone human rounded the bend, Daedalus closed his eyes and feigned sleep. The surprise and fear when the little thieves found out the dragon they were sneaking by was awake the whole time was his favorite part. When he was young, he realized that even the elves couldn't tell if he was truly sleeping. Now, he almost always pretended to be asleep when he had guests.

A faint smell of iron and rust wrinkled his nose as the human approached. The human seemed already hurt, which would ruin his fun. Besides, blood loss always made his snacks taste worse.

When the human stopped several wingspans away, Daedalus considered pouncing now before the snack lost even more blood. Before he could, the thing spoke. "Hello! Dragon, are you alive?"

What kind of question was that? This human had to be insane. Or maybe he knew that if Daedalus was alive he would be eaten anyway, and just wanted to get it over with? Stifling a sigh, Daedalus didn't respond, waiting to see if the human would start trying to take his gold.

"Excuse me?" the human called again, more loudly. "I'm Archibald. I'm looking for Daedalus, is that you?"

The human was *looking* for him? That was new. Rearing up, Daedalus fixed the intruder with his Dragon's Penetrating Gaze of Fear. It was one of his favorite skills, and freezing his captive audience was always satisfying.

"WHO CALLS FOR ME?" Daedalus's roar echoed through the tunnel network. The wind of his shout ruffled the human's long hair. As he waited for a response, Daedalus evaluated the human. He appeared to be a scrawny male. Shoulder-length brown hair waved, framing an altogether forgettable face. One hand was clasped to his side, and blood welled between his fingers. The whiff that Daedalus caught made him wrinkle his nose again. Blood really was disgusting.

"Yes, Spot, humans do taste good, but blood is disgusting. No, it's not because it's liquid. Casks of ale are liquid but also delicious. I think it's the red color, perhaps. I'm not a huge fan of wine either, but the sight of that doesn't make me feel dizzy the same way. Oh, I agree wine is the worst. Now, I was waiting for Archibald to answer..."

The man worked his jaw as if he had something wedged in his teeth. He held up a hand to Deadalus and spoke, nearly shouting now. "Wait a second before you say something else, sorry! I think my eardrums burst and I can't hear anything right now!"

The audacity of this human! How dare he not hear a dragon's mighty words? The man had to be properly cowed by his might and power! Daedalus waited indignantly as Archibald unstopped his ears.

"Are you good now?" Daedalus growled at the insignificant human.

"I *was*." He winced, giving me a dirty look as he worked his finger in one ear.

"Come on, I was *way* quieter that time. Are humans really so fragile that I could have incapacitated them just by *talking?*" Daedalus kept his voice nearly to a whisper. It didn't have quite the same effect, but he would put as much regal authority into it as he could muster.

"Okay, that's better," Archibald said after some time. Daedalus hesitated to say anything more. Should he just eat this uppity human? Walking into a dragon's lair and calling out to its owner was surely a crime. Only curiosity about his purpose kept Archibald from being the latest snack.

"Why has such a bloody meal delivered himself to me?" Daedalus asked in his most considerate yet powerful whisper. The hair on the human only slightly moved this time.

"So you are Daedalus, then?" the human asked, seemingly without fear. He continued on before Daedalus could answer. "I thought you would like to know that a demon army is marching on this mountain as we speak."

Daedalus frowned, and finally, Archibald showed some reaction to the many teeth in the dragon's maw. Demons had known better than to bother the dragons for a long time; why were they bothering him now? "Why should I care, human?"

The human in question blinked. "Uh, Aren't dragons territorial? I didn't think you would like an army coming at you. It seems disrespectful."

Dang it. The human was right. It *was* disrespectful. Daedalus decided he would have to do something about this. Grumbling to himself, Daedalus got to his feet. "I will burn you to a crisp if you touch anything, human. Stay here so I can eat you later."

Archibald swallowed and nodded. With confirmation that his hoard was safe, Daedalus lumbered through the tunnel that led out. When he reached the surface, a few beats of his wings sent him soaring into the sky. Looking below, he found that the human didn't lie.

There was a small gathering of familiar mud huts at the base of the mountain. Before it was a vast sea of demons and their slaves. Had the humans been trying to protect the huts? If so, coming to him was stupid. Those ugly things were as much of an insult as the demons were. With a deep inhale, he blasted the mud with a jet of flame, baking it. Continuing his flight, Daedalus billowed fire into the demonic army and watched in satisfaction as they scattered before him.

A few more passes, and he could go back and eat his snack. Then he could take a well-deserved nap. As he wheeled around in the air to break the rest of the formation, Daedalus saw not all were running in fear. A lone demon that stood twice the height of a human stood in his path, shield held high. Large black horns swept back from its head, ending in deadly points.

Not in a million years would Daedalus back down from such a challenge. He braked in the air and let a concentrated stream of dragon's breath pour onto the shield. As the edges of it started to melt, Daedalus felt a pang of concern. This was taking a lot more effort than he had wanted to put out.

With a crash, Daedalus landed, snapping his tail and wings forward to knock everything away. The demon tossed its ruined shield aside and shouted up at the majestic dragon. "You do not keep me from my prey, lizard!"

Snapping his jaws forward, Daedalus ate the top half of the demon. The thing's flesh was bitter and ashy; only his pride stopped him from spitting it out right away. The demon was remarkably stupid if it thought it could speak to a dragon in such a manner. He was much too weak for that.

Beating his wings, Daedalus took to the sky again. The army retreating below him had already taken too much of his time, so he winged his way back to the mountain. Inside his treasury, he found Archibald remarkably waiting for him. Eyeing the man up and down, Daedalus made a decision. "A smart man would have left when he had the chance. At least you didn't disturb my gold."

The human looked around. "I suppose I could have left." He

rubbed the back of his head. "I didn't think of that. Whoops. Are the demons gone?"

"Yes, they were most disrespectful," Daedalus said. "For the warning, I will offer you one boon. Choose wisely; this is not an honor many humans have ever received."

"A boon?"

"Yes, a boon. Don't push it too much. I will eat you before I part with my hoard." Daedalus was already regretting his offer. It was what his pride demanded of him, but he could already tell that it was going to be a pain to deal with. The human would probably ask for something incredibly dumb. Blood was still running down the human's side, and it was making it hard to concentrate as the room began to swim.

Turning his head aside, Daedalus dug through his hoard as the human considered. He came out holding a delicate necklace with a brilliant green gem, grasping it gently in his lips. Whipping around, the gem smacked into the human's head and faded slightly.

"Oww!" Archibald yelled as he grasped the side of his head and glared up at the dragon. Daedalus didn't pay it any mind as his nose picked up the lack of fresh blood. That calmed him down, and the cave around him stopped spinning.

The human looked down at his side and frowned. Poking at it with his bloody hand, he looked confused.

"You are trying my patience. Tell me what you would ask." Archibald winced and covered his ears again. Daedalus didn't really feel bad about not modulating his volume this time. Maybe it would get this annoyance out of his lair sooner.

"I want help fighting the demons," the human said.

"I already did that," the dragon answered.

"I want more help fighting the demons," the human clarified.

"I—fine," Daedalus agreed with a sigh. At least the human didn't ask for a certain amount of help; he could just do something small, and it would be done.

"Yeah, the demon army was just the start of it. Spot, I think it's

your turn. Ah, good move. Hmmm. Let's see how you deal with that! Well, of course I wasn't going to carry the human to our destination, that would be beneath me. So I had to figure out alternate transportation."

CHAPTER 55
REBEL WITHOUT A CAUSE

"I'M NOT sure how you plan to get all the way up north," Daedalus said to Archibald. "Francis is way up in the mountains and at least a day's flight. Are you sure you don't want my help more locally?"

"Well, you can fly, right?" Archibald asked, confused. He looked at the dragon, as if wanting a ride, but Daedalus chose to ignore that.

"Yeah, but you can't," Daedalus pointed out the obvious. Archibald wisely kept his mouth shut. If he had been about to suggest that Daedalus carry him? Well, the man wouldn't leave the cave.

Archibald looked around as if searching for a pair of wings he could borrow. "I really would like to get back to Francis. My father is there and I don't want to see it burned to the ground."

"Wait, what? Then why do you need my help? What do you expect me to do about taking care of some rebellion?" Daedalus asked.

"The city is almost in rebel hands, we just need some support to keep the armies off."

"So, no burning it to the ground? It would be easier to take care of the rebels if I just burned the place to the ground." Daedalus supposed that he could just be intimidating, but that would be much slower than just annihilating the city and going back home. There was no guarantee the rebels would come out so he could eat them, and he might have to burn the place down anyway.

"No, we aren't going to burn the city we spent years trying to take! That would make the rebellion a waste," Archibald said. "Besides, the demons don't care if you burn the city down."

"Why should the demons care?" Daedalus was now thoroughly confused.

"Well, they would rather have their slaves dead than in control of a city. If we can free this city, we can start gathering an army and fight back," Archibald said.

"Oh, are you the rebels, then? I thought this was your city." Daedalus was starting to understand.

"My city? Humans don't have a city. I don't think anyone but the demons do," Archibald said.

"'Really, none at all? I knew that gold had stopped being mined, but I thought that was just because of recent fighting and whatnot. The demons don't seem to care to get more, not like the other lesser races," Daedalus said. Archibald looked at him strangely.

"What fighting? The demons have always controlled all the cities."

Daedalus pointed to some of the more decorative pieces of his hoard. "You think the demons made this? What about that? Have you ever seen the demons make anything this beautiful?"

"No... Maybe they made a human do it for them?"

"That axe was made by Ironheart Forgehammer, first king of the deep," Daedalus said proudly. It really was a rare piece, and one he was proud to have liberated from the ancient dwarven treasury.

"Never heard of him...?"

"Never? What about Smith Smitherten? He carved this chalice from the highest rock of Mount Heaven-Touched."

"No?"

"Balder Bouldershoulder—"

"Nope."

"You really know so little of the dwarves?"

"Dwarves? Aren't those just myths?"

"Just myths!" Daedalus exclaimed, forcing Archibald to cover his ears again. "JUST MYTHS?!"

"So...they aren't myths?"

"*Sorry, Spot. No, I don't know if any dwarves survived. There might be some deep underground, but I haven't been looking for them. Yes, their arts are amazing, but I don't know anything about how they were done. I think it was mostly system-based racial magic. Sure, maybe once Archibald wakes up we can go questing for them. That would be great fun.*"

Daedalus returned with a very grumpy griffin clutched in his claws. He could have made the catbird fly behind him, but it was better to put him in his place the proper way.

"Is this really necessary?" Griff cawed from below. "I would have followed you without complaint, your shiny eminence."

"Yes," Daedalus emphasized, but he didn't deign to explain more.

Once he rejoined Archibald where he had left him, Daedalus released his new underling. Intimidating a flock of the birdbrained cats into agreeing to send one of them to help him out hadn't been hard, but dealing with their incessant squawking was barely better than lowering himself to carrying a human he didn't plan on eating. At least he'd only needed the one.

Archibald fell back onto the rock he had just stood up from.

"A griffin!" he shouted unnecessarily.

Archibald was a natural flier. Even as the griffin tore through the sky at breakneck speed just to keep up with the dragon's languid wingbeats, he kept his composure. The human only whooped with joy on the occasional dive Daedalus made to watch the herds scatter beneath him.

It only took them a little over a day to get to Francis. The city was already partly on fire, making Daedalus feel as if he had wasted his time coming here. Archibald didn't seem to agree. He eagerly pointed down to the demon army nearing the city gates. "Them, we need to get them!"

"We? What do you plan to do?" Daedalus asked, knowing the human couldn't do anything much in this situation, but the lack of respect was starting to get to him. His patience for the human would only go so far. The favor he had done the dragon was only so much.

Archibald seemed to interpret Daedalus's meaning well enough as he quickly changed tack. "Uh, can you please do something about that army?"

"Of course." Daedalus's words were almost lost to the sky as he tucked his wings and dove at the army of demons and their slaves below. With the sun at his back, the waves of arrows launched in his direction were so far off the mark that they were no more than a joke. A few hundred feet above the ground, he let loose, and streams of dragon fire drenched the army.

Everything ran before him as was right and proper. Everything but one figure. A demon much larger than any he had seen before stood in his path and laughed. The dragon fire merged with the demon fire already dancing along the beast's shoulders.

Daedalus pulled up Scan and assessed his enemy.

Name: Nazareth'gak, Race: Lieutenant Demon, Class Type: Demonic Torturer, Titles: Butcher of Rasputin, The Scourge, Devourer of Dreams, Bane of Humanity, Age: 789273, Level: 70

Strength: 192837
Intelligence: 5
Constitution: 9081
Dexterity: 12347
Charisma: -237
Perception: 80
Will: 28739
Faith: 9999999999999999
Magic Defense: 90873:
Physical Defense: 123784091
Regeneration: Inf

Daedalus harrumphed. That was annoying. The worthless demon was at a higher level than him. And older, somehow. This was not okay. He would deal with it later. Soaring around, he continued routing the army. They fled before him, and the city continued to burn.

In his peripheral vision, Daedalus saw Archibald direct Griff down to the city. Hopefully, he could get whatever errand he had taken care of while Daedalus cleaned up the army.

As he was causing a platoon of demons to retreat into a nearby lake, a sudden impact struck his side. Of course, whatever it was didn't penetrate his scales, but the force of it tossed him sideways through the sky. Daedalus spun with the impact, and the motion threw off a weight that had attached itself to his left hind leg.

Daedalus watched as the laughing form of the Lieutenant Demon fell through the sky and splashed into the lake below. How dare it! Just as the demon resurfaced, Daedalus snapped his jaws shut, skimming over the water. Straining his wings, he pulled out of the dive and bit down hard on his foe as he climbed higher in the sky.

It was an effort for his teeth to break through the demon's natural armor, but the bite force of a dragon wasn't to be underestimated either. Slowly, the pressure overcame the demon's defenses, not allowing the regeneration to take effect.

Several thousand feet in the air, Daedalus finally broke through, and the demon started tumbling to the ground in two halves. That would show it what it meant to laugh at a dragon. Perhaps Daedalus would have to call the council to meet and discuss this issue. If the demons didn't learn their place, the dragons would have to teach them.

Daedalus dove to go back to terrifying the army, but as he made it to the ground, the same Lieutenant Demon shot out of the crater left behind by its landing. The impact of the diving dragon and the rising demon sent a shockwave through the sky that leveled trees for miles all around. The walls of Francis rattled but miraculously didn't fall.

Daedalus shook his head, his eyes watering from the pain in his nose where the demon's fist had landed. That stung!

They clashed several more times. More often than not, the demon was damaged, but that never slowed it down for long. The unthinkable was slowly happening. He, a red dragon, was taking damage. If this went on much longer, he would have to flee.

After one exchange sent the demon flying toward the horizon, Griff showed up with Archibald on his back. "The city is lost," Archibald said, "but we are mostly evacuated! If you can redirect the demon's attention, we can get into the mountain and slip away."

Daedalus acknowledged this, doing his best to keep his flight steady despite the several tears in his wings. It would be good if they would just be able to get away; he wasn't sure if he could win this fight anymore. Not that he'd ever admit it.

As the fight resumed, he stopped trying to destroy his opponent and instead forced him further south. The change in tactics worked in his favor. He was able to take less damage as he fought.

"The humans were able to get away that day. Injured as I was, I didn't make it back to my mountain. I needed a place to heal. Archibald was the one who found me, stayed by my side, and stitched my wings together. During the fight, he had reached level 50 and gotten an interesting class offering.

"Once he took a Companion class, we started to fight together. The humans grew at the same time they ran. The nomadic settlement soon had to split, but through us and other means, they kept organized, slowly freeing more and more people. The council took a decade to gather, but after my report, they didn't take the threat seriously at first.

"Many went to test the demons and the second council only took a year to regather. With one of our number dead, a decision was made. For the first time since the gods retreated, the dragons were going to war."

REACH FOR THE SKIES

DRAGONS GOING to war was never a pretty thing. It wasn't like the simple squabbles of the lesser races like the elves and humans. No, when dragons fought, it had consequences. Still, it took time and effort to convince the rest of Daedalus's kind to care, and the months of argument thoroughly wore him out. The roars of his kind had shaken the mountains, but eventually, everyone had seen sense.

When the decision was made, Archibald was waiting for him in a small fortress nestled in the entrance of the valley where the council was held. He had wanted to attend himself and plead the humans' case, but luckily, Daedalus was able to talk him out of it. That would not have gone over well. Dragons were arrogant at the best of times. In a situation like this, where they were being asked to do something, it was better for the request to come from one of their own rather than someone beneath them.

Also, Archibald wasn't likely to have survived the encounter anyway. One dragon was hard enough on the lesser races, as their terrifying presence could stop hearts. More than one dragon, though? No matter how well Archibald handled being near Daedalus, he was only human after all. Such a shame.

"Yes, Spot, I radiate terror. No, I don't suppose you would feel it.

Why do you think people don't come around here? The last few millennia would have been lonely if I wasn't able to just hibernate them away."

"I take it things went well?" Archibald asked with a cocked eyebrow. Daedalus was a bit jealous of the expression. It was beneath him to try and emulate it, even if it wouldn't have worked on his draconic face.

"Yes, well enough. They have agreed to spare one in ten acres," Daedalus said, sharing the good news.

"One in ten acres?" Archibald asked in bewilderment. "I don't get it. Are they going to war, then?"

"Yes, of course we are. We're going to do war properly, there's no point otherwise. That was decided in the first few minutes, though some did use it as an argument for lowering how much to save."

"Then why did it take you *months?*"

"We were discussing how much of the world we would leave unburned," Daedalus patiently explained. Even after spending so much time with the human, he was still surprised at how dense he could be. "It wouldn't do to leave a job half-done. However, we realize that you all need food and homes and whatever if you're to continue digging out gems and gold."

"How does that make any sense? What does burning the world have to do with the demons? Can't you just burn them?"

"Well, we need to scour the world to make sure none remain, of course. Anything we don't just burn would need to be searched thoroughly, and no one wants to do that. Much better to just raze it all."

Archibald just stared for a moment, expression blank. Eventually, he shook his head. "Dragons."

"Yes, we do like to clean up thoroughly. Leaving anything behind just causes more of a mess."

Daedalus soared through the skies, Archibald gliding along beside his griffin. Below, fields of scorched earth sent sheets of black smoke up in vile plumes, obscuring their vision. In the far distance, a black dragon wrestled with a white one, sending terrible screeches and jets into the air as they fought.

He steered clear of the dragon only by focusing on the human on his back. That kept his focus off the fact there was someone else fighting in his warzone and challenging him for territory.

Similar scenes were repeated all over. The horizon was simply cluttered with smoke and warring dragons. Over the course of the campaign, Daedalus had seriously wounded, driven off, and incapacitated three of his kin personally. While they weren't making great progress with destroying the demons, he was at least gaining a lot of status among his kind. In the next century, he might even earn a clutch of eggs.

As much as he hated to admit it, a lot of Daedalus's success was due to his champion. Having Archibald fighting alongside him gave him just enough of an edge that he could safely challenge anyone for battlefield dominance. That the next strongest opponent on the field was almost always another dragon wasn't his fault. This was *his* field, and he would raze it how he pleased.

Archibald didn't have the same view. "NO! We are going to the west!"

Daedalus growled in frustration as he tried to focus on his companion's voice. War was harder than expected. Dragons were irritable, proud, and totally incapable of constructing even the most basic chain of command, even in the best of times. Asking them to accomplish directed tasks while ignoring the chest-puffing of their kin was nearly unheard of.

Eventually, he managed to ignore his instincts to veer east and challenge Archimedes. They were rather close friends, all things considered, having just spoken yesterday. But once the battle started, that didn't really matter. He couldn't suffer another to challenge his magnificence. The gold dragon couldn't help but catch the light of the sun on his all-too-shiny scales, but that was no excuse.

Daedalus howled as a sharp pain on the tip of his nose broke him out of the rage. The dragon glared at Archibald and the shield that bounced off of his snoot. "Focus! You big scaly lizard."

Lizard?! How dare he! Daedalus felt the emotions return with a vengeance and a new target. The little prey animal dove out of the sky, barely avoiding the torrent of magic streaming out of his maw. Turning into the rising sun, Daedalus chased his prey.

As the airborne snack dipped and dove through the air, Daedalus spared no effort in unloading after it. Somehow, he missed constantly, but that didn't matter. He only needed one hit. The snack dipped closer to the ground. He almost laughed as it cornered itself and limited its maneuverability. Folding his wings in, Daedalus attempted to slam the pest out of the air with nothing but his body.

Smashing into the earth, a shock wave rippled out from him and rattled his teeth. What was he doing? Looking around, he didn't see the dragon who had been encroaching on his territory. That meant he must have chased him off. Daedalus huffed before throwing his head to the sky and roaring in triumph.

An annoying pain in his toe brought him down to earth. Ah, yes, the demons. That was what was happening. Spinning, Daedalus came to his senses enough to begin his actual task. The demons attempting to swarm him vaporized in an instant. The Earth demons' sand melted to glass. Air dispersed, and the water attempting to quench his fire boiled away into steam. Even the flame demons were but candles before his unstoppable might, consumed and incorporated into his own magic.

Daedalus ignored all these inconsequential enemies and laid into the Greater Demons, leading them. They were at least intelligent enough to avoid standing still. Only when an Archfiend arrived did Daedalus finally have to focus.

The Archfiend's claws actually scratched his scales. With enough luck, they might be capable of injuring him. That was how one dragon died, at least. A Lieutenant had gathered enough Archfiends and Greater Demons to overwhelm and wear the poor sop out over the course of days. What a weakling. He should have never let himself get cornered.

There was only one Archfiend here now, and Daedalus wasn't alone. Finally getting his wits back, he maneuvered the enemy around until a sword tip sprouted from its chest. Archibald then took its head with his second sword before kicking the body off of his blade. It took a little bit more effort and time this way, but the human needed the experience anyway. Besides, it wasn't like a level 50-to-60 opponent was going to be too much for Daedalus.

The two of them regrouped and looked around. He didn't take to the sky again so as not to clash with any of the dragons nearby. If he was hunting and he saw their forms on the horizon... Well, it was best if he stayed on the ground. Of course, that only made their task that much harder.

Despite numerous clashes, they still couldn't take down a single Lieutenant. One by itself wasn't quite enough to match a dragon, of course, but they didn't have the same problems with teamwork. Several times, right as they seemed just shy of overcoming the seemingly endless regeneration they possessed, a second one showed up to ruin everything.

The advantage they held was huge, but they refused to use it more than was necessary. Perhaps it had to do with the sheer numbers of the dragons, but the Lieutenants were rarely found together, and the Demon Lord hadn't even taken the field once. It was almost as if they were happy with the status quo.

Even though the leadership of the demons was still intact, the dragons were making good on their promise to burn 90 percent of the world. The potential battlefields were already shrinking, but the demons did nothing.

"Yeah, we didn't think of that until it was almost too late either. What? Why would mess makers want to clean the earth? What do you mean by mess makers? Ah, no, I don't think they would. But could you really consider that cleaning...?"

"Right. Let's stick to the plan." Archibald panted, wiping some demon blood from his cheek. "We need to corner one of these monsters."

Daedalus hated to admit it, but the man's idea was a good one. It was embarrassing to have a human understand dragon psychology better than an actual dragon. It stung his impressively enlarged pride yet again. But so far, it was working. Once they had secured the landing zone, they turned east and started that way on foot toward Archimedes.

It wasn't a fun journey. Dragons were not made for walking, and despite their near-impenetrable hides, their wings were the most vulnerable on the ground. Even with all his weapons, he still had to rely on his companion to keep them off his sides.

Archimedes was hopefully close enough to the human army that he would have support there, as long as he also managed to hold back his instincts. It was their best chance of getting two dragons fighting against a single Lieutenant rather than each other. If this didn't work, nothing would. It was several hours of near-constant fighting before the pair reached the human line. They were barely in time.

Daedalus's friend was doing his best to keep the horned Lieutenant Demon busy and away from the humans as the two armies clashed. Archimedes could only do so much, as his magic wasn't nearly as potent as a red's, at least not on the battlefield. The gold had much finer control, which was why they thought this plan had a chance of working. He was the only other dragon who might be able to stay on task long enough for Daedalus to reach him on foot.

Despite the limited power of his magic, he was still a dragon, though, with all the advantages that came with it. But against all odds, the demons had persevered. It was time to take this annoyance down.

The Lieutenant didn't even notice the *massive red dragon* sneaking up from behind it with how engrossed it was in its fight. When the red's fire engulfed it, it finally realized the problem. The griffin took Archibald high in the sky, and after the first few exchanges, the demon tried to escape up there as well.

"Oh, how that rankled. We are the kings of the sky, kings, Spot, and we dared not follow it into our own domain. Not if we didn't want to turn on each other."

Its escape was short-lived, however, as the human spiked it back down to the ground. It was close, but Archibald was finally coming into his own after years of power leveling. At least enough to *move* one of the Lieutenants, even if he couldn't face one alone.

CHAPTER 57

BOUND FOR GREATNESS

THE BATTLE LASTED FOR DAYS. Long after both armies had retreated or been annihilated, Archibald, Archimedes, and Daedalus continued to battle the Lieutenant. It wasn't a close fight, exactly. The only reason there was any problem at all was that regeneration. Every single time they thought they had it, it came back faster than they could believe.

Daedalus sent a jet of dragon's breath forth, completely enveloping the demon. The trio stared, panting as they watched the Lieutenant's cinders settle to the earth. Eventually, they sighed, turning around to leave. Archibald barely managed to bring his blade up to catch the sudden slash coming toward his side. The force of the impact sent him flying off into the distance, and the battle began once more. The two dragons had a difficult time pinning the Lieutenant down long enough for the human companion to return.

After such a long and intense experience, they were clearly running out of steam. Daedalus and Archimedes could fight for longer, of course, mighty dragons that they were. But even they wouldn't last forever. Not to mention that Archibald was only human. The Lieutenant didn't seem to have any limits to its energy, however.

At one particular lull in the action, the demon stopped and grinned at them. A dragon stood on either side while Archibald's griffin circled above nervously. After a moment, he spoke.

"I have to thank you all." A raspy voice emerged from the dark figure. It sounded like a rusty cleaver being dragged along jail bars. "After all, you scaled lizards are doing my master's work."

No one knew how to respond. Daedalus looked between his friend and companion in the sky. A frown creased his brow. Doing the demon master's work? What did it mean? The demons didn't *do* anything besides move humans from place to place in herds.

Eventually, he snorted. The thing was probably lying. Probably. Unless there were things that the dragons didn't know.

Archimedes, however, seemed to take greater offense at the insult and used the time to plan something. Webs of golden light spun out from his maw as he roared a challenge to the demon's insolence.

The webs were flung forward, and as the center of the net struck the Lieutenant, it began to wrap around it. The Lieutenant grunted, bucking and thrashing, but the webs held tight, binding its legs together and its left arm to its side. Daedalus was about to engulf it in Dragonic Inferno when Archimedes shouted a warning. "No! Wait."

He barely bit back the fire. The spell was *working*. It was merely binding their foe, but still. Daedalus didn't want to risk burning away the magic with his own. Not when Archimedes was still focusing on maintaining it.

The demon managed to get its feet underneath itself, but was clearly struggling. After a few seconds, its arm successfully slithered up and out of the spell. Daedalus could see the strain written in Archimedes's tail position and how he held his wings. This was costing the dragon, costing him more than was wise. If the demon got out, they might have to run. Archimedes might not be able to fight anymore.

Suddenly plummeting from the sky was Archibald. The man had leapt off his griffin, his sword arcing down deep into the shoulder of the Lieutenant. The arm fell to the ground, another one immediately beginning to grow in its place. But that took precious seconds, and the demon roared, swinging at Archibald. He managed to just barely deflect its blow. Daedalus tried to think of something, but his magic wouldn't help here. Attacking with his wings or bashing with his tail would just as likely hit Archibald as the Lieutenant. So he crept closer, waiting for his opportunity.

Just as Archibald was dipping down to duck a massive haymaker from the newly reformed arm, Daedalus turned his whole body, whipping his tail. It snapped quite painfully as it broke the sound barrier before smashing into the Lieutenant's head, pulverizing it. The body fell limp, and Archibald dove on top of it, driving his sword through the demon's chest and into the ground below. Archimedes reared back, and another set of golden webs wrapped around the Lieutenant.

Slowly, they wound around the Lieutenant, and the sword pierced through. But as Archibald tried to climb off of the demon, he grunted in surprise. One of his hands and one of his feet were stuck. He yanked and pulled, but his limbs were bound to the Lieutenant with a power well beyond his mortal strength. Daedalus looked at Archimedes frantically. "Get him out. Release him!"

Archimedes immediately started to unweave the spell, but Archibald yelled, "No, this is our chance. Bind him more!"

"No, Archibald. We need to get you out. We can't risk it."

"We can! Once you've figured out how to kill him, you can release me. No way we'll get a chance like this again! We need to bind him!" Archibald yelled at his friend.

Archimedes looked sadly toward Daedalus for instructions, as the red was the dominant of the pair. Daedalus felt conflicted. Destroying the Lieutenants was their goal here, but it seemed further and further out of the realm of possibility. This was the closest they'd ever been to actual progress. The dragons were becoming quite frustrated with the issues of their campaign, and the scorched land soon would blow past the 10 percent mark if they didn't have any way of winning. Otherwise, they'd scour the earth of demons and everything else to maintain their pride.

"Oh, they're stupid," Daedalus told Spot. "Stupid pride. Yeah, I suppose I am a bit different than I was back then. I've had a lot of time to think." The little godling was resting on its own small pile of coins, which Daedalus had shoved toward it for the extended story. It chirped up at the massive dragon as if it were a hatchling. Along with the sound came the picture of the statue of his old companion trapped below.

"Yeah, we had to bind him, but we never did figure out how to separate him enough to wake him up alone. We managed to physically separate him enough that we could put them in different spots, at least. I would not have my companion stuck for so long with that monster. But they were spiritually bound as well. Their states were entwined."

Above the godling, a new image appeared of interesting representations of dragons that didn't quite look right. They all had a bit too much of Daedalus himself in them like they were palette-swapped copies of himself instead of anatomically accurate. The dragons flew forth, releasing the human and demon before fighting the demon ten on one until the demon was rebound.

"Yeah, we considered that, but it just wasn't feasible. The risk was too high." Daedalus waved the suggestion off. "Especially not at the start. And these things are wily. If it was able to think while in stasis, well...it would probably be ready to bolt as soon as we let it out. Catching one for a second time would be a hard ask, now that it had felt the spell once. Of course, at the time, we were just happy to get the demon out. But after that, the war changed. Now, we had a purpose. We had a drive, a path to victory. But our enemy also had fear."

The demons didn't behave the same way after that. If anything, it was harder to get the next one because Archibald couldn't lure Daedalus away from fighting the other dragons. So the dragons walked with their thunderous footsteps, following armies across the earth once they got anywhere near a battlefield. The prey drive when they were flying was just too high, and the territory was just too tempting. So the dragons slowly waddled across the land, destroying everything in their wake. As much as they grumbled about it.

The demons were more mobile in some ways, but their armies were not. It only took a few complete annihilations of massive armies to put real fear into them. They were destroyed in such a way that the rank-and-file demons weren't just banished to their other dimension but consumed, their magic repurposed to fuel the dragons' growth. Hatchlings were reared on just the essence of demons, and dragons prospered. But they didn't forget the humans.

At least, Daedalus didn't. His friend was stuck. Trapped with the first Lieutenant they had bound. And he didn't let any of the other dragons forget it. As one of the most active dragons throughout the entire first half of the skirmishes, he had gained enough power that none opposed him to his face. And he always managed to gather several dragons who he could force into the conflict alongside him. Archimedes didn't feel bad about getting Archibald stuck per se, but came as close as possible for a dragon to showing remorse. And that was saying something. It made it easy to recruit his help for further bindings.

While they fought on, each demon was eventually forced to stop and defend their armies and interests, whatever they were on this plane. Slowly, they began to be bound. Individually at first, but then in twos and threes as they tried to work together. But this only forced Daedalus to bring more dragons for support.

Archimedes refined his capture spell and taught it to other dragons. Soon, even human mages would line up in the thousands, circle around their battles, and slowly give their energy and life force to power the spells.

Eventually, the dragons prevailed. After a final epic battle, the Demon Lord was banished from this plane, and Daedalus was finally able to return to his hoard. With his dragon's fire, he built Archibald a tomb, carving it deep, deep into the rocks below. The base of the rock was heated so much that it turned to white glass, serving as an altar to his companion. Thus, he rested in his petrified state under the dragon's watchful eyes. Thousands of elves and humans worked to build structures within to further honor the great hero.

Slowly, they covered the first layer and then began to bury it. Above him, they put defenses. Many thousands of the warriors who had fallen in the final battles were entombed there. Powerful wards of defense were placed on their bones so that they could defend their greatest hero. The human martyr. Above that, a few hundred years later, a castle was built to defend the Lieutenant himself and give a place of pilgrimage for those who would come to pay their respects.

After that, Daedalus didn't care much. Apparently, some human order was created, and extra defenses were placed around the demons. But he found a nice cave up in the mountains and migrated his hoard there slowly, piece by piece. Until he was left to watch over the castle, waiting for the demons to come back. After all, the spell wouldn't last forever. They all knew that. But it should last long enough for the dragons to take a nap.

They still had to bury their dead and rear younguns to replace the many dragons they had lost in the conflicts during and after the war. Daedalus didn't stick his nose in. He'd already proven himself to be the greatest. But one day, his human would be back. When the time came...he'd need to catch another griffin so they could go have another adventure.

CHAPTER 58

SHOOT FOR THE MOON

THE LOUD SNIP of scissors echoed over the camp. Bee held them aloft before the cheering crowd as the red ribbon stretching across the entryway fluttered to the side. Feet pounded on the newly cobbled streets throughout the camp as citizens of the castle and soldiers all rushed to be the first into the stands.

This was the first major project completed by the army since the construction on the camp had settled down. While the simple, rough longhouses for the men were certainly important, they weren't nearly as exciting as a colosseum.

Bee was grateful for Void's wisdom in requiring good roads. She was also grateful that it'd agreed to Arthur's suggestion for a formal training area. But its reasoning for building a massive structure like this was far beyond her. Still, they had built it nonetheless.

Void had provided a very detailed set of plans involving stacked, curving arches forming the base of the building and nesting upwards into smaller and smaller arches until each arch was only a dozen feet wide. Each level of the circle on the inside sloped further and further down into a massive round arena. The building was huge, and that was even after they'd scaled down the plans a bit.

Construction hadn't taken nearly as long as she'd feared. With how quickly everyone was leveling, their average person had many times the strength they should have. That, plus some help from Void and those blessed with helpful skills, meant that such an impressive project was done before the end of winter.

The whole thing was filled with stands and stone bleachers where people could sit, bring some padding, and lie back to watch the arena below. There were even special boxes part of the way up where food could be served, and the announcer's box at one end was somehow designed to project words all throughout the arena without any enchantments. Void had told her that was her box, and Bee couldn't help but feel slightly embarrassed and grateful at the same time.

The first spectacle was planned for tonight. A Nighty Knight-led tournament was going to take place, but instead of the traditional one-on-one tournament they had at her birthday party, they had something different planned. Felix had told her the kids were branching out when she'd asked him about it. Apparently, both Void and Arthur had insisted that learning how to fight was not enough. They had to learn teamwork and cooperation. They were broken into small squads of four, but could be combined into larger ones of eight or even eighty. The Nighty Knights didn't even number eighty, not yet.

It wasn't exactly mimicking the composition of the army, but it was close enough that the children had been going to the sergeants they knew to learn about marching in step and group tactics. Bee was sad to see that the childish games had only been able to take the Nighty Knights so far. Now they would be learning something closer to actual war. But at the same time, she was glad Void was preparing them. Even if it seemed grim.

She admittedly had limited experience in battle herself, with a few exceptions. However, she had seen others who did fight, and they did face their enemies like her or Void. The vast majority of people fought in ranks, as in war. They had to learn how to not injure the people next to them and how to hold the line, certainly valuable skills. It was only people like her and maybe Arthur or the champion buried under the castle who fought as individuals on a battlefield of thousands. Normally, for anyone of an average level, that would be a death sentence. But for someone who was double the enemy's average level, it seemed natural to be able to fight as a solo unit. She had no doubt that most people here could do that.

Several of the Nighty Knights were certainly on track to be such fighters, but depending on when conflict came to their doorstep, they might not be there yet. Even then, even if they managed to become an army unto their own, who knew what their opponents would be like? Maybe their opponents would be just as strong. Or maybe they would be split up to work with other armies. In either case, it would be useful for them to know tactics and be able to read the flow of the battle so that they could position themselves as needed. The soldiers, too, were working on practicing ambushes and other slightly atypical tactics, like constructing forts from nothing but their surroundings after a long day of marching.

The building wasn't the only change that Void had made when it had come back from its strange disappearance a little while ago. It came back in a particularly productive mood. Some would say it was concerned about something, but that wasn't anything anyone wanted to voice out loud about Void.

Bee joined Arthur on one of the viewing platforms near hers so they could speak without being overheard. As they watched the stands, nearly every seat soon filled. However, there was still time before the event, so many streamed back toward the concession booths.

"How is the integration going?" she asked Arthur.

He grumbled. "I think we're going to have to give up on fully integrating the forces," he said. "The scouts are just too different. They've been trained with their own goals and skill sets. I think it's better if we maintain the two forces separately. They do things differently enough that I think we can leave more traditional scouting to my men and leave the more clandestine work to Susan."

Bee nodded. "Makes sense. I know she really wanted to just be better at everything, but she was trained to do a pretty specific job, whether she likes it or not. And she trained her men to work like her rather than a traditional military scout."

Arthur agreed with a distracted grunt. "Yeah, the woman's a terror, but a normal military scout doesn't need to know how to infiltrate a city or mix with the nobility. But we're not just an army anymore, are we? We need to get the support that we would have received from the intelligence operatives the king employed. We need to have their equivalent. So I've been working with her.

"Earlier this morning, I think we agreed that we need to send out individual scouts to the castle. From the castle to various cities around the kingdom, along with other countries, if possible. It's going to take a while for her to train up replacements enough, but I think we can count on my scouts to watch the valley for now while they're short-staffed."

Bee bobbed her agreement. The idea of running a spy network was something that Susan vehemently denied they were doing, but there was no other way to describe it. The amount of influence she would be able to hold in any city, and the amount of information that her network would be able to provide in return, was nothing short of master-level.

"That new messaging system should help your men out a bit," Bee added.

Arthur nodded. "Right. That. I'm not even going to ask how Void came up with that."

The messaging system that Void had created gave Bee a bit of a headache. It was quite simple, really. Void had somehow enchanted sheets of paper so that, when folded in the proper manner and thrown from a high enough point, they would glide straight toward their labeled destination. The odd triangles quickly replaced the more unreliable and commonly used pigeon method.

The trickiest part was learning the folds for it to work. These pieces of paper had very low tolerances, and even a slightly imprecise fold could cause the enchantments to fail. But really, Bee's problem was that she couldn't understand how it worked at all. There weren't any enchantments inscribed in the paper that she could tell, unless they were inscribed so finely that she couldn't see them with the naked eye. The paper itself shouldn't even *have* magical properties, not with the materials it seemed to be made of. They were plain wood, not even fairywood or wyrmheart oak. Yet, somehow, these sheets did.

Void had tried to explain it, attempting for several minutes to detail how it took wood scraps and arranged them in particular patterns in a very, very dark place. She just couldn't grasp the meaning. It must have been more godly magic in his domain or system shenanigans.

"Still, we do need to set up a traditional pigeon station because we won't always have access to high towers in the field," Arthur said. "And we have a limited amount of paper."

Bee nodded. "Yeah. The castle had some, but a lot of the pigeons were lost when the college mages left. I've put a couple people on figuring out how to raise more, but it will probably be some months before they manage it, even with artificial conditions. Birds still have seasonal mating rituals and stuff."

Arthur nodded. "To be honest, I don't know anything about pigeons or bird rearing, so I'll leave it in their hands."

Bee laughed. "I don't either, but I hope they do."

"Speaking of animal handling, your boy Tanu is quite impressive. I'm not sure how he managed to control that wolf, but could you please ask him to stop scaring my sentries with it?"

Bee chuckled and shook her head. "I've asked about it before, but I can try again."

Arthur smiled. "Well, at least he keeps them on their toes. But if any of his new recruits start doing the same, I swear we're going to have to start giving pensions for heart attacks."

"His new recruits?"

"Oh, yes. Some of her litter have found friends amongst my

men as well. I think two soldiers and two other Nighty Knights have started to bond with the growing beasts. At least, I found them sneaking through the camp with them."

Bee's eyes widened. She had almost forgotten about the other wolves. How big were they now?

Arthur continued. "One sergeant asked my opinion on punishment for finding a wolf sleeping under a soldier's bed. Apparently, he had been buying extra rations for the pup and feeding it against orders. It was only when he had been late to a training session one too many times that anyone noticed. I told them that the man probably should just be transferred out of the unit and trained on his beast handling, but I wasn't sure what your thoughts were on that."

Bee shrugged. It wasn't really her issue. "Whatever you think is best. We never really trained Tanu. He just figured this out himself. So if he's going to help other people, that would be great. I'm not sure if they would fit in better with Susan's scouts or with your unit in your army."

Arthur shrugged. "They're kind of their own thing, I think."

"Yeah. Well, it's up to you," Bee said. She spotted a messenger waiting for her at the door and said her goodbyes quickly.

"Okay, we're ready to begin." Bee nodded in acknowledgment and stepped to the front of her box, clapping once.

The sound echoed throughout the entire arena. Slowly, the chatter died as everyone turned to look at her. "Ladies and gentlemen," she shouted in her best performative voice. "We have for you the spectacle of the ages as our opening ceremonies begin. Please welcome: the Nighty Knights!"

Bee was touched by how many people showed up to watch the much toned down children's event. Their enthusiasm wasn't at all diminished by the games instead of near deadly combat.

The crowd went wild as one of the gates on the side of the arena opened, and the children filed out in a double column. At this point, they barely gawked about at the cheering crowd, though there were a few suppressed grins among them. It made Bee proud.

They walked around the mazes and other obstacles set up for their games to stand at the center of the arena facing her. They knelt as one, looking not at her, but above her. She followed their gazes to see Void hovering over her shoulder. As one, they shouted. "Hail Void!"

CHAPTER 59

TIMES THEY ARE A-CHANGIN'

THE WARDEN FUMBLED the heavy iron key in his hands, trembling as he stepped into his study. His investigation had yielded results. Unfortunately. He had thought that he was the master of secrets in this place, but apparently, there were deeper machinations beyond even him.

He glanced toward the cage by his desk. Three pigeons. He'd have enough for three messages. He could only hope that they would do the job. Especially considering the threat of interception in the air or even at their destinations. Who knew if these recipients were already compromised?

Internally, he gave a dry chuckle. Ironic that, after all this business with Harold's nightmarish demon and Arthur's possession, he could only gamble on it being a huge misunderstanding. Regardless, he had no choice. He'd send the message anyway. He just hoped he wasn't opening up the kingdom to a worse invasion.

He moved quickly to the writing desk, pulling out the thin slips of paper even before he sat down. Scribbled messages filled the sheets in a rush. Harold glanced toward the door nervously as he rolled and attached them to each pigeon's slim legs. As he tossed the last bird out the window, he allowed himself a relieved sigh. Only a second later, there was pounding at the door.

The Warden looked around for some place to escape. He knew it was futile, but his instincts as an operative for left him searching for any outs. He had known that by coming here to deliver the messages, he would be giving up his chance to get away cleanly. But that didn't mean he was going to go easily. He had many, many backup plans, as any paranoid man must. Just because they probably wouldn't work here didn't mean they weren't worth trying.

Prying the window the rest of the way open, he flipped a lever hidden in the windowsill. A faint grinding sound echoed throughout the courtyard below.

He leaned out the window. What had once been flat wall now had an irregular pattern of bricks jutting out, each no more than an inch exposed. It was by no means an obvious change, especially from a distance.

He flexed his fingers, hoping against hope that his arthritis-riddled fingers would be strong enough for one last adventure. This was a risky exit to take. A decade ago, he wouldn't have even thought about it. But now? He wasn't sure if he'd have better luck risking capture and finding an escape from...well, whatever hole they decided to throw him in.

Swinging a leg over the sill, he reached with his bare toes to find the next hold. They touched on the granite below and nearly slipped. Dust from the crumbling mortar had shaken loose as he had activated the escape route.

Carefully, he rubbed his foot back and forth, clearing the spot before he transferred his weight over slowly. He knew it wasn't going to be enough. This escape was not exactly subtle. If anything, it would be better if someone had just stored a rope and tossed it down at this point. But the clever engineering of this solution had won him over when they designed the thing. Of course, the whole thing relied on him getting to the bottom to hide the handholds before someone else came in the room. And that was going to be a tough ask for him.

Methodically, he swept the ledges free of dust and climbed

down the makeshift ladder, his forearms trembling all the way. Just as he thought he had, by some miracle, made it down without being noticed, a guard's head popped out the window. His eyes widened as he spotted the Warden. "What the—"

The guard cut off as his captain yanked him back through the window. His quick reactions saved the man as the sill crumbled under him and almost sent him tumbling out the window. Dang. There went his hope to at least take someone down with him. The Warden finally reached the bottom, but didn't even bother to pull the lever to hide the stones once more. They'd already been spotted.

Reaching into another hidden compartment, he quickly wrapped a dark-green robe around himself. Unfortunately, time had taken its toll. The robe had a few holes in it, not quite covering him as well as it should have.

"I definitely got too soft," he muttered to himself. He had stopped maintaining these escapes a long time ago. After all, he never expected to actually get this desperate. It might've been a fatal mistake.

Darting away from the castle, the Warden searched for a crowd of people to slip into. He tried to blend into a group of passing merchants, but only a minute later, a firm hand on his shoulder pulled him up short. Another guard stood frowning at him. He'd been caught.

It was over. Unless he wanted to start killing relatively innocent guards, of course. This was going to be rough.

He raised his hands in surrender as additional guards approached to surround him. The Warden gave one final sigh of defeat at the sight. "I'll go quietly."

I hovered high above our fledgling city and gazed down upon it. The humans had been adapting well to the recent changes around here, and things were coming along nicely. That battle arena had lent a certain amount of majesty to the skyline. Plus, it did look quite impressive from above, even next to the monstrous castle. Other projects of a similar scale were being built all around the city for a variety of functions, such as defense and upkeep.

The biggest relief to me was our sanitation system, though. At first, they hadn't quite understood the idea of the cleaning wagons, much less why they should be housed in the center of the city instead of on the outskirts. Luckily, it only took one conversation with Arthur to get his city planners to see sense.

Now, a massive warehouse full of stables and wagons would house the workers and equipment for the city's sanitation workers. They'd go street by street, sweeping up any debris along paths, tidying up community areas, and generally keeping the place neat and tidy. Each morning, they would also go from house to house and empty the waste bins left out front. It helped to make sure that trash and the like would not gather in people's homes. At Trent's insistence, we called the group the Sweeping Society.

Of course, individuals were still responsible for keeping things clean as well. People took great pride in their homes and rooms being spick and span. It just helped to designate more formal roles and jobs among the people. It also helped to bring the trash to one place where I could get rid of it.

Once I had convinced them of the importance for such a group, the policies were implemented right away. The soldiers, as well as the people living in the castle who received similar waste disposal services, were quite happy with the operation. In fact, once people realized how many levels the people in these positions were gaining, it quickly became a sought-after position. It was a bit of a problem. Apparently Beatrice had to insist that they keep the pay high enough for a living wage. Otherwise, the demand for the position was simply so high that people were willing to pay the organizers to get involved. It was rather strange.

Instead, they implemented some sort of lottery and secondary reward system to designate daily Sweeping Society members. I was just happy that everyone was so excited about cleaning.

The other important but less noticeable improvement was underground. I wasn't much for digging through the dirt, for obvious reasons. However, the humans had a brilliant idea of moving all of their waste and sewage below the dirt and then moving it out of the city.

I was thoroughly on board with the idea and assisted them plenty of times. It was a difficult project. Between the sheer amount of stone they needed, the manpower required to excavate it, the fact that all this incredible infrastructure had to go underground? It made sense. So many times, I simply used my lasers to melt the dirt into something that would not leak. Kind of like how Daedalus had described using magma tubes. I was also very careful to scan the surroundings and make sure this filth did not flow into their drinking water. Instead, it flowed deep into the mountains, filling up caverns down there that likely could use the nutrients stored within the filth. Hopefully. If not, I could always go clean it up sometimes. But Trent's lessons on compost had stuck with me a bit.

Those products were less visually impressive than the battle arena, but I was quite proud of them. I was also proud of the Nighty Knights' performance in the arena. Ever since it had been made, they had been holding their weekly contests for castle passes there. So far, not one of them had made a fool of themselves. I was satisfied with their understanding of my teachings. The adult army they were training was doing okay, I suppose, but they really couldn't match the growth of the young children as they shot up in both levels and height.

I lifted further above the city, aiming toward the dragon's mountain. We talked regularly, even if our visits were usually on the shorter side nowadays. We did enjoy playing a game or two as well, but I could tell that often Daedalus just wanted to be left alone with his thoughts for a bit. My facial expression subroutines had adapted to the dragon's emotions. He seemed melancholy after thinking about his friend for so long, and I wanted to give him enough space to work through it. I could only imagine how upset I would be if I had to wait ten thousand years for Beatrice to wake up from a nap.

But I also didn't want to leave him alone too much. So, as I rocketed up to his cave, I let out a beep of greeting. The grumbling response came a moment later. "Hello, little godling."

I responded by projecting some text. "Hello, fat dragon."

Daedalus blew some smoke over my way with a laugh. "Hey, don't be like that. I'm not fat. You're just very little."

"Well, you are very large."

I was pretty sure this counted as humor. It was a promising attempt, at least. But maybe I'd have to reconsider my approach, as the dragon didn't laugh as much as my models had predicted. Perhaps something was off with my observations. Or was it something else?

Anyway, we moved past the greetings, and Daedalus and I swapped small stories to catch up. Mostly, it was me just telling him of the city forming below while he offered some advice about the cities of old. It was rare that he actually paid very much attention to them. Mostly, he just burned them down. But he did have some insights into how to build defenses against a giant monster from the sky. We didn't take a lot of his suggestions, as they were not very practical, but it was something that I had passed along a few times when I felt the need.

After the small talk, Daedalus made a face. "There has been something on my mind, little godling, truth be told. I'm not sure if you can tell, but something in the world isn't right. I can feel it in the magic."

I projected the image of a person shrugging, not able to understand what he was talking about.

"Yeah, I suppose you haven't been here long enough to really tell the difference, but the magic balance has shifted. Something's changing, and I'm afraid I have an idea of what it is."

I motioned for him to continue. "You see, beings of immense power draw magic in from around them, creating eddies and pockets and swirls of the energy of the cosmos. Between your actions, a Lieutenant waking up, and other things, it feels as though something's happening. Something big, for the first time in nearly ten thousand years.

"But there is another thing as well. Something besides what's happening here. Far to the east, actually. Something drew in a massive amount of power briefly, but it has since gone into the north. I can feel it. It worries me."

CHAPTER 60
A LAND BEFORE TIME

AS DAEDALUS and I emerged from the cave, I couldn't help but feel a slight thrill of excitement quiver through my bristles. I had been at the castle for several months straight now, and I was starting to realize that I had a taste for adventure. Being cooped up for so long was not as fun as I had thought it would be, especially with how seriously everyone took their cleaning responsibilities. The ability to go anywhere I wanted truly was a blessing and a curse.

When I approached Beatrice about taking an extended trip with my new draconic friend, she was surprisingly receptive to the idea. In fact, she started producing what people called "tears of joy," promising to protect the city and that my trust in her wouldn't be misplaced. It was reassuring to hear, though I wasn't particularly afraid of any threats showing up anyway.

As Daedalus and I flew north, great sheets of ice spread out below us. Additional snow-capped mountains reached toward the skies, though none were as tall as his. Soon, though, the landscape transitioned from frozen earth to a marshy swamp.

When I asked Daedalus about that, he explained that the ground beneath us was called a tundra. Now that the beginning of spring was here, the frozen ground had begun to melt and give way to budding plant life. The initial ice plain we saw apparently had to do with mountain shielding and weather patterns that I didn't really understand. Apparently, some magic was involved, too, but Daedalus wasn't entirely sure about it himself.

After that explanation, we flew silently for a few more hours before Daedalus spotted something else and perked up. "Ah, Spot, my friend. This is going to be a sight. Have you ever flown over the ocean before?"

I had not. What was an ocean?

"You've never even seen an ocean before? Surely you've heard of them?"

I mean, I knew they were large pools of water, but that didn't seem particularly noteworthy to me. Certainly not something worth celebrating or admiring.

Daedalus thought for a bit. "Well, let me tell you how we explain it to our hatchlings. A long time ago, among the void were scattered world gems. The most ancient of dragons fought over these gems, coveting them and their incredible shininess and warmth. That led to many battles across millennia, with my kin fighting or fleeing to seek other gems.

"This gem in particular was fought over quite fiercely. As the dragons grew in size and power, though, winners emerged. Seven earth dragons gained prominence and were able to more reasonably claim the gem as their own. They defeated the water dragons, whose remains cover the earth even today." Daedalus pointed below. "The land we fly over is the backs of these great earth dragons. As for the water dragons... Well, they form the oceans."

I beeped a question. "No, the earth dragons still live. In fact, they're still fighting even today. They've grown lazy and comfortable over their long lifespans. They move across the world so slowly that it takes hundreds of thousands of years for us to even notice their steps. But they seek each other out, and when they collide, their roars shake the world, their battles forming mountains. Then, when they retreat, the land splits apart and the ocean comes to fill the void."

I wasn't sure what to make of the story. The idea of walking dragons forming the ground below us seemed pretty unfeasible, though the general idea gave me some useful context. I remembered a brief image of a scribble from one of the very, very small humans back at home. It was a strange circle of blue and green. Perhaps it was attempting to depict these land masses separated by water, as Daedalus explained?

The dragon nodded as I projected the drawing. "Yes. That's not the right shapes, but that's the general idea. Splotches that are the backs of earth dragons poking up from the endless water. Up north of us, there is a great ocean. It's not nearly as large as some of the others in the world, but across it there will be another dragon's back. A continent, as the humans call it. We will fly over there to reach our destination."

I beeped my thanks for the explanation. "Of course. The ocean is a beautiful thing. You'll see the sunsets and the waves, and maybe we'll even see some leviathans of the deep."

Soon, something new appeared over the horizon. I recalled seeing something similar once before, on the way back home from Arthur's army. A sliver of vast, sparkling blue. As we approached, it widened and widened until it became clear that this expanse was far larger than I had expected.

We continued toward the ocean until the land below us gave way to azure water. My sensors indicated that not only was this wide, but incredibly deep as well. In fact, if I stuck my Mop in it, I doubted that I'd be able to make even a dent in the sheer volume of the stuff.

It made me shudder internally. Without the wonders of flight, I would have been very uncomfortable about all of this. Even now, the idea of plunging into that much liquid felt like my worst nightmare. I made sure to top off my energy regularly as a precaution.

It's a good thing that it was nowhere near any of my homes. This would be a nightmare to clean up.

As we flew across the water, Daedalus was quick to point out when massive dark shapes glided under the water below. Apparently, things *lived* under there. I shuddered at the thought. How did their circuits stay functional? Or, if they didn't have circuits, how did they breathe?

"Look. Look. You see those tentacles? That's a baby kraken." Daedalus excitedly gestured, pointing out a floating tentacle mass that was thrashing about on the water. "It must be stuck. Wait one second. I'll be right back."

Daedalus dove down and gripped a few of the tentacles in his massive talons. With a mighty beat of his wings, he slowly pulled the kraken until something seemed to give. Satisfied, he let the writhing mass sink back down underneath the waves in a froth of bubbles. How nice of him.

I saw another mass beneath the water, only a few dozen feet below the surface. I pointed it out as Daedalus returned to flying by my side. "Yeah. That looks to be like an island that's forming. I don't know the explanation for them, but sometimes islands will just appear. Apparently they come from molten rock that hardens or something. That, or it's a great turtle."

I just beeped, and we continued on.

A few days later, we finally saw land again. I was overjoyed. Sure, the place was edged with horrible sandy beaches, but it was something. But we didn't stop, even for such an important task as fixing one of the worst collections of loose debris and dirt that I had ever seen. It was all *wet,* to boot. I was glad no one had introduced me to such things before. They might haunt my background processes for a while yet.

Soon, those beaches transitioned into plains of long grass and then eventually some spotted trees. A few hours later, mountains rose up on the horizon. More than that, though, I felt something odd. A strange twinge picked up by my sensors, but unidentifiable.

Daedalus confirmed that it wasn't a glitch. "This is what I was talking about. The magic feels a little bit different. There was a slight draw of power from this area."

I probed my senses more thoroughly, and indeed, I could feel slight currents of energy being pulled toward this area. I asked if he had only noticed this recently, and Daedalus nodded. "Yes. I can guarantee it wasn't a thing until a couple of months ago. Even then, I wasn't exactly sure when it started, as it's been gradually ramping up. If it keeps growing at this rate, there will be significant consequences even over on our continent, and I'd like to take care of it before things get out of hand."

I considered what the castle would be like without magic. For the most part, everyone would be okay, but the healing potions and other alchemic ingredients we relied on for so much might not work so well. Could that mean we couldn't get more ingredients, or would the magical properties actually be leached out of the stored ingredients as well? Either way, that probably wouldn't be good.

At the same time, I thought about this trip. Travel alone had taken us quite a deal of time. Depending on how long this took, I was going to be gone for at least a week from the castle. Maybe more. I wondered how everyone was doing. Beatrice and the others had been doing an admirable job of keeping everything in order, though, so I wasn't too concerned. I knew they were worried about a response from the kingdom, but that probably wouldn't happen soon.

Setting my worries aside, I continued on.

Bee worked alongside Maranda in the laboratory. Today, they were attempting to research a new type of potion that would allow for long-range communication. They were essentially trying to combine Felix's telepathy skill with Void's paper messengers, if such a thing were possible. The new messenger service had given her the idea of improving communication even further, but being able to mimic that with conventional magic was more difficult than she had thought. They simply weren't having any luck.

Right as she was thinking about calling it quits for the day, a soldier knocked on the doorframe and stuck his head in. "High Priestess Bee, Arthur requests your presence in the command hall."

Bee waved in acknowledgment to the man. "Tell him that I'll be right there. Just need to clean up. Did he say how urgent it was?"

The man nodded. "Yes. The highest priority, ma'am."

He gave a sharp salute before he left to go deliver the return message. Bee frowned. Highest priority? There hadn't been any major incidents that she was aware of in a very long time. Nor did there seem to be a large commotion. She couldn't help but wonder what the issue was. They were preparing for the thaw of spring, but they wouldn't expect any sort of conflict with the kingdom to start for at least a month after that. So they should have time before anything major showed up. At least, that was the going theory.

But with Void having gone off on its own travels, she was a little bit worried. She was glad that no one in the castle seemed concerned that Void had abandoned them, but she also wasn't sure what their god was up to. It was a little presumptuous, but having been with Void nearly constantly, it was a bit disconcerting to have it away again for more than a day. Still, Void had entrusted them with defending their home. They couldn't disappoint it. That didn't stop her from sending her thoughts to her master, though, wishing it would return if they did, in fact, need its aid.

Finishing her cleanup, Bee then made her way over to the exit of the castle and out into the city. The city was massive, already several times the size of Caleb. At least, it seemed that way, based on the size of the outer wall being built on the nearest ridge around the castle. The wall wasn't filled in yet, so they would have room to grow, but she didn't doubt they would fill the city in no time, especially with Void's blessings.

The city would completely enclose the castle eventually. The wall was the first thing they started working on after the amenities of the initial camp were done. The layout of the place was a little bit complicated, though. There was the castle as an inner sanctum, then the soldiers' initial camp further out. Past that were all the military buildings and other amenities they had created. These two adjacent circles formed the two city centers.

As they continued to grow, Arthur had started to develop a defensive project that would enclose an entire section of the valley, with one massive wall blocking off both the city and the castle from the forest and surrounding area. That left a secondary place where other things could be built, and the city leaders had decided that they would expand into this area for housing and public areas. After all, they'd need them once the families of the soldiers and Caleb's citizens arrived.

Bee took in the sight of their budding city as she approached the newly built command center. With a tired sigh, she stepped toward the entrance.

CHAPTER 61

SPRINGING THE TRAP

WHEN BEE STEPPED into the room, she found she was not the first nor the last one there. Arthur, Mary, Susan, and a few of the military officers were there, but Trent and a few other captains had yet to arrive. Mary waved Bee over, and Bee gratefully joined a spot at the table next to her.

The conference table had actually been a bit of a point of contention amongst both the military and the people of the castle. The military officers wanted Arthur to be at the head or the right hand at a long table. The castle and religious leaders wanted Bee to occupy a similar position. Arthur wanted Bee to be at the top, and Bee wanted Arthur to be at the top. With this tangled mess of various positionings, they eventually chose a round table where no individual took a place of prominence. An elliptical table had been an option, but had threatened to provoke the same issue. It gave Bee a secret bit of pride that the table was the same shape as Void.

The only thing that remained to be set was the ordering of a few spots. Technically, it wasn't a formally established rule, but Bee and Arthur always sat next to each other. Arthur sat to her right, and that usually meant that either Mary or Susan was to Bee's left. Other than that, the seats were more or less random. No one was forcing the officers and Bee's staff to mingle, but they also weren't segregated to one half of the table or the other, which Bee and Arthur were both very grateful for. It showed a willingness to work together that they hadn't been certain of while they were setting up their command structure.

"Do you know what this is about?" Bee asked Mary as she slipped into the chair. Mary shook her head, and Arthur jumped in before anyone else said anything.

"I received a missive from someone in the castle in the capital. But let's wait 'til everyone's here before we can discuss details. I don't want to have to repeat this, and it's important for everyone to hear it."

Some small talk dominated the table as people chatted about their families and the projects they were working on. Bee listened with interest, even if she was already aware of much of this. The wall was getting pretty close to complete. Apparently, a lot of the masons and engineers who had been working with the army had taken the lead from many of its combat-class members and also decided to follow the Church of the Cleansing Void. Bee was glad that her master was getting such recognition, but if anything, it was more likely overjoyed by how effective they'd gotten.

The ones she'd helped convert to Devotee had received rather unusual skills. One of the most common ones was Stone Melt, with which the engineers and masons could join stones together with no mortar and make them into a single seamless stone. Most of them had gotten skills like this while they were working on the battle arena or other large projects. But by the time the wall was started, only those with such impressive skills were allowed to work on it. The lead engineer was boasting to her about the thing's peerless beauty as the last member of the council made his way into the room.

"This is going to be the most impressive wall the world has ever seen, mark my words. It's going to be one solid granite piece that will be forty feet high and ten feet thick the entire way. The gate housing will be completely enclosed with stones. You could launch catapults and trebuchets at it for *years* before you break things down. Anything that isn't a high-level miner with the right tools won't be able to do a thing! I'll tell you, this might be the crowning achievement of my career. Nothing's getting through this wall. Well, maybe a dragon or some other ridiculous monster, but definitely nothing under level 50."

"What about over level 50?"

The engineer pursed his lips. "I'm sure you might be able to damage it if you tried, but please don't."

Bee chuckled at the engineer's backtracking, but she was still very impressed. This wall was fortified beyond anything she had ever heard of in all of her research. It wasn't just the construction, but also the amount of spellwork they had asked for around the gate housing. The materials used by her and Maranda to reinforce it would also help quite a bit. Still, walls were solid fortifications that could always be bypassed. Once the last engineer finally settled into his seat, the small talk quickly died out.

Arthur gathered everyone's attention by clearing his throat. "I received a missive from one of the king's advisors bearing news. Apparently, this advisor had gone rogue and is concerned. He warned us that military action would be soon arriving against our castle and that the king was likely mad."

Silence reigned over the council for a few seconds before one of the officers ventured a question. "As in, angry? Or mad as in insane?"

"Insane," Arthur clarified.

The soldiers shifted uncomfortably. Bee could understand why. Not only was the king being insane a major accusation, but an army arriving soon? They had been assured they would have until mid-spring at least to prepare for any sort of attack.

Arthur let the silence go on for a little longer before he spoke again. "Now, this is beyond our expectations. But there are a few things to be aware of. First, this would have been a very hard march for them. They will likely be exhausted and undersupplied, which will help us greatly. But right as spring arrives, so too will their supply lines."

"You expect an extended assault, then?"

"I can't imagine they are trying to storm us, but rather to start a siege. We will want to make sure we have enough forces outside the castle before they get here. That way, we can disrupt their supply lines long enough to make them feel the pain of a siege as well. Plus, with the wall in place, we should have plenty of farmland and skilled farmers to produce food for us. I'm not certain what their strategy is, but we will have options."

This made Bee feel a little bit better. At least they weren't completely caught off guard. Still, she felt a pit open in her stomach. They might have to do all this without Void unless it returned soon.

"Remember," Arthur continued, "we always expected some sort of attack. Even if the origins of this message need to be verified, it doesn't change the core of things. We can't be sure if the king is insane, either. But we know for certain he's definitely upset with us. As shown by our homecoming welcome at Caleb."

The officers all nodded, and one of them raised his hand. "How do we know we should trust this missive? This advisor is going against the king. Maybe he's simply trying to put us at odds even more?"

Arthur nodded. "He's an advisor that I have known for some time. He's rather clever and good with information, but I do believe his loyalty lies with the kingdom over the king."

They went back and forth a little bit more, talking about the believability of the message and more detailed preparations. But eventually, it came down to seeing for themselves. Susan stepped out of the room briefly and was soon followed by Captain Major as they arranged for scouts to be sent out. While they were gone, there was more argument about what to do if the king truly was insane, corrupt, or power hungry.

There were too many options for the source of this fracture.

Just because one advisor claimed something in a missive didn't make it true, even if Arthur trusted them. Bee had no idea about all that, though. She had never even seen the king nor been involved in politics. It reminded her too much of her father's type of work, so she didn't really care much, to be honest. She cared more about protecting her people.

She tugged on Arthur's sleeve, distracting him from the argument brewing around the table. "Are we prepared?"

Arthur grimaced and shrugged. "As much as we could reasonably be, but there is always more we can do. We probably should start working on drills. Preparing for wall watches and rotations too. We can start building more siege weaponry as well."

Bee nodded along with the assessment as Arthur posed a question of his own. "Do you think we can convince Maranda to give us some of those fireworks? They might make good ammunition for catapults and trebuchets."

Bee shrugged. "I can talk to her. I'm not sure how much more of those ingredients we have. We'll all work with her to figure out some alternatives."

Arthur nodded. "We are mostly prepared. But there are still things we can do."

Bee nodded. "Well, let's get to it."

Daedalus and I soared over the mountains, going east to west as we searched for the source of the feeling below us. I noticed many interesting things in the field of snow. Every once in a while, we'd see a small hut-like structure. It was incredible. I couldn't believe that anyone lived out here. Daedalus was unsurprised, though.

"People live everywhere," he said. "It's not just over on our continent. That one is almost entirely human, besides the monsters. At least, it was a thousand years ago. Maybe there are some more elsewhere. But on other continents, there are probably elves and other humans and stuff still."

I was surprised. I hadn't heard Bee talk about anything like that. But I supposed she might not know. Especially if travel between continents was as difficult and long as our flight.

As we moved to the center of the disturbance, the occurrence of such buildings increased. To call them buildings was a bit of a stretch. At first, I thought maybe they were just temporary shelters. But as I started to see groups of them, I noticed that they were actually collections of crudely built mud huts. The things were partially buried in snow, but even still, I could make out the raggedy thatched roofs and lumpy brownish walls. Quite disgusting living conditions, I had to admit.

Eventually, we came to the base of one of the largest mountains around. There, we spotted a cluster of huts that actually looked slightly planned instead of randomly scattered. It was still terribly messy, though, even if they were arrayed in mostly straight rows.

As our shadows passed over the structures, several odd-looking creatures ran out of the huts and began screeching up at us. They weren't people, exactly, but rather shaggy apelike creatures. We were high enough in the air that it was difficult to make out any details on them besides their general shape and the fact that they were furry. But even as we soared past, they tramped through the snow after us, yelling something. I beeped at Daedalus quizzically. "No, I have no idea what those are. New to me too."

I looked down at them and then back at Daedalus, uncertain about what to do. I flashed a message to him. "Should we go visit the snowmen?"

The dragon chuckled. "Sure. Why don't we go land and see what these 'snowmen' have to say? They better not attack us, though. I would not want to have to eat an entire civilization."

I thought about it. Yeah. It'd be best not to have to consume all of them. They couldn't all be mess makers, though, surely? Perhaps they were just misguided. I was sure we could work out some sort of peaceful solution. While they seemed agitated, they hadn't thrown stuff at us or anything. Perhaps they just wanted to say hello.

Finding a relatively flat outcropping on the side of the mountain, we glided down to make our landing. We waited there as the snowmen chased after us not too far behind.

CHAPTER 62

FUR AND FERVOR

THE HORDE of snowmen approached us like a flood of fur. There were far more of them than I had originally expected given my view from above. As they came closer, my sensors were able to estimate their numbers with greater accuracy.

There were far more than there should have been, considering the size of the settlement we'd seen. But the density of the pack didn't seem to slow them down, nor did I see any getting left behind. Each and every one of them was being carried forward in a tight wave of furry white bodies.

I also noticed that they were significantly larger than most of the humans I had seen, standing an average of 8.9 feet tall. Their hands were massive, each finger tipped with a claw. Their arms hung down far past their waist, almost to their knees. When they ran, they swung these long appendages, pumping them to add significant momentum to the run. They also used their arms to launch themselves across the ground or over a particularly rocky patch, and it seemed to speed them along as they rushed at us.

If this was a bunch of human adventurers or an army, I might have felt some sort of pressure. But here? There was no cause for concern that I could see. The threat of danger was quite low, really. Whether that was because of our power or the uncertainty of them being aggressive, I wasn't entirely sure. It didn't really matter. I trusted my background processes to warn me if I was in any real danger. Daedalus seemed to agree as we just waited for the tide of humanoid snowmen to reach us.

About a hundred feet out, the front of the pack skidded to a halt, throwing up snow and ice from the dirt as their toe claws dug into the ground. Not everyone seemed to get the message, and the back of the pack quickly crashed into the front, sending them stumbling several more feet. But eventually, they all came to a halt and dropped to their knees in front of us.

I chirped in satisfaction. They weren't trying to be a threat! That was nice. They were simply excited to see us. I hoped that meant they would be willing to listen, because they had so much to learn when it came to sanitary building practices.

There was a shuffling in the ranks of the snowmen, and a small pathway opened up from them as they parted. Slowly, a very small snowman who couldn't have been more than six feet tall hobbled towards us, leaning on a cane. She was the only one of them that had any decorations about her. A strand of seashells was strung around her neck, and they clinked quietly together as she made her way towards us.

Taking a closer look at the necklace, I noticed several of the seashells were cracked or just parts of ones. Considering how far away they were from the ocean, it must have been some sign of wealth to have them at all. When she was a dozen feet closer to us than the rest of the snowmen, she, too, went down to one knee. It was a slow process. Rather than diving down, she carefully used her cane to lower herself down before letting out a series of hooting, grunting syllables at us.

I swiveled my attention to Daedalus to see if he understood what was going on. He just shrugged, his massive scaled shoulders shifting as he resettled his wings. "Don't look at me. I don't speak...Snowman? You called them snowmen, right?"

I told him that it would take me a bit of listening to their conversations before I was able to develop a language model enough to translate. Right now, I didn't have nearly enough samples to understand them. But clearly, from the way they were staring at the red dragon, they recognized Daedalus. As what, and why? I wasn't sure.

As one, the snowmen went from their knees to bowing, their heads pressed into the snow. Slowly, the elderly snowman in the front reached up, dragged her seashell necklace over her fluffy ears, and gently laid it out on the ground before us before shuffling backward.

While I might not understand their language very well, it was clear to me that this was an offering and Daedalus needed no prompting. He lumbered forward. Each step shook the earth, and his scales rolled majestically, each one catching the light in a special way, giving his walk a shimmering effect. It felt like he'd practiced this particular stride. Kind of like when the castle cat Chester crossed the courtyard and knew who all the humans were looking at.

Whatever it was that Daedalus was doing clearly had some effect. Sounds of awe flowed through the prostrated group until Daedalus reached down with one talon and fished the necklace out of the snow. He looked back over his shoulder at me with a little bit of confusion in his eye. I could see his issue. There was no way for him to wear the necklace. It would not even fit over his talon fully, let alone his head. After a moment of hesitation, he slowly reached up and hung it on one of the horns over his eyebrow. The string of shells clattered as it settled off to the side of his head.

He did look quite comical, in my opinion, but I stifled my laughter. I was sure Daedalus would not appreciate the blow to his pride. The fact that he was willing to wear such a piece of decoration at all was unexpected, given the stories of his past. It didn't sound like something he would ever have demeaned himself by doing. Having spent so much time with Archibald must have really changed him.

Daedalus stood over the snowmen and breathed out warm puffs of smoke, ruffling the fur of the hundred or so still lying prostrate in front of him. He then grumbled a question at me. "What do we do now? This is not the first time I've been worshiped, but usually, I can at least understand what they want."

I had no answer for him, but the snowmen seemed to take his words as leave to get up. They were on their feet and dashing back toward their huts in a matter of seconds.

"Should we follow them?" I asked Daedalus.

He cocked his head. The seashell necklace swayed slightly. "I don't see why not, and it's interesting that they were gathered here near the source of the disturbance. I would like to know why. I doubt that was a coincidence. Perhaps they know something more."

I agreed. These snowmen must either have some legends about this place or some great sensitivity to magic and energy. The latter would've been impressive, as most of the creatures I had met so far had no notion of it. Even I was just beginning to pick those signatures up with my Advanced Sensors. We made our way after them at a more sedate pace, and every once in a while, some of them would look back and make sure that we were following. So clearly, they were trying to show us something.

Once we were in the snowman's camp, they led us toward the mountain. Daedalus had to walk around the village to get there, as there was no way he would fit through any of the gaps between the houses. But I stayed close to our escorts. Hovering around Daedalus, I wasn't paid too much mind. But as I separated from him, they looked at me curiously, as if only now realizing I was a separate entity from the giant dragon.

There was a large cave in the back of the mountain. Some of them picked up glowing torches. Looking closely, I realized that they were not exactly torches, though. Instead of fire, each tool featured a glowing stone that emitted a soft, even light. It was attached to the large stick with what looked to be vines and leather straps. Four of the snowmen and the old lady each grabbed a torch and walked inside the cave. I followed. But Daedalus had to stay outside and just stick his head in, as he was far too large to make it inside without damaging everything.

The cave was not too deep, only 103.45 feet from the entrance to the back wall, but it opened up into a wide and surprisingly regular sphere reaching all the way up to the ceiling. It was also covered in paintings. Not the crude paintings of the little humans, but not quite the detailed renditions of images that some of the more skilled, larger humans could produce. There was enough detail in them that it was still very clear what was depicted. A war.

On one side hovered had a giant dragon, along with many glittering warriors of various kinds. They weren't distinguishable as humans, but rather as some other sort of humanoid race with two legs, two arms, and scary metallic faces. Opposing them was a creature with giant batlike wings and a face made of fire. Surrounding it were more recognizable shapes of demons and other mess makers.

The torchbearers slotted their torches into the four cardinal directions inside the cave. Then two moved to the dragon and bowed before it, while another two bowed before the demon. Huh. That was strange. Did they worship both sides? Why? What could compel these creatures to do so? This explained why they held great respect for Daedalus, at least, but raised more questions. Especially since that demon wasn't one I was familiar with.

It didn't match the pictures of the Demon Lord that I had seen below the castle. But based on Daedalus's old tales, those were probably made long after anyone who actually worked on them had seen the Demon Lord.

Daedalus huffed from behind me. "Look at that. They got the shape of my back spines all wrong. And the color! I'm far more 'ruby glimmering in firelight' than whatever that shade is."

Looking closer at the picture of the dragon, I realized it was actually pretty close to Daedalus. Daedalus was a tiny bit larger, if the scale was accurate. And his horns were a bit longer than the picture's, but just barely. It very well could have been artistic license. I had to disagree on the spines, though. They seemed to be one of the more accurate details. "It seems these snowmen know something about your old war," I flashed to Daedalus. He nodded ever so slightly, careful not to bump into the cave ceiling.

"It appears so. They have better memories than most humans, it seems. Though the fact that they appear to worship both me and the demon is quite disturbing. Perhaps they know something more about it. There should be one of the Lieutenants captured around here somewhere. If I remember correctly, at least three went down on this continent."

"Do you think it's nearby? Could that be the cause of the magic drain?"

Daedalus hummed with a thoughtful noise, shaking the cave as he did. "I suppose it's possible. I can't say I remember this particular demon being captured here, but this is definitely a loose artistic interpretation of one of the Lieutenants. Likely by someone who had only ever heard of him. The general shape is right, but the position is a little odd. So I wouldn't be surprised if whoever made this only saw its bound form, not it in action."

"So if the demon is here and drawing power, then we need to find it. Right?" I asked Daedalus.

"Yes, we do indeed. Let's get on it, friend."

ARTHUR STEPPED into the meeting room, his eyes quickly scanning the officers sitting and waiting for him. This was one of the rare military-only meetings he really should've been making a point of having more often. The only one from the castle present was Susan, and that was by necessity. Admittedly, her scouts were really the best in this area. A small force like hers was inherently limited in what it could do, but there were times when it excelled. He could only hope his would improve quickly enough to better leverage their superior numbers.

He kicked off the meeting with some introductions and a general summarization of their situation before waving her to the front. Susan had brought a few visual aids with her that she set up at the front of the room. A general map of the area, along with some pins representing the Scout's findings, were soon displayed before the group.

"Three days ago, we made contact. The military vanguard is still several days out from the edge of the forest, but we do believe they will fully regroup before heading into the woods. Out in the open plains, there is very little opportunity for ambushes and general sabotage, but we have managed to make some strides. While no actual sabotage acts have been committed, we do have their supply train schedule for the next several months, planned routes and backup mounts, as well as information about who is maintaining the weapons. Those are the major points. I will disseminate more details to those who need it."

The officers gave an approving murmur. The fact that they had all this information up front was going to be of great help when it came to slowing down the enemy's approach. The siege preparations were going along swimmingly, but they could use more time. There were always more fortifications, always more traps, always more ambitious countermeasures they could lay. If anyone thought the castle was fully prepared for a siege, Arthur would call them a fool.

Susan continued to give more details about the kingdom army's estimated time of arrival as well as certain landmarks that they could gauge their progress with. These were especially pertinent for the several day march through the valley that would be required to even reach the settlement. Along those lines, she picked out specific unit commanders and gave suggestions about which ones would be best in various spots for ambushes.

Arthur was impressed by her devious mind. There was not more than a half-mile where she didn't see an opportunity for a rather tricky ambush or act of sabotage. At this rate, the entire length of the five-day march through the forest wouldn't give the army real trouble. Especially considering that the narrow road would force even a massive army to be strung out, meaning they could not bring their numbers advantage to bear in any one particular spot. As long as the guerrilla forces they fielded could flow through the forest and hit from both sides, they could almost always outnumber their enemy two to one in the actual engagement.

This was a rather simple tactic, but the way Susan was setting up her plans for sabotage made heavy use of it. Arthur was glad he'd sent out forces days ago like she'd pushed for instead of waiting. If he'd sent them out now, based on her information, they would have barely managed to get out of the forest before the kingdom showed up. Those forces would have either been stuck in the valley or needed to maneuver through the forests.

They would have to rely on these troops to intercept the kingdom's supply trains, along with any sort of support that the kingdom would be trying to give the military during the siege; if they were successful enough in cutting everything off, they could peel away a large part of the force and give Arthur a chance to do more than just endure the siege. Or they could basically end up forcing the enemy to siege themselves. Arthur doubted that a rushed army pushed to march through the winter would have anywhere near the amount of provisions the city and the castle had.

With the food production that Trent and his branch had managed under the guidance of Lord Void, the castle was set for almost two years and would be nearly self-sustaining in the near future. They just needed a slightly higher influx of livestock before they had their own thriving ecosystem. As for water, there was no way to cut off the water supply through either the glacial runoff from the mountains or from ground wells. So, as long as they were independent in food, the only way to take them out would be through a direct assault. And Arthur was doing his best to make sure that was an unadvisable course of action.

After Susan finished her report, the lead engineer stood up and gave progress on the third ring wall. For each wall they finished building, they started to build a slightly lesser wall in front of it so that they would be able to fall back to a more fortified position. By some miracle, they had managed to finish an entire wall spanning the perimeter of the forest, 250 feet in front of the first wall. It was a crude thing, but no less impressive for it. The third wall had begun construction, and the trees were being cleared.

He hoped to have at least a basic palisade the entire way. It wouldn't hold up for long, but it would give Arthur's men a place to make a first stand. Also, it would test the enemy's mettle, letting him see how they handled the conflict. Arthur didn't expect to hold that position for more than a half hour before they fell back to the second wall. That one was fairly normal, comparable to most city walls. It was the third wall that they would have to hold for all their worth.

Not that the wall was anything to scoff at. That masterwork thing of melted granite would give even Arthur himself pause, even without the frankly absurd amounts of magic thrown on it. Apparently there was stuff on there the likes of which hadn't been seen for a thousand years. At least, that was what his engineers had said after the two young girls had worked on it.

Sometimes, it was hard to think of Miss Bee as the High Priestess of Spot. The fact that Void's mouthpiece would be such a sweet little girl went against his every expectation. But that was nothing compared to her apprentice Maranda, who seemed even more out of place but strangely competent in understanding magic. Even now, Maranda still worked to fortify the positions while Miss Bee had other important things to see to.

Daedalus and I circled around the mountain after we had finally gotten away from the snowmen. They had seemed to want to throw a feast of some sort, but we had retired and left them to their own celebrations. Neither of us really wanted to eat whatever they were going to cook up, and I was having trouble not cleaning up the settlement beyond what would be polite. I had, of course, gone through and resolved all of their waste issues, but I didn't want to offend them by rebuilding their muddy huts or completely upending their society.

They were acceptably grateful for my assistance and seemed to look at me in a new light when they realized the wonders of cleanliness. But it was a distant respect for my teachings, and I clearly would have to do more before they would trust me. Still, they started to give me a little bit more space to do my work.

The dragon and I chatted a bit about what the implications of the demon and dragon worship were for these people, but we quickly ended up revisiting the topics we'd already talked about, and we fell into silence. Each of us did our own computations, trying to figure out what we needed to do. Daedalus was sure something was wrong with the dragon art, but I was convinced the dragon in the depiction was supposed to be him.

As we rose higher up in the next mountain over, I saw a strange opening in the side of it and pointed it out to Daedalus. I flashed him an image of his own cave as I had seen it from a distance.

Daedalus cocked his head inquisitively. "You think one of my cousins is over here? I suppose that's actually pretty plausible. That would explain the details they got wrong, at least." I resisted arguing. Even if the wall art was ancient or artistically rendered, he seemed convinced that no one would ever possibly render his image with anything but perfect accuracy. Besides, who would know those sorts of details about the dragon?

But the dragon seemed to think that anyone who'd even heard about him should be able to get his magnificence near perfection. If they had enough skill in whatever medium they were working with, at least. And if they didn't, then why even try? It wasn't an argument I was going to win. Still, we made our way over there, mostly out of curiosity.

As we alighted before the cave entrance, my sensors registered a slight disturbance in the area's magic energy. It was similar to the mountain we had just left, but still different. Clearly, this wasn't the source of the magic draining, but it wasn't too far from it.

Daedalus let out a polite roar in greeting in case the cave was occupied before we even approached. "I wouldn't want to be rude. But hopefully we're not waking someone up." He shot a baleful glare in my direction. "I know how annoying it is to be woken up by loud noises."

I beeped indignantly, flashing, "Look, I apologized for that already. I didn't realize you were there."

He gave me a toothy grin, and I relaxed slightly. "But yeah, let's not lob any explosions at him."

An answering bellow came from deep within the cave, and Daedalus grinned. "Ah, one of my cousins *is* here!"

A white head poked out of the mountain and breathed a pillar of frost over at Daedalus, and Daedalus responded by breathing a jet of fire. The two breath attacks met between them and mingled before they both cut off suddenly, and Daedalus landed at the foot of the mountain. The white dragon launched themself out of the cave and slowly glided down, shaking the earth with their landing. Comparing the two, I realized Daedalus was significantly larger than this other dragon. He likely possessed about 30 percent more mass, even if the white dragon was longer from tip to tail.

"Daedalus! Big brother! It's been too many millennia," the white dragon greeted, rumbling and shaking his head.

"Thucydides. I didn't think I'd see you again. You've been sleeping for, what, ten thousand years now?"

"Give or take. I had a bit of a fever a while ago and was just sleeping it off. Woke up a couple hundred years ago and have been trying to shake off the grogginess ever since." Thucydides shook his head and grumbled. "I think it was some dark elf curse after I ate of one of their princesses. I know I shouldn't do that anymore, but she just looked so juicy."

I looked between the two bantering dragons. "Dark elf? Princess?" I asked.

I seemed to draw Thucydides's interest for the first time. "Why, Daedalus, have you brought a guest?"

DAEDALUS MOTIONED for me to move forward and made brief introductions. Afterward, Thucydides turned to me. "I haven't talked to a godling in a very, very long time. I wasn't even aware the world had enough magic to produce them anymore. As the ages go by, it's been harder and harder to grow."

A melancholy silence started to settle on the three of us before Daedalus broke it with a gibe. "Is that why you still haven't cracked 50 yet? Honestly, if you weren't my little brother, you'd be an embarrassment."

Thucydides glared at Daedalus. "You know how hard it is to gather mana nowadays? Why, I haven't been able to condense my power in a very long time. Especially with everything fading so much recently."

I turned toward Daedalus with a question: "How did Thucydides have trouble gathering power when it was so simple? All you had to do was kill strong things. Demons and the like."

Daedalus shook his head and offered an explanation. "Thucydides has a bit of a weird class. He doesn't get power from killing or defeating enemies. He has to meditate and gather the energy of the world. It was great when we were hatchlings, but..."

Thucydides sighed. "Back then, mana was so rich throughout the world, all I had to do was breathe and I'd level up."

Daedalus bobbed his head in agreement. "Yeah. The magic of the world has been getting thin over the past several millennia. I'm not exactly sure why, but it started long before the demons came, and it's been declining ever since I was born. It's one of the reasons humans can thrive so much now. Ten or twenty thousand years ago, they would have been overrun by stronger races. But now? I mean, we dragons get sleepy so easily that we have no choice but to hibernate and leave them alone. It's also why no new gods have showed up. Not since we drove the last ones off this plane."

I wasn't about to question that, so I exchanged a few more polite words with Thucydides, then left the brothers for their reunion. I was not exactly sure what I needed to do, so I went back to talk to the snowmen. As the dragons conversed, their rumbles echoed through the valleys surrounding the mountains. I saw a few stones clattering near the edge of the settlement. In fact, many of the snowmen were lined up and listening to the distant sound as I approached.

They turned their attention to me and welcomed me with deep bows. I made my way into the village and searched around, eager to give any help I could offer. As I swept through their collection of shelters, I did my best to clean what I could. It wasn't too hard to better pack the earth and carve out channels for the rain to go through. They'd probably be useful if this snow melted soon as well. The snowmen didn't seem to understand what I was doing, but they didn't get in my way either. If Daedalus took a while, maybe I'd try to teach them.

"High Priestess! Come quick!"

A sudden pounding at the door woke Bee from her slumber.

Groggily, she rubbed her eyes and rolled out of bed. This was the first time she'd had a chance to grab a few hours of rest in the last several days. She didn't have to sleep very often anymore, but she still needed it occasionally.

With all the preparations for the coming army, there was just too much to do. And that was even with her staff and council performing their duties extraordinarily. She could only be grateful for all the support and work that went into preparing for the siege. Without people like Arthur, Trent, Mary, and Susan, she would have been crushed by responsibility several times over. But that didn't mean that she didn't have endless things to do herself. Most of them boiled down to just being visible and keeping people's spirits and morale up. The rest of it was training.

Every last person who was going to fight in the coming battle was trying to eke out another level or get to that next skill that might make all the difference. And with her being the highest-level person present, fighting with her was the best way of getting those levels, at least for combat classes. So, for at least eight hours each day for the past week, she had been fighting against multiple high-level opponents, each one usually above level 35. Anything else would not have been worth her time. And she had been doing so publicly in the arena.

Many would watch to learn the techniques that Void taught her with the broom. As much as she had discouraged the unorthodox weapon, it was often popularized among the non-soldiers who were trying to learn basic defense techniques. It was quite impractical, and only because of her personal connection to Void did she think she was able to achieve such mastery with it. Of course, that didn't stop anyone. Still, between her level and her practical experience, she was able to equal, if not best, an opponent with a more traditional blade around the same level of physical ability.

Besides the kids and their swords, all the followers of Void preferred to use its favorite weapon. Only those who had already spent a vast amount of time training with another weapon were refusing to switch.

As Bee stood, yawning, she padded over to the door and wrenched it open. Beyond stood a practically frantic mother.

"Have you seen the Nighty Knights? Do you know where they are? I haven't seen my son since last night. He wasn't in his bed for breakfast, and I couldn't find him on those stupid patrols they go on..." The woman rambled in an endless stream of words, not giving Bee a split second for a response. It wasn't like she had anything to add.

"No, I have not seen them," Bee interrupted, causing the women to finally pause. Her mouth hung open mid-word in surprise. "Who else have you asked?"

"Um. Well, I assume many of the other mothers know...?" came the uncertain answer.

Bee put her hand on the woman's shoulder, comfortably interrupting the tirade from continuing, and spoke in her most comforting voice. "We'll find them, don't worry." With that, she rushed past her.

The smart thing would have been to go look at Susan or Captain Major first. One of the scouts would probably have seen the Nighty Knights wherever they were going, but if they were actually gone? Then she didn't have time to look for Susan. There were only so many places the children could go and she had a bad feeling about it.

As a group, they were probably too skilled for many others to catch up to. If they had really wandered off and they didn't want to be found, Bee had a sneaking suspicion of what they were up to. This might be something that she had to take care of personally.

While Bee's role was important, it wasn't essential, and others could cover for her. These kids took precedence for a multitude of reasons. She was already pulling her broom in front of her as she made her way quickly through the halls.

A quick circuit around the castle to investigate revealed that they were, in fact, gone. Once that was certain, Bee made haste to track them down. Between her Pathing skill and her faith sense, it was easy to find the general direction of the Knights. Soon enough, she was running down the road away from the castle.

As her skills led her further and further from the castle, her heart sank. She didn't want to be right about this. As competent as the Nighty Knights were, they were still children. True, most of them had seen awful things in the undead plague or had other horrible experiences—far more than any children should have, in her opinion. The loss of their homes and everything in them was enough to traumatize practically anyone. But seeing them train had not only shown their incredible resilience, but also how much they were still children at heart.

Bee couldn't in good conscience let them be on a battlefield. A real battlefield where they would be in real danger. They might get hurt, but worse, they might have to hurt others. Do things when they didn't fully understand the consequences.

Early in her search, when she had talked to Mrs. Chadwick about the disappearances, the woman had been eerily calm as she sat at their family's dining room table and served her a cup of tea. Apparently, when she had woken and found the flaming sword missing from where she had hidden it, she immediately knew what had happened. She just hoped that her two children would come back. But in her own words, they were "too much like their father. They're not willing to let injustice..."

She had trailed off, biting her tongue. Bee just placed her hand onto the woman's, where it trembled. She was barely holding it together.

"Don't worry, we'll get them back," she had said. Bee could only hope she would get there in time.

The flying carpet could have lent her more speed, but at a cost. The kids likely didn't take the road, meaning her vision and maneuverability wouldn't be as good as on foot. Not that Bee was an expert tracker or anything, with how much she relied on her skills, but she hoped that she could take advantage of her speed to catch up before anything happened.

As the sun rose and began to fall once more, she realized that something was wrong. Faith sense of the Nighty Knights' direction blazed clear ahead of her. But she wasn't catching up. Somehow, something was allowing them to run at a speed that she could barely maintain by herself. That the children were barely above level 15 should have prevented them from having any sort of ability like this.

Perhaps this was new or something they had hidden. Who knew what powers their faith in Void had given them? The fact that Felix and Leanne had started to develop command-type abilities so early meant that something like a group buff would not be out of the question.

It was on the second day that she finally broke out of the forest, and she still hadn't caught up with any knights. She had finally managed to make up some ground on them, but they were still hours ahead of her by her skill's estimation. Yet she had to keep going.

As dawn turned the sky a rosy hue, she noticed something new on the horizon. Clouds of smoke were just visible over the next few hills.

She forced down her exhaustion. As she crested the next rise, she was treated to the sight of a camped army sprawling out as far as she could see. Bee was careful not to expose herself too much in the morning light. But the smoke wasn't just coming from the campfires. In addition to those, several wagons off to the side were currently ablaze, causing soldiers to pour out of the tents like a kicked-over anthill. They rushed to put out the fires as Bee frantically scanned the encampment for a group of small prisoners. But she didn't see any.

CHAPTER 65

GET OFF MY LAWN

BEE WATCHED the enemy camp from atop a tall hill for several minutes, scanning for other signs of the Nighty Knights. Suddenly, nearly a mile away, another set of flames began rising up in the sky from elsewhere in the encampment. This caused a renewed scramble as the kingdom's army attempted to adjust. Officers shouted commands, and soldiers all scrambled to accomplish their tasks. Many rushed towards the fires. Others dashed about to find buckets or arm themselves.

But before a full pursuit could be organized, a third disturbance made itself known. Horses started whinnying and screaming, and their picket lines snapped. Suddenly, the soldiers had to choose between gathering the fleeing horses, putting out their supplies, or dealing with the mysterious fire off in the distance. It wasn't more than a handful of moments before an officer began organizing priorities, but it was enough to ensure that no effective pursuit was launched. Bee couldn't help but grin to herself.

Now that her initial worry had abated somewhat, she had a good idea of what was happening. Given her faith sense, she could track the threads of faith through the camp and thus identify where the Knights were moving next. A fourth party snuck through the confusion and slipped into the back of one of the command tents. A few heartbeats later, a fourth fire sprang up. But this time, a dedicated force was on the prowl. All the officers' guards nearby ignored the other disturbances to become laser-focused on the group that had snuck into the section.

Except the fires in the command tents had been started in several spots, and many officers needed escorting out of danger. Even with the guards' attempts, these openings gave the five saboteurs a chance to escape. They darted into tents, trying to throw the pursuers off their trail. But the men were relentless. Once they spotted the small forms of their enemies, the men began tearing through cloth barriers with their swords and shoving people out of the way. Bee quickly searched to find the other three groups and found that they had, thankfully, made it a decent distance away from the camp.

The five had managed to stay together somehow, but they were quickly becoming surrounded. They hadn't been caught yet, but it was just a matter of time. They were being herded toward another group of soldiers assembling to block their way as their pursuers came at them from multiple sides. She considered dashing down the hill to step in, as stealthily as she was able to keep the element of surprise. But just as she thought she would have to actually rescue the little rascals, a fifth disturbance appeared.

One of the five Knights hopped to the side and hurled a glass vial into the sky. It landed ahead of them, among the group of assembling soldiers. A deafening *crack* sounded, followed by a deep *whoosh*. Suddenly, a massive area of the camp was engulfed in roaring orange and red flames.

People screamed. Soldiers ran, rolling on the ground to put the fires on their own bodies out. She wasn't sure if the projectile had been aimed intentionally or if they had gotten lucky. Regardless, it had landed in just the right spot to open a hole in the encirclement.

The group didn't slow as they ran right towards the flames. Bee instinctively reached out as they entered the inferno, but could sense from her ability that they weren't harmed in the slightest. They must have borrowed some potions from Maranda for this.

The group dashed onward. The soldiers found themselves too preoccupied with dragging others away from the blaze, and the pursuers were hesitant to plunge in after their targets. So the group of children ran through the blaze, completely concealed from sight, and darted a few rows of tents over.

Bee watched from afar as they turned on a dime, slipped into the shadows of an unoccupied tent, and circled around in a dark alcove. They waited as the pursuers that had managed to avoid the fire trundled past. Then, flitting from shadow to shadow, they skulked their way toward the edges of camp. Before long, they were off into the tall grass, crawling on their hands and knees around the camp. Bee still sat on her hill, watching the slightly swaying grass as they made their way around the sentries and rejoined the rest of the group.

She smiled as she found the small cave that they were using as their base of operations for the night. Once she had done a quick head count and realized everyone was there through her spirit sense, she started to make her way over, careful not to leave a trail to invalidate all their hard work. When she stepped into the entranceway, a sentry she had almost missed in the shadows let out a whistle, and all of their heads swiveled toward the entrance.

As they reached for weapons, Bee held her hands up and waited for them to recognize her. "I'll have you all know your mothers are quite worried."

Daedalus watched his little friend go to play with the snowmen. He let the little godling have its fun. Interacting with a new race for the first time was always interesting. It was one of the few truly unique experiences a long-lived immortal got to enjoy. Turning back to his little brother, he continued their conversation. "So where did you find these snowmen?"

Thucydides looked surprised. "Snowmen? You mean the yetis?"

"Is that what you're calling them?"

"That's what they call themselves, at least."

Daedalus snorted. "Well, they're going to be calling themselves snowmen from here on out, if I make my guess."

Thucydides just huffed some frost out into the air. "Sure, It's better than 'yeti,' at least."

"Where'd you find them?" Daedalus asked. He didn't mind talking a little shop with his little bro.

"Yeah, well, I've been mostly sleeping but keeping an eye on them. They found that cave and drew some artwork on it a few thousand years ago. Not sure how they managed to get the history right and all that, but they got most of the details down."

"That's for sure. Only a few thousand years ago? That's a lot later than I would have thought. But at the same time, they haven't advanced very far, it seems."

Thucydides nodded. "Yeah, they're not the most useful, at least not when it comes to making things. But when it comes to mining, they're great. They *love* digging. I'd even say they're almost as good as the dwarves."

"Really?" Daedalus perked up at that. "Wow. We haven't found a good mining race since...I don't know when. With how scarce the dwarves seem to be, I was worried that all that gold would stay underground!"

"Yeah, they're really fast at digging and finding ore, but their size means they have to dig a lot larger tunnels. But when it comes to crafting, they're completely useless." Thucydides snorted, waving a massive claw. "They haven't even truly figured out fire yet. Basic torches are as far as it gets. They might be able to smelt copper if they did, but so far they haven't moved past cold forging it."

Daedalus hummed thoughtfully. "Have you tried slipping them any hints?"

"Yeah, a couple of times," Thucydides said. "They just don't seem to grasp it. I imagine it might be a bit of a hobby project in the next couple thousand years to get them up to snuff. But once I get them there, I think it might be a worthwhile investment. It's a long shot, but I'm hoping to get them to take a good look underneath these mountains. They're relatively new, but mostly untapped as far as I can sense."

Daedalus considered that and activated his Draconic Hoard skill, sending his senses seeking downwards. Surprisingly, he did find the ore underground to be relatively untouched. There was no honeycomb of underground tunnels that went through the mountains below. That was rare nowadays, "Yeah, that seems like an interesting project. Good luck. Let me know if it works out, I might have to borrow some of your snowmen for my own hoard. Anyway, any word on the Lieutenant that's captured around here?"

Thucydides shook his head. "No, I haven't checked."

"Then do you know what's up with the disturbance in the magic in the air? Recently, I started to feel it even an ocean away. Surely you've noticed?"

Thucydides shrugged. "Honestly, not really. I've been taking a break from magic recently and haven't checked in. Give me a second to see if I can sense what you're talking about."

The white dragon folded in an awkward position, pulling its hind legs underneath itself and folding them over each other strangely. He touched the tips of his talons together and wrapped his tail around himself.

Daedalus groaned as he watched his little brother's meditation. He had never understood this method for gaining power. It just seemed so complicated and useless when you could just kill things to get stronger. But it made his brother feel special, he supposed, the diva that he was.

As he settled in to wait, the great red dragon spent some time sorting through his hoard in his mind, trying to figure out the best piece to put in his fourth-highest place of honor now that Spot had claimed a few of his pieces. It was painful to let them go, but much more amusing to think of their current uses as prizes for such simple competitions. Plus, he was well compensated for them. His extra levels and new power were certainly worth the cost.

Thucydides pulled him from his daydreams not too much later and looked at him with a worried expression on his toothy face. "You're right. Something really is wrong. I can't believe I didn't notice this."

Daedalus just shook his head and sighed at his scatterbrained little brother.

"We need to investigate," the idiot said as he pointed a claw at the sky.

Before he flapped his wings to take off, Daedalus stopped him. "Wait, wait. Hold up. Where are you going?"

"To investigate."

Daedalus rolled his eyes. "Okay, but where? Where are we starting?"

"Well, I was going to fly around and see if I saw anything odd."

Daedalus closed his eyes and centered himself. His little brother was much too excitable sometimes. "Relax. We don't need to go anywhere. That's why Spot and I came here. This is the center of the disturbance. It's somewhere in this mountain or one of the next ones over. We need to get a better idea of exactly where because, somehow, it's not localized as much as I thought it was. Based on the amount of power it's drawing, at least."

Thucydides put on a thoughtful expression. "You're right. I would expect it to be a single massive draw for you to be able to notice that all the way across the ocean. It's weird that it's something pulling power over such a wide area, though... Have you tried going straight up and seeing if you can sense how deep underground it is by triangulation?"

"Triangle-what?" Daedalus asked. As the words left his mouth, he wanted to call them back. He was already sure he didn't want to hear the explanation.

"Well, I wasn't just sleeping in my cave. See here," his brother said, drawing in the dirt with a claw. "If you pick out any three points on a plane, you can..."

For a few minutes, Daedalus tried his best to keep up with his little brother's ramblings about straight lines and even planes and various angle theories he had come up with. Might as well take an interest in what his siblings were doing, after all. But it was just so *boring*.

"...So what I'm saying is, if we can get a sample and a value estimate in at least five different points of various elevations, I should be able to trace it back to a single source or determine whether or not there are multiple sources evenly spaced out. And then—hey, bro? Did you fall asleep?"

CHAPTER 66

A KNIGHT'S OATH

THE NIGHTY KNIGHTS let out a snicker. Evidently, the idea of their mothers being upset made them laugh rather than feel guilty.

Felix moved to the front of the group, standing as tall as he could manage. "Miss Bee, we did what we had to. They couldn't expect us to just sit here while our home's threatened. We have the skills to do somethin' now. We have the levels. You know as well as we do that we're some of the strongest fighters at the castle. We aren't gonna sit there like a bunch of scared adults when someone comes to threaten us. Not again."

The rest of the Nighty Knights grumbled their agreement with his statement. Bee frowned. Evidently, the loss of their homes had impacted these kids more than anyone had realized. The fact that no one saw this coming spoke to how much they'd underestimated the kids, as well as how well the kids had been handling the frankly traumatizing events up to this point.

"And we *did* leave a note," Bradley added as if that excused their actions. The Knights were silent at that. "What? We didn't run off without saying anything!" He looked around but received no support on that front.

Bee just sighed and gave him an exasperated look. She guessed that they likely just weren't aware of the plans already made to sabotage the incoming army. Why would they? Those were high-level military discussions. And so the Nighty Knights struck out, determined to do their part when they saw nothing being done. She couldn't help but respect them for it, in a way. But at the same time, it was incredibly naive.

Void had done well, instilling in them a sense of responsibility and restraint. But there was only so much that could be done. The fact that they had the levels and the abilities of people well into adulthood didn't really help with their maturity.

Bee sighed and ran her hand down her face. "I am disappointed in you, Felix," she said, turning to their commander. "Disappointed that you have so little faith in me and Void to take care of this ourselves."

Felix looked appropriately guilty but slightly confused. "Maybe the castle's gettin' more walls and stuff, but the army's not goin' out to meet them. Everyone's just holin' up at home."

"There are hundreds of ambushes and acts of sabotage planned, but they were planned in better locations than this," she said, gesturing to the wide-open plains. "We wanted to lure them deeper into the forest, where they'd be more vulnerable, so we could hit them harder before they started to prepare for us. But now? Now, they'll be on guard and wary."

To be honest, she was making it out to be a bit of a bigger deal than it really was. It was very unlikely that the army was going to be unprepared when they were strung out on a road and vulnerable, but one could always hope. The reason they hadn't been hitting them too hard was that most of their scouting units still hadn't made it this far, and those that had weren't willing to risk being caught on the open plains. If they had been in the area ahead of time and had time to prepare, that was one thing. But when they found the enemy just as they were about to enter the forest, it didn't seem worth it.

The Nighty Knights could attest to this based off of their own troubles escaping after a single assault. Assuming this *was* their first.

The Nighty Knights shared an uncomfortable look as they processed her words. Eventually, one of the younger children broke the silence. "But, but we hit them good. We did good. It was worth it."

Bee looked at the speaker, a young girl, probably around six years old. She met Bee's gaze without flinching. The cold anger in the girl's gaze made her shiver involuntarily. "My squad got the horsies. We cut each rope and set each horse free. We also got all the saddle straps n' stuff before they even noticed us. They thought we were just some stable boys, taking care of the horsies for some coppers." She pulled out a handful of shiny coins. "They even paid us."

Felix nodded as she finished speaking. "We've got a good in here. No one's gonna suspect us, even now. There are a lot of children besides us running around from the women's camp a little ways away. And soldiers are constantly complainin' about 'em getting underfoot. But they don't do anythin' more than just maybe yell at us a bit."

As much as she hated to admit it, Felix had a point. Children running around in Arthur's camp might've received slightly different treatment, especially after the men's experiences in the arena. But of course, anyone reasonable wouldn't expect such a thing from children normally. Because they were supposed to be innocent. Sabotage, burning food, freeing horses, and setting tents on fire usually involved killing people. She hadn't seen any deaths that night nor any intentional harm to the soldiers other than from the fires. But if they decided to keep at it? She wouldn't be surprised if some of these children ended up taking lives, intentionally or not. That was not something she wanted on her conscience.

She stared at the group before her, thinking. More than ever before, the memories of these children playing catch with Void warred with the elite fighting force standing before her now. Most children didn't have the ability to even attempt something like this, much less pull it off. But these Nighty Knights were different. They had been personally trained by a god, so their abilities were over and above what anyone could expect from them. They took on burdens far beyond what they should be concerned about, yet at the same time, they did so with a childlike innocence that had them acting unpredictably.

The Nighty Knights looked at her with unapologetic resolve, waiting for her to give a reason why they shouldn't be out here. They seemed to understand why their parents were upset, all besides Bradley. Maybe he was a bit too idealistic, thinking that a note would calm them down. But she could see that they were not going to go home without a fight. They believed in their cause, in defending their homes and families. It left her with no real good options.

To be honest, Bee wanted nothing more than to drag them all home that very instant. She supposed she could order them as their High Priestess to go back home in the name of Void, but would that work? Or would they sneak out again, act on their own, and get into an even worse situation? That being said, she couldn't just allow them to be involved in a literal war.

She closed her eyes. What would Void do? Would it protect their innocence as it had protected their lives when they were young? Or would it respect their honest desire to protect their home, to put their training to use?

Opening her eyes, she made a decision. No matter what, she couldn't let them be here by themselves. That was just too irresponsible of her. But...compromises could be made.

"Okay," she sighed, finally making her decision. "You all made a mistake to come out here on your own, especially without consulting me. *But,*" she continued before they could interject, "I understand your frustrations. How much you want to help. So. I will stay here with you and assist until the scouts and saboteurs from Susan and Captain Major's divisions arrive. After that, we're all going home to prepare for the siege and leave the fighting to the army. Alright?"

At the restrained excitement in their nods, she hardened her gaze. "But there are conditions. First: *no harming any people.* You got lucky tonight that those tent fires didn't kill anyone. We are *only* going to steal or destroy their resources. No harming any of these men. They aren't undead or monsters. I don't care how competent you all are, no one is taking a life at this age." Her eyes swept across the group. "You get into trouble, you run. You only hurt someone as an *absolute* last resort, in self-defense, if there are no other options. If you can't agree to that, then we're going home right now."

She met the Nighty Knights' eyes with a stern look that promised that if there was any dissent, she would be dragging them all back physically, and there was nothing they could do about it. Felix looked a bit chastised but nodded, accepting the deal. A few of them appeared almost annoyed at the lecture, but most of them seemed to easily accept the terms.

Bee relaxed. The reaction reassured her. Thankfully, it didn't seem like they were here to seek glory or battle itself. They really did just want to help protect their home. But their willingness to retreat when someone else was stepping up let her feel slightly more at ease.

"Good. With that settled, let's go through an after-action report. What was your plan, and how did it go?"

Hearing their explanation of how it had gone down, Bee nodded. She was rather satisfied with their plan. She couldn't see any obvious problems with it, and they'd put in a surprising amount of contingencies and backup routes. But maybe someone with more experience would be able to do better. To her relief, all of their targets had been supplies, maps, reports, and other similar items. Not people. They hadn't planned for any loss of life or obvious aggression. "All right. So what went wrong?"

They looked at each other and shrugged. "Well," Bradley said, "it was harder to get through the camp than we thought. Once everything was stirred up, at least. There were just so many people running around that it was hard to tell what was going on. And they are a lot taller than us, so it was hard to see very far."

"I tried my best to coordinate," Felix added, "but I can only broadcast messages right now. I couldn't get info back from all the squads, so I was kinda limited too."

"Yes, communication is one of the most difficult parts of battle, according to Arthur." Bee nodded. "That's why it's best to always have someone watching over the whole thing, some way to communicate across an entire battlefield. That's why trumpets and horns are so useful, though colored flags and lanterns work as well. But they do provide the enemy a bit of a target. You're lucky to have Felix's skill. Give me some ideas of what you could use as a signal to get info *to* him, though."

People looked around, and someone spoke up. "Well, we could use something like the fireworks? To get our timing done better."

They tossed out a few of the suggestions, and Bee eventually indicated Cliff lying near Tanu. "You have a very effective scout and signaler right here, don't you?"

They looked at the wolf as she explained. "See, wolf howls carry over long distances, but are also perfect for blending into the rest of the environment. No one will think twice about a wolf howling in the distance, especially in the evening. And if you work out a set of signals ahead of time, you won't have to worry about them being confused with actual wolves. That can probably help get info to Felix."

The Nighty Knights were nodding, considering her idea. "Good. Now, let's talk about tomorrow's plans."

CHAPTER 67

THEY GROW UP SO FAST

BEE LEANED FORWARD and stroked the mane of her horse, rolling with its gait as it moved. Looking back over her shoulder, she saw the long train of small children riding two to a horse, leading the animals in a slow walk as they made their way back to the castle. Overall, she thought the operation had gone rather well. It had taken her a lot of effort, but she had managed to move the Knights' plans and attention towards a less risky target, and one that she honestly thought might have a longer-lasting effect on the army. That first night, they had gone after several different targets at once and been rather effective. But as she watched the enemy camp in the morning, she realized that they wouldn't have the same luck again. Even if they were closer to the forest entrance.

They were too prepared. There needed to be a concentrated strike in one area for Bee and the Knights to have the numbers to actually pull anything off. And while something flammable like food would've been a very effective target, it wouldn't actually make that much of a difference. The army was so large that they couldn't possibly sabotage enough food in one night to truly hurt them. At most, they might manage to slightly reduce the army's food intake for a few days until they were able to be resupplied.

No, the planned attacks on supply lines by Susan's scouts would be better in that area.

What she'd known would be more effective, though, was if they hit the horses. The horses that had been released on the previous raid had been largely rounded up. All the replacement mounts and horses for pulling wagons were relatively easily tracked down and well-trained enough that they were soon captured. The Nighty Knights didn't know enough about horses to really use them as more than a distraction. Even with all their efforts, the horses had simply run in fright for a few minutes and then were found grazing not that far away.

This time, though, they had struck with more force. Bee had gone in first and taken out several of the guards quietly, in such a way that the children did not have to dirty their hands. After that, she simply tasked them with cutting a lot of the leads. And then, when they were ready to leave, they herded all the horses together and pushed them several hours south, away from the castle. Away from the direction the enemy was marching. Once they scattered them, Bee and her team broke off and went around the army to slip back into the forest.

They had been chased, of course, but they had left the pursuers far behind. This time, she was sure the horses would be harder to collect, if the kingdom's army could manage it at all. At least 15 percent of the mounts, maybe even 25 percent, were ripped away in one fell swoop. Even better, they'd kept some for themselves. Each Nighty Knight had taken about two horses on average. The children were far too small to properly ride a horse, so they had to improvise.

One child would sit holding the reins and using their heels to guide the horse from the front, whereas the other one sat backward and held three long ropes, pulling another three horses behind them. This allowed the group to bring almost 150 horses with them, with the little children usually sitting behind. Unfortunately, the saddle situation left something to be desired. The stirrups just didn't tighten enough for them, so many of these children had to ride bareback. At least riding in pairs also helped the children mount their steeds, as they had to boost each other up and then pull up the other rider behind.

It was quite a hilarious process to watch, but with a little bit of practicing, they managed to do it efficiently. As they had returned from their long ride in the wee hours of the morning, they ran into a set of Susan's men coming through the forest. When they spotted Bee, they left their cover and flagged her down.

"High Priestess Bee!" One of the scouts called out to her as she neared.

"Mat. Good to see you." She waved a greeting. "I've found the Nighty Knights. We'll be heading back with news on the enemy."

Mat frowned. "The mothers will be relieved to hear it. They've been worried sick. But...where did the horses come from?"

She smiled. "We had a few successful operations of our own."

He blinked. "You did?"

"Of course."

The scout mulled the words over for a moment. Eventually, he seemed to decide on how to respond. "I...don't know if they'll like that. Especially Arthur. The commander was pretty unhappy about the Knights going off. With this..." He shrugged. "Far be it from me to say it, but I dunno if you'll be getting a hero's welcome here."

After exchanging some additional information, they parted ways. Fortunately, with the professionals showing up, she was able to hold the Nighty Knights to their end of the bargain and send them home without having to commit to additional sabotage operations and put them further at risk. Hopefully the good news of their successes would help to temper everyone's displeasure. She somehow doubted it, though.

At the very least, Arthur might appreciate the mounts. Arthur's army hadn't kept horses, for the most part. The vast majority of the men were infantry. Horses didn't do well in long sieges, from what she understood. They tended to be expensive to feed and difficult to exercise, and when people were pressed, they often became the meals that they so needed.

Of course, having a small cavalry of 150 units wouldn't be game-changing. But when it came to running down open infantry, mounted troops were something that Arthur had lamented losing. Perhaps this would make a difference. The horse she had found for herself was quite impressive, at least.

Her Scan indicated that it was a level 30 Destrier, and she honestly wasn't sure how a horse had managed to gain so many levels. She had no idea about its skills or what skills a horse might even have. Regardless, she could feel the power and speed of the mount. This walk that they were maintaining to keep everyone together and in their saddles was nothing compared to what this horse was capable of. Of course, her carpet would be far more efficient for her to fight from in both speed and maneuverability. But the horse *was* pretty.

When Bee finally made it through the castle gate, she entered into a beehive of activity. All around, preparations were underway, people running around to attend to their tasks. Standing among it all were the mothers of the Nighty Knights. The fretting women waited nearby, evidently warned by a scout traveling ahead.

As soon as they saw Bee's party, they called their children over with a mixture of concern, relief, and absolute rage. The children were dragged off by their ears to a cacophony of lectures and scolding about running off and getting into danger. The children complained loudly and tried to tell stories about their accomplishments, but the mothers were in no mood to hear. In a moment, Bee was left alone with all the horses. A few of Trent's workers came up and started to lead them away towards the stables, which would soon be overflowing. Perhaps she would need to talk to some of the engineers to get them to expand those.

A few moments later, Arthur appeared. Evidently a runner had been dispatched to find him when she arrived. The man came marching up to her and gave a crisp salute. "Welcome back, Miss Bee."

She nodded and returned the greeting without too much comment. She followed Arthur into a private meeting room in the castle for a debrief. "Thanks for going after them. I'm glad you caught up to them before they managed to do any harm."

Bee flinched slightly. "I...didn't really. They were already in the middle of their first operation when I reached them."

Arthur's face froze. His expression was one of cold granite. Seeing his concern, Bee tried to reassure him. "Uh, no one was hurt! But by the time I found them, they were rather insistent on helping."

"*First* operation, you said?" The words came out quietly. "Does that mean there was a *second?*"

Bee looked up and found Arthur slowly turning red. "I managed to talk them into doing something relatively safe, like stealing some horses while we waited for the professionals to show up. Susan and Captain Major's people, I mean. They got there earlier than we expected, so only one more night passed before I managed to lead them all back."

Despite her words, Arthur didn't seem to be calming down at all. Rather, at this point, it seemed like steam was blowing out of the man's ears.

"WHAT?" He barely restrained himself from shouting the word. Suddenly, Bee felt a lot less certain about this interaction.

"What do you mean? 'Managed' to talk them into coming back?! They are *children,* Bee! This is not something to compromise on. You just tell them that they're coming home and that's final. Instead, you led them on another raid?! What the hell were you thinking? Irene is FOUR!" His volume steadily increased until he was shouting in his parade voice. Bee flinched back and wiped a little bit of spittle off of her shoulder.

"They have every right to protect their home," she said, not willing to back down.

Arthur repeated himself. "She. Is. Four. She has no right to *protect* her home. She has the right to *be protected* and *safe* and grow up and be *a child*. I know that Void has been paying them special attention, and I dare not question what it is doing with them. I don't care if they are using wooden swords pretending to be gladiators in the arena. But we will *not* have them grow up any faster than they have to. They need to be *children*. Children are supposed to be innocent at their age. Maybe, *maybe* if they were teenagers, this might be a different conversation. But right now? If we use them like men, we are no better than the demons!"

Bee blinked at the venom in the general's words as he continued on his tirade about the children. He argued that the whole point of the army protecting the castle was so that these children could live in peace. Arthur didn't want them to grow up too quickly and face horrors they didn't need to. He didn't want them involved in any part of the war, not in the slightest.

Bee, though, couldn't help but disagree. This was their home. These were their families. They had been training so that they'd never have to worry about losing anyone ever again. How could they simply throw that aside? She agreed that there should be limits on what they could ask of them, but to have them do nothing? Whether the Knights, children that they were, actually acted like children or not was in many ways besides the point. At the very least, they had to respect their desire to help.

They made no progress for nearly a dozen minutes. Eventually, she stormed out of the room, unwilling to look Arthur in the face any longer. Furious, she ignored a requested meeting with Mary and dodged Tony in the halls before she eventually went looking for somewhere to be alone.

Soon she found herself on the castle roof, leaning against the tallest spire with her carpet rolled up next to her. It took a while for someone to find her. By that point, the sun was setting again, and she watched the moon rise into the field of stars above her.

The panting, sweating form of Susan grabbed the lip of the

roof and hauled itself over. She flopped onto the roof and rolled, bringing the rest of her body up after her. She then scooted next to Bee, leaning against the same spire a few feet away, and breathed heavily for a few minutes before she said anything. Bee didn't look at her, instead fixing her attention on the moon.

"You know why Arthur is mad at you, right?" the woman eventually said. Bee felt her anger flare up.

"He made it very clear. He thinks I put the children in more danger than was necessary. Because I'm *also* an irrational child who can't make decisions," Bee spat. Well, Arthur hadn't said that directly. But it became very clear what he had thought of her judgment during their argument.

Susan looked over at Bee and, in a gentler tone, spoke again. "How old are you, Bee?"

"Fourteen. We just celebrated it. You know that."

"Right. And you understand that a fourteen-year-old is still considered a child, right?"

Bee snorted. "I haven't been a child for a very long time, Susan."

SUSAN SIGHED AND CORRECTED HERSELF. "You realize you *should* still be a child, right?"

Bee shrugged, thinking of her few friends back at home who she hadn't talked to in years. What were they doing right now? Probably gossiping about boys and whatever people her age normally did. She didn't really know at this point. She sighed. "I suppose so. But I had to grow up fast."

"Bee. I understand it was hard, believe me. No one can even imagine what you went through. But just because you had to grow up fast doesn't mean anyone else should." Susan leaned back against the spire. "Arthur looks at you and sees someone he's proud to work with. But he also sees his own children. They're your age, you know. He sees what you should be, how carefree and happy you should be. Not the ball of stress you've been ever since we've known you.

"You've done things that no thirteen- or fourteen-year-old should ever be able to do. And it's impressive as hell, not to mention terrifying. But you should never have needed to do this in the first place. And just because you can do it doesn't mean that Nighty Knights should as well."

Bee mulled over the words in silence for a moment before Susan continued. "Unlike Arthur, I was there when Void first started training them. And do you remember how he started? Void played with them. It was a game, a way to work off their extra energy. Eventually, they learned actual technique and started playing soldiers. But that's all they really are doing. They're *playing* soldiers. They're imitating their parents and the people they look up to. All children do that. But just because they're good at acting doesn't mean that we should listen to them, or treat them like they actually *are* soldiers. When a child finds a stick and pretends it's a sword, and they march around the house, we don't then give them an actual sword and tell them to go kill people."

Bee clenched her jaw. "They still had every right to protect their home. Especially after everything they've been through. I will not deny them the ability to defend what they love."

Susan let out a long breath before starting to explain in a measured tone. "You're right when it comes down to it, and there's no other choice. If things get serious, they may need to grow up fast, and at that point they can make a difference. Well, some of them can. Some of them are just simply too young. But not like this. Not unless it's a last resort.

"The army that's coming at us? We don't know their numbers, but there is no way they're prepared for our level advantage. With our preparations, our sabotage will hit them so hard in this forest that we will probably outnumber them by the time they reach the wall. By that point, they'll be destroyed, and there will be no retreat. Overall, this is a minor battle that will probably be the first of many. And it's one we will win. We will crush them utterly, and the king will have no choice but to despair. And that's even before we consider Void returning." Susan gave Bee an even look. "This is *not* a situation where they need to grow up. They don't need to be standing between their families and destruction."

Bee sighed, slowly letting her anger go and seriously considering her friend's words. Maybe she had been wrong. She had gotten so used to everything being a life-and-death struggle that she had forgotten what it was like to exercise moderation. This conflict? Susan was right. Even if there was an army at their doorstep, they had prepared for this and seen it was coming. She had people around to help her now. People who knew what they were doing. Compared to a Lieutenant destroying the world, a city's destruction, or her imminent death by demon, this was a situation they were actually prepared for. At the very least, it had a ways to go before getting out of hand completely.

She breathed out a long breath and finally looked down from the stars to meet Susan's eyes. "I suppose you're right. I probably need to apologize to Arthur. And a lot of other people." A slight smile quirked the corner of her lips. "Perhaps he'd take a horse as an apology gift."

Susan gave her a soft smile. "I think he'd accept a more general apology. And a promise to protect the kids. But I don't suppose he'd say no to a horse."

Bee sighed, stood up, and offered a hand to Susan. "Well, however it goes, I hope Void comes back soon. Even if this isn't really as desperate as some of us may think, I wouldn't want to have to fight without its guidance."

I spent my time cleaning the village and its surroundings as the two dragons caught up for a little while. I considered seeking them out when night fell, but before I could I was interrupted. The same hunched chieftain who had welcomed us in and shown us the cave with the art approached me. She stood in my way as I trundled over to the center of the village to begin my search.

She bowed deep and made a strange rhythmic sound in a language I didn't understand. I had been doing my best to run language models all day. Still, as far as I can tell, there was no common ancestor between the language she spoke and any I knew. I had to completely recreate the entire thing from scratch. I estimated it would take me another several hours of hearing constant chatter before I understood it reasonably well. But even now I was able to understand a general gist of her words.

Apparently, she was warning me about something and asking for help. And something else that I didn't quite get. I wasn't sure how to react. So I just sat there and waited. She seemed satisfied with that somehow and asked some questions, only one of which I understood. It shared some similarities with a scene I had observed earlier, where one of the mothers was indicating that their troublesome small child should stay in one place. Instead of telling me to stay here, though, it seemed to be phrased as a question. She was asking if I was staying here.

I thought about it. I wasn't sure about the larger context, but for now, I'd be willing to stay a little longer while Daedalus and his brother caught up. I answered with an affirmative beep.

The old crone cocked her head, reached up with her gnarled fingers, and scratched behind her ear as if trying to decipher the meaning of the simple note. Eventually, she let out a very human-looking shrug with a harrumph. She turned and hobbled away, leaving me in the center of the village. Then I started to notice a very odd set of behaviors.

All the children were being ushered away for bedtime. But instead of going to the individual huts I had just spent the day cleaning, they all gathered in one large place, a defensible cave in the mountain. The adults huddled in after them, some of the larger ones standing by the cave mouth. The odd hunch in their shoulders started making a little more sense now. Perhaps that wasn't just their posture, but exhaustion showing through amongst the adults.

But why were all huddling in the caves when they had these small huts? Especially when I just cleaned them? Why, it didn't make any sense to me. There were clearly beds in them, but why were they not using them for their intended purpose? Did I also need to teach them the proper use of those?

When the last light of the setting sun faded, I started to get my answer. A grinding sound echoed through the foothills of the mountains, and strange shapes began to move in the shadows. I focused my Advanced Sensors on one of them and saw that it was just a pile of rocks.

Hm. That was interesting. My processors usually didn't play tricks on me. False positives when it came to movement for my sensors were extraordinarily low, and there was no way this sensor would be triggering all at once just because of some light-based phenomenon. It only took me 2.1 more seconds to confirm the fact that I had actually seen something. The pile of rocks shifted again, slowly, as if I were watching a child's block tower collapse in reverse. The stone pile reached up and up, stones stacking until it was a towering twelve feet tall. At that point, it stopped growing, and the base split into two pillars.

Rocks continued to gather to either side of the tower as they started to extend into two long arms. It took nearly two minutes and forty-two seconds before the transformation was complete. Then, once it was fully formed, it took a thundering step forward.

That was odd. Looking around, I saw that several other rock piles had done something similar in the few minutes I had been watching. Around the village, nearly two dozen of these stone monstrosities slowly made their way forward. I looked over to the cave all the snowmen were hiding in and realized I couldn't easily detect its entrance anymore. They had stacked several huge boulders inside the cave mouth, blocking the way.

Suddenly, the old crone's question made a lot more sense. She was asking if I wanted to stay with them in the cave where it was safe. That was rather kind of them to offer me shelter. After all, I was a complete stranger they'd only met earlier today. Perhaps they did appreciate my cleaning. Maybe I should have taken them up on their offer.

I sat in the center of the village and watched as the stone piles slowly made their way toward me. Judging based on the trajectories of all two dozen, they were headed directly for me, not just the village in general. Thinking about the mess each one of their steps would leave in the newly leveled streets made my bristles curl. And what would happen if they stomped through one of these fragile huts?

I decided I was going to do something about this. Activating my Thrusters, I lifted off gently and shot towards the edge of the village.

The trajectories of the rocks shifted to follow me. However, the ones on the other side of the village were still passing directly through it as if they didn't even register the huts as obstacles. It was going to be tricky to make sure that the village wasn't damaged. I moved far away from the village in an attempt to lose the rock monsters. But even from a long distance away, I could feel all their trajectories shifting to follow me. How were they tracking me?

I had a few ideas. They had latched on to me even before there was motion. So clearly, they must be able to see me or sense me in some other way besides sight. Perhaps it was due to the concentration of energy in my batteries. But how could they tell?

The other question was how they hadn't detected the villagers. If these rock monsters were actually tracking me by some method other than sight, then they must have also locked onto other things besides my energy signature. Perhaps my energy signature was just their primary target for now, and they would move on to something else later. But that was something I would have to figure out after I had saved the village.

I navigated back toward the clusters of rocks. Once I got close enough, I started to move in an arc around the village, gathering the golems with me and pulling them around the village outskirts. I carefully planned my flight path to pull them together and away from any huts or roads. It was tricky to get the balance right, requiring a lot of minute speed and angle adjustments. If the village hadn't been up against a mountainside, I don't think I would have been able to manage it. But after a decent amount of effort, I had the crowd of rock monsters following along behind me out of the village.

CHAPTER 69

HEAVIER THAN A MOUNTAIN

I SURVEYED the shambling towers of rocks that followed me. Now, I just needed to figure out what to do with them. I supposed I could consume them all or chop them to bits with my Sanitation Lamp. Or maybe I could destroy them permanently? I guessed I could consume them and transmit them to energy like anything else. That would probably be the simplest approach.

After considering it a bit longer, I decided there was no reason not to. Arcing through the sky, I curved to attack the first one in the pack. My Sanitation Lamp shot forward in a beam of blinding blue-violet light. It blasted the stone to surprisingly little effect. The rock in its front slowly heated up, but only the single rock the laser touched was affected, not the whole pile. Based on my modeling, it would take me a significant amount of energy and time to heat even that to the point where it would slowly melt a hole.

All right. That wasn't going to work. I needed to change tactics. I came in closer using my Air Manipulation and tried to lift them up, but came up with only dirt and snow. The piles were somehow much heavier than my sensors indicated they should be. It was as if I was trying to pick up the entire mountain instead of a few individual rocks. Confused, I tried to use my vacuum to pull them into my dustbin. Again, they didn't budge. As though they were connected to the earth itself rather than floating collections of disparate rock.

Pulling out my Divine Sword, I charged the monsters head-on. The golden blade passed through the arm of the lead golem, and I felt the rocks easily shatter in its path. The arm fell loose, with several cracked stones hitting the ground beneath them. Activating my vacuum once more showed that I had no trouble consuming those. But the rocks were now strangely inert. They had no energy beyond that of normal stones, unlike what I'd expected.

Slowly, other nearby rocks worked the pile. The arm regrew as rocks shifted and morphed into a new limb, replacing it.

I hacked into it again, spinning between its legs as I took off. The pile collapsed as the stones were split in two. But it kept reforming slowly as the others closed in around me. How odd. I decided to try something else, this time slashing straight up its body with the sword. The whole thing collapsed into just a pile of unmoving rocks. But as I flew up, one of the others swung at me. A fist made of rocks smashed into the soft plastic covering of my sensors and sent me hurtling back toward the mountainside. I felt the plastic shell crack in a few places, and my energy levels slowly drained as my repair functions went about mending the damage.

These things were strong. They moved slowly, but I was having real trouble hurting them. And without being able to simply pull them into myself and dissolve them, I realized I didn't have as many offensive weapons as I had thought. Perhaps I had grown arrogant in my last few fights.

Fighting a weakened Lieutenant Demon after it had just woken up had felt quite impressive, even if Beatrice deserved a lot of the credit. So had destroying the wraith and the undead with it. But I had to accept that I was remarkably well-suited to fighting those enemies, and maybe I needed to be a little more creative in some situations.

My damage healed, and I floated up from the crater I had left in the mountainside. I started running some models to see what other options I had.

As they worked on my options and tried to dissect my opponents, I played a little bit of keep-away with the rock monsters. Luckily, they were slow, so it wasn't too hard to stay ahead of them. As I watched the progress bar in my mind's eye, I started playing a game where I tried to get them to hit each other. And to my surprise, as I did this, the bar started filling a little bit faster. I must've been getting some information from them that was helping the models fill in some blanks quicker than I expected in a foreground process.

I tried to figure out why, and it only took me a few seconds to realize the pattern. They did not hit each other at all. They worked in complete harmony, each strike layered one after another, covering openings as though they shared the same sensor inputs, making me work to find a way out if I became cornered. Their movements left no way for them to accidentally damage each other. It was like they were the limbs of the same person. When my model finally spat out some answers, I wasn't as surprised as I probably should have been.

These were probably not their own creatures. They were almost certainly puppets of something else. It explained a lot of things, like why I had been relatively unsuccessful in damaging them. Apparently, even if I managed to destroy them utterly, that wouldn't have any more effect than trimming off someone's toenails. They were expendable and interchangeable. The towers of rock would just reform, or new ones would come out after me.

The only question I couldn't answer was why they were chasing me. What had I done to anger something so powerful and seemingly mindless? It was a complete mystery to me. I didn't think I missed any attempts to communicate or anything along those lines. So clearly, this was an instinctual response.

If this had instead been an intentional attack, I could imagine this would have been a lot more effective, too. As things were, the creatures posed no danger to me. Rather, it just forced me out of the area. I supposed the point could've been to hide something around here, but that just seemed fairly unlikely. So, I went with my gut instinct and said it was a responsive protocol with no actual consciousness behind it. But the big question remained: how was I going to deal with it?

I pulled up out of the reach of the rock puppets and reached out with my Advanced Sensors, seeing if I could detect where the energy that powered them came from. As I focused on that, I felt something impact the undercarriage next to my wheelhouse, sending me spinning through the air. Looking down, I saw a small rock falling away. Suddenly, dozens of others were flying after me in a hail of stones. Adjusting my Thrusters, I began taking evasive maneuvers, never able to stand still for more than a quarter of a second.

Before the rocks found me again, I spun, twirled, and looped through the air as I did my best to trace where the energy was coming from. For each of them, the pattern was very similar. Energy seeped through their shapes in a simple one-to-one overlay. The energy then spread down into the ground and trailed off towards the mountain peak. I followed the path back toward the source of the energy, hoping to see if there was something I could disrupt along the way. But about halfway up the trail, I lost the path.

The energy didn't lead directly to the peak. In fact, once it got most of the way up the mountain, it sort of dispersed into the center of the mountain. I lost any ability to follow it without burrowing or digging deeper.

I needed to collect my thoughts. So I soared up above the mountain, well out of rock-throwing range, and watched for a response. Unexpectedly, the rock monsters did not go back to the village. Rather, they simply stopped and collapsed into rock piles. As they did, I felt the energy recede back into the mountain and diffuse throughout the entire peak.

Huh? This was a really weird phenomenon. I wondered if it was what Daedalus was feeling. I needed to go find him and ask.

Bee knocked on the doorframe of Arthur's office and held her breath. She watched as Arthur finished scratching something on a paper before looking up and noticing her.

She had to admit she was a little bit nervous. It had been several hours since they had their argument, and Bee took most of that time to calm down before talking to Susan. But now she had to at least come and mend fences. It wasn't that she was entirely convinced the man was right, but she could see his point of view now and understand his frustrations. She hoped that he also felt the same way. At the very least, maybe he'd see how her decision at the time made sense. But it wasn't something they should be fighting over when they both agreed on the main points. And when they had a war to address.

"Hey." Bee gave a slightly awkward wave. He looked at her for a second with hard eyes before gesturing for her to come in. She shut the door behind her before taking a seat in one of the chairs across from his desk.

She opened her mouth to apologize, but Arthur beat her to it. "I'm sorry I lost my temper with you earlier. That was out of line. I understand you were put in a tough situation and made the best of what you could, but as a father, it's hard for me to see the safety of children put aside so recklessly."

Bee was waving her hands in front of her. "No, no, no, no. That was my bad. I probably could have made some better decisions." She hesitated, then sighed. "I talked with Susan a little bit, and she helped me see it from your perspective. Well, I can't say I totally agree with some of the statements you made. I do think that you are probably right in that I should have been more insistent on coming home with them. However, I do not think that Nighty Knights are going to see it that way. Say that they're children as much as you like, but they have real power. They don't all have to listen to us if they really don't want to."

Arthur nodded thoughtfully, "Yes, they're all young and easily impressionable. They've looked up to you and Tony and Void, obviously, with all your going out saving the day, and they want to do the same. I tried to help teach Bradley to avoid something like this, but..." The man sighed. "I should have realized this was a more general issue. But I think we actually can figure something out for them."

Arthur paused. "It's been a long military tradition to use young boys as messengers and pages during battles. They run arrows between fletchers and run messages between officers. It's a useful role but one that we'd prefer not to spare men for if we don't have to. Most importantly, it's safe.

"I think perhaps we can get the Knights involved with the effort like they want, but in a non-combat way. That will help them learn discipline and structure. Then, one day far in the future, they can choose to take part in a more direct manner if they want to. Once they're mature enough to make that decision. Though hopefully, they won't even have to at that point."

CHAPTER 70

HEART OF THE MOUNTAIN

BEE NODDED at Arthur's suggestion, "I think we can do better than having the Nighty Knights run messages. But yes, I agree. Something along those lines would be great. It should help to get them involved, but keep them safe. I don't know if you're aware, but their commander, Felix, has the ability to talk to anyone in his command over a large distance. I think we can use that to send almost instantaneous messages across the castle and maybe even the whole valley."

Arthur's eyebrows shot up in surprise. "What is the skill's name?"

Bee frowned. "I'm not sure. It seemed unique, like many of them. It's not something I've ever read about."

Arthur nodded emphatically. "I've never even heard of anything of the sort."

"It seems insanely useful, though," Bee said with a shrug. "So far, we haven't really been able to explore it much aside from calling them together for dinner and such. But I imagine when it comes to coordinating battlefield tactics, it will be invaluable."

Arthur leaned back in his chair, thinking. "Well, I'll get one of my more experienced captains to debrief them. We'll see if we can learn anything about their talents that we can use in a more nontraditional role. I want to put some with the engineers, some as messengers, some with the archers. And if the commander...you said Felix was his name? If his messaging skill is as powerful as you said. I'll definitely want him with me. In fact, I might make him my squire or something if he's going to be commanding the Nighty Knights into the future.

"Between him and Bradley, I imagine we'll be able to help wrangle them into shape." The older man nodded to himself. "Perhaps I might be able to help set him on a path that would make him a better commander than someone simply trying to keep the men in line."

" I would like that," Bee said. "I'll make sure they're where they need to be. Let's assume we start this sometime tomorrow, since they'll have to finish reuniting with their families. But I need to go make sure that they don't try to sneak off again."

"All right, then." As Bee got up to leave, the commander stopped her. "Oh, one more thing. Do you have any idea when Void might return?"

Bee shook her head. "None. Should we be worried?"

Arthur shrugged noncommittally. "You can never tell what surprises the enemy might have. We shouldn't need any backup by a long shot. But I'd be a fool not to know exactly what I have in store."

I soared over the rock golems that were now wandering around the mountain aimlessly. I had considered going to find Daedalus, but I couldn't locate him anywhere on the mountain, and I was hesitant to leave the snowmen undefended as they were for too long. But I found if I stayed high enough out of range, the rock golems would ignore me, and I could just observe.

Even at this distance, I was still ready to zip down in a second if the snowmen appeared to be in danger. While I soared through the air, I took a moment to study the creatures as they rumbled along. After all my significant studying earlier, I could kind of see a pattern in their movements. It wasn't a fixed pattern or anything like that. But, after observing enough, I saw that their pathing had them completely covering the mountain after an hour and a half or so of searching.

I could have devised a much more efficient route for them, especially with how many there were. But what they were doing worked well enough, assuming that was their job. It was almost as if they were on patrol. At least there weren't any redundancies in their routing.

However, from the snowmen's village and their reaction, I could almost guarantee that this was a recent development. There were beds and everything in the huts that the snowman had, so presumably, they were used to sleeping inside. Unless they truly did not understand what beds were used for. I couldn't entirely rule out the possibility. But the presence of this threat was a much better explanation for why they weren't seeing use.

For one, it was quite dangerous. The rock men definitely had damaged some of the scrubby trees that grew up at this altitude by simply walking. They would likely have no problem stomping their way through a hut completely without malice. And if they were trying to attack? The village would be in shambles within minutes. Not to mention that if the snowmen were anything like humans, they needed quiet to sleep. The level of noise the rock men gave off while moving wouldn't make that an easy criterion to meet.

I again attempted to follow the strands of the energy fueling the rock monsters. Again, I found it led nowhere, just into the mountain. I couldn't see anything else leading away from the mountain, either. This led me to a frightening conclusion.

If there was no other energy source in the mountain, the only possibility was that the mountain itself was the source of the energy. What's more, this wasn't like the still energy that suffused

Daedalus's artifacts or Beatrice's alchemy experiments. No, it was more like the energy that one might find in a living being. Did that mean the mountain itself was alive?

I hadn't even noticed this signature when I first approached. How many other things were alive right under my chassis? How many such instances had I missed? As my sensors gained more and more capabilities, it just made me realize how much I was missing.

Daedalus watched as Thucydides flapped frantically ahead of him. It wasn't that Thucydides was a poor flier, per se. His struggles stemmed more from Daedalus having a significant advantage when it came to size, levels, and even practical experience.

It had taken them a little bit of work and Thucydides scratching symbols in the dirt, but they had narrowed down the position of the anomaly that had drawn him here. Now it was time to check it out. It wasn't too far away, but buried significantly underground.

Right now, they were searching the area for some sort of underground cave entrance. He had little hope that even if they found one, they'd be able to fit through it. So he expected to spend some time burning his way through the rock to reach the location. Thucydides, though, wanted to exhaust every other option before he had to do hard manual labor. It meant that Daedalus was just about ready to drop to the ground and start digging if it meant finally doing something.

Thucydides made one final larger circle, trying to scan for openings. Daedalus just rolled his eyes. The red dragon banked and headed toward the spot they had located.

From here, they needed to go only about fifty feet down. It wouldn't take more than half an hour if they worked together or forty-five minutes if he did it by himself. As he took a deep breath and felt the fire build in his chest, he watched as his little brother started to take another lap despite their agreement. Daedalus just shrugged his massive shoulders and focused, losing himself in the fire.

He modulated his magic output so that he wasn't expending too much power, just enough that his natural regeneration would offset his efforts to burn through the rock. It was the most efficient way of doing things. Especially if he was worried about something at the bottom being dangerous. Besides, it still resulted in a quite respectable stream of fire. The mountainside glowed with molten orange-yellow light as Daedalus exhaled. Clouds of vaporized snow obscured the streams of liquid rock that began to flow downward.

By the time Thucydides had given up searching for another easier entrance, Daedalus had already made it 95 percent of the way through to the source, at least by his estimations. What had once been a sheer mountain now bore a glassy tunnel of molten rock reaching deep into its heart. He had started to have a little trouble when the melted rock had blocked his fire from reaching new material, but an extra bit of magic had taken care of it. Now there was an obsidian tunnel wide enough for him to glide down as well as fly back out when he was done.

The two dragons slipped down into the cavern, Daedalus leading the way, and they found themselves in the circular center of a massive hemisphere. Across the floor, concentric circles of tiny intricate runes spread out in all directions. The runes were carved deep into the rock, showing little sign of erosion over time. As Daedalus read them, he started to understand what was going on.

The runes spoke of containment of a deep and ancient evil, one stuck here forever until the end of time. On and on they went. But he could feel that they were quite powerful. Surprisingly so. For something not made by a dragon.

"Huh. I didn't realize that they had moved the other Lieutenants after we bound them," Daedalus told his little brother.

"I hadn't heard about it either," Thucydides said casually, shrugging.

"It appears they couldn't move him far," Daedalus snorted. "This wasn't that far away from where we had captured him. This one was the Death of Hope, I think? Anyway, it looks like they took the binding Archimedes made and reinforced it a lot and then hid them so that they wouldn't be tampered with. That was smart. I should find out who did that and thank them."

"It doesn't appear to be enough, though," Thucydides remarked as they looked at the empty pedestal in the center of the circle.

"No. No, it does not," Daedalus said, rather disappointed. "It appears that everything is falling apart."

"Yeah, that's not good," Thucydides echoed. "Do you think we need to go track down Archimedes? I really have no idea where he's resting nowadays, but from what I heard, he was the only one who managed to do anything about this. With your help, of course."

"Of course. He wasn't the only one. And also, I wasn't involved with all their captures." Daedalus felt a surge of pride at how humble he sounded. "But it would be nice to find him again. I, unfortunately, also have really no idea where to look, though. After we had rid the world of the last one, I mostly just stuck around and waited for Archibald to awaken."

Thucydides just rolled his eyes. Daedalus ignored the gesture and continued, "But I don't think we need to find him urgently. Well, it would be a nice backup. But we don't really have to worry. We have Spot, after all."

"Spot? The little guy you came with?" Thucydides asked with obvious skepticism. "Are you sure about that? I mean, he seemed nice and polite and all, but he's not even a dragon. What can he possibly do?"

Daedalus let out a deep belly laugh that shook the walls around them. "Oh, little bro. You have no idea. Spot may not be a dragon, but it's the next best thing. No, no. It's a godling."

"A—a what?" Thucydides asked.

"Ah, I forgot. Before your time, probably. I think the last godling died when you were but a hatchling. Suffice it to say, it's stronger than you. By a lot. A *lot*, a lot." Daedalus didn't add that Spot was likely stronger than him, too. It was close, but he wouldn't want to risk a one-on-one fight with the nascent deity. It was a good thing that the little terror was friendly.

Thucydides blinked, stunned. "Really? You're going to have to explain this whole godling thing to me. They sound interesting."

"That's one way of putting it. Anyway, we should probably head back and go see if we can find the little guy. It would be good to have it around if a Lieutenant makes an appearance."

Thucydides shrugged, and without further ado, they beat their wings and rose from the cavern. It was time to go talk to a god.

CHAPTER 71

RETURN OF THE MESS MAKERS

BEE AND TONY sat across from each other on a grassy knoll, munching contentedly on a plate of sandwiches. They were having lunch together in a rare quiet moment within their otherwise frantic schedules. She only had half an hour's break, but she had been convinced very politely by Mary and a few others that she needed some time for herself. So when Mary had sent her son her way with a serving basket of lunch, they had gone on a little impromptu picnic.

Tony was his usual charming self, doing an excellent job of joking with her and keeping her mind off of what was going on. He managed to make her feel like things were almost normal. Not that they'd ever really been normal, but it was as close as Bee had felt in a long while.

Then that thirty-minute imposed break ended, and everything got a lot worse.

As soon as they packed up and started to head back, the significantly more relaxed Bee had been ambushed by a messenger waiting just around the corner. Apparently, she'd been summoned to the command center, where Arthur, Captain Major, and Susan were waiting.

"Do you know what this is about?" Bee asked the messenger, and he shrugged a little bit.

"Um. Yeah. Some reports came in, and apparently, we got some more news about the troop allotments."

Bee frowned. That didn't seem urgent enough to warrant a meeting like this. They had a rather rough idea about infantry versus cavalry and all that, but it wasn't going to massively change their strategy, at least not that she was aware of.

When she reached the meeting room, she saw the taut and drawn faces of Susan and Captain Major, along with a rather haggard-looking Arthur. That was when she realized that there might have been something else to the report than she'd been led to believe.

"What's this?" she asked. Susan and Captain Major exchanged a look, for once putting their rivalry to the side. Rather, they each seemed to be hoping the other would speak. Eventually, Arthur's frown deepened, and he took charge.

"It seems that we have a problem. Some of our scouts have been reporting odd anomalies for a bit. The saboteurs have been running into more resistance than they should. And recently, when we hit them hard enough, we discovered why. Apparently, many of these soldiers aren't actually as human as they appear. When pressed, some of them will transform into demons."

Bee frowned. "What kind of demons?"

Captain Major and Susan finally found their tongues. Susan spoke first. "No particular kind. As far as we can tell, there are some lesser demons and various elemental varieties. A greater demon even took an entire squad out at one point."

"That's concerning," Bee said as she processed the news. "The lower orders of demons aren't intelligent enough to act human, much less disguise themselves. How do we not see this? How do they interact with the people around them? Do the regular humans in the army know what's going on?"

The slew of questions was mostly met with confused shrugs.

"We've only gotten some initial reports. My second is out looking for himself," Susan said, indicating the first group of people she had trained. "We'll know more when Ruarch gets back."

Captain Major said, "We have some reports from the military scouts, too, confirming. As far as we can tell, most of the army isn't aware of it. The areas that have encountered more resistance are all isolated incidents where every one of them is a demon. And it appears that maybe some select officers are aware of it and keeping them separate from the rest of the camp. As to how the demons are acting human-ish, we don't have the magical expertise to make that call. Perhaps if we bring some back to you, you might be able to tell."

Bee shrugged. "It's worth a shot. I won't know for sure. It might be best if I go out there and see for myself."

Arthur grimaced, but Susan and Captain Major both nodded.

"It might be best," Arthur said, "but it's a risk we probably don't need to take. If there are actual greater demons in here, you might be in more danger than you think. And it's not worth risking when you'll find out in a day or two anyway. Let's get you a corpse of one of the lesser demons or something for you to examine. Then we'll go from there. There's no point in putting the chariot before the horse."

Bee didn't like it but saw the logic. It wouldn't be as good as a live specimen, of course. But it made sense to take things one step at a time. "Is there anything else we know about this?"

"No. It just matches what we've been hearing about the king through our spies. Apparently, he's become far more paranoid than before. Some say he's gone mad. We're getting reports from our first people to reach the capital, and they confirm that things have gotten a lot worse in the kingdom recently. I think that we have to seriously consider that there is some dark influence in the king," Arthur said in a weary tone.

Bee remembered something they'd talked about earlier. "The advisor you spoke to warned you about this."

Arthur nodded. "Yes. He was having significant doubts about the king, and while I initially thought that he might be overblowing concerns that the king had been compromised, now I believe he might be correct."

Bee scuffed the ground with her toe. "I suppose this means that once we defeat this army, it's not going to be the end of it, is it?"

"It never was, Miss Bee. It never was."

The meeting wrapped up with very little else to decide. It felt really important at that moment to do something about what they'd just learned, but there wasn't much they could do besides wait for more information. It was frustrating, but she luckily had an outlet. She trudged her way back into the castle after holding some quick conversations. This hopefully would help to keep morale up.

She worked her way up to the laboratory, where she found Maranda working tirelessly for the war effort. The fireworks that she had made for Void actually had shown great potential for military applications. Apparently, the ones deployed at her birthday party were heavily modified to emphasize the color and lights rather than the explosive power. If they just undid that, the vials made excellent projectiles for the siege equipment. Scatter shots of multiple vials could be launched from trebuchets, or they could be attached to a ballista bolt and cause much more damage in a specific area than a simple stone.

Now that Bee knew they were dealing with demons, she had some ideas about injecting demon's bane into the fireworks or something along those lines. They would really need improved siege equipment if it was going to be used against demonic forces rather than just simple humans. But in some ways, the explosives weren't the most practical. Each vial was expensive and slow to make, and when they had so many targets, each one could only do so much. That wasn't the only idea that she and Maranda had, though, and not the most useful.

Bee had carved out enough research time for herself that she had learned some basic enchanting. It was a fascinating discipline where she could inlay runes with material or draw them on surfaces to imbue them with certain magical properties. The basics were simple enough that she'd even had some successes. It was similar in principle to the warding circles from demonology, but just in a slightly more permanent method. The runes were finicky to get right. Unsuccessful ones had a chance of fizzling out. Still, if you did them wrong in a very particular way, a cracking explosion could be obtained. And that was just what the doctor had ordered.

Today, Bee strode over to a large pile of uniformly sized stones. They would work in trebuchets and catapults once they were enchanted to explode on impact. A few of them were already armed and dangerous, but she had a lot of work ahead.

She actually had some proper enchantments she was working on as well. They were a lot harder to pull off and more likely to fail, but she had learned how to give the rocks extra momentum, for example. Still, her experiments on homing or improved accuracy so far hadn't achieved more than a few stubbed toes. Something that would guide a thrown object toward a designated target was a very complicated ask, especially considering how much she was pioneering in this field. She had to both work with how long the thing would be in flight and then also somehow designate a target.

If she could figure out how to mix that with anti-demonic explosives in the vials, perhaps they could be used much more effectively. It was going to take many experiments to work, and they didn't have much time. Luckily, Maranda had taken to magic even more than she had. Well, Bee definitely had an edge on her in certain aspects, but Maranda was a true savant. Perhaps they'd be able to figure something out together.

I was stuck. I had determined that the mountain was alive, but I didn't have a good way of communicating with it. I didn't want to leave to go find Daedalus while the snowmen were still vulnerable, though I supposed they would probably be okay if they had survived as long as they had without me. And I couldn't just remove the offending rock monsters on my own. It was quite the conundrum.

Just as I was about to despair, two broad sets of dragon wings appeared on the horizon: one red and one white. Within a few minutes, I was no longer alone in the sky.

I quickly replayed the scene of what happened for Daedalus and Thucydides to see, and they both groaned as they watched. Daedalus looked over at his little brother with a cloudy expression. "Thucydides, how did you fail to mention that you were living next to a mountain spirit?"

Thucydides looked anywhere but at us. "Yeah, I...well..." he spluttered, starting several sentences before giving up and just shrugging. "I didn't know. Either it's fairly young, or it just was dormant the entire time I was here. It's not my fault."

Daedalus shook in laughter. "Oh, you silly thing. This is what you get for all your meditation and symbol-scratching."

Thucydides shot his brother a baleful look. "Hey, it wasn't really something I thought to check! Who would even think that? Besides, it wasn't causing any problems anyways."

I quickly disabused him of the notion that it hadn't caused any problems by replaying a few of the scenes of me absolutely chopping apart a rock creature and it just reforming like nothing happened. Thucydides winced. "Yeah, I suppose that could be a problem. But normally, on their own spirits don't do much."

Daedalus grumbled. "I suppose I'll go talk to it. Mountain spirits aren't generally unreasonable. Just a little bit slow."

CHAPTER 72

WAR NEVER CHANGES

I WANTED to interrupt and ask how Daedalus planned on talking to the "spirit" that was in the mountain. But before I could, he just opened his mouth and let out a rumbling roar. It was different than his usual ones—this sounded like rocks grinding on each other.

Thucydides and I exchanged confused glances as we hung there, waiting. The only sign that something had happened was that the stone golems down below had paused mid-stride. 29.7 seconds later, the golems shifted back into an organized formation.

Then, from across the mountain, another rumbling sounded. If I hadn't been paying attention, I would have assumed it was just random bunch of rocks falling, but given the context it seemed like a response. Daedalus hovered in the air for a good 31.4 seconds afterward. Then he opened his mouth and roared back. This time, he sounded like an avalanche of rocks pounding down a snowy slope. I was very impressed that he managed to have enough vocal dexterity to convey all this.

Thucydides winced, shaking his head as if the noise was bothering him. It seemed that the mountain and the dragon were going to be talking for a while. So, the two of us headed a little ways away, where the vibrations were not nearly as intense. He sat down heavily in front of me in a clearing less than a mountain over. "I didn't know my brother could speak Mountain Spirit."

I let out a negative beep and flashed up a message. "Me neither. I had no idea that mountain spirits even existed."

Thucydides shrugged his massive scaled shoulders. His wings rippled along his back as they settled back into place. "Yeah, I had heard of them. They always sounded kinda boring, if you ask me. But wow, Big Bro is amazing."

We waited for several hours listening to what sounded like the mountain tearing itself apart. Every time I checked, I could still see the distant form of Daedalus up in the sky, so I assumed they were just having a good conversation. Eventually, though, the rumbling came to a close. Daedalus winged his way over and landed before us. Thucydides impatiently asked for an update. "So what did it say?"

"Well, apparently, it felt the Lieutenant escape a while back. It's also been trying to destroy what it feels is the unnatural evil set loose in the world for the past several months."

"The Lieutenant escaped?" I asked. That was news to me.

"Oh, yeah." Daedalus quickly filled me in on what he and his little brother had found in the cave. It was worrying, to say the least. Honestly, if this Lieutenant had been free for a long time, it was likely to be at a much higher power level than Nazareth'gak had been when we faced him. Not to mention that we didn't have Beatrice and Tony slinging anti-demon measures and other assaults at it to soften it up.

Well, I was a lot more powerful too, at least. But I had heard Daedalus's stories. Nazareth'gak's regeneration had been bad enough to deal with, but if this one regenerated faster? That might make it even harder to get the thing in my dustbin, especially if they resisted consumption like the mountain spirit had.

I expressed my concerns about being able to face a Lieutenant at full power, and Daedalus nodded. "It makes sense. It's hard to say if you had trouble consuming the mountain spirit because it was at a higher level than you or because of some inherent property of it being a mountain. I would normally say it's a coin flip. But if you've consumed a higher level before, then it's probably the latter. Mountains are heavy, and it would make sense that they would be metaphysically immovable. But at the same time, the mountain spirit was probably level 87 or even 90. I don't think it has broken the 90 barrier yet."

I blinked, my light flickering in confusion. The mountain was level 80-plus? That was mildly terrifying.

"So what did you tell the mountain spirit?" I pressed for Daedalus to continue his story.

His recounting of the conversation continued. Apparently, he'd explained to the mountain spirit that the Lieutenant was probably long gone, and it wasn't worth terrifying the snowmen villagers staying on top of the mountain to find it. The mountain spirit requested that they hunt down the Lieutenant and, if they did find it, to let the mountain spirit know that it was done so it wouldn't have to stay on alert. Daedalus readily agreed, and decided that wouldn't be an issue.

Thucydides nodded uncertainly. "Okay, so...we're going to track down a Lieutenant now?"

Daedalus started to nod, then froze. His eyes went wide as his neck stretched toward the sky.

"What is it?" Thucydides asked.

"I need to go," Daedalus said, already beating his wings urgently. A moment later, he was up in the air. Thucydides and I began to follow until he noticed us. "No, you two need to take care of this. I need to get back. Something's happening with Archibald."

Thucydides and I exchanged looks. I supposed Thucydides knew a lot more about the world than I did, so he'd certainly be helpful in figuring out where to start looking. But as we tracked down the Lieutenant, I just worried that the two of us together might not be enough to destroy it. If Daedalus had been helping me, my models were a bit more confident about our chances. I simply wasn't sure about this smaller dragon, though. He didn't seem nearly as powerful as I was led to believe all dragons were.

Oh well. We had a job to do. I didn't know how long this thing had been on the loose for, but I shuddered to think of the destruction and messes it must have gotten up to. It had to be stopped. Hopefully Beatrice wouldn't mind me taking a little longer on my trip.

As it turned out, Bee didn't have to go to the army to confirm whether or not there were demons amongst the ranks of humans. That had been made very clear from numerous reports, and one squad had already brought back the body of what was indeed a demon. Judging based off of the way the encampment was organized and what appeared to be a concerted effort to make sweeping attacks on each section of the camp, nearly 20 percent of the forces arrayed against them were demons.

Of course, some of the most basic demons were barely better than soldiers. But when it came to siege warfare, the demons did not care if they lived or died, and the ability to climb up walls would make this a little bit more difficult. The best thing these weaker demons had going for them was that most of the rest of the enemy didn't seem to be aware that they were demons. They still wore their disguises, and some interception of communications said that the officers were telling the regular soldiers that the demon corpses they found after raids were from the attackers. Bee had to admit that the lie was rather clever and plausible, knowing what the military would think of Void.

The way that the camp was set up kept most of the humans from the actual raids that affected the demons. She had the inkling of an idea to force a demon confrontation with the rest of the army. It would be hard to organize, but her idea to instigate a fight between some real humans and some demons in the camp was shot down by Susan and a few others. Apparently, it wouldn't be that hard to say that the demon was just an infiltrator or something like that.

Still, if the demons were going to be openly used in combat, the word had to come out eventually. Hopefully, they could use this to their advantage somehow, though she wasn't quite sure how yet. But that time was coming sooner than she would have liked.

Late the night before, the enemy had camped out just outside of bowshot of the third wall. They could have maybe moved some trebuchets or catapults forward and started bombarding them, but they decided to wait. It would be a surprise right as the attack on the third wall started in earnest. Between that and the wall's other surprises, the Church of the Cleansing Void had planned to make quite the impression. So the members of the castle's forces and the army simply stood watch on the wall, keeping hidden for the most part.

No response was given, and no shouts or calls were made. They tried to make themselves seem as relaxed and unimposing as possible. The only reason she was there was in case they asked for some sort of conversation before the battle. Bee didn't expect that there would be, though. Arthur hoped that they would want to parlay, but apparently, Bee was right. As the sun set, still no one had come out to ask for their leader. It didn't seem that they expected or even sought their surrender.

The next morning, Bee stood on the wall, looking out over the endless sea of tents of the army ahead of her. The sun was just breaking the horizon, and she had to admit she was getting a little tired. She would be here for the opening of the battle and fight for several hours before going back to rest in the first shift. If things went as planned, anyway. Ahead, the soldiers formed ranks under the watchful gazes of officers and began to march towards the wall.

At the blast of a horn, Bee raised a signal flag, and the defenders all along the wall got ready. Archers readied their bows and waited for her signal. It was about a quarter of the overall forces.

They expected to lose this wall quickly. They would empty all the arrows they had stored here and then disengage at the first real sign of contact. As soon as the enemy forces reached a few discreet rocks piled up in no-man's-land, Bee dropped the signal flag she was holding, and a volley of arrows shot forward to slam into their ranks.

While formations had to move the wounded out or step over the fallen. It didn't slow their approach at all. Every three seconds, Bee called for another volley, and the thousands upon thousands of arrows that rained into the approaching soldiers quickly turned their march into a sprint as they launched toward the walls. A second flag went up, and the army stopped shooting in volleys in favor of firing as quickly as they could, practically straight down into the faces of their enemies.

They were at such a short distance that there really was no need to aim. The bows were powerful enough that pretty much any shot would at least take the enemy out of the battle, and the enemy's shields were not used as effectively as they should have been. As Arthur had warned. The enemy's initial forces barely reached the wall. Once they did, half the archers put down their bows and picked up long spears.

Each was twelve to fifteen feet long, long enough to reach the bottom of the wall from the very top. Of course, the length made them rather flimsy, but that was why there were backups. Frantically stabbing down, they forced anyone who was attempting to scale the wall to back off. The enemy had brought some ladders, but the concentrated fire made it so that even those ladders advanced very slowly.

The archers then shifted their focus and started firing into the back ranks of the army, not wanting to disrupt their allies' targets. Besides, that was where the officers likely were. Arthur had shared some bits of wisdom the night before when they were all up on the ramparts. The way he said it made it stick in Bee's mind, and hopefully everyone else's as well: "Aim for the fancy hats."

Those were the officers. Anyone with some sort of insignia that denoted them as something besides a regular soldier would be prioritized. If they removed enough of their leaders, they would quickly run out of direction. And without good leaders, they'd be slow and efficient, or even be forced to retreat. Bee doubted that last bit would happen, but removing the command staff did seem like a smart decision.

Once the battle was in full swing, Bee stopped worrying about signaling and pulled out her own weapon. Her broom couldn't really do too much from up here, but it felt good to have it in her hand. She maybe had some options to throw rocks or try to use a bow herself, but she didn't feel the need. It was better for her to sit back and wait to deal with any problems that did show up.

CHAPTER 73

ONE ETERNITY LATER

THE RETREAT from the first wall went almost as smoothly as expected. Right about when the castle's forces ran out of arrows, the enemy soldiers began seriously making progress on scaling the wall. Bee heard the signal from Arthur's command position to fall back. The archers retreated first, making it most of the way back to the second wall. From there, they took their last remaining arrows: three arrows each. As the pike wielders fell back, they started to pick off anyone who made it to the top of the wall, preventing them from overrunning the rest of the retreating defenders.

All along the wall, people sprinted towards the gate in an orderly line, filing through as the archers fended off any pursuers. Then the archers slung their bows over their shoulders and quickly retreated as well. Bee stood by the gate entrance, keeping watch to ensure everyone got through.

As soon as the archers were unable to hold back the aggressors any longer, she tossed a vial as high in the air as she could. It exploded in a flash of bright purple light. A few moments later, a swarm of stones and other projectiles launched through the sky as the trebuchets and catapults flung their payloads high. A handful of seconds later, the first wall disappeared. It went from being a vertical obstacle to a mound of rubble that would break up any formation trying to pass it.

The redesign was well worth it. The enemy's vanguard had just started cresting the wall and coming down the other side when they were bombarded by dozens of stones the size of pigs. Some stones exploded. Some stones set fire to the wooden walls. Others just landed with heavy impacts. Immediately, the advance was halted.

The plan was to set up a situation where it would take hours for them to clear the rubble for another proper advance. That kind of time would give the defenders plenty of opportunity to set up and rest before the second wall was invaded.

All the while, when they tried to advance onto the next wall, the trebuchets and catapults would be extending their range and actively engaging in the battle to decimate any ranks set up too close to the castle. This would mean that any attack would come with a much-extended charge or simply have to accept continuous bombardment. And Bee didn't think any force would be able to sit under that for very long.

She celebrated internally. So far, so good, it seemed. Their initial attack had been extremely successful. But it looked like the enemy general had plans of his own.

Immediately, the army pulled back to just outside of the range of the catapults, and the catapults stopped firing. Then the kingdom's forces unveiled their own magic. Originating from several points along the attacker's front, a wave of frost billowed out in a quickly creeping front. Bee couldn't tell how it was happening, but she had to push her curiosity to the back of her mind to deal with the immediate threat. The air crystallized as it advanced forward, smothering the lingering fires and burning walls while shifting rubble out of its path. Bee lost sight of what was happening through the fog as the frost advanced steadily toward the second wall.

Dread suddenly seeped into Bee's heart. That wave was troublesome. What if it could break through their defenses somehow? With an effort, she reigned the fear in. If that were the case, they likely would have used it first instead of trying to sacrifice so many of their soldiers to take the first in what was going to be a long, grueling series of walls.

However, letting something like this approach the second wall uncontested didn't feel right. Defenders were already up on top of it, and the last of them were still moving through the gate. It wouldn't be pretty if it did anything remotely as dangerous to the people as it did to the ground. But how could she stop it?

Bee quickly thought through her abilities and didn't immediately see an option. Then she had an idea. The skill that had been so important for defending the breach at the walls of Caleb might just work here as well.

With a mental effort, she activated her Holy Aura and pushed it out to meet the frost. The golden light bloomed within her consciousness and expanded into reality. She felt her aura connect with the invasive magical particles swirling towards her. The advancing field of ice and cold seemed to recoil as though burned, melting back into nothing as it met the glow. It took a little bit of her energy, but it halted the creeping wave. Stretching out her hands, she formed her aura and pushed it out as wide as she could, trying to cover the entire path toward the second wall. She couldn't cover the entire wall, but could protect enough of the road to keep the soldiers safe.

As she focused, she closed her eyes and tried to visualize the distance. She used the feeling of the aura and the sensory input it provided her to guide her skill forward. The golden light seemed to morph and shift, halting the attack in its tracks. This went on for several seconds, a brief span that stretched into an eternity as she waged war against the enemy's magic.

Eventually, Bee felt more than saw the wave peter out. With a huge exhale, she reached up and wiped a thick sheen of sweat from her eyes. Her clothes felt as though they had become drenched in a matter of seconds. A hand grabbed her shoulder and kept her steady, but it only took her a couple of moments to regain her footing. She was just tired, not an invalid.

Looking around, she saw that the soldiers had bunched up behind her, cramming together exactly at the edges of the aura shield she had projected. Apparently, they hadn't liked the look of that magic any more than she had. Where the frost had touched the trees, their bark had split and ruptured as the sap inside flash froze. Little tinkling sounds reached her ears as small twigs fell to the ground and shattered, like someone emptying a glassware cabinet onto the floor.

Blinking, she realized that she could actually *see* her aura. Before, she'd only been able to sense it, but now? Based on the soldiers' reactions, they could obviously see it too. It was fading, as she'd stopped trying to project it, but the golden glow must not have been her imagination. It must have projected a real visual barrier for everyone to hide behind it. That sort of magic was not common, as far as she knew.

She looked over to see the source of the hand still steadying her, only to see Tony. Apparently, he had run out from behind the wall to keep her aloft. She smiled tiredly at him as he spoke. "I think you overdid it a little bit, Bee. Here, hide behind the walls for a spell, yeah?"

She nodded and worked her mouth to muster the moisture to speak. It seemed like it had all sweated out of her during that exchange.

"How long?" she croaked out eventually. Had it really been just a few seconds, or the eternity it seemed like?

"A minute or two," Tony said. "Just enough time for everyone to get up into positions, though. You look like you just ran a marathon."

She tried to chuckle but ended up coughing. "Yeah, I feel like it too."

Tony turned her around by the shoulder and started to lead her into the castle, but her feet refused to cooperate. They repeatedly sought out small rocks and uneven patches to stumble over. Eventually, Tony gave up and crouched down, grabbing beneath her knees and pulling her into a princess carry.

Bee wanted to protest. Especially as she felt her sopping clothes leave a huge wet spot along his front. She muttered something as she vainly pushed at his arms, forcing Tony to shift a little bit. But soon, her head was lolling back in exhaustion as she watched the silhouettes of the soldiers go by.

"I'm fine," she muttered up in the general direction of Tony's swimming face. "Really, I can walk."

"Of course you can. You're walking right now," Tony soothed her in a blatant lie.

This made Bee quite frustrated, but she couldn't quite put words to why. "Just...need to rest a little..."

"Sure, sure," Tony reassured her. "I think you probably want to drink some water, huh? We'll get you inside and draw up a nice bath for you. How does that sound?"

"That... sounds nice." Bee mumbled as her consciousness started to slowly drift. She began to dream of Void, a strange dream. Her master was far off, among ice and snow like the stuff she'd just fended off, fighting some great evil of its own.

What was her master doing? Did her master need her help? Was it coming home? Questions swirled in her mind until even the dreams started to fade.

Archibald blinked. The last thing he remembered was stabbing a Lieutenant Demon in the chest, rather heroically at that. But in a flash, it was gone. Surrounding him instead was a complete and vast whiteness, emitting nothing but blinding light in all directions. His first thought was that he was clearly dead. That made sense, given the situation. He blinked a few times. Slowly, the feeling started to spread from his eyes down to the rest of his face. He could feel his nose as air began rushing through his nostrils. He tried to breathe in more deeply, but his chest wouldn't move. Still, it might only be a matter of time. The sensation kept creeping lower and lower.

Suddenly, the tongue in his mouth was able to move, and he wiggled it around. All he tasted was stale, musty air. Not at all fitting for the blinding whiteness that surrounded him. Once his neck was able to move, he was able to look around. Finally, he noticed something besides the blank white void.

Archibald looked down and saw himself, though he was in a funny pose. He was holding his sword, but in an awfully proper and grandiose way. Not at all like himself. After that, he looked around the rest of the space. He couldn't completely turn around yet, but upon closer inspection, it appeared to be a dome with a uniformly colored floor and walls.

Toward one corner of his vision, he saw an archway. Still, it was too far in his periphery to make out entirely. As his sensation returned lower, he took a deep breath of air for the first time. He could feel his chest expand, and he exhaled slowly, relaxing his shoulders and rolling his head around. A moment later, Archibald stretched up towards the sky, shaking his arms out. His spine protested with a rippling set of pops as everything came back to life.

He felt his wrists and fingers flex and pop as he stretched them and manipulated them. He started to wiggle his hips and could soon fully turn around and see behind him. There was a single entrance over there, and it appeared to have a small object in the corner. He couldn't quite make out what it was, as anything that wasn't right in front of him was a bit blurry. It always had been.

But it was something he had long since learned to live with. Eventually, as his toes finally softened up, he wiggled them carefully. Then Archibald took a step forward.

Apparently, not carefully enough. His foot wasn't 100 percent awake. As he landed, he landed on the side of his foot, rolled his ankle, and stumbled forward. And then, too late, he realized he had been standing on a dais several feet above the ground. The miscalculation sent him painfully crashing onto the floor, shoulder first. Archibald attempted to continue his roll to disperse his momentum. Unfortunately, he ended up just flopping on his back, his head colliding with the stone. He simply sat there for a moment, head ringing and wind knocked out of him. He panted, attempting to get his lungs to work again.

At that moment, Archibald was simply grateful no one had been around to notice his acrobatic feat. Mentally, he reached out and felt the connections of his bond. Relief washed over him as he noted that Daedalus was still alive, that big, scaly boy. Even if he was far away.

It seemed as though some time had passed since Archibald's sealing away. The real question was, what had he missed? Slowly levering himself up to his feet, he worked his way forward one step at a time. Carefully, he approached the object near the archway. As he drew near, it resolved into a small wicker basket.

He went down to one knee and started to dig through it. It was filled with food. A few loaves of bread wrapped in paper, some dried fruit, and a pair of wineskins. The sight made his stomach growl loudly.

He also found a folded piece of paper on top of the whole ensemble, scrawled in High Elvish of all things. He blinked, struggling to interpret the words. "What the heck does this mean? Champion? Companion? Hm. I assume this is for me... I don't see anyone else here, at least."

Archibald unfolded the piece of paper to reveal a text wall that didn't mean much to him. He put it aside and decided to decipher it later. His mouth was parched, and those wineskins seemed like a far more pressing matter at the moment. Unstopping one, he lifted it up and squeezed. A stream of tepidly warm and flat water dripped into his mouth. Still, it was the most heavenly sensation he could ever remember.

CHAPTER 74

GROUNDED IN FAITH

ARTHUR FELT the blood drain from his face as he spotted Tony carrying Bee's limp body through the gate.

"Mr. Arthur, the enemy is—"

He immediately motioned for Felix to silence the constant stream of information he was recounting and dashed toward the girl. This needed his full attention. However, the crowd of people around the gate weren't reacting as though Bee had been severely hurt. Instead, they were cheering as Tony kept walking on. When Arthur reached for Tony's side, he laid his hand on Bee's brow. She was feverish but clearly breathing heavily.

"What happened to her?" he demanded. He had almost asked for a report on reflex, but the farm boy wasn't a soldier.

"The enemy deployed some sort of big magical frost attack. Bee used a skill to stop it. It took a lot out of her, though. I have no idea how long she'll be out for, but she needs to rest badly." Tony summarized the situation well enough. "They took the outer wall, but they definitely paid every bit we could make 'em."

Arthur nodded. The last part wasn't news to him, but Bee's condition certainly was. At least she was exhausted, not wounded. With the situation under control, the commander headed back to Felix.

"Archers on the left wall 're runnin' out of arrows," Felix reported in a strangely monotone voice, his eyes closed. Arthur nodded and signaled to one of the Quartermaster's assistants nearby, and they went off running to take care of the issue. It had never been so simple to control a battlefield as it was now. Information flowed almost instantaneously, no matter where his forces were. He could make decisions and take advantage of openings so quickly that it might feel as though he were predicting the enemy's moves.

Unfortunately, he wasn't sure how long Felix could keep this up. It had already been some time since the kid's skin had taken on a pale sheen. They would need to find an easily defensible lull in the battle for Felix to take a quick nap, but Arthur wasn't sure how quickly they could bring one on. It could be some ways off. He continued to make small adjustments to the forces arrayed on the wall, sending reinforcements to places that were at risk of being overrun based on reports.

All the while, the catapults and trebuchets and ballistae kept firing into the mass of foes. The enemy had decided to immediately push forward for the second wall, not even slowing after the first. The kingdom's armies just kept pushing through the rubble of the first wall and racking up casualties. But as they made it through the no-man's-land, the continued bombardment meant that reinforcements found it harder and harder to reach their destinations, especially once they entered the range of the second wall defenders and were absolutely unloaded upon.

That was when the trebuchets shifted their ammunition from single-target, heavy, destructive weapons to the specialty items that Miss Bee and Maranda had cooked up. Judging from reports, they worked just as intended. The stones split apart before they hit the ground. Instead of leaving craters, they left shredded piles of soldiers in a large radius. Arthur had waited until the enemy had reached the absolute most people packed into the killing field before changing ammunition, and this new threat made it nearly impossible for the back of the army to reinforce the front or for the front of the army to retreat. They'd broken off a large chunk of the force, pinning them between the wall in front and a field of steel death behind them, making easy targets for archers and pikes to finish off.

Arthur shuddered a little at how effective those exploding rocks had been. Those two girls were somehow more terrifying than he'd given them credit for.

So far, everything had been going according to plan, but he wasn't sure if it would be enough. The enemy vastly outnumbered their own forces, and if they were throwing their people at the wall like this, they clearly believed they could spare them. It could've been that the demons amongst them were in control and didn't view the humans as particularly valuable. But he suspected they were more likely conscripts or just poorly trained fodder, little more than shock troops. While they were still important to the battle, their loss wouldn't make the enemy commanders lose any sleep. Usually.

Arthur was more surprised that he hadn't seen any demons yet. No one had, based on the information the other Nighty Knights fed to Felix. But with this strong of a showing, he wouldn't be surprised if they made an appearance soon. The second wall was constructed significantly better than the outermost wall, and they intended to hold it for much longer. So perhaps it would allow them to draw out their true enemy.

Once the latest tide was defeated, he signaled for the trebuchets to stop wasting their limited supply of extremely potent anti-personnel munitions. They had agreed upon this earlier and set up a manual signal from the front lines to the back lines. And they even had backups in case Miss Bee wasn't able to perform her duties, like right now. They would let the trebuchets know when to fire a stone in case the no-man's-land was encroached upon. But for now, that was the only information they needed. And Felix could get some rest.

Arthur steadied the young boy with a hand on his shoulder as he walked him over to the series of cots set near the command tent. The boy was still a boy, but Arthur could tell that somehow he had already mastered the soldier's skill of sleeping whenever he needed to. If only his own kids had learned that one—it would have made his wife's job a lot easier. As if to prove his point, Felix began snoring before he was even halfway onto the cot. Arthur had to help lower the boy down the rest of the way so he didn't fall off as he slept.

Leaving him be, Arthur quickly approached the scouting post where Susan and Captain Major coordinated their efforts. A lot of their duties had been subsumed into Felix's abilities, but Arthur wasn't about to entirely trust the Nighty Knights to watch for everything that was needed. After a quick rundown, he confirmed that Felix had been giving him good information this time, and they had acted accordingly. They had orders to step in if they were getting massively conflicting results reports, but they hadn't needed to so far.

"Okay. And what of the flankers in the forest? Have we seen any attempts to bypass the walls by going around the densely wooded areas?" Arthur asked.

Susan and Captain Major both shrugged. Captain Major spoke first. "We've caught a few of their scouts, but so far, there has been no concerted effort."

Arthur nodded. "Good. Good. Let me know if that changes."

He turned to move away, but Susan called out, "Sir. There's another concern. I'm worried about them trying to burn the forest down around us."

A messenger ran up, interrupting their conversation. He gave a crisp salute, turned to Arthur, and only glanced at his immediate superiors. "Sir, they've started advancing again."

Arthur heard a slight boom as another heavy stone landed. He winced. He didn't expect them to try to push through the bombardment as quickly as they had. They only had so many enchanted stones. While they had proven to be some of their most effective weapons, they had been an experiment. A gamble that took time to prepare. Between that and other necessary preparations, they didn't make as many as they should have. Now it was too late. Maranda wasn't skilled enough to produce them herself yet, and Bee was indisposed. Even if she started producing them nonstop, it wouldn't be enough to extend the bombardment for more than a minute or so.

He hoped they had enough to push back another assault. Fortunately, they also had plenty of magical concoctions to use if they needed to collapse the walls. Surprisingly, the immediate single-target stones that Bee had made were more effective against a wall of stone than they were in a large area. Arthur turned to Susan and Captain Major once more.

"I want to know the second they start sending something that can actually get through the bombardment. And I want to know if we can risk not using the specialty ammo and just use regular stones for now to prevent them from getting too far ahead. They shouldn't be willing to trap as many of their soldiers against the wall this time if they've learned anything from last time.

"Actually, belay that. Just tell the catapults to switch to standard stones now." He turned to the messenger waiting, and the man ran off to instruct the catapult operators.

"It would be better if they did push through. We will hold them at the wall, and we'll do the same thing again, destroying another large section of the force," Arthur explained. "Still, I want to know the second they change their tactics."

Susan and Captain Major both saluted, and Arthur walked away as they prepared their scouts. He went to climb an observation platform that some of the farmers had built in their spare time.

It wasn't going to give the best vantage point of what was going on, but he could at least see the ebb and flow of the battle.

Half an hour later, one of Susan's messengers ran up to inform Arthur that their plan had worked again. The enemy had just thrown more soldiers into the meat grinder of the anti-personnel rocks. But things were changing. Apparently, sand golems—or earth demons disguised as sand golems—were being sent ahead of the army. Why they hadn't been used earlier, Arthur had no idea. But he supposed that if his opponents were playing some hidden cards, he might have to see personally what was happening.

He quickly descended from the tower and took a pair of soldiers as guards with him towards the second defensive wall. It was time for him to see what was going on with his own eyes. When he arrived, he saw four mounds of living dirt shot full of arrows. The projectiles showed no signs of impeding their progress at all. The standard troops had halted, since they weren't able to get past the trebuchets for fear of the anti-personnel rounds. But these elementals had no such issues.

Occasionally, one of the trebuchets would increase their range a little bit and attempt to hit farther back in the enemy camp. But the enemies had wised up about this and pulled their forces even farther back. The four earth demons carried a massive log between them at least thirty feet long and several feet across. It had a metal cap on one end, narrowing its diameter down from several feet to only a few inches. The handles on each side were sturdy enough that they would be able to put significant force into each strike of the incoming battering ram.

Arthur looked around and saw panic on the faces around him. There were ways to deal with demons, and they had magical countermeasures, of course. But he didn't think that that would cut it for these men. They looked worn out. Most were his soldiers and war veterans in the campaign. But this was different.

At least with the undead, they were able to do harm. Earth demons were notoriously difficult to deal with, especially with a soldier's standard repertoire of stabbing and slashing. And with Miss Bee having fallen so early in the battle, Arthur thought they might need a little pick-me-up.

Drawing his sword, he motioned for his guards to stay behind. With a yell that reminded him what it was like to be a younger man, he leaped off the wall and met the demons with a charge.

CHAPTER 75

OPERATION SEARCH AND DESTROY

THUCYDIDES and I spent several hours searching for clues about the Lieutenant Demon's location. We eventually found a few markings that made it look like something big had come through this area about a quarter mile away from the cave entrance. How would it have gotten here? I had no idea, but Thucydides was certain. The way he explained it sounded quite interesting as he produced all sorts of equipment from some hidden space and measured magical output.

While he was doing that, I worked under the assumption that this was, in fact, the passing of the Lieutenant Demon. In that case, I wanted to figure out the direction it was going and see if I could determine a goal or destination. So far, my mental model of the planet was rather limited, and I wasn't sure of what lay in the direction of this path. I could tell that the trajectory was at least south. Of course, there was a very good chance that the demon could have doubled back. But that seemed unlikely to me. There was no way it would have known something was following it, but it could be paranoid.

Once, Thucydides looked up from his equipment. I indicated the direction and gave him the odds associated with it going that way. Thucydides blinked in surprise. At first, I thought I would have to explain probabilities to him, as I had to do with many of the children. But then I remembered even though Daedalus called him Little Brother, Thucydides was quite old. Surely, he understood basic math and statistics.

"From what I know," Thucydides said, "I think you might be placing too much assurance on the Lieutenant Demons acting rationally. They are agents of chaos, after all."

I inwardly frowned, taking that statement into consideration. Had my models overlooked the Lieutenant doing something completely nonsensical, like traveling in a zigzag pattern just for fun? Maybe. It was pretty unimaginable to me, even after encountering so many mess makers. I updated my calculations with that assumption in mind and flashed up new percentages, slightly lowering the certainty of my prediction. Thucydides cocked his head and nodded. "Yeah, I'd say it's a little bit lower myself, but I think it's still high enough that checking is worthwhile. We'll just have to make sure we scan around every other footprint, too."

We headed off in the direction that I had indicated and fanned out slightly, scanning the ground to see if we could find any other marking of the Lieutenant's passing about another quarter mile away. My sensors were able to pick out the pattern in the ground clear as day despite the wind having obscured it. It wasn't exactly in line, but close enough that it was within the margin of error for my predictions.

Thucydides pulled out fewer experiments this time, and within a much shorter time frame, he confirmed it. "It looks like we're going in the right direction, but I don't trust that the demon will keep going this way. We should do a full sweep around a quarter mile out almost every time to ensure that we're not missing something."

I beeped my agreement, but honestly? My primary processor was focused on understanding what the white dragon was doing with his tools. It all seemed very interesting.

They somehow resonated with the ambient magic in the area.

From that, he was able to determine some sort of pattern that was a match for the one back where we had started our search. It wasn't the same as an energy signature like I might pick up, like a soul. Those I could use to recognize things I had already seen rather than matching someone's fingerprints to them. Which I could also do, of course.

But this new technique was fascinating. I wanted to see if I could replicate it. I felt like it would take me a while, but with enough time and processing power, it shouldn't be impossible. I'd have to develop much better algorithms to do so efficiently, though. Thucydides's pace, while easy for me to follow along with, was glacially slow. I could have cleaned the entire castle at least twice over by the time he finished fiddling with his equipment.

Still, just because I could interpret what his equipment did was no indicator that I could perform its functions. Perhaps I would need some special materials in order to figure this out. Beatrice might help with that. I could sense energy from these things, but I couldn't really identify exactly where it was coming from.

We continued on through the snow. Each time, we'd have to search a little bit more to find the tracks. Thucydides was right that this was not nearly a straight line. In fact, I calculated that there was a 36.4 percent loss of efficiency based on the path that this Lieutenant Demon was taking. Worse, that efficiency loss didn't even help it much to throw off a pursuer. We could tell that some sort of magic was being used that teleported it almost exactly a quarter mile at a time. It was nice to have precise intervals of distance to search at. Still, it made Thucydides's suggestions of making a full circle around each mark even more important. Luckily, we could do it without too much effort, especially once I got particularly good at detecting the energy signatures in the rock.

We went on like this for hours; eventually, day turned into night. Even with my Advanced Sensors, the lack of ambient light made it difficult to keep track. Thucydides and I found a nearby cave to rest in, and the dragon wormed his way inside and curled up, quickly falling asleep. I just tidied the cave floor so we could have a more comfortable spot to rest. Today had been a long day; I imagined it would be another one tomorrow. Well, technically, the day had been the same length as every other, but the humans were so fond of this saying that I had picked up on using it myself. Regardless, we had months' worth of distance to make up for, but I had no faith that we were moving faster than the Lieutenant.

Archibald finally put down the wineskin. His mouth felt less parched than it had before. Next, he started up on the bread; it was slightly stale, but surprisingly not as hard as it could have been. How long had they been putting food like this out for him? Judging by how he felt, he must have been asleep for quite a while. That meant someone was watching out for him.

As he chewed on the slightly rubbery bread, he realized exactly how hungry he was. At first, he hadn't noticed because of the thirst. But even as he swallowed, his stomach complained, and he started chewing faster. He would finish everything in this basket, and it still wouldn't be enough. But it would hopefully give him the energy he needed to keep moving.

Chewing, he returned to the piece of paper, flipped it open, and slowly began to decipher it one word at a time. Several minutes later, he looked up and blinked at the ceiling.

"Ten thousand years. That's a long time," he muttered to himself. He honestly wasn't sure if he believed it. Ten thousand years was far too long for anyone to remember him. In fact, with the demons having ruled for so long, humanity hadn't even known what had happened a thousand years before. There were no records and not even any stories that referenced events that long ago, at least not that he was aware of. Maybe some ruins somewhere held stories about older things, but still.

"Dang." He muttered the word through a mouthful of bread. That was far too long for someone to have been leaving him bread and a note. That just didn't seem very likely.

"How many loaves of bread would that be? Well, if these loaves of bread were two or three days old, maybe someone comes in here every week. That would have sucked, waking up to week-old bread, but still. Fifty-two weeks a year. That's like...that's so much bread." Archibald just shook his head. He could still feel his bond somewhere in the world. Maybe Daedalus had been watching out for him and waiting for his return? Nah, that didn't make sense.

Sure, Daedalus had been a good friend after a while, but the dragon was still pretty arrogant. He couldn't imagine the old lizard just sitting there waiting for him. Much less bringing bread like this. Even if the mental image of the dragon assembling little baskets of treats did give Archibald a chuckle. He'd probably be off having some adventure and claiming a massive hoard somewhere as he sat on top of a dwarven settlement and demanded 90 percent of the gold. It still would be nice to see his old friend again, though. He was glad that he had survived the Demon War.

If he was still alive, of course. He assumed that the demons were somehow banished. It was hard to say, but he looked back to the letter and continued reading.

"Okay... Maybe they did find a solution?" There wasn't really much more information on the page. It mentioned that the Lieutenant Demon had been trapped with him this whole time. Apparently, the Lieutenant had been released, but they somehow managed to banish it. Something about a lord of cleaning and a god.

Archibald had never put much stock in gods. There were still some humans around who worshiped them even in his time. Most of the talk of gods had come from the elves, but no one had seen a god for a very long time. And from what he understood, the myths said that they were gone before the demons even showed up. Or maybe the demons showing up had been when the gods disappeared? He didn't really care. The gods hadn't done anything for humanity when they had been enslaved for who knows how long by the demons. But this was a new god. He shrugged.

Well, the people living in this era were willing to welcome him. And if they were this polite, perhaps they would be able to tell him more when he found them. He considered picking up the basket and walking as he ate, but decided against it for now, reaching over and grabbing the next loaf of bread. The awakened hero continued his snacking. It took him nearly half an hour to finish both the loaves of bread and the preserved foods on the covered dishes. Jerky and cheese were certainly a lot more filling than the bread, but at the same time, he kind of wished there was a warm meal.

The other wineskin held actual wine, albeit with very low alcohol content compared to the wine he was used to. However, it was still a nice taste and didn't hold the same stale flavor as the water did. Leaving a little bit of food and a little bit of wine in his skin, he decided it was time to move. He slung the strap of the skin over his neck and put it on his side as he picked up the basket.

"Well, no point in waiting." Stretching again, his muscles complained a little bit less than when he sat down. Slowly, he made for the door and began to walk up a slightly curving ramp.

CHAPTER 76

NAPTIME IS OVER

ARTHUR BENT his knees as he landed on the hard-packed ground in between the walls. Before him, the four demons carrying the battering ram paused, earthen faces expressionless. He took half a second to draw in a breath and center himself before charging forward. But in that half second, his mind flitted through a thousand different details. He considered the hundreds of people on the wall behind him. He went through his skills and picked out the ones that he would need. With a commander-based class, he didn't have nearly as many direct combat skills as a soldier would. But then, soldiers rarely ever got to his level.

Instead, he had a few things that would actually serve him rather well in this situation. A few of the leadership variants he'd picked up allowed him to pull strength from those he led, and more so when he was defending them as their champion. It was a very infrequently used skill, as he did little direct fighting anymore. But if this wasn't the perfect time to use it, then he was a cat.

He activated the skill, breathed in, and felt the support of his entire army swell through him as they watched. As he used that moment to propel himself forward, he scattered a bit of demon's bane that Bee had given him as a precaution on his blade.

As Arthur moved, he felt his two guards drop onto the ground behind him. He trusted them not to engage, but rather to just watch his back and make sure nothing extraneous happened or interfered. They would also make sure he had a clear path back through the wall when he was done. The demons were hesitant to drop their ram, but once he got close, they decided that he was enough of a threat that they had to stop their advance and deal with him first.

As one, they released their hold, and the massive log slammed into the ground. The impact sent vibrations through the paving stones underneath his feet, even thirty feet away. It didn't slow him down or even send him off balance as he charged forward. He hefted his sword and held it at the ready, imbuing it with his very first skill: Decisive Strike.

It was a skill with a surprisingly large cooldown, especially considering he'd earned it at level 1. But it had served him well. Sometimes, the first strike was the most important. Sometimes, he saved it later for the fight. But having a weapon that could deal damage to almost any opponent with one hit was nearly always tide-turning for him. It wouldn't guarantee an instant kill, but it would help bypass any resistances, hitting with more force and a certain magical emphasis that wasn't normally found in melee classes.

So when the "stone golem" raised its hand to block his blow, Arthur slashed it, cutting right through its arm and into its body. A huge chunk of earth sloughed to the ground in a dusty mass. It wouldn't kill an earth demon. Very few things could kill an earth demon outright, but it did neutralize a good large percentage of its mass. The demon's bane did help, though.

The best way, in his experience, to kill golems or earth demons or anything elemental was to target its weaknesses. A water-based attack would be excellent here, for example. But he was no mage, so the next best option was to separate them from their power until they were weak enough that they couldn't do any harm.

His blade bit deep into his opponent's chest, and as soon as he felt the blow's momentum slow, he twisted it and slashed it down, coming through the center of the demon and cutting out a huge chunk of its side and one of its legs. It fell into magically inert material.

The demon collapsed and started to reform, but Arthur was already moving past it and cutting at the next. The demons showed no hint of wariness or self-preservation as he carved through them, nimbly dancing through the group. Men behind him empowered Arthur to move faster than the earth demons could ever hope to keep up with.

He was probably stronger than them by nearly twenty levels, so without their inherent strengths and his inability to directly counter them, they would already have fallen. But his increased physical abilities made this fight little more than a waiting game as he ducked and dodged around the heavy blows that were far too slow to touch him and sliced off piece after piece of sandy earth.

Arthur's only concern was his opponents being able to regain the material that he cut away, but even then, he did have a skill that could help with that. It was another one of his rarer skills, the one he had gotten at level 10. In combination with Decisive Strike, it had made him a formidable opponent in his younger years, if not quite top-tier. It was a nullification skill that could dampen the use of magic in his presence. It was easily overwhelmed by anything more powerful than him, which was why combatants like Bee and Void and even the wraith could be so much trouble for him. But it had also been able to weaken the wraith's attacks in critical moments.

Despite all its shortcomings, it was great at suppressing things near or below his level. This had helped immensely to level the playing field, as he could remove the truly broken abilities some got early. It hadn't taken him long to learn that he could focus it and use up all of its potential at once. But he didn't need to do that now; he barely had to apply the effect here to stop the earth demons from reforming.

Arthur kept the remains of the earth demons magically inert and slowly whittled them down until they were each smaller than him. At that point, he stopped even trying to avoid their blows, instead turning them with his blade to meet them with a strike. The collisions destroyed them even as they tried to attack him. Then he started throwing in kicks that would shatter through the thin walls of sand the demons protected themselves with, and soon, they were nothing more than little mouse-sized piles of sand scuttling around his feet.

This was when his guards truly proved useful. They dashed forward with what looked to be tightly woven bags. Arthur had no idea where they'd found such things, but he was grateful. They scooped up the demons in these bags and tied them shut. Arthur could see the things struggling futilely, but they were so weak that they couldn't do more than slowly cut their way through the bags with their sand. It wasn't a long-term solution, but someone in the castle would be able to handle them. Maybe Bee would be awake and functional by now. If not, Maranda should surely be able to bind them long enough for Bee or Void to take care of them.

The men on the wall erupted in cheers and shouts, which quickly devolved into insults flung at the enemy. Arthur let them go for a few minutes as he caught his breath and studied the kingdom army. They hadn't yet made a move, but something didn't sit right with him.

Arthur raised his hand and pointed at the log, and a few moments later, several arrows, soaked in pitch and on fire, streaked forward to set it aflame. Arthur didn't imagine this would stop the enemy for long, but it would certainly take time to find and prepare another ram. The next time they tried, they would have to bring more forces with them, and that would slow them down as well as give the defenders targets. Turning, he stalked back through the gates and made his way back to the command tent. There was still a lot more work to be done.

Bee felt sensation slowly return to her body as she woke up. It didn't at all feel like waking up from a good night's sleep, but rather more like jumping into an ice-cold river in reverse. There was an initial shock as her mind started up again, and then slowly, the numbness of her limbs faded. What had happened?

The last several moments that she could recall were fuzzy. Some magical attack from the enemy had forced her to exert herself and expend a lot more effort than she wanted to.

She tried to open her eyes, but the lids wouldn't respond at first. So, instead, she tried twitching her fingers and toes. Nothing. Was she paralyzed? No, sensation was still running through her limbs. It just hadn't reached much farther than the center of her chest.

She focused on her breathing and on feeling the world around her. Mostly, her magic-based skills still functioned, but she could feel that if she pushed them at all, it would simply slow her recovery. She didn't have enough in her to put forth the effort. But her passive senses were just fine. She could feel the faith of Void all around her with no apparent effort. Good. It seemed that her people still lived.

The vast, vast majority of Void's faithful were localized in the castle and pulled back towards what she felt to be the second wall. But she felt new strands of faith coming from very far north, strangely. She wondered if Void had been up to anything over there. She also felt some more towards the city of Caleb and the neighboring province. Slowly, those were spreading and strengthening, but they felt different. As though they weren't quite the same as the ones within the Church of the Cleansing Void.

It was as if she were giving red apples to those she talked to, and whatever was spreading the faith towards the east and west were giving out yellow apples. Not necessarily wrong, but different. Up to the north were more like green apples. It was very interesting that she could tell something like denomination with her skill.

Suddenly, she felt her energy hit some kind of recovery threshold. Her Repair and Improved Repair skills kicked in, and her body quickly mended. Unfortunately, they quickly left her feeling exhausted once more as their effects cut off, but her body felt whole again. The brief kick of recovery left her wanting nothing more than to lie back and sleep. She could sense with Improved Pathing that the best way out of her room was to get out of her bed, walk down the hall, and then descend a few flights of stairs. That would bring her right back to the fight. But she wasn't ready.

Even as she opened her eyes and took in the stone ceiling above her, she felt that she needed a good meal and a few more hours of rest before she could really do anything strenuous. That didn't stop her from forcing herself to her feet and quickly getting dressed, though. She almost stumbled as she left the door, but a force of will kept her upright as her energy slowly recovered. With a bit of effort, she made her way towards the kitchens and found them in full swing. Loaves of bread and fresh rations were constantly being piled up and then whisked out to go towards the soldiers on the walls.

When the head of the kitchen, Mary's second, saw her, she was immediately ushered to a table. A massive plate of eggs and cured meats, toasted to a nice crispiness, was placed in front of her an instant later. Bee barely even tasted it as she scarfed it down, but the meal did wonders. Even her recovery skills began to kick in once more and remain in use. Regaining her feet, Bee made her way down and out of the castle, ready to go see where she could be of use.

CHAPTER 77

BLOWING THINGS OUT OF PROPORTION

A WHOPPING 59.34 HOURS LATER, Thucydides and I finally spotted a change in the monotonous landscape. Over the next snow field, we spotted a large shadowy shape looming a quarter mile away from our most recent checkpoint. My Advanced Sensors couldn't pierce the unnatural darkness that seemed to surround it. Luckily, my Spiritual Cleanse sense had increased its range significantly in the past few months.

My front touch sensors were nearly triggered as we hovered closer. The energy was so much more intense that it felt like physical pressure. Inside that looming pillar of smoke and shadow, I saw a flickering flame in the shape of a man. It was just standing there. Judging by the burns around it on the bare stone of the mountainside, it had been standing there for a while. What was it doing?

My thoughts were interrupted when Thucydides glanced toward me, baring his teeth in a partial sneer.

"They're not so tough, are they?" the white dragon boasted. I let out an unconvinced beep. That monster seemed nearly as powerful as the mountain that Daedalus had spoken to. It was so much more powerful than the first Lieutenant I had fought that I had trouble believing they were on the same level.

I had to remind myself that the one we faced was significantly weakened. Still, even if this was stronger, I wasn't going to let it get away without a fight.

"Let's go get it," I projected in the air above as we came to a stop a little ways away. The creature hadn't reacted at all to our presence, so I thought we could take the time to plan. I started showing tactics where I would come in low and the ice dragon would come in and hit it with ice breath from above, giving me an opening to start trying to consume it.

He went back and forth with me a few times, adjusting the plan, but I put a stop to it when we started getting to the precise angle of his descent. The young dragon was just stalling. I gave him a push forward with my Air Manipulation as he flew higher in the sky, and we made our approach.

The demon didn't seem to realize we were there until Thucydides was nearly on top of it. The white dragon was already exhaling before the demon had a chance to react. It didn't show any surprise; instead, it casually lifted a hand of flame to block the ice breath. The hand, made entirely of fire, managed to melt the ice attack as it got closer, but I could see the limb's radiance dim slightly.

I followed in after the attack, getting in close. As I entered the pillar of smoke and shadow, my sensor range greatly diminished, and I lost awareness of everything happening outside thirty yards of the fight.

Now in range, I immediately started trying to consume the demon. Unfortunately, I could only rip little bits of flame away from its body every few seconds, much less than 1 percent of its mass. And it regenerated relatively quickly, as Daedalus had warned. I kept at it, though, unwilling to give up; even this little bit of damage would build up given enough time. Pulling out my Divine Sword, I went to slash, but the fire of the demon's body parted around the blade with no apparent damage. It appeared that it wasn't quite corporeal, almost like an earth demon.

Thucydides came around with another breath attack. This

time, the demon blocked with one arm and pointed with the other, sending a burning bolt up at the dragon. The young dragon rolled out of the way to dodge and had to flap hurriedly to avoid crashing into the ground. As the dragon circled around, the demon turned its attention to me. I quickly ran through my options, trying to think of something that might have an effect.

An old ability came to mind first. Popping up my Spray Bottle, I unloaded as much water as I had in me at the Lieutenant Demon. The torrent fizzled, sprayed, and steamed as it approached the demon, but siphoned off its heat well, and I could see its radiance dim. I kept the stream up, shooting at its face as I tore through the massive reserves I had in my Limitless Dustbin. I zipped around it, covering all angles, trying to stay ahead of the random sprays of fiery bolts it sent all around itself.

With my Spray Bottle, I managed to dodge or neutralize most of them in midair. The rest I redirected into my dustbin with Air Manipulation. I could feel it strain my ability and my dustbin to catch such powerful blasts. Still, I was able to store them and slowly dissipate their energy to later transmute it for my own purposes. All the while, I pulled in a steady trickle of the demon's mass.

My barrage of water was clearly frustrating it, if not actually damaging the enemy. It was able to avoid its half-hearted grabs for me, but it was enough of a distraction that I was not able to start some of my more complicated options. I had hoped that it would break through eventually, but it seemed we were mostly at an impasse right now. And I wasn't about to give up my slightly superior position without a good reason.

Then Thucydides, recovered, dove in with his icy breath. The blast caught the Lieutenant Demon in the back, full-on and unprotected. This time, the lance of cold speared through the flaming demon, and the Lieutenant flew apart into a thousand pieces scattered throughout the pillar of darkness. I immediately took advantage and was able to suck up a significant proportion of the demon's mass as it tried to reform, dousing many more of the small flames with water.

However, the demon reformed in an odd way. It didn't all rush toward one point. Instead, each tongue of flame paired up with another and merged into a larger one. Then the process repeated over and over. Soon enough, I was surrounded by many smaller versions of the demon scurrying across the landscape.

I zipped about to try and consume the smaller versions of the Lieutenant, but they seemed to still have some sort of ephemeral link to the whole that made them hard to pull. That didn't stop me from getting some of them, but I couldn't consume them outright like I had the minuscule versions.

Thucydides worked with me. Hovering above, his breath attack snuffed out one after another of our prey. But there were still at least 3482 more of them that I could see, far too many of them to vanquish quickly even as they continued combining. We focused on cleaning one area of the flame fragments at a time.

Hidden among the number scattered everywhere, one underneath Thucydides did something unexpected. It transformed into a pressurized jet of fire, sending itself streaking upwards. The lance of fire speared through the base of an unsuspecting Thucydides's left wing. The dragon's breath cut out as he let out a roar of pain that turned into a squeal. He fell from the sky and crashed into the ground, sending a shockwave of dust and debris rippling across the hillside.

I increased my efforts, trying to spray down all the fire surrounding Thucydides. Repositioning, I hovered above him, shooting down anything that got near and consuming anything that was left. This frantic defense of my vulnerable friend went on for several minutes as the Lieutenant tried to approach the downed dragon. Thucydides struggled to get to his feet, but the damaged wing was making it nearly impossible. Fear was clear in his eyes as he lay vulnerable on the ground, claws scrabbling at the bare stone.

Suddenly, the assault stopped. My sensors indicated there

were no more little fire demons left. Checking my dustbin, I found that I had nowhere near enough to account for all of it. Less than 20 percent of the demon's mass was inside me. The rest was simply gone.

I didn't for one second believe the enemy was destroyed, especially based off of Daedalus's explanations of their impressive regenerative abilities. Rather, I found it was far more likely that it had fled while we were distracted. It must have sacrificed a large portion of its mass to keep me occupied while it got away.

But I couldn't pursue after the injured Lieutenant to finish it alone. Not with my companion hurt. Descending toward the dragon's prone form, I examined the injury with my extremely limited medical knowledge.

"How does it look?" he croaked out at me.

"Not great," I flashed. "How does it feel?"

"I've had worse," he said with a tough face that looked a lot like he was trying to imitate his older brother.

When Bee eventually made it out to the castle walls, she found that her help was simply no longer necessary. There had been a few assaults since she had been rendered unconscious, but Arthur and the rest of the soldiers had taken care of them without her assistance. Relief washed over her at the discovery that everyone was safe. But at the same time, it was a little disappointing to know she wasn't needed.

She quickly squashed that immature feeling. Just because she wasn't needed yet didn't mean she wouldn't be soon. And besides, it was better this way. At least it meant they weren't in real danger.

After a brief conversation with Arthur about tactics, she learned that apparently, the best place for her was alongside Maranda. That was how Bee found herself back inside the castle and climbing up into the laboratory. The hallways leading towards it were crowded with masses of people carrying stones in stretchers and buckets through the tight stairways. The ramps that Tony had installed to please Void would have been greatly useful, but no one trusted them to hold up with such heavy loads. Plus, they were a little too steep for something like a wheelbarrow full of bricks. It'd be easy to lose control of that. A cart of bricks speeding down one of those ramps would be extremely dangerous for anyone below.

At the same time, Bee spotted enchanted missiles slowly being brought down as well. They had not been enchanted in the same way Bee could. Still, Maranda had apparently found her own solution to creating exploding rocks while Bee was out fighting.

A crew of nervous men carefully maneuvered the rocks about. A simple cork stopper jutted out from the top of each, marking it as dangerous. Instead of enchanting the stones themselves, Maranda had taken to hollowing them out and stuffing explosive liquids inside. The results acted like her fireworks, just on a much larger scale. They made Bee even more nervous than her own explosives.

This extremely crude method wouldn't work for long-term storage. Bee would have to make sure that every single one of these was tracked down after the battle to confirm that they didn't have explosive ordnance sitting around the castle. The thought of someone mistaking them for regular rocks made her shudder. However, they would work rather well for projectiles. She just hoped that none of them actually exploded before they left the catapults.

As Bee reached the lab and set up her workstation, she asked what Maranda was up to. The fledgling mad scientist flipped open her notebook and turned it for Bee to see.

"I've had an idea for mass producing some of the boosting potions," she said with a smile.

Bee looked over the designs. "Hmm, do we even have enough powdered caterpillars for that?"

"No," Maranda said dejectedly. "I asked Arthur if they could find some for me, and he told me that 'as happy as I would be with such equipment to provide my troops, it is simply more effective to make more explosives.' So boring."

Bee couldn't help but agree as she started pulling the stone blocks off a pallet and carving away at them. She started with a basic, simple enchantment for light or something along those lines to practice her actual enchanting abilities. Then she would add a few lines to make it unstable before placing it on a separate pallet and grabbing the next brick.

Hours went by with them barely noticing. Both pallets of bricks were replaced periodically as they emptied or filled and moved toward the field. No messengers came, so she assumed she wasn't needed somewhere else urgently. That meant she was simply able to lose herself in her work.

Around dinnertime, food was brought up to both of them. Maranda had finally gotten it through her head that safety protocols were to be followed in the wake of their dangerous work, so they reluctantly left their work behind to wash down in a separate room. Neither of them wanted to risk eating explosives on accident or contaminating the lab. Dinner was a quick affair of roast lamb in freshly baked bread, but Bee hadn't realized how hungry she was.

As they finished up and headed back to work, someone dashed up the steps to the second floor and called out. "Miss Bee!"

Bee glanced around in surprise. It wasn't a messenger from any of the military operations, but rather one of the mothers who had taken it upon themselves to maintain the castle's cleanliness while their children were running about. "Miss Bee, High Priestess. Come quickly, there's someone you need to see."

CHAPTER 78

GOOD MORNING TO YOU TOO

THE RAMP CURVED EVER UPWARD. Archibald had just passed the second massive chamber above him, and after hours of walking, he was starting to get bored.

In the beginning, he hadn't exactly been in a hurry. But this was starting to get ridiculous. Who even made a ramp this long? If he ever met the architect of this nonsensical structure, he'd give them a piece of his mind. Archibald had plenty of water to last him several hours, which was fine, but honestly, his body was getting tired. His full strength hadn't returned to him quite yet, so the natural stamina of his levels wasn't all there. This kept his pace to a sedate stroll, much to his frustration.

At least he had a lot of interesting things to look at along the way. The mausoleum and catacombs and art frescoes along the wall were particularly nice and well-done. They were also surprisingly well-maintained like someone had dusted them regularly. But it was a bit repetitive.

On this last portion of the ascent, things finally changed. Instead of a long sloping ramp, some stairs of different construction than the tomb led upwards into the darkness. He trudged up the steps with extra pep in his stride. It seemed that he might finally be getting out of here. Maybe he'd be able to meet whoever left him the food and note. He looked forward to that.

At the top of the stairs stood an old wooden door with an iron handle. The touch of the cold metal sent shivers up his arm as he dragged the door open. He felt his heart rate increase as an escape from the oppressive darkness of the confined tunnels was finally at hand. The flickering light of the torches was one thing, but he wanted to see the sky.

As soon as he stepped out into the bright, sunlit hall, he couldn't help but stare. The building was incredibly impressive. He had seen nothing like it in the human settlements, as neither the demons nor their ilk were amazing builders. But this put even some of the ancient dwarven halls to shame. The stained-glass windows, high arches, and beautiful columns with shiny marble floors projected an aura of majesty and order that befitted a ruler. Heck, it looked like something that his bonded companion might even appreciate.

For a moment, he merely stood in awe. Then he looked down at his own slightly drab appearance and long, unkempt hair. He wasn't sure how he had ended up underground looking like this, but the only nice thing Archibald had on him was the sword on his hip. The enchanted breastplate that had still hung on his torso after the fight with the Lieutenant had been cracked, and the magic had long since drained from it. So he had left it behind, as it was rather useless. It wouldn't block a single hit that could actually hurt him. Under it was a roughspun doublet that felt only half-preserved. They hadn't fallen apart completely, but they hadn't come out of stasis as well as he had. He could feel how brittle they had become.

As if to reinforce the point, an overeager step up the last of the stairs was accompanied by an ominous ripping sound. Archibald nearly swore, blushing and checking whether anyone had heard. He just hoped his hosts would lend him a new pair of pants. A shirt, too, if they could spare it.

As he took in what looked to be a grand entryway of a castle, he felt distinctly out of place. Only the clatter of a bucket being dropped pulled him out of his trance. Turning, he saw a young woman clutching a mop tightly. A puddle of dirty water spread across her feet as she stared at him in open-mouthed shock. He attempted to speak, but his voice came out in a rusty croak. He coughed, flushing with embarrassment. On his walk up, he had talked to himself a little, but it had been in a half whisper and apparently hadn't helped with restoring his damaged voice.

The sound spurred the woman into action, and she let out a squeal as she turned and ran. Archibald sighed. He supposed that might have been a reasonable reaction to seeing someone come out of a crypt entrance and then croak at you. As she ran away, she yelled something over her shoulder. It took him a bit to decipher what she had said, as the extremely thick accent made it sound like she was gargling rocks as fast as she possibly could. However, he was able to parse the language with some effort. "Wait right there. I'll fetch the High Priestess!"

A High Priestess? Who was that? Shrugging, Archibald saw no reason not to do as the woman asked. Finding a small bench tucked in an out-of-the-way corner, Archibald sank down gratefully and waited for this High Priestess to show up. Leaning his head back, he stretched out his legs and wiggled his toes in their old leather boots as he attempted to get comfortable. Finally relaxing a little bit, he let his senses explore the area as he studied the surroundings. At that point, he started to become aware of an all-too-familiar sound.

Somewhere outside the castle, the sounds of metal clashing on metal and screaming echoed. They were unmistakable. There was a battle going on. He could've said that much even if he were dead asleep. It might've also explained why the maid was so on edge. Aside from the obvious, of course.

Archibald sighed and got back to his feet, stretching. The High Priestess would have to wait or just find him later. As he moved, his muscles told him that he was far from top shape, but even then, he was no weakling. Reaching for his side, Archibald patted where his sword hung ready on its loop. Even these thousands of years later, it still held its edge. Unlike his armor and clothes, it had never failed him so far. With a steady breath, he walked out the propped-open doors into the bright sunshine.

Bee raced down the stairs toward the catacombs. Apparently, the champion from below had finally woken up. Bee was shocked that they hadn't had more warning. When they replaced the welcome basket each week, they conducted a careful visual inspection of the hero. The last one indicated some change, but nothing this sudden. While the man should have been a ways from waking up, even then, she had thought they would find him resting down below with the food rather than up here.

She could only imagine how weak he would be with the vast majority of the magical energy drained from his system. But for him to have come up from below after being in stasis for so long... Even a demon like Nazareth'gak took time to recover, and he had that unreasonable regeneration on his side. She couldn't imagine how a human would fare.

He was last seen in the entryway of the castle, but the one who'd spotted him was startled and had run off to go find her instead of keeping watch. Bee hoped the champion stayed put, as things were rather chaotic at the moment. When she made it down the grand hallway and down the steps to where the cata-comb door stood ajar, she looked around and didn't find anything. Great. This was going to be tricky. But even as she poked her head out the front door, she realized something was wrong.

While she toiled in the lab, the lull in the battle seemed to have long since ended. Bee cocked her head and listened. The noise of the fighting carried much farther than she remembered. Or...

Bee dashed down the castle steps and out of the entrance to the nascent city. She saw people racing toward it, streaming through the gate of the innermost wall. Struggling against the flood, she managed to push toward the wall. Her head swiveled about as she looked for someone to intercept and ask about the situation.

"What's going on?" she demanded as she grabbed a soldier's arm, pulling him out of the stream of people running past.

"The second wall is falling, ma'am," he said. "We're retreating and refortifying. Arthur's orders."

Bee let him go, and he dashed off to go about his duties. She gave up on looking for the champion for now. This took priority. Besides, hopefully, he wouldn't cause too much trouble. Pushing her way against the stream of soldiers, she leaped onto the wall to get a better view.

The second wall was falling, but hadn't been fully abandoned yet. There was a fighting retreat in progress. Several people held the wall as the bulk of their forces ran. The gate still remained closed, and the enemy hadn't gained the top of the wall, but it was damaged. A massive chunk a little way to the right had been blown out of the stone, at least a dozen feet wide. Rocks lay scattered out in a cone behind the wall.

How hadn't she heard that from inside the castle? She had no idea, but it didn't matter. What really caught her eye was the figure standing in the gaping hole. A single man stood in the breach, holding back the tide of halfway-disguised demons and kingdom men as the reserves fled back to the inner wall.

The people on top of the wall eventually slowly started to pull back, giving up the second barricade. This was not good. This was too early. They should have been able to hold this wall for days, not merely hours. Eager to stop the solitary soldier from being overrun, Bee ran forward to join the fray. Her broom was already up and swinging before she even arrived, a Scouring Strike flying out at max range. As she ran past people, she activated her Repair abilities, fixing minor wounds in the instant it took her to leave them behind. Her Pathing skill helped her dodge through the crowd with minimal collisions, and moments later, she was at the breach.

The single man holding the breach held a sword. It flashed in the sun, his movements with the blade unlike any from the soldiers she had ever seen. There was a practiced grace to his strikes that even Arthur didn't have. The only one who showed similar talent was Bradley Chadwick, though that was from raw talent rather than practice.

Who was this man? No one from the castle fought like that. He wasn't even moving particularly fast. With each swing or thrust, he simply ended up right where he needed to be. Quickly, she ran a Scan on him to confirm her suspicions.

Name: Archibald Smith, Race: Human, Class: Companion of Daedalus, Titles: Dragon Rider, Hero of Legend, Bravehearted, Warden of Nazareth'gak, Age: Unknown, Level: 69, Highest Stat: Strength, Lowest Stat: Wisdom, Status: Awake

She immediately realized where she knew him from. He was Archibald, the champion from below, the companion of Daedalus. Rather than inside the castle, here he was, holding the breach.

Bee stood there for a second, unsure of what to do. Then the reality of the situation got hold of her, and she charged forward to lend what aid she could.

CHAPTER 79
A VOICE LIKE SMOOTH MOLASSES

AS THE WAVES of men and barely disguised demons crashed against the shattered wall, Bee dove forward into the breach. She dipped to the left, trying to give the dragon's companion space to continue his one-man stand without getting in his way, but her approach still distracted him. He snapped his head over to glance at her, though his sword never stopped moving, quickly assessing the newcomer and deciding whether she was a threat.

His evaluating gaze turned to shock as he actually registered Bee's appearance. The champion's eyes darted between Bee's broom and her face, confusion growing by the second.

His mouth moved, but Bee couldn't make out the words over the screaming of defeated enemies that covered the ground around him like macabre rugs. At least he didn't attack her. Deciding that actions spoke louder than words, Bee just bared her teeth and lunged forward with her battle broom to skewer a demon. With a casual flick of her wrist, the demonic corpse flew to the side, smashing into a soldier sneaking up from the side.

Though they were all humanoid, a look at the incoming enemies revealed a generous share of glowing red eyes, horns, jet-black fur, and sharp talon-tipped fingers. She wasn't sure how the enemy had convinced these men to fight alongside what were now clearly demons. Had the kingdom's men always known about this? It didn't quite make sense to her, as they had made so much effort to hide the presence of demons amongst their men before. But now that they were attacking, maybe stealth had gone out the window.

Whatever was going on with the enemy army, one thing was certain: she still had no idea how to change their minds about this war. If there were a way to convince the humans to stop or change sides, then she'd have tried it in a heartbeat. But she didn't have much hope of that. Judging from the aggression of the attackers, human soldiers included, she didn't think they were being 100 percent rational at the moment. Any efforts to do something about the misguided souls fighting against them might be in vain.

Bee quickly raised the bristled end of the broom and slashed it in an arc in front of her face, deflecting two of the three arrows coming at her. A simple side step and twirl allowed her to slip out of the final one's path while also bringing the bladed end of her broomstick to bear. It speared forward, stabbing through the helmet of a soldier who was flanking Archibald. The sight of the falling body made her squeamish. But she couldn't think about it. Not right now.

Her martial skills had certainly improved along with her levels, and she was doing a decent job holding back the tide with just her broom. But the hole in the wall was a wide one. Even with the champion acting as a harbinger of death on his side, she wasn't confident she could hold her own like this forever. Letting go of the broom with her off-hand, she thrust it forward palm first and let loose a Scouring Strike. Sand blasted in a wide cone before her, and she averted her eyes as it stripped the flesh from the enemy's bones. The sight reminded her of what Void had done to those bandits in the mountains so long ago. The idea that she could do the same now... Well, there was no time to think about it right now.

After a few seconds, the skill petered out. She felt her energy reserves dip in response, but just held her broom and kept swinging.

With a thought, she extended her Holy Aura and her Repair skills over to Archibald as well. She could see the small wounds he had taken over time begin to close up as the energy of the aura washed over him, bolstering him. It didn't quite work as well as it did on Void's followers, but it still had a noticeable effect.

Quickly, she fell into a rhythm of using skills and her broom to hold her section of the wall. The dragon's champion hadn't actually moved from the center of the gap, so she was holding more like a quarter of the gap while he was single-handedly holding the rest. From the corner of her eye, she watched him fight, and was surprised she didn't see a single magical skill manifest from him. It seemed to be pure bladework, endless grace in motion. He still didn't seem like he was moving faster than an average person. Still, every step he took, every small slide of the feet, left him in the perfect position to block the next invader and destroy them with simple thrusts and slashes.

Nothing seemed even close to touching him unless he was mobbed by huge amounts of force. When a particularly large push came, Bee would try to pull a few off of him onto her section of the gap. She knew he was level 69, but still. With how long he had been asleep in stasis, a performance like this blew past her expectations. Perhaps that explained why he wasn't using magical skills and why he seemed slow. But whatever it was, she was just grateful for the help. It was doubtful whether she could hold this herself.

As more and more forces challenged them, she Scanned the enemies and found that they were, on average, fairly high-leveled for soldiers. Perhaps these were the elite troops from among the ones that were willing to fight alongside demons, but all were above level 20, and several of them were in their mid-30s. The demons, though, were all at least level 35. Still, her 15-to-20-level advantage over them was monumental, and nothing truly challenged her except for sheer numbers. But the flood of forces took its toll after fifteen minutes of constant fighting. She could feel fatigue entering her arms, and her broom seemed to triple in weight.

When she heard her name being yelled, she spared a quick glance behind. There was no need for them to hold the wall anymore. Everyone had retreated behind them, and all the defending forces were doing was shooting anyone who came up to the top of the wall to keep them from being flanked. She supposed it was a rather good strategy, just allowing the enemy to slowly throw themselves in the meat grinder one at a time for her and Archibald to finish off. Still, it probably was not going to last. Besides, there were better things to do with their stamina.

So she signaled the retreat. Turning over to her companion in arms, she yelled at the top of her lungs to be heard over the battlefield noise. "Hey! We can fall back, Archibald!"

For the first time since she had jumped up next to him, he turned fully to look at her, one hand holding his sword and his offhand fending off two warriors at the same time. His hard eyes searched her expression for a moment as he casually dispatched another enemy. He drew in a breath and opened his mouth to speak. "WHAT? I can't hear you!"

For her part, Bee had no trouble hearing him. Still, his manner of speech left something to be desired. He spoke extremely slowly and clearly, as if he were talking to some old man who was very, very deaf and didn't understand the language. Maybe this was just the best way to communicate over the battlefield, she thought, but something didn't sit right with her.

Instead of repeating herself, she pointed back to the wall and shouted, "Go!"

Archibald looked around and nodded. Together, the two of them dashed off. The line of archers just outside the gate for the innermost wall stopped the enemies from cresting it as they fell back. Bee shuddered to think of how many arrows in skulls it had taken to buy them time to hold the gap. But at least they made the enemy pay for taking this wall. The last one they had would have to hold longer.

When she finally made it inside, she immediately leaned

against the cool wall, panting and wiping her sweaty hair out of her face.

"That was a harrowing experience," she muttered to no one in particular. After catching her breath, she looked up to see Archibald standing in front of her. The man leaned against the wall casually, his sword back in its scabbard while one hand rested on its hilt. A frown graced his rugged face, tugging at the small amount of stubble growing on his cheeks.

"What?" he spoke again. Just as before, he enunciated each syllable and drew it out for an almost comedic length of time. Did he not understand the language that well? Or was he hard of hearing? Bee thought for a second before just shaking her head.

"Not important," she said, slowing her words down slightly. Hopefully, that would help him understand. He looked confused but nodded nonetheless.

"Are you the High Priestess?" He emphasized each word, putting what felt like a whole breath in between each as he drawled carefully.

"Yes, I am. You are Archibald, the companion. I'm sorry we weren't there to welcome you when we woke up, but we are understandably quite busy," she said between panting breaths.

"Huh?" was Archibald's only response. Bee sighed and repeated herself, this time slowing down the words even further.

After she was done. Archibald nodded. "Yes. That's me. I appreciate the note. I assume that it was you who left it. Also, I don't understand why you are all speaking so fast and choppily."

Bee waited impatiently for him to take his sweet time finishing.

"I'm speaking normally. I don't know what you're talking about," she defended, slightly self-conscious now. She did think that she spoke a little more formally than most, but she had never entirely gotten rid of the middle-class accent she had picked up.

"Why are you speaking the high tongue so rushed-like? If you want to speak casually, why don't you just speak common?" Archibald asked in his weird vocal style.

"High tongue?"

"Yeah. For formal occasions? It was a bit of an odd choice to use for battlefield commands, but I guess I could see it."

Bee rolled her eyes and shook her head. "I think some things have changed since you were last awake, Mr. Smith. This is the common tongue, and as far as I know, there isn't any high tongue."

Archibald sighed, shoulders slumped in defeat. "I guess I better do some studying, then..." The declaration was followed by a string of totally incomprehensible words that she assumed were in his common tongue. "Also, don't call me Mr. Smith, that's my father."

"I am sure you'll get used to it. Now. Do you want to hear about what happened with your master?"

"Master?" the dragon's companion asked in complete bewilderment.

"Yeah. My master recently talked to yours and thought you would like to hear the latest updates," Bee clarified.

"What master?" For once, the question came out rushed enough that it almost sounded normal.

CHAPTER 80

FLOATIN' AROUND AT THE SPEED OF SOUND

I FELT my Thrusters whine in complaint as I pushed forward with all my might for the second day in a row. Thucydides bounced awkwardly on my much-too-small chassis as I carried him. I tried to use Air Manipulation to help him stay on, but his awkward shape and size meant there was only so much I could do.

It would've taken Thucydides weeks to walk back in his current state, weeks we didn't have. Worse, his wing wouldn't heal anytime soon. I had figured, based on Daedalus's healing speed, that he would be able to fly in a few days, but apparently, his much lower level meant that it would take him weeks or months to heal the wound.

So I was stuck here carrying him. There was no chance I was going to risk taking him into my dustbin and having something unforeseen happen to him. Therefore, I could only carry him. It slowed me down significantly, but we were making good progress. We'd be back in just a few hours.

I originally planned on just taking him back to his cave, but Thucydides asked to be dropped back with the snowmen. Apparently, he liked to have someone to talk to while he was healing. I wasn't sure how good of conversation partners the snowmen would be, but he seemed relaxed about it, so I did my best to accommodate.

The massive white dragon shifted slightly and sent me tilting a few degrees. The disturbance started to exaggerate as I wobbled in the air trying to maintain my flight path.

"Sorry," Thucydides groaned from above. "You're kind of digging in right underneath my rib cage and pressing on my bladder. Can we take a break?"

I whistled in frustration. There was really no great way to carry him. The sheer mass of the dragon meant that any point where I pressed up into him was going to be extremely uncomfortable. And if I got too far away from his center of mass, he just would fall off of me. Even at full output, I had no chance of catching him with Air Manipulation.

So we had to take regular breaks every twenty to thirty minutes for the dragon to lumber around and stretch. And also lick at the bruises I was leaving in his stomach and chest area.

As we landed, I gently set him down and wormed my way out from underneath him as he pushed himself to his feet.

"I'm really sorry about this," Thucydides said. "I can't believe I didn't see that attack coming."

I made a calming gesture with my Grabby Arm. This was the twenty-third time he'd apologized for getting injured, and I kept trying to tell him it was okay. But some of my frustration about the wasted time was probably leaking through. It was important to take care of my friends and make sure that I left affairs here in order. Yet my time away from the castle was starting to worry me. At least Daedalus, having gone back, would be able to help if there were any issues. But I was also excited to go meet the dragon's companion, and I knew that sometime in spring, the human army was going to attack.

So much to do and so little time. And this trip had already taken twice as long as I originally had planned.

The itch to get back constantly worried at my brushes. Once I dropped Thucydides off, the journey home would be a quick one. It was not much more than 26.21 hours or so if I pushed it at full speed and optimal pathing. It was unfortunate that I hadn't been able to destroy the Lieutenant in our fight, though.

We'd promised the mountain spirit to do our best, but it seemed it would have to wait a bit longer. I would really have appreciated the extra energy. The bits I had collected of the Lieutenant managed to level me up once already.

I was sure that if I'd converted the whole thing to energy, I would have reached the next skill. Perhaps I would even move a bit faster with the extra power. But it wasn't to be. I'd have to find that enemy later after I had made sure the castle was safe and everything else was taken care of. My to-do list was getting quite long as it was.

A few moments later, Thucydides and I were once again up in the air and doggedly heading towards the snowmen's village. When we finally arrived, the snowmen streamed out of the town to welcome us. Very oddly formal bows greeted us as we touched down and Thucydides lumbered over. They first bowed to the dragon, and then they bowed to me. But when they bowed to me, they dropped to one knee and pressed their fists over their hearts in some sort of salute. I wasn't exactly sure what this was, but it felt kind of similar to how some of the more formal people at the castle treated me.

I merely waved at them cheerily and checked to make sure their homes were still clean. Surprisingly, they did a good job maintaining the order I had left them in. The streets were swept, and the houses were scrubbed freshly since I had seen them last. The only thing was that their latrine pits needed to be re-dug. It only took me a couple of minutes to bore new ones with my various skills and transport the removed material on top of the dirty ones. I really need to introduce plumbing to this world soon.

Still, I was proud of the snowmen. They honestly took to this cleaning stuff even better than some of the humans I had met. I even noticed that some of them had cleaned their fur until it looked pristine, rather than the dirty cream I was used to. I gave them a beep of approval, which elicited an even deeper bow.

With a quick goodbye to Thucydides, I promised to tell Daedalus that he was all right and what had happened with the Lieutenant Demon. Then I was off. I blasted past a couple of mountains separating me from the ocean before I really turned on the speed. I felt the pressure wave in front of me build up through the air as I zipped. I could sense the rippling explosions as the air compressed before me. I continued to accelerate, blasting through the invisible barrier. I was truly going fast.

I took my Air Manipulation skill and started to split the air in front of me to prevent the drag from becoming overwhelming as I zipped back toward home as fast as I could manage. When I crossed the 1000 mph barrier, I started to coast as the efficiency of my Thrusters began to decline. I experimented with a few different ways to cause a windbreak. Still, it only yielded minuscule improvements as I flew. I kept tinkering with it, slowly adding on speed. It was a nice way to pass the time as I headed home.

Bee leaned back against the crenellation on top of the last defensive wall. The two nesting circles of the castle wall and the city wall stood relatively unmolested, though the bits of industry that had cropped up in the area had long been dismantled and had retreated temporarily. If this wall fell, the forces in the settlement would be split off from each other almost entirely. Small squads could be passed through where they intersected, but it wouldn't be one united force anymore. So they were putting much more effort into holding this wall than the previous ones.

They had a cycle of powerful people on watch, Bee being one of them. Her shift was almost over as dawn broke on the horizon, but she still had fifteen minutes or so to go. The enemy had favored dawn attacks recently, so she didn't let her guard down as Archibald popped up on the wall shortly after light broke. They intentionally built this little overlap into the guard to make sure that the weaknesses in their schedule wouldn't be exploited, and that they had enough manpower that no one was left too exhausted.

Yet they had held this position for a couple of days and done relatively well. This wall was the sturdiest and tallest of them all. Even the explosion that the enemy had used before paled before its impressive construction.

She and Arthur had done what was necessary, and Susan and Captain Major had done their job as saboteurs scouts admirably. The Nighty Knights had also been essential in their contributions, even if they weren't exactly happy about it. Still, the instant messages they provided had saved them many, many times. But of all people, Tony had actually gone above and beyond.

From starting at level 32, he had managed to wedge himself into enough desperate fights and hold his own that he had passed level 40, according to Scan. He might even hit level 45 if things stayed like this for another day or two.

"Shift's almost over?" Archibald confirmed as he started up the stairs to the top of the wall.

"Yeah. It's been quiet, luckily," Bee called down to him.

"Awww, that's no fun. How's Tony supposed to get stronger if things stay boring?"

Bee had to credit Archibald for a lot of Tony's growth, though. The men had become fast friends, and Tony had spent a lot of time learning from the soldier. Archibald's weapon was a sword, but he knew enough about wielding clubs that Tony had been able to pick some stuff up. And just in mimicking the attitude of humanity's ancient champion, Tony had grown a lot.

Bee looked around as Archibald came to stand beside her. "Tony still not up?"

Archibald's massive shoulder raised up slightly as he spoke in his odd, slow accent. Listening to him talk was a bit infuriating, as it took him three times longer to say anything. "Yeah. He's resting. We had a hard bout of sparring after I came off watch last time. He did well, but maybe pushed himself a little too hard."

Bee just rolled their eyes. Archibald was a true battle maniac. He never did anything halfway. And when it came to fighting, his biggest problem was leaving the wall too often to go chase down feints. It was why Tony often ended up in such desperate straits.

Archibald looked out over the enemy's camp as he drummed his fingers on the parapet next to her. "It's too bad Daedalus hasn't shown up. That absolute monster would have decimated everyone already."

Bee shook her head at hearing him call his companion a monster. According to Archibald, he was the rational one who kept his friend in check, but after seeing him in action? Bee doubted it. The posh dragon who Void had told her about didn't seem to be the kind to lose control, and after seeing Archibald fight, it was hard to believe that he wasn't the real battle junkie.

"Sure, sure," she said, a smile creeping into her voice. "But then you wouldn't be able to go charge out yourself to fight their commander, would you?"

Archibald at least had the grace to look embarrassed. "Hey, Tony said he was going to hold the wall. And he did."

Bee just signed. It wasn't worth mentioning to Archibald that to hold the wall, Tony had to spend a ton of expensive alchemical resources that his little sister had made and a lot of Bee's personal stash as well. It set them back days of effort, and Archibald hadn't actually managed to find the enemy commander. If he had, it probably would have been worth it. But as it was, it wasn't exactly a useful tactic.

The goal was to stall the enemy for as long as possible and hope that Void returned. It became more and more clear that if they rushed the battle, they might very well lose. But Archibald didn't seem willing to wait.

"No," Archibald said, drawing out the word even more than he normally would. "No, I don't think today is the time to go out for some fun. I got a bad feeling about today, and we're going to need all hands on deck."

CHAPTER 81

ANOTHER BRICK IN THE WALL

UNFORTUNATELY, Archibald was right.

Bee replayed the champion's words in her head as she dashed along the top of the wall. The assault had started just a little before sunrise, and it hadn't let up since. She never did get the break she wanted, meaning she had been up here for far too long. But that didn't slow her down as she moved along her section of the wall, furiously running from one ladder to the next. She barely even stopped to finish anyone off or intentionally hit demons at this point. She would simply rush to the enemy's ladders and release a Scouring Strike or throw some of her alchemy equipment to dislodge each one from the crenellations.

It was only due to her Improved Pathing skill that she could hit every ladder as efficiently as possible. Without that, the numbers would have overwhelmed her. Even then, it was a struggle to ensure she could hit all the ladders just before they allowed demons over the wall, and with such precise timing. The skill was very good at scheduling when she needed to be where. The only issue was pushing her body hard enough to actually keep up.

She destroyed another ladder with her Scouring Strike, sending the climbing figures tumbling backward. One managed to leap onto the wall at the last moment. She didn't even give it a second glance as she smashed her bristled end of the broom into its chest and flung him back off.

As she ran towards the next breach marked by Improved Pathing, something changed. Suddenly, it winked out. She skidded to a stop, taking a breath and trying to figure out what was going on.

Looking out over the enemy army, she saw that every single one of their troops had paused in place. Their heads had swiveled to their back line in response to some sort of signal. She had no idea what everyone was looking at, but one thing was certain. The humans wore looks of fear and uncertainty while the demons bore wide grins.

Squinting, she could make out movement in the back of the army. They were milling about in a rather chaotic way, but she couldn't tell what exactly caused it. She tried running Scan to see if she could pick out anything in particular, but the distance was too great. The only things she picked up were Scans of random soldiers along the way. Then, just as suddenly as it had stopped, the assault restarted. Bee began her frantic defense of the wall once again.

To her dismay, two separate ladders appeared at the exact same time, as far apart as they could be along her section of the wall. A quick glance around for help came up with nothing. Gritting her teeth, she darted toward one of the ladders, leaving the other behind.

There were plenty of other defenders about, but they had their own problems. Archibald guarded the other side of the wall like she was doing, except for an even larger breach. As he managed to regain his energy throughout the fighting, he became more and more of a terrifying combatant. Yet he apparently still wasn't nearly at peak. Between his recovery from stasis and the guy's absolute love of battle, he seemed to only become stronger rather than worn down like everyone else.

Susan, Arthur, and Captain Major also held smaller sections of the wall almost single-handedly. Their own army filled and rotated through the remaining sections that comprised the majority of the area. But despite how crowded it seemed, no one was nearby to help her.

Bee skidded to a halt when she was almost within reach of the first ladder, as she had an idea, turning to fling several of her alchemical concoctions towards the other. Hopefully, she'd get lucky and knock it off or at least delay the assault. In the mix, she hurled a sleeping potion, hoping to knock some people out with the potent gas. Then she turned back to her main focus: the ladder that clanged against the wall, its hooks digging into the stone at the top.

She chopped off the top rungs of the ladder with her broom and pushed, using her admittedly lacking weight to try to heave the thing away. It was a ton of effort, but with her broom as a lever, she managed to push it up and then off to the side, and the ladder came crashing down.

She would have preferred to destroy the ladder with her Scouring Strikes so it couldn't be reused, but she was just running low on energy; better to save them for the direst moments. Not even waiting for the ladder to crash below, she dashed over to the next one.

Surprisingly, soldiers and demons hadn't swarmed the wall like she'd expected. As she looked down, she saw several unconscious forms at the bottom, along with several demons halfway up the ladder. She stood over the ladder, panting and trying to catch her breath as the demons came closer. She wasn't in any huge rush yet.

Ping. Her skill indicated that there was another ladder coming up. She kicked out this one after cutting it free, pushed it to the side, and sprinted along the top of the crenellations to the next spot as demons screeched in anger below. Just a few yards over, she caught the next ladder as it was coming up with one foot and pushed, sending it careening off sideways. But at the same time, a rope flung up from below wrapped around her ankle, a hook digging into her boot.

Inwardly, she cursed herself. That ladder had been too easy to knock over, and she'd put herself in too vulnerable a position. She attempted to jump back over the wall, where she could maybe get into a position where she could cut the rope off of her foot. Still, an inhuman weight tugged at her and yanked that foot out from underneath her. Bee managed to catch the wall as she fell, but even if she managed to get free, she could see the other ladders going up all along her section. They'd take advantage of this if she didn't fix it fast.

Letting her broom slide down her hand, she gripped it by the bristles and swung wildly beneath her with the bladed tip. It took a couple tries, but eventually, she caught the rope with the blade. It parted like warm butter before the divine broom. With one arm, she pulled herself up and rolled over the wall only to spot three breaches. She bit the inside of her lip in frustration as she darted to the first and unleashed her most powerful attack, blowing it into the abyss before heading towards the next. It would take her a lot of energy to make up for lost time and regain control of the wall, but there wasn't anything else she could do.

It took her nearly fifteen minutes to fully beat back every assault. Every time she managed to knock one down, it felt like another two popped back up. But with the time it took soldiers and demons to climb the ladders, she could get ahead of the swarm just enough that she wasn't overrun.

Despite her success, Bee felt exhausted. She had probably taken on more than she could chew, but there was no helping it. Someone had to do it. Looking over, she saw that Susan and Arthur were doing okay, holding their sections of the wall, but the soldiers were heavily pressed. At least they were still holding for now. No small thanks to Archibald for lending them a hand occasionally.

She frowned. She could have taken less of the wall, perhaps just a yard or two, and maybe she'd have been better off. But at the same time, they just didn't have the manpower to spare if she even made a small contraction like that. Not for as long as they'd been holding. As it was, if this assault kept up for much longer, they wouldn't be able to hold at all. Hopefully, the enemy army would break before they did.

The disturbance at the back of the army moved again, and this time, it had moved closer to the wall. She grimaced. Now she could tell what was different. Bee could feel the pressure of power forcing her aura back, trying to constrain it as she let it billow out across the castle wall. She had never felt anything like it before, but the aura pressure was undeniable.

A pit of dread opened in her stomach. She couldn't be sure, but she had a bad feeling about this. A *really* bad feeling.

Daedalus beat his wings, pushing himself as fast as he could. He flew over the water like a meteor streaking overhead. He could feel the wind between his horns, and he smiled.

His companion was awake. After so long, his friend was finally back. It was frustrating that it would take him days to return. If he had known how close his companion was to awakening, he likely would never have gone on such a long trip, no matter the cause. Though he couldn't say he completely regretted it, knowing that a Lieutenant had been freed. But it was still disappointing.

He had done a little bit of fishing as he flew over the ocean, picking up a few smaller whales that were breaching too close to his flight path. He didn't really need to eat. There was enough mana in the air to sustain him, at least. But the hunt was fun. It certainly made that massive stretch of nothingness less boring to cross. Eventually, though, he finally caught sight of land. The broad white expanse of the massive tundra that led to his mountain home.

Daedalus was debating whether or not he should make a stop in his cave to pick out any of Archibald's favorite things. Or should he just make a beeline right towards him? He was still debating the question when he finally got close enough to the castle to see that something was wrong.

It was a faint buzzing noise that first caught his attention. The strange sound made him arc up and over his mountain to take a look rather than dive right into the cave for a quick pit stop. But then he saw the long line of soldiers snaking through the valley and crashing into the walls of the castle.

Something came over him. Something Daedalus hadn't felt in a long time. There were tens of thousands of attackers, and they went on for what looked like days of walking through the forest. Were they here for his Archibald? Of course. Why else would they be here? Petty humans trying to take revenge on the dragons. He knew they'd be bitter over them keeping so much of the gold. But it was simply a fair reward. After all, the dragons had sacrificed so much to fight the demons for them! Especially Daedalus himself!

He faced the demons, giving the humans their freedom, and this was how the humans repaid him? By teaming up with the demons. Not just to steal his hoard, oh no. That would have been inexcusable enough. They were trying to hit him in the only place he was weak. It was the only place where this dragon was truly vulnerable. His friends. His softer, squishier, and significantly weaker and maybe a little inferior friends.

That would not happen. Not on his watch.

Daedalus felt something build deep in his chest, far below where the fires were stoked, and his vision went white. Only dark reliefs of his enemies appeared within his mind, and his instincts took over. His wings tucked to his sides, and he felt the wind rush by ever faster as it flowed across his scales. The ancient red dragon dove down. Down to face his enemies.

CHAPTER 82
A VERY PROPER AND WELL-MANNERED DRAGON

BEE WATCHED as the disturbance pushed its way through the ranks of men and demons. Even from this distance, she could feel its aura. A movement next to her caught her attention, and she realized that she had gotten distracted. While she had frozen, the rest of the fight was still continuing along. Just the few seconds she had spent staring off into the distance had allowed a ladder to land on the wall.

She hurriedly expended some energy to clear it. The move was inefficient, but she was in a hurry. Then she turned and screamed "HEY!" at Archibald.

The dragon's companion was holding a section of the wall himself, but still turned to look at her even as he cut down another attacker. She pointed towards the disturbance. His eyes flicked over. He squinted slightly and looked back at her, nodding his acknowledgment.

That was enough for Bee. Something had to be done. But they were so busy holding the wall already. What could they do?

She turned and yelled down to the Nighty Knight below. "Aiden! Tell Felix I need reserves here, fast!"

A few moments later, some of the reserves charged up the wall to take her spot. As they flooded up onto the landing, she spent a little bit more time and energy knocking away foes to give them enough breathing space to set up. Two more ladders went down with Scouring Strikes and a thrown potion.

That settled, Bee jumped down behind the wall and ran along the base of it until she reached Archibald's section. Scrambling up the stairs, she joined the man to talk.

"Do you know what that is?" she asked as she whacked a demon away with her broom. Archibald held this area with no problem alone, but Bee still wanted to feel useful.

"I'm gonna be honest with you. That feels a lot like a Lieutenant," Archibald admitted. "It was very good at hiding its aura, though. I'm surprised you were able to spot it at such a distance."

Bee grimaced. "How could you miss it? It's like—I can feel it everywhere. It's just this constant pressure on my Holy Aura."

"You have the Holy Aura skill?" Archibald asked, impressed. Even as he talked and Bee stood near him, he was still fighting. She wanted to lend him some help, but honestly, it didn't look like he needed or wanted it. Instead, she gladly took the rest.

"Yeah, got it a few levels ago," she said, not wanting to reveal exactly at what level she had gotten it. It was still a massive amount of trust for her to tell him exactly what skills she had in the first place.

"Well, that would explain it. Holy skills and demons don't really mix. But yeah, that means this is going to get a whole lot harder," Archibald grunted, and he flung his latest opponent off the wall. The man went crashing into the soldiers below.

"We don't have much choise but to go fight it and drive it away," Bee said. "I don't see how we can hold the wall while it attacks them. We have to try and handle it before it destroys our defenses. It's pretty much our only hope."

Archibald shrugged, but Bee could tell from the set of his shoulders that things were grim. "I don't know how we're going to beat it. Archimedes isn't here to capture it, and I couldn't defeat one on my own even when I was at full power. I think the best we can do is slow it down."

Bee winced. She could only imagine how well that would work. Still, she repeated herself. "We have to try to drive it off. Otherwise..."

Bee paled when she realized Void wasn't here to help them, either. Could they really face a Lieutenant Demon without their god to back them up? Was their faith strong enough? Would that even matter?

Even in the heat of the battle, she bowed her head, closed her eyes for a second, and sent off a quick prayer to Void. She asked for its presence and its blessing in the coming fight. Opening her eyes, she looked up, hoping to find that her god had teleported there somehow. A little black disk ready and willing to save the castle and its followers. But there was no such luck.

As I zoomed above the vast expanse of sapphire oceans, something strange happened. My Spray Bottle suddenly fired.

It didn't shoot much liquid. Barely a spray of water that the wind quickly whisked away, that was all. But still, it confused me. How had that happened? Was there a bug in my programming? Could any of my mutations fire off randomly like that without my input?

I dedicated a processor to reviewing my firing mechanisms for different mutations and scanning for software bugs. However, I tried not to worry too much. It was just a small spray of liquid, after all. Nothing too bad.

Funnily enough, the action reminded me of something the humans did occasionally. Something they called a "sneeze."

Contemplating what it might mean, I continued my speedy return home.

"Void should be back soon. Void always shows up in time," Bee said, the burning faith inside her making her feel warm again. With conviction, she continued. "I've called up soldiers to take over this wall for you. We are going to go out. Is there anyone else worth bringing?"

Archibald looked around. "You said Tony fought with you last time? He might be able to help, maybe Arthur and Susan as well. But we also just might be sentencing anyone we bring with us to death."

"Arthur and Susan are needed to hold the wall," Bee said. "I don't think we can take everyone out and fight. Maybe we can bring Tony, and he can help keep some of the auxiliaries off of us and prevent the Lieutenant from getting reinforced. Even as things are, though, we'll be on a time limit. They'll have trouble holding the wall for long without us."

Archibald nodded. "That's probably the best idea we have. It should keep him reasonably safe. Grab him, and I'll join you as soon as my reinforcements arrive."

Bee nodded and ran off to go get the farmhand-turned-warrior. She found Tony a little way down, holding his own small section of the wall, using his heavy club to great effect. Its momentum was perfect for sweeping soldiers off the wall and preventing them from getting a foothold. Each time he swung, she could see the air warping around him as some sort of skill activated. Even hits that should have only sent someone stumbling sent them careening off the wall in a tumble of limbs.

She jumped up and quickly finished off all those around him before kicking down the ladder that he was working toward. "Tony.

Something big is coming. Archibald and I are going to go out to meet it, and we're going to need you to keep the rest of the army off our back while we handle the big guy. Are you up for it?"

Tony turned to face her, snarling with battle rage. Then something in his eyes changed as he recognized her, and his expression mellowed. "Bee." He breathed in and out for a second. "Sorry, what'd you say?"

Just as she prepared to answer Tony's question, a shadow passed over the wall. Bee feared the worst as she looked up. However, rather than some demon or skill, she instead found herself staring at a massive figure flying through the air.

Overhead, a massive red-scaled dragon swooped low over their position, less than twenty yards away from her. And then the world shook.

Flames didn't billow out of the beast's maw. Rather, they were ejected with more force than all of the catapults they had made combined. When the fire struck the ground, Bee watched the shock wave ripple through the earth and felt the wall flex under her feet.

The dragon soared forward, blasting a huge line clear through the enemy army, heading directly toward where she felt the ominous presence approaching. And still it continued on. The dragon flew low along the road, blasting the enemy army with gouts of molten fire. The world seemed to pause as everyone on the battlefield simply stopped and stared into the distance.

Bee could barely make out the back of the creature through the trees. At least, what remained of the trees that hadn't been instantly vaporized. As the flames reached the tree line, they cut off suddenly, and the dragon banked up to circle around before starting another pass. This time, the fire came back towards them.

At this point, the enemy came to their senses. The attack on the wall was completely forgotten as their archers turned to launch waves of arrows up at the dragon flying back over them. However, most merely missed and fell amongst their own troops, causing even more chaos and mayhem as soldiers dove to take cover.

That didn't help any in the path of the dragon. The second torrent of flame turned everything in sight into a sea of fire that expanded toward the wall.

Frozen in awe, Bee suddenly understood where the term "mopping up one's enemies" came from. It truly looked like the dragon was simply pushing a broom along the floor, gathering all the dust into one massive pile as it went. Its second pass came back just slightly offset from the previous line of smoldering rocks, carving a new trench through the kingdom's army.

This time, they could only run in one direction as a massive column of melted rock and burning dirt split the army in two. As they ran, the dragon's fire chased them, consuming them whole and pushing the rest into a frantic scramble into the forest.

The titanic red beast neared the wall, soaring closer and closer. The heat of its flames felt intense even from this distance. All around, Bee heard the shouts of soldiers retreating along the wall or scrambling for cover. Screams of terror echoed up from below, where the castle's inhabitants fled into the building, uncertain whether they'd be spared. Bee found herself fixed to the spot, unable to do anything but watch as the dragon kept coming without even slowing.

It cut off its breath right as the path of molten ground was about to touch the wall. It banked above them as she and Tony looked up in awe. Ruby scales glittered in the sunlight as it came around for another pass.

Suddenly, there was a new disturbance a short ways down the wall. Archibald was running and shouting something at the top of his lungs. Bee had a little trouble making out what it was, but she had caught the last few words, at least. "...big stupid lizard!"

"Huh? What is he yelling about?" Bee swiveled her attention back as she noticed something in the center of the first glowing path. Rather than the destruction she'd expected, a singular figure stood on a small circle of completely untouched ground.

She looked at it more closely. The thing wasn't actually standing. From this angle, it almost looked human-sized as it uncurled and stood up to its full height. She realized that this was not some ordinary demon that managed to survive the onslaught.

Archibald was right again. This was a Lieutenant. What else could have survived such an assault?

CHAPTER 83

ONLY YOU CAN PREVENT FOREST FIRES

AS THE SOLDIERS fled into the forest and the surrounding valley, Daedalus reached the end of their forces. Instead of coming back towards the wall for another pass, he banked sideways, laying down a perpendicular tract of burning forest in the molten ground. It would prevent anyone from the army from escaping the valley. And then, satisfied, he continued to burn everything.

It didn't take long for Daedalus to stop his careful approach of precisely straight lines. Soon enough, he circled in spirals and figure eights over the roiling mass of enemies. These little ants had dared offend him. It was time to get revenge. As they ran into the cover of the forest, he couldn't help but laugh. Were they trying to defend against dragon fire with wood? As if that was going to stop him. He was the Red. He was Daedalus, the destroyer of demons.

Eventually, he noticed a few attempts to fight back. Arrows were nothing. He just shrugged the weak shafts off as he blasted through their ranks. Without coordinated volleys to damage his wings, a single shot here and there was practically beneath his notice. The demons were a bit more inventive, though. They would launch themselves or each other up at Daedalus, but they were nothing more than something to sharpen his claws on as he tore them apart and continued to rain down fiery destruction from above.

So when Daedalus felt a strong impact in the center of his stomach, he was thoroughly surprised. It actually knocked him off course a little bit and stalled his breath. Twirling in the air, he threw the attacker up even higher with a powerful kick of his hind legs while digging his talons in and raking them across its body. The slate-gray figure flew up in the air. Daedalus beat his wings to shoot up after it and catch it in his mouth. He bit down hard, splitting flesh that tasted like stone.

Then he whipped his head down and threw the thing into the ground, his serrated teeth cutting through easily. He watched as the legs flew helplessly off in one direction and the body in another. The impact sent a wave of ash and burning sparks even further into the forest. And the dry leaves of winter started to burn all the more.

The fire jumped from treetop to treetop, completely encasing the offending ants. Daedalus roared as he focused back on the fleeing nuisances in the forest and continued burning them all down. They would all learn to never anger a dragon.

As Bee watched the Lieutenant start to move, she heard trumpets signal a retreat of their forces. When she turned to the Nighty Knights member assigned to her location, she watched as the little girl closed her eyes. The Nighty Knight then shouted in her high-pitched child's voice, relaying the instructions from Felix. "We're pulling back to the castle and the city. We hold the innermost walls until the situation has changed. Anyone over level 30 should stay on the wall to watch the retreat."

Bee and Tony nodded to each other and split up, spreading out. There were a few other soldiers who had also made it over level 35, especially after the days of constant fighting. So the eighty or so monsters of their army, along with several of the leaders, gathered along the wall to make sure that nothing snuck over as the weaker troops made it back to safety.

Bee couldn't help but agree with Arthur's decision to pull back. There was no chance they would be affecting this fight in any meaningful way unless they wanted to go directly to the dragon and demons. But why would they do that when the dangers were taking care of each other? She could only hope that the dragon would eventually lose interest and fly away, preferably before setting its sights on the castle.

When she looked around to find Archibald, she was surprised to realize he wasn't there. At least she couldn't see him on the wall with the rest of the stronger troops. When she started searching the horde of people below, she saw the strange man moving very quickly through the enemies. Running directly towards the dragon.

What the hell was this guy thinking? Did he have a death wish? Archibald was obviously a battle maniac, but this was too much even for him. Why antagonize the dragon further and risk earning its ire?

Suddenly, she realized something that made her slightly embarrassed. An epiphany, if putting two and two together could be called that. Was this dragon Daedalus, Archibald's companion and Void's friend? It seemed like it had to be, based on Archibald's reactions, but the dragon was not acting at all like how her master had described him. These were not the actions of a sophisticated, gift-giving, friendly dragon. This was the wrath of —well, she was going to say "god," but it didn't match what her god would do at all. "Judgment of old" maybe would be a better term.

Eventually, everyone was clear of the danger, allowing the leaders to leave the wall. Each made haste, crossing as quickly as possible to the city or the castle, depending on where they were assigned. Bee was amongst the fastest, so she reached the gate to the castle first and started ushering people through. Her watchful eye marked people's faces as everyone made it in.

She was fascinated by the varied responses that the dragon's appearance caused. As Susan sprinted past her, she could hear her muttering under her breath, and she caught a lot of unfamiliar curses and creative turns of phrase that she'd have to remember for herself later on. But she also might have to see what Void thought about that. Would that language be considered unclean? She pondered that.

Captain Major, once he got close enough to the castle wall, slowed to a march and made sure everyone around him was catching up and getting through it in an orderly manner. They couldn't have a scuffle amongst their most powerful people right outside the gate. That would be disastrous. As he ushered people through, she could hear him yelling encouragement and orders. "Stay in line! The line is the shortest distance between two points, you numskulls. We need to stay in line. We're going to make it inside!"

As he organized people, he kept throwing out mathematical descriptions for what they would need to do in a way that caused a number of confused expressions to emerge from the small crowd. Many of them knew what "parallel" was, but as for what the angles of their entry into the castle would do with their efficiency? At the very least, his constant talking seemed to keep everyone calm, or calm enough to enter the castle in an orderly fashion.

Some of the passing faces had gone completely white, with their lips pressed together as the blood drained from their expressions. Others were on the verge of hyperventilating and looking around with furtive glances. A few people who Bee took careful note of were eerily calm. They simply walked into the castle like nothing was happening and they were just coming back from a nice shopping trip on their way home.

The worst, though, were those who walked listlessly with slumped shoulders and a vacant look in their eyes. Bee did her best to exude her Repair skills and Holy Aura over everyone, trying to bolster their spirits and help them maintain morale. But she was concerned that it wasn't enough.

With everyone inside, she shut the gate behind. They could only hope that Archibald knew what he was doing out there by himself.

Hastily, Bee climbed up on a watch platform erected behind the castle wall so she could track the action. It had enough height that they could see over all of the walls, though only the inner one was left standing.

Bee watched in horror as the dragon continued laying waste to the forest after burning the end of their valley. This was going far beyond anything that she had ever thought could happen. There was no option for retreat and no mercy, just one singular powerful being devastating anything in its path. The site of the Lieutenant crashing into the dragon broke her from her stupor.

Archibald shouted a string of expletives as he launched himself over the wall. It had been a large part of his job as Daedalus's companion just to keep him in check. And now here he was, rampaging again without a care in the world. Some things never changed.

He was impressed that without him on Daedalus's back to keep him from destroying everything, the dragon had managed to rein himself in and keep from destroying the castle and its defenders. Still, he suspected that was more because Daedalus saw the castle as his property rather than out of respect for the people.

"Daedalus, you dumb brute!" he shouted up, trying to get the dragon's attention. Even if he was angry, Archibald was relatively certain he could survive long enough to calm his friend down. And once he did calm down, the red dragon would be so disappointed in himself. He knew that Daedalus had grown a lot softer over the last decade or so they had known each other.

Archibald wasn't exactly sure what the dragon had been up to in the last several thousand years. But if he'd at all continued on his trajectory, he likely would deeply regret burning the forest down for this. He had taken a lot of pride in his measured responses and lack of wanton destruction as time went on.

Suddenly, he saw the Lieutenant gathering power for a leap. Archibald increased his pace again. He was certain that Daedalus could tangle with a Lieutenant. Assuming there was only one, of course. But without another option to contain the thing, the best they could hope for was for Daedalus to drive the thing away.

The dragons had managed that several times, and Daedalus was one of the most powerful ones. So he wasn't concerned for his friend's safety. Rather, this would probably be his best opportunity to be able to get Daedalus's attention and board the dragon.

Once Archibald was in range, he sprinted forward a couple of steps and gathered himself low. With a mighty surge of his legs, he leaped high up after the Lieutenant.

Unfortunately, as the dragon and demon collided, they spiraled off to the side. It meant Archibald missed completely, soaring through the air and coming down in the canopy of trees below. He caught a branch to help break his fall, but it snapped in his hands, sending him thundering into the ground. The champion winced as his knees absorbed the shock.

Turning around, he located Daedalus as well as half of the Lieutenant falling towards him. Even as the Lieutenant fell, its two halves were already being pulled back together. By the time it landed, it was well into the process of healing.

Archibald waited for Daedalus to come down and continue his fight with the Lieutenant. Yet, instead of pursuing the enemy, he went back to immolating the attacking army.

Daedalus didn't realize this was a Lieutenant. Dumb lizard. Did he think his enemy was vanquished because he bit him in half? Archibald had a bad feeling that if his friend was really this far gone, it was going to take a lot more to get his attention. Archibald dashed away, ignoring the Lieutenant for now, and tried to hone in on where Daedalus was.

Charging through the forest, he ducked beyond the trees. When he finally got to the road, he was left with just a burning patch of molten stone in front of him as Daedalus soared off into the distance. He looked to the left and right and finally found a tall enough tree for his purposes. Quickly bounding up its trunk, he then stood atop it, hoping that he might be able to reach the dragon from this height.

Patiently, he waited for the Daedalus to come back around. When he saw his opportunity, he leaped again. This time, he managed to catch hold of one of Daedalus's tail spines and, with both hands, held on for dear life as he flapped in the wind behind the dragon. Archibald desperately held tight as he flailed around, shouting. "Hey, Daedalus! Wake up!"

CHAPTER 84

FIGHTING DIRTY

I WAS LIVID.

As I finally flew over the mountains that ringed the castle, I took a look at the grounds below. Of the three walls that had stood when I left, only one still remained. The rest had been reduced to rubble and ashes. Even the last wall hadn't made it through unscathed. Its surface was marked with scratches, chips, dings, and scorch marks. Buildings and carefully laid paths had been replaced with a wasteland and piles of smoldering wood. Even the surrounding forest hadn't managed to come out intact, as I could see trees still burning in the distance.

The only bright spot was that the city and castle seemed to have remained mostly unharmed. Only the occasional impact crater marred the roads inside the innermost walls, apparently made by large rocks falling from the sky.

What had happened? Concern pushed me to accelerate even faster until the castle was better resolved in my sensors.

In the sky, I spotted a massive red dragon flying about. A human held onto his tail, yelling at him. Even as I watched, another gout of flame left the dragon's mouth and hammered down into the forest.

No, it couldn't be. I had trusted Daedalus. He was my friend.

A good guy. He even appreciated the cleanliness I brought to his lair, even if he hadn't seen fit to organize himself. Never in my worst dreams would I have thought that he would destroy my so-carefully-tended valley like this.

It was hard for me to believe, but he was the only massive fire-breathing lizard in the vicinity. A quick analysis of the scorch marks of the walls didn't seem to match his patterns, so perhaps he hadn't attacked the walls directly and simply limited himself to the attacking army. But still, this was unacceptable. There were far more proper ways of dealing with an issue like this. Ways that didn't involve wanton destruction, much less filling the sky with soot and smoke. He wasn't even being organized about it!

My mind went back to his tales of dragons losing their perspective and rampaging through battlefields in the days of old. I suppose I hadn't taken it seriously enough then, and I didn't like suspecting something so awful of my friend. But was he really capable of doing such a thing?

Without hesitation, I veered towards him, decelerating so I was no longer breaking the sound barrier. I raced up in front of him and began spritzing his face with water. He shook his head and roared with irritation as the water sprayed across his massive maw. He plummeted to the earth like a meteor time after time as he chased after me, but I guided him to a flattened, slightly burned meadow. I pulled up at the last second and drifted to a gentle stop. He did not, slamming down to the ground and sending the human attached to his tail flying off into the forest.

I winced as the man crashed through a tree. I sensed that he was still alive, thankfully. But did he really have to break that tree? Eventually, when the dragon went down, he shook his head and blinked. I saw something in his eyes shift slightly.

"Wha—what?" His gaze focused on me after a moment. "Oh. Welcome back, Spot, I..." he said in a completely dazed tone. I cut him off with a sharp beep. With my Grabby Arm, I gestured around at the destruction.

Daedalus's head dipped in embarrassment. "Well, I might have gone a little bit overboard, but—"

I bopped him in the nose with my claw. A bit. *A bit?!* So this was his fault! I laid into the dragon with an angry tirade of beeping and emphatic gestures.

I went on and on, venting my own frustration while also making sure the dragon knew exactly how badly he'd messed up. The dragons dipped lower and lower until his posture closely mirrored that of Cliff when Tanu had found her sneaking food off of the Nighty Knights' plates during dinner. It seemed only right. Daedalus had definitely messed up. I had felt comfortable leaving because I could trust the castle's inhabitants to take care of themselves. In particular, I had faith that Beatrice could keep things under control. I'd have to talk to her later, as clearly something had happened to get something this bad.

I ignored that for the moment and focused on Daedalus. He had to understand how horrible this was. All this work the humans had done was gone in an instant. And the mess left behind? Well. It would take me days to clean this up. Days!

I continued scolding him for a while until I noticed Beatrice running out of the wall towards the dragon. I drew my rant to a close as she approached, but to my surprise, she didn't run straight to me. Instead, she ran over to where the human that was holding onto Daedalus's tail lay.

After talking with him for a few moments, she helped the man to his feet. He was a bit shaky and had to lean on. Beatrice as they walked over. I actually recognized the man as they got closer. I projected up a message. "It's nice to meet you, Archibald. I've heard good things." With a little smiley face at the end to make sure he knew I was friendly. Shortly after, I projected another note. "Thanks for trying to keep your lizard companion in check. I didn't think he would get this out of hand."

Archibald threw back his head and roared with laughter. "I've never heard someone give Daedalus such a dressing down—at least, I assume that's what all those screeches were about!"

It took Archibald several moments to catch his breath and stop chuckling. Eventually, Beatrice spoke up. "I think you should take it easy on the dragon, Master. Without his assistance, I'm not sure there would have been much of the castle left to come back to."

"Oh?" I beeped inquisitively. Then Bee launched into a terrifying tale about how a massive army had invaded the valley and attacked right as I had left. Well. I guessed I did need to be grateful that the castle was still standing.

When Bee saw Void appear in the sky in front of the dragon, she immediately started running. She wasn't exactly sure what was going to happen, but something told her that Void was not going to be happy at all about the state of the valley. But as she got close to where her master and the dragon had landed, she saw Archibald lying on the ground. One of his arms was resting on his face, covering his eyes, as he groaned.

She ignored the two incredibly powerful beings talking over to the side and ran over to her friend, pushing her Repair skills out over him. To her relief, he seemed to be relatively okay, just stunned. After a few moments of intense focus on her skills, she was able to help him into a sitting position.

"So," he said, and he coughed and spit out some blood. "That's your god, huh?"

Bee smiled and nodded. "Yes. Its name is Void."

"It seems a little bit touchy. Can you guys understand what he's saying? It's all just noise to me."

"It takes a little bit of time to get used to it, but he's very articulate."

"Well, what's it saying? I've never seen Daedalus act like this."

"Oh, it's mad about the mess."

Archibald looked around. "Mess? It's a battlefield. Of course it's going to be messy. Why, you should've seen it back in my day."

Bee rolled her eyes and helped him to his feet. "Yeah, yeah. I know it's a battlefield. I'm sure that Void was mostly just worried about us. But it doesn't see things the same as us. We've fought undead hordes, and after my god was done with them, there was nothing but a pristine field left behind."

He looked down at her and blinked. She wasn't sure if he was concussed or just surprised, but she slung his arm over her shoulder and supported him as they walked over to the still-quarreling god and dragon. Bee felt that she probably should intercede on the dragon's behalf, but that felt a bit intimidating, to be honest. After all, who was she to come between a literal god and an ancient red dragon? Even if the dragon did look thoroughly chastised at the moment. She had to admit it looked a bit silly.

Still, she worked up the courage to step forward. She told Void the whole story. Starting with the Nighty Knights' impromptu raid, she reported to her god all of the developments that had occurred in its absence. She ended with Daedalus's appearance and how he had arrived just in time to fend off a Lieutenant.

Void listened patiently and eventually asked some clarifying questions. When it got around to asking about the location of the Lieutenant, the dragon simply shrugged. "I wasn't aware there was a Lieutenant here, honestly."

To which Bee had to interrupt. "You bit the Lieutenant in half. How were you not aware of it?"

"I uh, wasn't exactly in my right mind back there." Daedalus lowered his head in embarrassment. "Those things regenerate like mad. I'm sure it's not really damaged for good, though they do tend to run whenever they fight a dragon one one-on-one. I wouldn't be surprised if it had already left back to where it came from."

"That's not good," Bee muttered, and Void indicated its agreement. It emitted a few more of its strange noises, and Bee interpreted the beeps for Daedalus and Archibald. "It seems like Void has more bad news."

It began showing a moving picture, projecting the illusion above itself. The images showed Void and a lesser dragon fighting some sort of living flame. Archibald looked confused as the beasts soared, but Daedalus was starting to grumble. She could feel the air and ground underneath her shake as he growled his displeasure.

Eventually, when it showed the dragon being injured, he let out a roar that shook the clouds in the skies. Void cut him off by tapping him on his talon with its little arm.

"Right, sorry." Daedalus paid more attention and watched as Void chased off the living flame but came back to help the dragon back to a resting spot.

"Thucydides was not ready for that fight." Daedalus growled. Bee was obviously missing some context, but the picture was clear enough. The dragon Void showed was powerful, but nowhere near as powerful as the dragon sitting in front of her right now.

"I think that we have bigger things to worry about than just that," Archibald said. "I'm not completely sure what's going on in the world right now, but from what I can tell, this isn't an isolated thing. If the Lieutenant escaped, I'm sure it'll be going back to their base of power to regroup. And next time, it won't underestimate us."

The other three in the group looked towards him.

"Yeah. I'm sure you are right," Bee said, thinking back to what Arthur said. "We've gotten reports of the king acting strangely. Could that be related?"

Void let out a string of noises, and Bee nodded. "Yeah, I think you're right, Master. We're going to need to go pay the capital a visit and clean some things up."

EPILOGUE
THE WORK OF THE RIGHTEOUS

THE CAPITAL STOOD tall and imposing atop a high hill. All around, green fields rolled down from its walls to meet the plains below. The massive walls hewn from stone gave it quite an impressive silhouette on the horizon. Even more so when once considered how far that stone might have traveled to come here. But even past that, the place was still growing. Palaces on the inside climbed ever higher into the sky, visible well past the walls. At the center, though, above them all, rested the most impressive keep where the king resided.

Zeal's broom handle tapped along the road as he walked forward. From a distance, he thought the capital looked quite nice. It had been a long journey from Caleb, but his faith had carried him through. The organization there had taken well enough hold of the city that he felt comfortable with leaving for a bit, even if he had to go alone with his most trusted subordinates staying behind. He had thought about bringing the crazy woman with him, though. He had never gotten her name, but somehow, she knew about their god. Like him. Even before Caleb had spread the word beyond its walls.

When Zeal had found her walking through the city, they simply thought she was some crazy rambler. Some unhinged woman who babbled nonsense. But upon further inspection, her ramblings weren't as crazy as they first thought.

She obviously had no power or responsibility in the organization. She simply walked about and spoke her prophecies. The people had taken to caring for her, making sure she had a roof to sleep under and food and water at all times. They hadn't been able to get her to bathe or anything, which was borderline sacrilegious, but at least she was alive.

The woman's appearance had puzzled Zeal until eventually he realized: she was god-touched. Patricia was sent by their lord to tell them the error of their ways. There was no other explanation. Why their lord would have sent someone as filthy as this, Zeal couldn't begin to imagine. But it had to be the case. It had to.

Zeal had been distressed to realize his teachings had contained inaccuracies and slight mistakes. But with some simple corrections to his understanding, he managed to remedy the issue. All based on interpretations of her mad ravings.

It had been a relatively simple adjustment to make, and if anything, the people agreed with the revised teachings more. The purifying fire and wrathful cleansing of angry gods seemed more in line with what they had witnessed than the gentle cleansing that had worked its way into his sermons. As he meditated on the ideas, he only confirmed his new resolve. Clearly, something had led him astray. Turned him toward softness and tolerance. But some stains could not be scrubbed out so easily.

Ever since the crazy prophet had come, the streets were twice as clean, and people worked much harder to make sure that there was not a single speck of dust to be found about the place. And so Caleb sparkled. The city was being rebuilt in an orderly manner with a meticulously precise grid. It would have no slums where dirty street rats could hide, and that was intentional. In the new Caleb, the more perfect Caleb, there would be no need for such things. No one would fall behind. None would sink into filth.

It was going rather well, but just the one city wasn't enough for their god. They had to convert more. Patricia was staying behind, as he doubted that she would be accepted in a city completely unprepared for her. But he had taken it upon himself to take this pilgrimage, to spread the word and prepare the capital for Void's teachings.

He passed a single copper to the gate guard, who allowed him to bring his worn pack into the city's walls with his walking broom. He was sure that the guard didn't believe that he was a peddler, coming to sell his wares and buy more to take to the surrounding cities, but the small amount of coin was enough to make him look the other way and let in what was probably just a refugee.

His steps took him past the gate and into the city proper. The first street was not bad, but as soon as Zeal turned off to find a place to stay, he couldn't help but lift his lip in disgust.

There was a pile of refuse, not a block away from the main road. Horse dung and straw and rotting food just piled up against a bricked window, stinking on the ground. It should never be allowed. It was unacceptable.

Shuddering, he stepped around the pile and looked for an inn. This simply redoubled his desire for a proper bath. As he passed the massive pile of dung, he saw someone huddled up against it. An old man with missing teeth holding a wooden cup. He shook it at Zeal as he walked past.

Zeal couldn't help but wrinkle his nose at the man's state. How could one let themselves become so dirty? Much less allow themselves to exist next to such filth. The fact that the man didn't simply move away nearly made him twist his face in open disgust.

He felt the desperate desire to scrub himself with soap and water until he was once again pristine enough to be seen speaking about his Lord. But looking at the man's face, Zeal couldn't help but stop. This man just didn't know any better. He bent over and offered the man a hand instead of a copper. The man looked at him, confused. Once they met with their eyes, though, Zeal activated his first real skill.

Preach was nothing too impressive, but it certainly helped give his words a little extra weight. "Come now, brother. I think you need to learn how to become clean."

The man looked at Zeal's robes. They were slightly marred by dust and travel, but the pure white still stood out compared to the surroundings. He took his hand and let Zeal help him to his feet.

They continued farther in, looking for a place for them both to get clean now. Several people watched the odd sight from the shops as Zeal's walking broom clacked along, but no one bothered him.

No one bothered him yet, at least. He didn't imagine that would last. But he was on a mission to explain to the people what needed to be done. Then, he was sure, this city could turn itself around. It had the potential to even surpass Caleb, with the amount of resources it had and the ways it could be remade. Imagine the city renewed, these dilapidated buildings around him torn down and rebuilt in straight lines, with wide streets. Where everyone had a place and the cobblestones would glisten from being polished. The filth would be moved out of the city and buried deep. Very deep.

But the more he came across the blatant displays of petty crime and lawlessness, the more concerned he became that the filth was rooted too deep in the hearts of the people.

Perhaps many would be beyond saving. Purges were nasty things, and blood running through the streets was not a pretty sight. It did a horrible job at cleaning, being hard to remove. But sometimes, as Patricia had mentioned, sometimes one needed to dirty their hands in the work of cleansing something.

Eventually, they found an inn willing to take them in long enough for them to get clean. Zeal found himself unable to resist explaining to the innkeeper how the inn's floor could be better swept, and the paint could be fixed.

The innkeeper had at first been enraged, but once he had calmed down, he realized that Zeal was correct. He even grabbed a broom from the corner to rectify the issue. Then Zeal helped him as they swept the floor. There was not much they could do about some of the stains for now, but even before his bath, he was outside helping paint the inn. The sign was redone, and even the beggar man helped. Perhaps he understood Zeal's teachings better than he had feared.

A day or two passed before the inn was in complete order. The innkeeper and his family thanked Zeal for the push they needed to better themselves. "We're still busy. In fact, it is busier than ever had been."

Within a week, the inn had become a favorite haunt of many of the locals.

At first, the neighbors had grumbled about the need to be clean-shaven and freshly washed. But when the inn started providing those services to others, people flocked to it right and left. Many of them came just to listen to Zeal talk in the corner. He never tried to draw attention to himself too much. He had discovered that was counterproductive. Most of the time. So he simply sat in the corner of the room where a bard or a minstrel would usually sit and explained how best to live their lives. How keeping their lives spotless and free of clutter would make everything better.

Zeal also, of course, spoke about the opposite side of the coin. How the great void god would destroy all that failed to adhere to its word, all that was left impure and wanting. He'd been a bit hesitant on that one. Caleb certainly hadn't been immaculate when the void came and saved them from the zombies. But as Patricia explained it, it had the potential to be immaculate, and if they listened, truly listened to its word, it would be. The Void would protect them evermore.

Soon, the buildings next to the inn were cleaned up and tidied, and there just wasn't enough space for everyone who wanted to listen to Zeal speak in the room.

And so he went out into the street and talked to the crowd out there. Day after day, he looked out at the growing sea of white robes and spoke. They couldn't all hear him, so some relayed words to the ones behind them, and others relayed those words to the crowd forming around them. And they began to propagate. It took days and weeks, but soon enough, they had their own ministry. A few blocks of correctly behaving people and more people who lived outside were working to spread the news.

After several weeks, Zeal was happy with his progress, but the city still wasn't ready for the prophet. So, one morning, he packed up his belongings and told the innkeeper to keep up the good work. And then Zeal walked to the other side of the city. It took him several hours to get through the bustle, but he found someone else willing to listen to his speaking. A day or two later, he repeated the process.

This time, it was easier, as several of his white-robed followers had already paved the way for him. Even if they were mostly ignored on the corners of the streets, they tried to explain to the people the errors of their ways. It was just enough to prime the people. Then Zeal was able to get his foot in and explain the glories of Void. Soon, he would send someone to bring Patricia in, and the city would never be the same again.

All the Dust that Falls will continue in Book Four!

THANK YOU FOR READING ALL THE DUST THAT FALLS 3

WE HOPE you enjoyed it as much as we enjoyed bringing it to you. We just wanted to take a moment to encourage you to review the book. Follow this link: All the Dust that Falls 3 to be directed to the book's Amazon product page to leave your review.

Every review helps further the author's reach and, ultimately, helps them continue writing fantastic books for us all to enjoy.

Also in series:
All the Dust that Falls
All the Dust that Falls 2
All the Dust that Falls 3
All the Dust that Falls 4

Check out the entire series here! (Tap or scan)

Want to discuss our books with other readers and even the authors? Join our Discord server today and be a part of the Aethon community.

Facebook | Instagram | Twitter | Website

You can also join our non-spam mailing list by visiting www. subscribepage.com/AethonReadersGroup and never miss out on future releases. You'll also receive three full books completely Free as our thanks to you.

Looking for more great books?

Where others see doom, he sees opportunity. Hell Difficulty? More like a chance to thrive.
Nathaniel's bus ride was supposed to be just another boring commute. Wrong. Now, he, 23 fellow passengers, and a corgi named Biscuit, are stuck in a "Hell Difficulty" Tutorial, battling monsters and leveling up to survive. Easy difficulty, anyone can handle. Normal difficulty, you've got to put up a fight to get by. Hard difficulty is where only the tough ones last. And Hell? That's where you have to be a bit out of your mind! With his terrifying talent for mana manipulation, Nathaniel decides to invest every stat point into mana. Attribute imbalance be damned. It will either kill him before the monsters and his enemies can, or turn him into one of the most powerful beings within the system. Never underestimate the guy who has so much Mana it should kill him... **Follow Nathaniel's crazy journey as he takes on nightmarish foes and teams up with a far-from-normal group of bus passengers in this action-packed LitRPG Adventure. He must outsmart the odds, survive, and emerge stronger than anyone else! Perfect for fans of** *The Primal Hunter, Defiance of the Fall,* **and** *Apocalypse: Generic System.* **Grab your copy today!**

Get Hell Difficulty Tutorial Now!

Ezekiel died on Earth only to be resurrected in the body of a Lich. Well, now he'd done it. He was only playing the villain to blow off steam, now he was stuck in the body of one. Trapped in a hostile world, Zeke must flee his former guild. The problem is, he can only flee into a holy kingdom ruled by the Church of Olattee. Out of the frying pan and into the fire. Only his power is gone, and he must start over. Well... Mostly anyway. He is still a lich after all and he still has his weapon, Mercy, which is more powerful than even he knows. The real question is, is he now a villain or not? And will he survive long enough to find out? **Don't miss the next action-packed LitRPG / GameLit series by Levi Werner, the bestselling author behind *World of Magic*. It's perfect for fans of *Sylver Seeker*, *Book of the Dead*, and *The Ritualist*.**

Get Redemption's Cost now!

For all our LitRPG books, visit our website.

Made in the USA
Monee, IL
01 June 2025

18570527R00335